Also by **Stephen Wright**

Meditations in Green
M31 : A Family Romance
Going Native

THE
AMALGAMATION POLKA

A LOFTY DESTINY FOR THE HUMAN RACE.—A clergyman at Milford, Massachusetts, called the Rev. E. S. Best, has published a sermon in one of the Boston papers in which occurs the following paragraph :—"This blending of the two races (Caucasian and African) by amalgamation is just what is needed for the perfection of both. * * You will then have the highest, noblest, and most God-like species of humanity. Such a race will constitute the real people of America. Here the human race will reach its loftiest destiny, and this nation become the glory of all lands ; the place which, above all others, shall most resemble heaven, and be nearest to it."

THE

AMALGAMATION POLKA

Stephen Wright

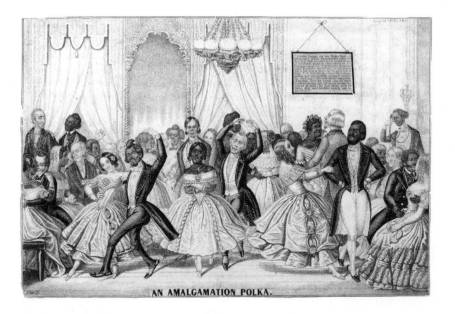

AN AMALGAMATION POLKA.

ALFRED A. KNOPF
NEW YORK, 2006

THIS IS A BORZOI BOOK
PUBLISHED BY ALFRED A. KNOPF

Copyright © 2006 by Stephen Wright

All rights reserved. Published in the United States by Alfred A.
Knopf, a division of Random House, Inc., New York, and in
Canada by Random House of Canada Limited, Toronto.

www.aaknopf.com

Knopf, Borzoi Books, and the colophon are registered trademarks
of Random House, Inc.

ISBN: 0-679-45117-X
Library of Congress Control Number: 2005938382

Manufactured in the United States of America
First Edition

THE
AMALGAMATION POLKA

The bearded ladies were dancing in the mud. Outsized country feet that just wouldn't keep still, strutting and reeling all along that slippery stretch of flooded road. Yellow paste clung to the hems of their gowns, flecked sunburnt arms and whiskery cheeks, collected in thick earthen coins upon the lacy ruffles of their modest chests like a hero's worth of medals artlessly arranged. A cold rain fell and continued to fall over the lost hills, the yet smoking fields, the rude, misshapen trees where light—vague and uncertain—struggled to furnish the day with the grainy quality of a fogged daguerreotype. And at the center of this dripping stillness these loud animated women without origin or explanation, refugees from a traveling circus perhaps, abandoned out of forgetfulness or deceit or simple spite, the improvised conclusion to some sorry affair of outrage and betrayal, and as they danced, they sang and reveled in the rain, porcelain pitchers of ripe applejack passing freely from hand to unwashed hand, the echo of their song sounding harshly across that desolate country:

> Soupy, soupy, soupy, without any bean
> Porky, porky, porky, without any lean
> Coffee, coffee, coffee, without any cream

On a rise back of the road stood a tall white frame house with long white curtains flung twisted and sodden from the open windows. A solitary blackbird perched atop the brick chimney, its beaded prismatic head jerking mechanically about. Several emaciated hogs rooted with audible vigor among the stumps of broken furniture, the puddles of bright clothing littering the trampled yard. From out the shadowed doorway flew an enameled jewelry box, bouncing once, twice, and off into the weeds. Followed quickly by an English plate, a soiled pair of ripped pantaloons, a clanging case clock, an oval looking glass that vanished upon an upended table leg in a burst of twinkling confetti—the house methodically emptying itself out. A pregnant sow shifted its spotted flanks, then resumed gnawing at the gilded frame of a painting in the grand style of Washington and Cornwallis at Yorktown. A bearded lady appeared at the door bearing before her a magnificent rosewood chair, the ruby red brocade of its seat and arms mounting up in lurid flame. The hurled chair landed upright in the mud where it continued to burn, to reduce itself to skeletal blackness, to pure idea. The bearded lady watched, haloed in the fires now leaping madly behind her. Curds of gray smoke were crowding out from under the cedar shakes. The house began to make a great whooshing sound. Flakes of wet ash blew down out of an opal sky.

The figure was already running when the bearded ladies glimpsed it, rushing slantwise down the clay slope as if materialized in midstride out of some adjacent realm of unendurable horror and perpetual flight.

"It's a nigger!" cried one of the ladies.

She was young and barefoot and clothed in woolen rags. The clear terror in her touched even them standing there astounded for once in their ruined fashions and waterlogged boots. They watched agape this sudden apparition go bounding up the road like a wild hare and as the size of her steadily diminished in the misting distance an unaccountable rage grew large among them. Without word or gesture they moved off as one in raucous pursuit. It was a remarkable sight. Splashing and howling, jostling for position like whipped racing ponies, all bobbing beards and bonnets, stumbling on petticoats, sliding belly down into the mire, they presented a spectacle of hermaphroditic frenzy such as few could imagine. In a moment they were strung out wheezing in the muck. All but one. Audacious in a poke bonnet and bombazine dress, she rapidly outdistanced the rest, she hounded her quarry, she ran like a mother possessed, in a fit of chastisement, hard on the heels of an impudent daughter. Over the near hill and down, up the far hill and gone.

When at last the others found them, they were fallen and half-buried in the melting loam of an eroded embankment, their partially clad bodies so slathered with mud as to be almost unrecognizable, ill-formed creatures who had failed some evolutionary test. The bearded lady was settled in between the girl's thin bare shanks and well into her work, the bonnet wadded fiercely into the girl's bleeding mouth, a crude brand of the letter D gleaming on the lady's exposed cheek. The girl's eyes were closed. She might have been unconscious. The stragglers stood about in an uneasy huddle, turning to study now and again the dreary emptiness of the road, the earth, the sky, waiting like patient cattle in the rain, the tattered remnants of contemporary finery hiked to their armpits, buttons undone on the filthy breeches beneath, waiting politely in turn, their pink manhood carelessly exposed. Someone belched; another laughed. Soon the last of the pale light would draw off into the pine hills, shielding from hostile eyes the occupations of these costumed shapes in a starless obscurity, in the cloaked freedom of the night.

There was a gorilla in the White House and a long-tailed mulatto presiding over the Senate chamber and the dreams of the Republic were dark and troubling.

He was born in the fall of the time at the end of time. The signs were plain for all with an eye to read: the noonday passage the previous spring of a great comet—"the marvel of the age!"—the swift echelons of croaking blackbirds flocking north for the winter, the collapse of the revival tent up in Rochester where, miraculously, not a single soul was harmed. Cows walked backward through the meadows; well water turned overnight into vinegar. Surely the advent of eternity was at hand. The vine was about to be reaped.

At dusk on the evening of October 22, 1844 (the date determined by the divine computations of an ex-sheriff and self-taught biblical scholar), the ascension-robed faithful gathered anxiously in churches and meetinghouses, along rooftops, the branches of trees and out upon high desolate hillsides—the nearer to glory—hymns and prayers keeping them through the final chill hours of that long last day until, instead of the Bridegroom, there appeared in the eastern sky the tentative kindling of just another dawn, proof that, for now, time would have no end, the body no release, and outside Delphi, New York, the disappointed crowd, waistcoat watches ticking steadfastly on, descended the knoll out of Briarwood Cemetery past the leafless, unscorched elms, the cold, unharrowed graves and into the welcoming arms of no company of saints but a taunting, unredeemed mob from town brandishing brickbats and stones.

So the trials of America were not to be so speedily concluded.

Hours more must be drowned in sin, the sun darkened to a seal of pitch, before God would deliver this errant nation from the wickedness of history.

Nine days later Liberty Fish was born.

His mother, Roxana, did not expect to survive the occasion, the birthing chair having served all too often as a makeshift gallows for women of the family, carrying off Grammy Bibb, several faceless cousins, a favorite aunt with dimples deep enough for planting and her eldest sister, Aurore, the blonde darling of Stono County, who stoically kneaded at her bedclothes for three frightful days before producing a male nonesuch that Father hastily wrapped in red flannel and buried in an unmarked hole behind the smokehouse on the morning she died, crying out at the end in a mystic guttural tongue none understood or recognized. Passage to that Good Land seemed to be neither fair nor fleet. The moment Roxana realized she was growing a baby she understood immediately what she must do: prepare herself like a warrior on the eve of battle. She had read *The Iliad* in the original Greek at the age of sixteen; she knew what was required.

The annunciatory instant, as clear to her now as present vision, occurred as she stood defiantly in the pulpit of the Pleasance Street Methodist Church in Utica, struggling to lift her modest voice above the clanging, the braying, the whistling, the clapping of the protesting horde outside. She had just finished reciting the Declaration of Independence—amazing the ardor those few simple words could still arouse almost seventy years later—when a boyish, moon-faced man in a rusty black coat climbed atop a pew and, shouting above the clamor of fists drumming angrily upon the walls, inquired of Roxana whether he could approach and feel her chin for evidence of a beard. A dozen men rose in outraged objection, and as Roxana waited patiently for the commotion to subside—a small, still figure at the eye of her nation's storm—she felt an unmistakable flutter of ghostly delicacy, a kind of spiritual hiccough, pass hastily through her frame, and at once she knew: a skull had begun to swell between her hips.

"Nonsense," declared her sister-in-law, Aroline. "No one's departing this household just yet, as long as I have any say in the matter."

"But I want this child," Roxana said in her soft drawl that always struck Aroline's northern ears as the sound a cloud might make if it could talk.

"And so you shall, my dear, and many more besides."

The thought depleted Roxana. Did she truly want even this one? She fell into a prolonged and uncharacteristic period of distraction. Days came and went, but she was no longer a passenger. The most trivial tasks eluded her. The careless placement of a spoon or cup on the kitchen table, a particular patch of sunstruck wallpaper, acquired a mesmeric fascination. She could lose herself for hours (and go she knew not where) in the view from her bedroom window, the barren hills lying motionless in the bleak February light like a corpse sprawled on its side. A single spider dangling on a single thread from a peeling porch beam was the saddest sight in the world. She kept misplacing her heavy ring of house keys. The pauses in her evening conversations with Aroline grew so lengthy she'd forget she was even speaking to anyone. At night, during those rare intervals when sleep actually came, she'd persist in dreaming that she was awake and rise in the morning achy and exhausted, a dark and haunted look hovering prominently about her solemn brown eyes.

Aroline did what Aroline did best: she worried. She left copies of *The Journal of Health and Longevity* or *The Cold Water Journal* or any of the sundry ultraist periodicals she subscribed to lying strategically around the house, pages opened to pertinent passages. Ever fashion's weather vane, she had already sampled a full course of the latest faiths, philosophies and fads, including vegetarianism, hydrotherapy, phrenology, perfectionism and harmonialism. She had been among the expectant number huddled atop the cemetery knoll, her presence testifying at least to the possibility, if not the hope, that the prophet's words were more than mere animal sounds but actual reverberations of gospel thunder, just as she was convinced there were embers of revealed truth in every belief fervently held. Fervency was the key, the sign incontrovertible of spirit leaking in through the cracks of this darkling world.

Roxana ignored the magazines, left the room at any mention of

Grahamizing her diet and, despite Aroline's pleas, refused to consult a doctor, seeing no reason for outside advice on a matter women had been handling quite well on their own since Eve birthed Cain. Her attention was wholly bent on registering the most minute operations of her Internal Monitor, a phantom elusiveness that communicated at confoundingly irregular intervals through either a sort of coded rapping upon the walls of her soul or, more directly, in an actual voice, never her own, a child's urgent whisper, so thin at times as to be practically inaudible. Such messages that she did receive—however obscure, paradoxical or contradictory—had always proven to be reliable governors through life's terrible riddle. So it was clearly disquieting to suffer her faithful Monitor behaving like an inept, even outright fraudulent, fortune-teller. Giddily, it swung first one way, then the other, as if her heart were the dead pendulum weight of a great faceless clock. The chords of her desires seemed far, far out of reach, and she felt hopeless, lost, utterly alone. The sun was an egg, the moon a bone, and she couldn't rid her mind of the singsong facts of that obvious perception. Such straw her head was stuffed with. But then, inexplicably, the color of her mood would flare into an afternoon's, sometimes a whole day's, conviction of supreme imperishability. Every significant event of her life, of everybody's life, was bathed in the hard liberating light of inevitability, and backward through the dark confusions of her past was opened a route to those charmed moments when absolute rightness descended like grace, the radiance she had migrated beneath after turning her back on hearth and home and, like the distraught heroine of an Old World romance, fleeing the gates of Redemption Hall forever, or the exaltation of her first galvanic glimpse of the young Thatcher amid the marble and potted palms of the Congress Hotel in Saratoga Springs, the nimbus crowning his head savage as hellfire. But then, as abruptly as a wind-extinguished candle, the sovereign light would go out and the night rush in, attended by a whole motley zoo of familiars—chattering doubt, thumping care, heckling vexation—and thought was an anarchy of remains in a moldering tomb.

When Thatcher returned, several months overdue, from his latest provocative circuit of western churches, he found his wife out back, coatless in the bitter air, unmittened fingers clutching the wooden rim of the well, her boyish body angled out precariously over the hole as if she were searching for something precious she had dropped. Her face was blotched and wet and he was surprised—he had never seen her cry before. When he took her in his arms, she began to tremble.

"My life is over," she sobbed. Around them the frozen trees swayed and creaked like giant chandeliers caught in a draft. Tinkling crystals of ice plopped without cease onto the thick carpet of snow.

"No, no," said Thatcher, his own voice a stranger's to his ear. "No." He had no idea what she was talking about and didn't know what to do but keep patting her mechanically on her quavering back, his uncertain hand running up and down the hard china knobs of her spine.

When Roxana finally dared to look up at her husband, her expression emptied of all defenses, she gasped, reaching out to touch the monstrous swelling around his half-closed eye where the skin bulged with organic color normally kept from view.

"It's nothing," Thatcher said, brushing her hand away. "The mark of Christian love. Tell me what's happened here."

So she did, and the very words themselves, spoken out loud at last to the one person they'd always been silently directed toward, settled like ballast deep inside her. "And I keep thinking," she concluded, in a surprisingly firm voice, "of all those babies who need me." She could see them, too, infinite acres of squalling infants, manacled each to each, horrible in number, every fresh tiny mind merely another receptacle of sufficient dimension to contain entire the whole of the world's pain, the chorus of their shrieks and wails rising like incense unto the stone nostrils of the father whose true features were perpetually obscured by the human mask of God.

Thatcher smiled. "This is wonderful news. But our child will need you as well."

"Yes," she agreed, and the look she gave him quivered for a moment and then broke, and there were tears on her face again. She was terrified of failing, of loosening her grip for even an instant on the file she had wielded for so many years, her heart's herald, the friction of her eloquence, rasping away in the gloom at the chain that bound up the land.

Thatcher hugged his wife tightly to his chest. "I doubt," he said, "that the country will begrudge you the time spent caring for your own."

"Is this pride?" she asked suddenly, pushing herself away, anxiously searching the mystery of his eyes. "Is this pride I am suffering from?"

A wind came up in a wild rushing from the valley floor, driving before it a hard, dry flurry, flakes as coarse as sand, stinging their cheeks, hissing across the sugary crust of fallen snow where the forked tracks of nameless birds and rodents traced a mad, illegible script.

"You are the least proud creature that I know," said Thatcher, taking her icy hand. "Come now, let's get back inside. You have to start taking better care of yourself. There's a needy visitor coming to our life."

They moved off, arm in arm, toward the tall stone house where from behind the curtains of an upstairs window watched the shadowy figure of Aroline, and the monotone sky moved over their bowed heads in a single seamless sheet of dunnest gray.

So, warily, with Thatcher at her side, Roxana settled into the facts of her condition. And as if to prove to herself that nothing had changed, nothing ever need change, she rediscovered the iron in her soul and, shamelessly exploiting her burgeoning belly as both shield and goad, ventured back out onto the lecture circuit, a leather fire bucket at her feet, delivering through the iridescent scrim of passing nausea a milky denunciation of the American Constitution. But the yeasty tide sweeping through her was undeniable, and as the shape of her body quickened and swelled so, too, did the shape of the world until both, strangely congruous, loomed large, unwieldy, insolently expectant. In other humors, however, she was attended by the notion that her being had been overmastered by a species of machine, the ruthless cogs and wheels of Nature inflexible, to which she must submit or risk prolonged breakage on the teeth of the mechanism.

One long unpleasant night Roxana passed under the shade of a terrible dream: the dreaded birth, pronounced a whacking success by the crush of obscure relatives and anonymous friends milling mindlessly about the bloodied bed, had come and quit with less fuss than a spring shower. The peril was past that she had, unaccountably, survived, and nestled in her arms lay the issue of all her anxiety: an infant well-formed and healthy and male and quite black—the latter trait gone strangely unremarked by all save Roxana, who had lately been seized by a nameless foreboding. She couldn't sleep, she couldn't unbend, her skin all full of furry spiders. In a panic, she stole her child and fled out into the countryside, past pasture and pond, down dark roads into darker woods. She ran and ran until her legs failed, and on the bank of a clear-rushing stream she placed the baby in a conveniently abandoned canoe and pushed it free of the mud on a journey to a far better shore.

She awoke with sweat on her brow and a trembling in her limbs, staring at the gray rectangle of her bedroom window until grayness dissolved in the slow, liquid light of dawn. She slept fitfully for weeks afterward, afraid of the places her dreams might carry her.

Then, one perfectly ordinary day, without fanfare or gonfalon, the great thing simply commenced. She was alone in the house at the time—Thatcher off on another hazardous mission across the Ohio, Aroline gone to town shopping—and she had been feeling slightly "vague" (there was no more precise word for it) since arising, a sensation she habitually associated with just being alive, when abstraction resolved itself into a pang, then another, and another, and she knew the contest had begun. She went out onto the porch and sat in the rocker watching the solid, solid hills and the bright autumnal sky. She was still sitting there waiting for whatever was to happen when Aroline, nose mask tied firmly across her face (a practical precaution she indulged whenever a nip entered the air), returned in the trap with a basketful of morally sanctioned supplies from the Required

Labor Grocery and Dry Goods Store and breathless news of the Grand Rally for Polk that had transformed their drowsy town square into a reveler's midway, the normal day's routine being apparently suspended for the duration. A Brass Band! Military Procession! Oratory and Cannonades! Oysters and Ices! Roman Candles at Eight! Then Aroline noticed what was written on Roxana's face and, recognizing the text at a glance, immediately hustled her protesting sister-in-law up to bed where she ordered her to remain while Aroline went off in search of a reliable physician.

Two agonizing hours later, reliability presented itself in the disheveled person of Dr. Timothy Margrave, a small, narrow, agitated man with big, hairy ears and a disconcertingly blank gaze typically centered on a point several feet behind the head being addressed. He was wearing a frayed, ill-fitting coat speckled fore and aft with whitish stains of indeterminate origin. If his manner seemed lacking even its usual gruff charm, he hastened to inform the women, it was due to his having been called away from treating a considerable wound to Mayor Twiggs's backside in order to observe a rather common labor. His Honor had just concluded a rousing stemwinder on behalf of the Democratic candidate for the presidency ("this loyal 'Napoleon of the Stump,' this fighting champion of independence, this patriotic foe of all foreign powers who would oppose our Union's triumphant march toward its divine destiny") and was basking in the cheers and applause, trying to collect his own breath, when a black-and-white mongrel no one in the crowd would claim ran up out of nowhere and planted a sharp set of little teeth into the invitingly ample seat of the mayoral pants. Town wags remarked that the animal must have been a Clay raccoon.

The doctor called for a sheet which he carelessly draped over Roxana's recoiling body and, studiously averting his eyes, proceeded, with cold, rough hands, to examine her "down there." Roxana stared at the molded plaster scallops on the ceiling and imagined herself up on the auction block, proud features washed and greased, enduring inspection by strange male fingers whose right to probe the very orifices of your flesh was sanctioned by law and blessed by the church. Dr. Margrave removed his arms from beneath the covering, announced that the business was progressing nicely and, clapping beaver to head, unceremoniously took his leave. He feared complications in the delicate case of that executive posterior.

The door had no sooner clicked shut than Roxana had sat bolt upright, torn the sheet from her body and flung the offending wad of linen into her sister-in-law's stoical face. Then, leaning from her bolstered bed, she let fly a healthy gob of spittle onto the exact spot where the good doctor had stood, declaring that should another medical man dare set foot in this house ever again she would personally stick him in the ass with his own catlin. Without a word of rebuke, Aroline rushed over to wipe up the floor with a lavender-scented handkerchief, few surprises left for her in Roxana's bag of tricks. My mother did this, Roxana declared fiercely to herself. She did it eight times. I can do it once. Trying not to dwell on such particulars as the roomful of family, neighbors, servants—women all—ministering to each of her mother's deliveries, fetching water, massaging limbs, diverting her mind with gossip, while she (Roxana) would be forced to abide her maiden labor alone but for a scatter-brained spinster whose notion of nonpareil care was a cold compress and an electromagnetic machine.

On the wall opposite the bed hung a framed lithograph of the *Water Witch*, a full-rigged, canvas-bellied clipper ship heeling majestically before the wind (another of Thatcher's divers fancies that he might, upon awakening, gaze dreamily from his pillow for a jeweled moment or two upon a reminder of realms the mind could populate to suit its occasional need for motion, space, unfettered light). A beveled tower of rounded sail and triangular line, the ship bore down upon the viewer like a charging elephant. From atop successively elevated peaks of pain and fearing the ranges yet to come, Roxana concentrated on the deceptively clean proportions of this picture, the geometry of rope alone offering numerous focal points within which consciousness might vanish, as the entire room moved and the air bloomed and the halyards sang and the pennants popped and the timbers groaned from truck to keel, amidships the atmosphere a virtual soup of noxious vapors (of garbage, feces, tar and mold), the day-world present, when at all, in a slender pole of piercingly bright light that shifted about playfully from an opportune knothole in the planks overhead, as if wielded by some mischievous fellow up top attempting to torment further this wretched company of prostrate gentlemen, unkempt wives of the once and future variety, and a dozen or so weepy indentured servants with a random touch of his magic healing wand. Too late for sister Rosetta, already gone over, in Paradise ahead of the rest, the wasted body she'd left behind attractive bait for ship rats big as terriers that grew bolder by the hour. Her own strength failing, she didn't know how much longer she could keep the vermin at bay. (Roxana realizing only now that this alien life she found herself occupying with such morbid intensity was, in fact, that of Great-grandmother May, braving Atlantic chop and the parlous unknown for one final turn of Fortune's wheel.) Her lips were cracked, her throat swollen, her stomach unmoored, the water in the drinking casks having long since turned foul, strung now with intricate webs of a white sticky matter too horrid to contemplate, let alone swallow, while under her, now and forever, the lift and pull of the sea shuddering through the hull ancient as time, the force of God's terrible hands moving mercilessly upon your body, and a voice cried out America! and, despite the captain's injunctions against passengers above decks, all who were able rushed up to the rail to behold the dim horizon line slowly spread and thicken into a vernal ache of purest wonder.

"It's a boy," Aroline declared flatly, thrusting into dramatic view a wailing, wriggling, shimmery thing of mottled red and blue that Roxana recognized instantly as a glistening piece of her own heart.

Liberty was always afraid of the dark. Even as a young man he required the company of an attentive flame standing watch over his bedded self because the night, he had come to know, was populated by a host of ravening forms and the fear of being *plucked*, stolen away physically, even spiritually, from the familiar, from the family itself, remained a sentiment not easily outgrown.

"Born with an anxious make," pronounced Aunt Aroline, "like all the Fishes—and no, don't for an instant suspect I am excluding myself from such a judgement."

It was a mother's tender stratagem that first coaxed the reluctant boy from the trundle bed at the foot of his parents' high poster and up the narrow complaining stairs to the snuggly roost prepared for him under the sloping rafters.

"This is the tower," Roxana explained, in her best maternal voice, "of a great castle. And this"—she gestured rather airily about the truncated space in which they stood like museum visitors side by side, mother and son—"is the hidden keep where the prince resides until the fateful day he is called upon to become king."

Liberty was skeptical; such a drab cubbyhole seemed, even to his untutored eye, to exhibit more of the characteristics of a prison cell than those of a richly appointed chamber for nobility. Roxana pressed a hand gently into the feathered ticking until it sank from view, demonstrating the sumptuous nocturnal pleasures awaiting a royal heir. She flung open the window, admitting the clemency of spring, its sweet pastoral breath, and the nervous twitter and rustle of sparrows on the roof. Liberty wheeled abruptly about and marched disdainfully from the room.

His inaugural night alone in the place, bound in a darkness so complete he might as well have been blind, he bawled inconsolably at such length and with such force he periodically lost his wind in prolonged fits of horrible gasping exaggerated only slightly for the benefit of any listening parental ears. Then, well past the death of all hope, the stairs awakened into their distinctive squeak, I'm coming, I'm coming, and the door suddenly swung open upon the forbidding specter of his father, splashed from the waist up in a wild fearful light that played eerily across his chest and cast the fond features of the paternal face into an inhuman mask of malign relief. Cupped in Thatcher's enormous hands like a transparent chalice of fire was a half-filled tumbler of water topped by a layer of whale oil upon whose trembling surface floated a cork disk, its perforated center containing a lighted wick that dangled down into the clear liquid like an undulating worm. Placing this improvised night lamp on a deal table beyond the range of Liberty's arm, Thatcher settled on the edge of the bed, took his son's warm, damp hand in his own and waited patiently for the boy's heaving body to subside. Then he asked, kindly, "Are you finished?" Liberty nodded. Unable to confront his father's gaze, the boy studied the seemingly autonomous motions of his own fingers, writhing and rubbing endlessly one against the other.

"I appreciate your position," began Thatcher. "Solitude, night, bumps and cries and all that, but I think you should understand there will come a time, believe it or not, when you will wish to leave home, to embark on your own adventure without comfort of escort or entourage. Remember, your grandfather Azariah didn't help Colonel Knox haul sixty tons of artillery three hundred miles over the Berkshires in the dead of winter for you to squander the precious nights of your earthly sojourn blubbering like an infant because your parents weren't snoring contentedly away in the same room with you. So, to help conduct you safely to the portal of that ordained future, I have brought you this lamp."

He then proceeded to instruct his son on the manifold hazards of combustion, especially the trickiness involved in keeping it tamed within doors. Did Liberty know the tale of Brother Latimer out on the Old Cayuga Road? Well, one evening not so long ago, far past the midnight chimes, the good brother could be found hunched at his desk, desperately laboring over his accounts, endeavoring by a fantastic stroke of the pen to convert two dollars into three, when, the hour late, his vitality low, Brother Latimer fell dead asleep facedown in the wet ink, and sometime before dawn his unconscious hand, reaching out for an object in a dream, toppled the candle and up went the books, up went the house and up went Brother Latimer, his wife and three children. Do you want to go up? Do you want your mother and me to go up? Then don't touch the taper.

Liberty's eyes were yet as big as boiled eggs when his mother joined them, enveloped in the restorative aroma of warm gingerbread emanating from the platterful of cookies she presented to her son, each cookie cut in the shape of a kneeling slave, shackled arms lifted beseechingly in prayer.

Liberty rode out the night in the embrace of several large pillows, munching beaverlike through one gingery figure after another, ever alert to the least fluctuation of that dim yellowy bead wantonly adrift upon its isle of cork over immensities of dream tide, until morning light found him asleep at last, a half-eaten cookie clutched in one chubby fist, the abandoned plate lying slantwise beside him on the bed, empty now save for a dusting of crumbs and a scattered cairn of neatly nibbled little brown heads.

Any wonder then that his earliest memory was baptized in the magic of fire? He was perched on his father's bony knee, clasped in arms of majestic strength, wine-scented masculine breath beating softly about his ears, the surrounding room hot, smoky, clamorous with strangers who kept approaching to pat his head, chuck his chin, screw up their faces and otherwise bleat, coo, croon and declaim, all of which Liberty pointedly ignored in favor of the intoxicating scene spread wide before him, the eternal drama of wood burning on the hearth where the wee orange people lived and capered among the crackling logs. Here was a world more real, playful strife and perpetual metamorphosis holding lovely reign, and as he watched, Liberty wanted to live there, too.

Framing this spirited show was a massive oaken mantelpiece darkened by time and heat and into whose scratched and dimpled surface had been incised a progression of geometric marks that years later, under his mother's patient tutelage, would, with the abruptness of distant objects brought to a startling clarity by the mere imposition of the proper lens, spring into the marvel of written language, the rude letters of the first words he learned to read hung in memory as a verbal amulet to be admired, even fondled when necessary, in the dark days of his future: Freedom Hath Been Hunted Round The Globe. O! Receive The Fugitive, And Prepare In Time An Asylum For Mankind.

The house he grew up in was an enchanted domain, a knotty warren of hidden passageways, secret stairwells, sliding panels, floor traps and peepholes bored into the wainscoting at assorted elevations from which disembodied eyeballs periodically gaped like living bosses of ornamentation.

One lazy sun-shot morning, sprawled on the green and white Kidderminster carpet in the front parlor and thoroughly engrossed in the patient composition of a lecture on the sanctity of mousey life he planned on delivering later that afternoon to a polite congregation of backyard cats, Liberty happened to glance up as an entire section of papered wall swiveled silently open and out stepped a tall, looming gentleman with clenched jaw and fists who directed at the boy a mad piratical glare, crossed to the doorway opposite and vanished—never to be seen again. Already quite accustomed to the odd comings and goings of perfect strangers of every age, gender and hue, Liberty wasn't particularly disturbed by this specimen. Furtive figures often came stealing in from the nearby woods to be admitted at the back door by Aunt Aroline and end swallowed up forever by the house. On occasion there'd be a whole family of novel faces seated around the supper table, solemnly chewing on warm Indian bread and barely uttering a word. Sometimes at breakfast Liberty half expected a fully clothed fugitive to come climbing out of the porridge pot, shake off his hat and demand a cup of fresh water.

At night, tending to his humble bowl of illumination, ever apprehensive that without the necessary fuel of his vigilance the precious flame might falter and die, he was frequently distracted by unsettling noises from up on the roof and behind the lath, the pattering of feet large and small, sinister scratchings, muted cries, irregular thuds and thumps, inarticulate whisperings of the air—a chorus of gothic notes he struggled in vain to separate and identify.

Endless hours on such watch left his nerves depleted, his sleep infected. Visiting dreams vivid as exotic sea creatures—scales intensely iridescent, eyes huge and lidless, gaping mouths lined with rows of sharp triangular teeth or, worse, cold ridges of slimy gum—gobbled him up into a labyrinth of entrails where raged vague conflicts of epic savagery and no clear resolution, desperate voyages over convulsive seas, frantic flight through narrow measureless spaces, as if just beneath the skin of the world a vast, ageless war contended and once asleep you were inducted into service in this great invisible clash. But on whose side? And for what cause? A duty permanent and timeless, broken only by the cry of a voice calling out your name, a mother's fingers hooked about the hunched blade of your shoulder and hauling you up into the light.

One long languid evening, either actually awake or mindlessly adrift down a dream of being awake, Liberty was roused by a volley of brittle noises approaching the house in the dark. What? What was it? Nothing but hooves, and the rattle of wooden wheels mounting the stony path toward the barn. Stealthily, he rose up in bed on his knees, leaned his elbows upon the splintery sill and peered anxiously out the window. The sky was clear, the moon full, seemingly doubled in size, mantling the scene below in layers of living phosphorescence, a coating of pure dream paint. In the bed of the wagon halted just beneath

Liberty's window, his father and a bearded stranger were stooped over a long, narrow box, bright as a bar of silver, prying the nails from the lid with the flat blades of their axes. Unable to budge from his vantage or even turn away, Liberty waited helplessly for whatever was going to happen, his breath clamped in a vise of tensed muscle, his heart at that moment the loudest sound on the sleeping planet. And when the lid was lifted away to reveal, resting peacefully amid a pile of wood shavings, an actual dead body, a rush of mausoleum chill went goose pimpling over Liberty's own warm flesh, and when the body sat up in its coffin and opened its mouth and spoke living words that his father then answered, a sound escaped Liberty's throat, an unrecognizable eruption from the darkest interior, and calmly the body turned its head and stared directly up into Liberty's wide astonished eyes. Immediately he ducked down below the sill, buried his face in a pillow and listened for a long while to the wind whistling in, whistling out of his squashed nose. And when he dared to peek out the window again, the wagon and its contents, the coffin and the body in the coffin, his father and the bearded stranger, all were gone without a trace. Was what he had just witnessed truly real or merely a bit of insubstantial mummery staged by the old sleep phantoms? At what point exactly had he come truly awake? How to know? He filed the event away with other curious matters requiring further reflection such as, Where does the darkness go during the day? or, Why can't people fly?

Next morning, at a typically gray and dismal hour, a rather pale, pink-eyed Liberty was collected by the man who lived in the root cellar. It was Fishing Day and time for their regular stroll down the dew-slick trail to the lake, where they would sit in communal silence atop a rock (their rock) with lines dangling optimistically down into the mysterious, velvety water. When the moment was favorable for talk, talk they would, on omnifarious matters great and trifling, until the whole brimming world to the pendent present was thoroughly sectioned, sucked dry and left as compost for tomorrow's yield.

His name was Euclid. A short, squat fellow with arms as well banded as his legs, he possessed just one good eye while the other, an oyster-hued globe behind a drooping lid, moved about in its socket like an object of foreign manufacture attached to an entirely separate being with a will and interests of its own. Of a pronounced mercurial temperament, as quick with a growl as a grin, Euclid suffered from rending tempests of the soul that left him beached, beaconless, besieged. Whole days he spent sequestered in his underground hermitage where he could often be heard furiously sweeping the dirt from wall to wall and back again, all the while cursing loudly in such strenuous terms that Aunt Aroline would be forced to stuff her ears with candle wax and Thatcher to descend the stairs and reason with the tortured man, all to no avail. Euclid's fits were occasions of nature which must, of necessity, blow themselves out.

Another hour might find him reclining tranquilly beneath the shaggy old walnut tree, lost in a private vista of such compelling intricacy it was useless to disturb him; he wouldn't answer, he would not be moved.

But when properly tenanted in his body, Euclid was as sociable a companion as one could hope to encounter in this flinty world. Often he accompanied Liberty on rambling walks through the woods and up into the craggy hills. It was he who instructed the boy in the multitudinous guises in which shy nature routinely sought to veil herself. He knew the names of trees, the uses of plants, the tracks of animals. He showed Liberty how to map the stars and how such a map could help guide one's wanderings upon the planet. And he introduced him to those measureless parts of the universe lurking malevolently in the pitchy places between the lights.

One large, brightly spangled, transparent morning, the boy of an age when budding curiosity breaks out in irrepressible interrogation, he asked Euclid about his eye. The man was seated comfortably on the back porch shucking a pile of peas into a bucket between his feet, the pods splitting neatly open beneath his broad thumbs like emerald wallets, the peas tumbling into the bucket as noisily as balls of shot. When he didn't answer, Liberty repeated the question. Without a word, Euclid rose to his feet, took Liberty by the hand and led him down the back stairs into his dwelling below the earth. One room for one man, it contained one each of the barest essentials—cot, chair, washstand, pitcher, trunk—and nailed to the wall the sole nonfunctional adornment, a crude woodcut torn from one of Aunt Aroline's reformist magazines, depicting an enraged husband and father about to hurl a stool at his cowering wife and children, this pleasant domestic scene entitled *The Evils of Drink*.

Euclid lifted the boy high into the air and set him down on the cot as he would a compactly bundled parcel of feathers. Standing squarely before him, his one sound eye fastened grimly upon Liberty's wavering gaze, he said, "Got that blasted glim same place I found this," then pulled off his shirt and turned around. His back was a hideous crosshatching of hard, ridged flesh, welt upon welt in random disarray, appearing much like the cameoed burrowings of some frantic creature permanently trapped beneath the exitless skin. "Touch it," he commanded.

Liberty refused, already gauging the distance between himself and the door.

"Touch," Euclid insisted, shoving his disfigured back into Liberty's averted face.

"I don't want to." Though his gaze, as if magnetized, kept returning to the dreadful scars.

Euclid reached out to seize the boy's hand. "Can't learn nothing of any account without feeling. Now, touch."

Liberty's fingers moved tentatively over the stubborn winding weals. They felt like dead snakes.

"That's slavery, boy, that's the kingdom come."

"Can I go now?"

At a brief nod of Euclid's head, Liberty raced up the stairs to the kitchen where Aunt Aroline, having scrubbed and polished the floor, was busy sweeping, with her usual meticulousness, the thick layer of white scouring sand into a great herringbone pattern through which the boy's obliterating feet went madly scampering, avoiding a near collision with a table corner, overturning a stray parlor chair, frightening the cat into a blurred leap out the window, strewn sand and Aroline's indignant cries in his wake, and on up to the secluded safety of his room where, bolting the door, he sat upon the bed in a vague displaced spell, thoughts all ajumble but presided over by one certain central fear: that his own delicate back might one day be set upon by the same malicious agencies that had so cruelly visited his friend, a notion sufficient to ice his body and glaze his brain.

Presently, though, time passing gratefully on, his darkly wrought attention began to gently unwind, and soon he was down on the floor rolling a toy wagon back and forth over the rough planks, bound for the Territory and a rendezvous with mountain men along the Green River. And not more than half an hour later he was back downstairs, dodging his aunt's ridiculous complaints, and heading out through the meadow to the secret pond at the bottom of the ravine where giant bullfrogs dozed in the stinking mud and speckled salamanders hung suspended in the clear water as if trapped in glass. And by the following day he was away with Euclid on a huckleberry expedition at his aunt's behest—her traditional Saturday baking ordeal drawing near—and he never again asked about Euclid's colorless eye or mutilated back.

His own parents so frequently absent, often for painfully extended periods, embarked on what they occasionally termed their "crusade"— Liberty had sometimes pictured them sword or lance in hand, hacking away at a wrathful dragon or, side by side, clearing a bloody path through a human wall of armed infidels—he understandably had come to regard the remaining adults in the house, Aroline and Euclid, as a perfectly acceptable set of substitute parents. And, accurately intuiting that his aunt's plentiful and intimate problems occupied a more generous portion of her day than even she might be willing to admit, the boy tended to turn to the older man when troubles plagued his mind and set his skin to itching.

"Euclid?" he asked, fiddling nervously with his line before allowing it to go slack and belly out into the wind. They had been seated quietly there on the rock for more than an hour, the sun mounting ever higher into a dizzyingly blue sky, the emerald flashings of countless dragonflies darting repeatedly across the eye. Neither had as yet detected so much as a nibble.

"Yes, turnip."

"Can a dead man talk?"

Euclid seemed not to have heard the question. He rubbed at his nose, spit into the water, glanced away at the far shore as if he'd just heard an interesting sound out there or momentarily expected some fascinating event to transpire among the distant pines. When he spoke, it was in the soft, uninflected voice he reserved for only the weightiest of matters.

"Dead man do what dead man wants to do. Why's a good boy like you fussing with such truck. These here're bones for the big dogs to worry at, and even most of them just trot right on by, don't want nothing to do with that stink-stick."

"Why not?"

"Why not? I'll tell you why not. Same reason they go whistling through the graveyard. This here is death stuff and common folk believe if you don't think about it, don't talk about it, you won't catch it, but what they's too scared to know is they already got it."

"Got what?"

"Never mind. That's enough philosophizing for one day. Now, where'd you see this dead man talking anyway?"

"I don't know."

The laughter rolled out of Euclid in big, generous waves. "Liberty," he said, wiping the back of a hand across his watering eye, "this must be why I like you so much. You are one fine, funny fellow."

"Are dreams real?"

"Look out," declared Euclid, ducking his head, "here comes another. How do you fit all these whopping thoughts into that little bitty nut of yours? Of course a dream is real. You saw it, didn't you? No different than anything else you see. If you saw a dead man moving around in there, he was real, too. Like I say, dead man do what dead man wants to do. But if you saw one standing up and walking about and talking plain to folks, most probably that's because he wasn't buried right. A man can't be buried crossways in this world. Got to be buried east to west so when Gabriel blows his horn at sunrise you don't have to turn your head to behold the jubilee. So much conjuring you got to do to keep the spirit from wandering. You got to have the shout, all the folks walking in a ring in the proper direction. You got to put the things of the dead person on top of the grave, so many things. And if the coffin ain't carried properly to the cemetery, the dead person's naturally all confused and upset. Might be able to find his way back home and bring all his troubles with him."

"Could he come here, to our house?"

"If he died here. But ain't nobody died here lately that I know about."

Liberty mused over these facts and said, in a quavering voice, "I think the dead man's in the barn."

"Well then, baby doll," declared Euclid, "reckon we'd better head on back and take a peek. Anyway, looks like our fishy friends heard us speculating about dead folks and got spooked. But they'll be back tomorrow and so will we."

Though the day was rapidly approaching the near shadowless glory of high noon, the woods seemed darker to Liberty coming back than they had going out and every slight crack and rustle sounded a clanging bell of alarm.

The barn sat isolate in a clearing up behind the house, implacable as a rock, old, gray, hard-edged by the sun, a structure obviously built to contain the meanest thing, no matter its size. The open door gaped like a devouring mouth, black, abysmal, utterly toothless.

Liberty waited outside, careful to keep Euclid's body between himself and whatever might come lunging out of those gloomy depths. He could hear Euclid's reassuring calls as he searched each dusty stall and corner. "Nope, nothing here. Nothing there, either." The wagon, partially visible in the shadows just within the doorway like a quaint artifact on display, appeared to have been neither moved nor touched in years. Its bed was empty.

Several weeks passed.

At last Euclid emerged from the barn, wholly intact and thankfully unharmed, shaking his head and brushing chaff from his hands. "Looks like that's one dead man done hightailed it out of here some time ago. Stepping lightly, too, didn't leave a single track. Don't look so disappointed. Never know when another dead man's likely to come traipsing through."

"I think he went away on the train."

"The train? What train is that?"

"The one Mother told me about, that runs under the ground."

Politely restraining himself, Euclid responded to this news with a considerate chortle. "Whew, you sure tiring me out now, turnip. What a heap of knobby stones you chucking at me today."

"I've heard it."

Indeed, he had often imagined the polished rails gleaming invitingly away down a dank, lamp-lit tunnel, and between futile wrestling bouts with his tenacious bed linen he had ruined the sleep of many a night, lying as still as he could, his breath controlled to an almost noiseless sigh, listening with every unabated nerve of his body for the telltale clack of the wheels, the rumbling chug of the engine, the long, piercing, seductive cry of the whistle.

"I ain't disbelieving you, Liberty, I've heard that blessed train, too. And so, I expect, has our dead friend, done caught himself a ride to the far place. But let me tell you, baby doll, you plan on passing along that particular route, travel light, get to the station early, don't argue with the conductor and be kind to those you meet along the line, 'cause you never know when that bullgine might blow up or the coach jump the tracks."

One evening in the late spring of 1846, Liberty not yet two, the ominous detonation of a giant's boots was heard thundering across the porch, over the threshold, down the hallway and into the parlor, where burst a big, loud, bushy man with guns at his hips and warts on his hands. He was wearing a crumpled oilskin cap of enigmatic hue and a ratty green duster. From a face dark and filthy, sprouting a black beard of such unkempt weediness it would have surprised no one had something wild emerged, a set of fierce, quick eyes blazed like coins at the bottom of a well. Through a hole in his boot you could see his sock and, through a hole in his sock, his foot. Uncle Potter. Thatcher's cousin, actually.

Aunt Aroline immediately excused herself, retiring to the genteel solitude of her room while Liberty, fleeing the friendly attempt at an ursine embrace, took refuge behind his mother's Windsor chair, from which crouching vantage he observed in a transport of unblinking wonderment not so dissimilar from his everyday consciousness at that age the extravagant style of this magnetic man whose mere presence seemed to fill the room to all four corners, his voice rattling nearby porcelain, every florid gesture of his body releasing into the air an almost visible trail of odor, each hardy whiff of human musk—stale tobacco, salt-rimed leather, lathered horseflesh or any one of a virtual olfactory rainbow of other, slightly less insolent fragrances—evoking in the impressionable boy whole worlds vast and complete, instantly apprehensible at a reach well below that of reason, though it would be years before Liberty would know what he knew.

And as Potter paced the worn carpeting before the dead hearth, his grandiloquence flew higgledy-piggledy in rapid volleys about the parlor—spittle-soaked verbal balls like "blood," "injustice," "barbaric" and "righteous" that these thin papered walls had safely absorbed a thousand times and more, and others like "Matamoros," "invasion," "Arista" and "Old Rough and Ready" that they had not.

Thatcher, half reclining on the balding horsehair sofa, his pale head floating within a perpetual cloud of pipesmoke, attended to his cousin's performance with bemused silence. Roxana, too, listened without comment, pausing now and again in her knitting (a task she absolutely loathed but one nevertheless she couldn't seem to keep herself from doing) to place a comforting hand on the hair-sleek crown of her son's head.

Suddenly Potter ceased in midstride, glaring down at Thatcher to demand, "So what do you say? Are you willing to strike out with me or not?"

Thatcher took some time removing the pipe from his mouth. When he finally answered, he spoke in cool, precise tones seasoned with nouns like "crime," "treachery" and "greed."

"Damn you," muttered Potter, and touching his cap and bowing slightly in Roxana's direction he strode decisively out of the room, out of the house, the front door hanging open behind him, and leaped onto his waiting horse and without bothering to pause in town to formally enlist (Fishes past and present always preferring to swim upstream far beyond the finely meshed nets of state authority), galloped off for the Big Frolic on the Rio Grande—days and nights with no more sleep than what could be stolen seconds at a time upright in a lurching saddle, rubbing tobacco juice on his eyelids to keep awake, the spirited discussions he conducted with himself a source of amusement and alarm to passing strangers who tended to give this wandering lunatic a rather wide berth—through storm and flood and impossible heat and actually arriving as far as the fair city of Cincinnati, the London of the West, where he could taste on his tongue the blood in the air and harried pedestrians jostled roving herds of pigs for right-of-way through the mud and manure of the streets, and rounding a corner he was confronted by a festering sump of bone, gristle and entrails, here and there a tiny wizened tail corkscrewing up out of the bubbling muck, runoff from one of the nearby shambles, into which his skittish horse placed one dainty hoof, instantly sinking in up to the fetlock before rearing back thoroughly spooked as an unruffled Potter simply sat there atop the anxious animal, his squinting eye caught by the colonnade of black-belching stacks rising up above the housetops at the end of the street—riverboats, an entire flotilla of them, lined up in docile formation down at the wharves like hogs at a trough—and beyond, through a dreamy blue haze, the distant wooded hills of Kentucky, and Potter yanked on the reins, swung the horse savagely about and headed back in the same direction he had come at half the gait, uttering not a syllable to another living soul until those same heavy boots remounted the same planks of the same porch, pounded down the hallway and into the parlor to wait for Thatcher to lower the book in his hands so Potter could face him directly and declare, "Damn you."

Thatcher, who had not bothered to rise from the sofa, waited a moment before replying. "There'll be other wars," he promised, "good ones, too, full of honor and glory and virtuous cannonading. You'll get your chance."

Potter turned and spat into the fireplace. "Not if I end up saddled with as many principles as you apparently labor under."

"Looks like you already do."

"Damn you," muttered Potter, and, as abruptly as he had appeared, he was gone.

When Liberty was six, his parents enrolled him in a local dame school of some repute operated by an elderly widow who called herself Ma'am L'Orange, though everyone in town knew she had not a dram of French blood in her veins and in fact nothing even remotely "orange" about her except possibly her head, which exhibited an alarmingly citruslike rotundity. She and her husband, Captain Fenn, had settled in Delphi more than two decades earlier, following the old salt's retirement from the navy where he claimed to have served with distinction aboard the famous frigate United States during its engagement with the British vessel Macedonia, personally fetching cups of water to the great Captain Decatur himself. Of course he also bragged of having been at one time a pirate, a spy, a poet and an attorney. Rumor persisted, however, that in his prime Captain Fenn had paced the quarterdeck of the good ship Constantia, an illegal slaver notorious from Hampton Roads to Hilton Head, and had been summarily removed from command when a consistently intolerable percentage of the "merchandise" either went missing or arrived at port in unacceptably damaged condition. Captain Fenn had embarked upon his own final voyage while on a semiannual visit to his brother Epheseus, a toper of the first reputation in southern New Jersey, when an extravagance of rum led to a nasty topple from the Philadelphia–Trenton diligence and the laying open of Fenn's skull upon an unfortunately situated post stone. Ten years had passed since the fatal accident without Ma'am L'Orange's once revealing to anyone even the most minimal satisfactions of proper mourning. Few were privy to the fact that deep in the throes of his increasingly frequent bouts with the ardent, the venerable sea captain was partial to chasing his wife about the house and grounds with a knotted carriage whip.

After his death Sarah Fenn changed her name and opened her school. The front parlor was readily converted into a pleasant classroom with several militarily precise rows of miniature desks facing Ma'am L'Orange's imposing escritoire, which stretched half the width of the room, and a mammoth slateboard with fist-sized chunks of chalk. Under the windows were shelves impressively stocked with books, and only a close perusal of the titles would disclose an odd and often decidedly unchildlike mix of volumes: Murray's English Grammar, The Bride of Lammermoor, Botanical Receipts for Cure and Custom, The Unknown Friend, Paley's Principles of Moral and Political Philosophy, The American Frugal Housewife and Tom Jones. Hung around the walls in haphazard fashion at a height of about three feet ("for the children's edification") was a series of illustrations to John Bunyan's Pilgrim's Progress that Ma'am L'Orange had drawn in a rudimentary but earnest style, each stick figure painstakingly labeled in an elegant hand: Faithful, Ignorance, Mr. Pickthank, Mr. Money-love, etc., Vanity Fair depicted as a sort of Brueghelesque Fourth of July picnic celebration, the City of Desolation indistinguishable from the Celestial City and both resembling Delphi itself. Her masterpiece, Christian's climactic combat with Apollyon, rendered the beast as a fanged snail with ludicrous curlicued bat wings.

But, in the end, this fine educational setting was rarely used. Most instruction took place upstairs in the mistress's bedroom with Ma'am L'Orange perched at the foot of her bed, the children arrayed before her on a motley collection of trunks, boxes, a carpenter's bench and a single rather unsteady stool once the property of her only son and heir, Winslow, upon whom manhood and gold-madness seemed to descend simultaneously, igniting an inner combustion that hurled him through the door all the way out to Californy and a disquieting silence unbroken by mail or hearsay for more than a year now. Strewn indifferently across the sills, the dressing table and the bare floor of this plain, undecorated room were—the sole touch of the personal—jars, cups, tankards and tumblers stuffed with garden violets, some sprigs fresh and startlingly purple, others wilted and tobacco brown.

A typical daily lesson consisted of Ma'am L'Orange reading aloud from the Bible for hours at a time in a chirpy soprano whose aspirations to the thrillingly theatrical tended to lapse promptly into the drearily vexatious. The children fidgeting on their hard benches, struggled, not always successfully, against the temptations of sleep and poking one another in the ribs. Then, in the midst of a passage, Ma'am L'Orange, having apparently attained a state of perfect exhaustion, would swoon back into her linen sighing, "Oh, children, children, children. It is a hard lot we have been assigned, devilishly hard. But do our duty we must and not a single tear will have been shed in vain." A second, greater sigh thoroughly deflating her body, she would lie there in absolute stillness, not a single pupil daring to stir, their innocent eyes intent upon this strange, mad woman laid out before them like a corpse awaiting resurrection—the frightening moment when Ma'am L'Orange would sit up with a start, as if catching herself in the midst of a great fall and, searching frantically about the bedclothes for her willow switch, seize in her bony grip the nearest hapless youth (never the agile, feisty Liberty whom she'd soon enough discovered wasn't worth the trouble) and commence whaling away on the unfortunate scholar's exposed backside as even untouched onlookers shrieked and howled in sympathetic pain. Suddenly the switch would cease in midair and Ma'am L'Orange would climb wearily back into bed muttering, "I'm so tired, children, so very tired." For days after such a vigorous demonstration of the disciplinary arts, a model of sullen docility reigned over the school.

Sometimes, setting her Bible aside, Ma'am L'Orange would entertain her charges with colorful tales from her past, whatever vague recollection, daydream, ill-lit fantasy or scrap of old gossip happened to be blowing through her mind at the moment. These recitations she called History.

"When I was a girl about your age the whole of this valley from

33

Mount Hook to the Kiawanna was still infested with raving hordes of wild savages. Half-naked and reeking of odors you couldn't squeeze out of a wet pup. They didn't care one jot what anybody thought of 'em. Their wolfish fingers perpetually curled about the neck of a whiskey bottle. A worse lot of lying, thieving, cheating demons you wouldn't want to meet—and those were the friendly ones. There seemed to be a dropped stitch or two in the knit of their souls long past right remedy. And their bodies, even in the ice-bound fury of a desperate winter, always a portion of tawny flesh peeking through the greasy rags. Agents of Satan's empire, yes . . ."

And her voice would trail off, and in the pause the children would begin to squirm in their seats, nervously studying one another until the voice would return from its hiding place, circling back cometlike, magically replenished, though settled decisively into another orbit altogether.

"Now up on a hill outside of town back in the faraway time there lived an old woman in a tumbledown thatch hut. If she had a name, it was not known to me. Old Skitteryclaws we called her, my friends and I. I couldn't even tell you for certain what she looked like because of the long white hair that obscured the features of her face and streamed down her back like a horse's mane. Winter or summer she always wore a long black dress and from the road at the bottom of the hill you could see her every morning sweeping the dirt from her door with a straw broom. At night her eyes glowed like a hell beast's and her horrible laughter scared the bark from the trees. And if you happened to be caught in that part of the country as the sun was going down you raced home as if your feet were aflame. Do you know why? That's right, children, because Old Skitteryclaws was a witch. Ellis Butts once stole some cherries from her orchard and she changed him into a snake. Many were the carefree boys and girls, much like yourselves, who, lost forever to their grieving families, came to live as hideously transformed pets under a rock beneath her wretched hut. And whenever she wished, Old Skitteryclaws had but to emit a single whistle between her two remaining teeth for this ball of poisonous serpents to uncoil and all come rushing out in an angry hiss, eager to do her infernal bidding.

"Last night, my dears, as often occurs in someone of my advanced years, I experienced some difficulty sleeping. The mind, you should understand, possesses a will of its own that not even prayer can always correct. So, as is my custom on such occasions, I sat for many an hour in my rocker in the parlor window, watching the dead wandering like fireflies among the stones of the cemetery across the valley. They can't sleep either, poor things. They're here with us, you know, every minute of every hour. No, no, don't bother twisting your necks about. You cannot see them from where you are sitting. If you could step outside of yourselves even for a moment and view the world through your spiritual eye, then all would be instantly apprehensible. This is heaven, children. We have, each blessed one of us, already been translated. Our earthly senses are like blinders beguiling us from the truth.

"Allow me, then, to pour into your porchlike ears an elixir of practical benefit. If ever you find yourselves preparing a batch of pumpkin cookies, I would advise you to omit the yeast and substitute instead a tablespoon of pearl ash. The baked result will be so much lighter—tastier, too—and your table will be adorned in a delightful spray of compliments."

One idle afternoon, several months after Liberty's passing under the tutelage of Ma'am L'Orange, Thatcher—curious as to the health of his son's academic life—inquired casually, "Who is the president of the United States?"

"Jesus Christ," Liberty promptly answered.

Father looked at Mother. Mother looked at Father. Liberty never saw Ma'am L'Orange again.

Instruction resumed at home under the watchful guidance of his parents and, in their long and frequent absences, Aunt Aroline, who was charged with an explicit list of prohibited topics, prominent among them her own string of modish hobbyhorses now temporarily banished to the barn. Society was diseased toe to crown, near and far leaking poisons perilous to the unformed mind. The general theory was clear to Aroline at least in principle—her own quest for physical and moral perfection yet another essay at warding off the fatal contamination—but the details baffled her. Alone in the big house with her impressionable young nephew often for weeks at a time, her overtaxed will further assailed by loneliness, responsibility and a host of other anxieties too dimly perceived to be even named, she couldn't help but seek to mend the empty air with certain navigational aids she deemed invaluable in negotiating the rapids of existence from genesis to revelations: don't ever eat anything red; kiss your elbow and your wish will come true; the Deity cannot commit a mistake; let the wind be your guide in times of trouble; the juice of one huckleberry will make you drunker than any wine; a cat is privy to secrets you and I will not be permitted to know until we are dead; the heart is a cesspool of verminous lusts; drink a gallon of water a day and you'll never be sick; God speaks directly through Senator Webster; the road to hell is paved with the skulls of infants; the seat of government is a Castle Misrule; dirt is the Devil's dandruff; your shadow is the robe of the angel watching over you.

As he had with Ma'am L'Orange, Liberty simply digested with serene impartiality whatever tidbits happened to drop onto his plate, from the valid to the fallacious, the modest to the exorbitant. Much of what he learned would be forever coupled in his mind with the memory of a specific setting: Latin and Greek at the kitchen table with his mother, geometry and philosophy in the study with his father, and of course the dizzying miscellany of Aunt Aroline's as she shooed the boy from room to room one step ahead of her chores. And then the countless books consumed in solitude out under the old walnut tree overlooking the east meadow or, with the dogs for pillows, prone on the floor before the hearth, munching meditatively upon a piece of fruit. For as long as Liberty lived, the god-haunted hills of Mycenae would always resemble the pine-capped round tops surrounding Delphi, just as the American Revolution would always be steeped in the humid flowery scent of ripe pears.

From the moment baby Liberty, alarmingly precocious in matters both physical and mental, achieved the capacity for locomotion of any sort whatsoever, it fell to supervising adults the tiresome necessity of assuming the posts of watchtower guards. An instant's inattention—a brief turning away to crimp that pie, search the cubbyhole of the desk for that recent letter from L. Tappan, toss a bundle of soiled linen out the window to Aroline boiling clothes in the backyard—and the boy would be gone, vanished beneath one's very nose. He seemed to enjoy an unerring instinct for doors left forgetfully ajar and would crawl, at a surprisingly energetic rate, through one beckoning portal after another, his progress usually checked at the routinely bolted front entrance, where he could be sometimes found gently bumping, bumping, bumping the soft crown of his finely haired head against the stubborn oak.

And, once the giddy pleasures of upright ambulation had been mastered, even a closed door presented a mere temporary obstacle, the cunning rascal having also speedily solved the slippery puzzle of knobs and locks. Liberty's endless waking hours required a vigilance nearly impossible to maintain. One exceptionally distracting morning, Roxana, in a gust of teary panic, rushed from the empty house to spy her wayward son some twenty yards down the pike, toddling briskly along on plump bowed legs, his arms in the air, and buck-naked. Racing forward, she snatched him up just steps ahead of the clattering wheels of the Albany–Schenectady coach.

"It's all your fault," Thatcher commented slyly, from behind the pages of the *Delphi Argosy.* "The boy's simply living up to the imperative of the name you christened him with."

"And if I had chosen to call him Patches," countered Roxana, eyebrow raised, "he'd have been obliged to scamper about on all fours and bark at strangers?"

Thatcher shrugged. "Who can say? In this world there is little of import we truly comprehend."

Such was the nature of their domestic exchanges at the time. Thatcher, ever prone to humors of diverse hues and strengths, was often brushed by the wings of melancholy, great batlike creatures who hung in shadowy suspension from the pocked and darkly gleaming walls of his caverned self, liable at the least provocation to spring into agitated flights of random duration. Despairing of the country, the crusade, his own meager abilities, he would indulge his innate propensity for frivolous speculation, drawing Roxana into extravagant colloquy over premises she doubted even he believed. When this mood was upon him, as she had learned over the years, the prudent course lay in quiet disengagement, a graceful retreat from the field. Still, she loved the man dearly, helplessly, having readily granted to him those portions of her heart untouched until their first meeting by human commerce, and if the thorns might occasionally obscure the blessings of the rose, she commanded the patience, the green thumb of a lover, and the wisdom to appreciate that in this mundane garden all was rankness and maze, an elaboration into ordained forms, outer and inner, to which we affix the name Destiny.

But what, finally, were they to do about their wandering boy? Nothing, apparently, nothing but watch over, fret about, hope for and endeavor to keep from as much harm as possible.

"Tether him to a rope," suggested Aunt Aroline, tactfully avoiding mention of her own experiments with this method of restraint when the parents were away.

"Like a dog?" queried Roxana, her shock at hearing such advice, from a close relative yet, largely suppressed.

"The boy needs to be taught obedience. There are rules in this world that must be respected, laws that must be mastered, without and within."

Roxana gazed out the window. The nearby hills, in their seasonal metamorphosis from white to brown, were beginning to exhibit the green fuzz of spring and appeared, strangely enough, closer than usual. A lone hawk, like some dark, defective piece chipped off the vault of perfect sky, descended in long, slow circles toward the valley floor. "There are no rules," she said softly.

"What? What did you say?" Aroline could barely contain her outrage. "I've never heard such nonsense in my life. Why, it's almost blasphemous, child—and I address you as 'child' because, evidently, your moral development has failed to progress much beyond the stage of your own untutored son. Is this what they teach you down in that horrid South? Is it?"

The wistful line of a smile materialized on Roxana's face, hardly cracking the glaze of her expression. "There is no place on earth more concerned with laws and precepts and maxims and regulations."

"The Devil's maxims."

"Yes."

The operation of memory, when Roxana came to regard it at all, seemed to her to be rather like the idle shuffling of an ever-thickening deck of haunted cards, some of course quite new regardless of age, figures and symbols still retaining a high gloss across years of hard usage, some gone missing entirely (thereby reducing one's chances in the crucial game?), while others, the bulk of the pack, simply gathered over time stains and smudges, layers of puzzling obscurities, edges slowly softening, detail fading, hands dealt and redealt in whatever grand, capricious, unknowable cycle it was that made up the contest of a life. But when she was visited by her distant past—which meant whenever she entertained thoughts of Carolina—the same unremarkable scene would be placed before her vision with curious and unchancelike regularity.

She must have been thirteen, fourteen perhaps, certainly some-where in that charmed interval between the gift of her first horse and her dreadful introduction to the smirking, doltish Cooper Beacham, her Intended, her parents' Intended actually, dubious product of one of the "finest families" of one of the "finest plantations" of one of the "finest etceteras" in a land plentifully stocked with etceteras. It was one of those long, hot, lazy, molasses afternoons in late spring just prior to the annual decampment to Charleston in advance of the heat, the bugs, the "summer sickness." Father and Mr. Dray, the over-seer, were up at the Point inspecting a dike that had collapsed overnight, Mother secluded in her chamber "resting her eyes," the boys off on a romp to the Pritchards "to see a man about a horse," cracked young Saxby, and the house, for a number of rare hours, was thankfully quiet.

Roxana was upstairs alone in her room, having curtly dismissed, over the usual childish protestations, her body servant, Ditey, who now lay curled up like an animal on the heart-pine boards outside the door, rustling and sighing in as obnoxious a manner as she gauged her little missus could safely tolerate. Ditey had also been sternly admonished not to go whining to Mother about this latest banishment from Missy Roxana's presence. "What in heaven's name are you doing in there?" Mother would demand, knuckles rapping sharply on the door. "Ditey thinks you don't like her." And Roxana: "Can't I steal a moment's privacy in this nosy house? Must I always be spied on by meddlesome eyes? We're watching them, they're watch-ing us, and no one relaxes for an instant. It's making us all ill." Mother: "I'll send for Dr. Groton." Roxana: "If you do, I'm going to start screaming and I'm not going to stop until I pass out." And so on. A conversation, of course, without any definitive end, variants of which had already been played out so frequently that Roxana simply could not bear another exhausting performance. She had promised Ditey a shiny new dime if she kept her mouth shut.

And what shady practice was Roxana attempting to conceal behind the locked door of her room? She was, dutiful girl, seated at the open window (the perpetually open window, sash and jamb warped together in perfect bondage since long before she was even born), the drawing board in her lap displaying an unfinished, reasonably accurate representation of the brown thrasher posed in regal solitude amid the leafy boughs of the white oak outside, beards of Spanish moss gathered in its limbs like hanks of collected time. She loved birds, always had, without quite understanding why. There was an essential mystery in their appeal beyond the proud elegance, the fineness of structure, the brittle beauty—qualities she sought to capture on paper in a recently embarked project, uncommonly ambitious in one so young, of documenting in her own hand the feathered species of the region. Once she completed a sufficient number of drawings, Father had vowed he would have the results bound and published in an actual book.

The thrasher cocked its head, training one hard pellet of an eye directly upon her. What did it see? Snared in the vortex of such a sharp, ruthless vision, how wan, soft, pitiably unfledged she must appear. What sort of rendering might a creature capable of flight make of her own earthbound flesh if it could draw? There are corners of this globe we are not permitted to inhabit.

More rapid than sight could register, the thrasher unfolded its wings, took an abrupt hop into space and was instantly swallowed up by the air. Roxana waited, patience being, as any devotee soon learns, the virtue of value in ornithological pursuits, but after several desultory minutes spent in observing the grand eastward processional of the clouds, imagining it was she and the planet she rested upon, not those heaped bolls of cumuli, who were actually gliding westward, as perhaps they were, she realized that this time the bird would not return.

Setting aside the drawing board and the box of colors Mother had bought for her in Philadelphia, she returned to the down of her great rumpled bed, crawled beneath the mended netting and, retrieving her copy of *Anne of Geierstein or the Maiden of the Mist* from among the sheets, composed herself upon a mound of pillows preparatory to her return to the crags and glens, the clans and clash, the lairds and their ladies with the pale, pale skin. As the skeeters went whining beyond the bar, she read a page, read the same page again and stopped. The book fell from her hands. A wave of near narcotic lassitude broke sweepingly over her stranded form, either the herald of some dread illness or her anatomy's shocked reaction to this early spell of August torpor. A day compounded of heat, thick, windless, all-reaching, its presence corporeal, cumbering objects, trespassing on thought, enshrouding even the narrative of her book in a repellingly foreign atmosphere. Yet beneath the weight of the weather, there remained something almost pleasurable in this dull oppression, something the land and the house had been built to contain, and, too weary to protest, she simply, willingly acquiesced, offered herself up to this secret sensation of sinking forever away. When, half an hour later, she woke, her face was bathed in sweat, her head throbbed, her skin itched. In a sudden surge of impatience she rolled out of bed and, crossing the room, divested herself of her remaining undergarments until she was quite perfectly nude. Positioning herself before the mirror, she regarded the reflection caught therein. All in all, a good body, agreeable in shape and proportion, despite the late changes creeping over it, the onset of her monthlies and her pains and the dark tendrils of coarse hair assembling in the fork of her legs, signs sure and unmistakable, tokening the future, her future, and, as she stood there, in all her flowing nakedness, pondering the perplexities of the body—our woefully inadequate conveyance through the medium of time—she couldn't help but wonder, in an impossible tangle of hope and apprehension, at what distant nameless station this onrushing futurity would leave her deposited.

One afternoon, plucked from the accumulated hoard of her youth so memorable she believed, because on this particular p.m., nothing, absolutely nothing, had happened.

As Liberty *grew,* so, too, did the radius of his rambles. By the age of ten he could have picked his way blindfolded through the surrounding woods and hills. When Roxana asked just what it was he did on these solitary excursions, Liberty replied, "Prospecting."

One clear summer day, utterly absorbed in following the track of some clawed, padded animal the consequences of a possible encounter with he had not given a single thought, Liberty happened by chance to notice, sprouting in the shadow of a large rock, a strange bushy plant of no recognizable species, a heap of gray, stringy tendrils and leaves that seemed, as he approached, to be exhibiting a slight quivering movement curious on such a windless afternoon. The boy hesitated. Had the creature he'd been tracking taken refuge inside this bush? Was it even now tensing for the wild leap out at him, fangs and talons bared? Then, just as he was preparing to back away, Liberty noticed amid the odd pile of breathing vegetation an eye of singular blue of a decidedly human character. He stared, rapt; the eye stared back. "Aye," declared a reedy voice from inside the bush as it began to increase in height and advance toward him, "you caught me, you did, fair and square, no denying that." A bony hand emerged from within the thready foliage which Liberty now realized was, in truth, an unbarbered cascade of gray human hair. "You are, no doubt, in a positive mystification as to whom you have the honor of addressing—Arthur Fife, gentleman of fortune, at your service, young lad." Liberty stepped forward, accepted the grimy hand, then examined his own and wiped it on the seat of his pants. "I've seen you before, lad, many a time, passing through the territory, but you haven't seen me, no, you haven't." He shifted restlessly about on filthy bare legs, the mass of hair swaying gently to and fro, parting just enough to reveal he wore no undergarments. "I've been the commissioned captain of this forest for more than half a century now. Try to guess my true age. Bet you can't. Go ahead, try." His bearded cheeks continued to move even after he ceased speaking, as if he were chewing on something particularly tough and sticky.

Liberty attempted to imagine an age of impossible longevity. "Seventy?" he ventured.

Fife responded with a chuckle that sounded like water rushing over a bed of stones. "I am one hundred and forty-six years of age. Incredible, isn't it? Do ye believe me?"

Liberty looked the man slowly up and down. "Yes," he said.

"Come, lad, follow me. Got something to show ye."

He led the curious boy up the steep hill through brambles and across fallen branches to the summit, where at the rotten base of a dead oak dismantled by lightning rested a bale-sized boulder that Fife pushed aside as easily as a bag of leaves, revealing a hole in the ground into which he disappeared quick as a frightened gopher. "Come, come," called his high, urgent voice from the darkness within.

On hands and knees Liberty scuttled through a short damp passage and found himself in a surprisingly ample underground chamber, the floor a soft carpeting of fresh moss, the walls reinforced with planks but for one side where an exposed network of roots bare and white as skeletal fingers held back the black dirt. The low ceiling was decorated in an expanse of embroidered white flowers, an upside-down field of Queen Anne's lace that Fife had obviously plucked and replanted overhead from wall to wall. The space was quite comfortable, large enough for a boy, though the top of Fife's head kept grazing against the pendent blossoms of those ornamental weeds. Fife himself was seated cross-legged on a pile of animal skins, having lit the stub of a tallow candle which, though sputtering, provided illumination sufficient to reveal the fascinatingly rustic decor of this furnished hole in the ground, as well as the queer smile fixed upon the proprietor's partially obscured face.

"I see you have discovered my treasure chest," declared Fife, gesturing toward a wooden box in the corner that Liberty had not in fact noticed at all. "All my worldly possessions are contained therein," he added, dragging the chest toward him. "Would you care for a peek? Frankly, my boy, it's not often I entertain visitors here in my dark abode, especially not ones so clever as you, cultivated lads who can appreciate the valuables collected over a bloody lifetime of frolic and folly." He leaned forward to offer a conspiratorial aside: "For I was a pirate, you see, under the black flag with Calico Jack and Bartholomew Roberts." With some degree of difficulty he managed to pry open the lid of the chest, releasing a choking cloud of fine dust and the perfume of the ages. Reaching inside, he removed a short cylindrical object which he presented with a certain ceremonial gravity. "The finger bone of Henry Morgan," he intoned. Liberty turned the object in his hand; to him it resembled a stick. "A lock of Teach's beard," said Fife, passing over a second relic. To Liberty, a piece of hemp. "A gold doubloon from Kidd's treasure." To Liberty, a clay-encrusted stone. "I was there, you know, when they turned the captain off the scaffold at Wapping. Terrible business. The rope broke, and they had to launch him out anew. Hope never to see the like again. It was a sordid life, lad, and I've been paying for it ever since. But there were times, oh, there were times, even though they put a pistol to my head to sign the articles, when the life was a glory never to be imagined.

"Now, of course, I'm the man marooned by society, and you, my boy, have found me out on my enchanted isle. Yes, I am guilty, a horrid sinner damned in the eyes of God and man. I deserve no better than what you see before you." He waved a languid hand about to indicate the mole's lair in which they sat.

"What are you guilty of, sir?" asked Liberty.

"Why a life of unrestraint, of course. I refused to acknowledge the word 'No.' It was 'Yes' with me, lad, 'Yes' forever and always. I knew no hindrances, I brushed aside all societal obstacles, people were as shadows before me. Those were the grand days of riot and debauchery. I strode through the world with flask unstoppered, cutlass unsheathed and breeches unbuttoned. Lookee here." Leaning out into the flickering candlelight, Fife pulled aside a curtain of hair to disclose, crudely etched into his very flesh, a primitively drawn skull and crossbones. "Old Inky did that on me at a table in The Flaming Bucket back in the roaring Port Royal times."

"But how did you end up here in upper New York?"

"How? How, you say? I suppose I took a wrong turn at New Providence." Then he opened his mouth, exposing a gumful of dark, ragged teeth, his begrimed face crinkled up as if in laughter while his shoulders shook, but not a sound could be heard. He searched around behind himself and hauled into view a white clay jug which he lifted to his lips, took a long gulp from and then offered to Liberty. "Care for some belly timber?"

Liberty, ever adventurous, swallowed a healthy sip. The liquid burned and smelled of turpentine and when he choked and coughed the droplets spewing from his mouth flared up brightly in the candle flame.

"Takes a mite getting used to," explained Fife. "But it clears the head and warms the soul. In a few minutes you'll be thanking me. They always do."

Through the prisms of the boy's tears Fife seemed to Liberty some hairy shimmering apparition that could devour him in one mad gulp. Then his vision cleared and Fife appeared much as he had before except that each strand of his numerous hairs stood out separate and lucent.

"And now," announced Fife rather eagerly, the glittering of his eyes a bit more pronounced than seemed possible in this dim tallow light, "now that we've properly introduced ourselves, attended to the required conversational strictures, shared a drink—care for another by the way? No? Well perhaps later—now we may turn to the reason I have invited you to my quarters today." From within his tent of hair he produced a leather pouch and extracted a sheaf of yellowed papers he dramatically waved in Liberty's face, then reverently placed in his hairy lap.

"I have often observed you traveling through these woods in the company of a black man. Once you passed no more than three feet from where I squatted, performing a rather successful impersonation of a pile of leaves which I had meticulously arranged throughout my tresses, and on more than one occasion I heard this man whom I noticed you were attending carefully, turn and call out to you, 'Liberty!' Is this not correct?"

Liberty, in awed silence, merely nodded his head.

"Is 'Liberty' indeed your Christian name?"

"Yes," the boy managed softly.

"So I assumed. You have been granted a great gift and a great responsibility. By the spark in your eye I see that you understand this. So, I now wish to honor you by officially inducting you into the ranks of the Liberi. Here are the articles." Again the sheaf of papers was flourished about. "Here, read them, examine them. I can assure you all is in perfect order."

The boy hunched forward into the light. Scanning the brittle pages, he saw the words: "Birthright . . . the Sweets of Liberty . . . the Fruits of Labor . . . a Share of the Earth."

"But what is this all about?"

"Ah, you are unacquainted then with the reputation of the great Captain Mission and his noble efforts to save humanity from itself?"

"Who is he?"

"It's 'was,' I'm afraid, boy, 'was.' Horrible engagement. Many a good lad gone to dive for the eternal peace. Last I saw of Captain Mission he had a saber in each hand, a gash across his cheek and a smile on his lips. A truer man never paced the quarterdeck. Under him we founded a paradise, can ye believe it? Libertalia, it was called, right there hard off the east coast of Africa, exactly where the ancient prophecies said it would be. Free and easy those times were, I'd give an eye to have 'em back again. Every man same as every other man. Share and share alike. What a wild larksome crew we were, white and black and yellow and red and all the shades between. A nation of

---

47

banded brothers slashing a lane of freedom through this shackled world. You should have seen the slavers running before us, hising up their skirts and scampering for home. And, do you know, not one escaped us. How can I explain to one so young the joy of the pursuit, the thrill of our cannons toppling those bloodstained masts, ripping through their ranks, the lead and splinters and screams, the jubilation of the slaves at their unexpected deliverance. Mental champagne I don't look to taste again this side of the bar. And every one of those slaves eagerly joined our crew, best damn sailors in all the world's navies. But what we would sometimes do to the captain and his mates would give a lad like you night fits for a month. One foul word to Captain Mission and off they'd go over the side to the fishies and the sharks. Once the slaves started talking we'd know who to do up right, haul 'em up to the yardarms, 'sweat' 'em around the deck. Not a pretty picture for delicate souls but, by God, the fun we had. And what was done to them devils was a precious kindness to what they done to the poor lads in the hold, but we rescued hundreds of 'em from the irons and I can live with that. Of course that's why they was all after us so fierce, not a country with ships on the sea didn't want to see us hanging in chains before the tide. This globe's a prison, child, and those who wish to break out are the sworn enemies of all governments.

"Now, from the look of your rigging and the company you keep, you strike this old dog as a lad enlisted on the side of malefactors one and all. And all you have to do to officially join up is place your mark at the bottom of the articles. Here." He thrust the sharp yellowy nail of his soiled forefinger down upon the bottom of the page where was gathered a bizarre collection of illegible signatures.

"But what shall I write with?" asked Liberty.

Fife plucked a random twig from his hair, held one end to the candle flame until the wood smoked and blackened. "Nature's writing implement," he answered, passing the twig to Liberty who, as conscientiously as he could, spelled out his name in sooty flowing script on the brittle parchment.

"Does this mean I am a real pirate?" Liberty asked.

"Welcome aboard!" cried Fife, solemnly shaking the boy's hand. "And now, lad, go and spread havoc throughout the main, always bearing in mind Captain Mission's immortal words, 'Death to all tyrants, freedom to all in bondage and to us a fat chest of glittering gold,' eh?" Fife eased himself back onto a bed of moss. "Go, I say," he repeated, making brushing motions with his hands. "Go, you've got important duties to be about."

Once home Liberty dared not tell his trusting parents he had from this day forth turned pirate. Let them continue to believe he still sailed under the old colors. That was how your true buccaneer operated, waiting until the gullible prey ventured too near to flee, then running up the Jolly Roger. This would be his special secret, a surprise to spring on unsuspecting malefactors everywhere once the time was ripe.

From the opening of consciousness Liberty had never known a home in which parents were not coming and going with casual regularity, so like all children he simply assumed that his life was the life of every child. Of course, he missed his mother and his father when they were away and though he had grown quite accustomed to their eccentric schedules, these frequent absences created holes in the evidence every child requires to try to solve that initial and most crucial puzzle of life: the mystery of parents.

His father was a big man with big hands and a big voice, but beneath his bigness was something small and quiet and tender which revealed itself most often when they were alone, in a certain look Thatcher passed to his son with the seriousness and gravity of presenting an invaluable gift, in the posture he assumed at his desk and the manner in which he gripped his pen when composing a speech, in the grace with which he modestly took Roxana's hand and held it for a moment in his own, and on countless other fleeting occasions when, with the humblest of gestures, the briefest of words, all that was good and true in human life was allowed to peek out for an instant from behind the bars that kept such recognition sadly, needlessly, cruelly, incarcerated.

But just as the sun must set and night come rushing in, there were periods of unfortunately longer duration when Liberty's father, or the self he chose to think of as his father, was partially obscured by what the family referred to euphemistically as Thatcher's "grumpers." Something deep inside the man became eclipsed by something else and the whole household had to move like mourners within its captive shadow. Then Thatcher sank into a curdled silence which no one dared break, stretched out on the worn horsehair sofa in his study, a wet cloth folded across his eyes. Liberty never really comprehended what was going on inside his father during these alarming interludes, but he did know this: Father, in this prone position, was not, under any circumstances, to be disturbed. No laughter, no loud voices.

But what Liberty would remember best was the feel of his own small hand gathered in the warm, comforting grip of the man, those times alone when all of Thatcher's potent attention was concentrated on his son, as something inside Liberty always insisted, occasionally to contrary evidence that it should be, their trips together, their talks, the information about the sorry state of the world Thatcher shared reluctantly, almost sadly, with his son and heir out of a conviction that I do not enjoy having to tell you these things, but it is important you hear this news, no matter how distasteful, because, unfortunately, it is the truth, whereas it is lies and the promulgation of lies that will make you and the people in your life sick.

From the front porch the lonely Liberty could often watch children passing along the road at the foot of the hill. Since his near accident with hooves and wheels he had been sternly and repeatedly warned by both parents and his aunt, under pain of a punishment so severe he could not possibly imagine it, to never, under any circumstances, dare to wander down onto that dangerous pike, no matter what the temptation.

Of course temptations were many and Liberty's years few, so eventually there came the day when, ignoring all adult authority, he yielded to his own. It was a warm, drowsy summer morning, banks of clouds sitting motionless off to the south like a succession of white reefs, Liberty on the porch rocking leisurely in his mother's chair and quietly contemplating the grasshoppers sailing erratically across the long uncut yard when two boys, shirtless and barefoot, came meandering up the road, brandishing sharpened sticks which each deployed against the other as if engaged in the most furious sword fight. Startled by their whoops and cries, a cloud of sparrows erupted skyward from nearby trees as the boys, thrusting and lunging, gradually disappeared from view. Not a thought in his head, Liberty abruptly stood up out of the chair and let his willful legs carry him down across the yard and onto the road, following the junior cavaliers at a respectful distance. At the crest of the next hill the boys turned, looked back at Liberty for a moment and went on. Insects buzzed in the weeds. Butterflies chased one another into the shadows of the woods. Liberty paused to retrieve a fallen branch which he waved dramatically about in the air as he walked. The boys vanished around a bend, and when Liberty caught up he discovered them posed on the front porch of a weathered frame house, one on either side of a lean, red-faced woman who was regarding him with the severe look normally reserved for cheating husbands, disobedient children and bad dogs. Bravely, Liberty approached. The boys looked expectantly at their mother. A large yellow hound slunk out from beneath the boards of the house and began to bark. "Hush!" snapped the woman, and the animal instantly stopped, sat back on its haunches and assumed a canine version of the same suspicious gaze mother and sons were directing at Liberty.

"What do you want?" the woman called harshly.

Ever the mannerly youth, Liberty replied politely, "I've come to play."

"Well, you get along now and go play somewhere else. We don't want your kind playing around here."

Each of the boys had taken hold of one of their mother's hands.

"Now go on from here before I sic Chester on you."

"Go back to your nigger hotel!" yelled the taller of the boys.

The smaller boy stepped down off the porch, picked up a rock and threw it at Liberty, which missile he easily dodged. But never having encountered such puzzling hostility, Liberty remained temporarily paralyzed, unable to move, unable to think.

The older boy was looking for a good-sized rock for himself when suddenly the woman shrieked, "Get him, Chester!" and in an instant the hound was up and bounding forward in a furry streak of fangs and claws, followed closely by the boys who, gathering stones as they ran, proceeded to let fly an erratic barrage at Liberty, now several hundred yards down the road, the maddened hound yelping, foaming, snapping at Liberty's feet and hands until one of the boys' rocks came sailing in directly on the pointed peak of its head and the animal dropped to the dirt like a bag of seed, horrified mother and howling sons gathered about the unmoving carcass as Liberty, with hardly a backward glance, flew over a hill and was gone.

For all its enthusiastic ferocity the dog had failed to even penetrate Liberty's skin. His wounds consisted of a couple bruises and a few angry-looking scratches which Thatcher washed and dutifully kissed, and then, sitting attentively in his study, with Liberty perched on a pillow in a chair opposite, listened to the sorry tale of his son's morning adventure. When Liberty finished Thatcher said not word, simply watched the boy's flushed face for a long minute. Then, sighing, he placed his hands on his knees, leaned forward and said:

"Now, Liberty, I have something of grave importance to convey to you and I would urge you to pay close attention. Are you listening?"

The boy nodded solemnly.

"Good. Now first, as an experiment, I want you to say the word 'nigger' for me."

Liberty stared blankly at his father.

"Go ahead, it's all right. I want you to say it for me."

"Nigger," Liberty said in a near whisper.

"Louder. Say it the way the boy said it today."

"Nigger," he repeated with a certain force and heat.

"Listen," Thatcher advised. "Listen to how you sound when you voice those syllables. See how the word seems to naturally lend itself to being pronounced with anger. Now say it again and notice how your lips, the muscles of your face, feel. To even mouth the word is to shape your countenance into a leering mask of ugliness and hatred. Now, most importantly, observe how you feel deep inside when speaking such a word, the ugly shape it makes of your insides, and imagine also what it is doing to the insides of the person so addressed. How did you feel when you heard your home called a 'nigger hotel'?"

"Bad."

"Yes, and though you didn't even really know exactly what the word meant, yet still it produced its intended result. So, I would like for you to always bear in mind the pernicious effects of this insult. Will you do that?"

"Yes." His voice barely audible.

"Because, as I hope you now understand, the word 'nigger' is the most foul sound that can be formed by human lips and tongue. There is no comparison with anything else. It is the verbal equivalent of a raised whip. Not all the blasphemies uttered by all the infidels of the world against God and all the churches and ministers and priests can equal the hatred embedded in that singular word. I don't want you to ever employ that word in any manner whatsoever upon any other person, no matter what slight or crime you think they may have committed against you. People who do so are callous fools deformed by ignorance and fear and not worth associating with by day or night. I know you feel bad about what happened to you today, but believe me, those boys would not have made suitable playmates. Their souls are soiled, as are no doubt the souls of their parents, their relatives, their friends. All touched by the curse that has been laid against this land. I know it hurts, but sometimes, Liberty, all one can do before such malignant idiocy is be polite as possible and gracefully withdraw. There are certain terrains where the wise general seeks to avoid battle. Because there will come other days, other fields, where one will be presented with the opportunity to beat back the tide of hatred and work to lift the curse that weighs heavily as chains upon us all, free and bonded alike."

One early evening in the late spring of Liberty's eleventh year, swallows playing tag over the peaks of the house, the limpid air marshaling objects near and far in sharply defined equidistance, cricket orchestra warming up in the dank pit under the front porch, Uncle Potter, who hadn't been seen by family, friend or local constabulary in more than a year and whose last known whereabouts involved a lengthy stroll down the Drummond Pike, a left at the North Fork and on out about sixty miles past the border of Nowhere, came thundering into the dining parlor, per custom, unexpected, unannounced and in an inveterate state of personal and mental dishabille at the precise moment Aunt Aroline, with the fussy ceremony of an anxious chef, was depositing upon the loaded table a great pewter dish out of which rose a steaming citadel of beef and bone set amid a delightful enceinte of boiled "sauce"—potatoes, onions, beets and carrots chopped and sliced and compulsively aligned in an alternating pattern emphasizing their natural chromatic harmony.

"As usual, Potter." Roxana smiled. "I must applaud your theatrical sense of timing."

The color in Aunt Aroline's round cheeks, already alarmingly high from an afternoon's labor at the oven, rapidly underwent several further degrees of pinkening. Delivering a fusillade of withering contempt in Potter's direction and muttering something obscure about "the improper domestication of beasts of the forest," she vanished into the kitchen, from which she refused to emerge for the duration of Potter's visit.

Halfway through slurping up his first of many bowls of over-seasoned pumpkin soup, Potter abruptly announced to the less than dumbfounded company that he had just about made up his mind to mosey on out to the Kansas Territory and try to bag him a puke or two.

"If the language weren't brutal enough," Roxana replied, "you must compound the crime with an act of ultimate violence."

"I would not have thought Mexico chafed so after all these years," commented Thatcher.

"What's a puke?" asked Liberty, instantly envisioning some bad-tempered collusion between a yellow-fanged mountain lion and a rabid timber wolf.

Potter's spoon busy ferrying gobbets of thick soup through the hair-curtained portal of his mouth paused in midcourse, and darting a bloodshot glance at the inquisitive boy he replied, "A puke is a jaundiced-cheeked, snaggle-toothed, scum-licking saucebox with a massy head and a wizened brain whose preposterous upright endeavors to pass as a man are incontestably betrayed by the bestial bouquet of his musk."

"I see you've given the matter some consideration," Thatcher said dryly.

"Really, Potter." Roxana's attention, as ever, focused firmly upon her mesmerized son. "I enjoy backcountry vulgarity as well as the next, but must we be so entertained at the dinner table?"

Potter, now hunched mere inches away from his bowl, was slurping up soup with renewed abandon. "A puke is a puke." He shrugged. "You can't pretty 'em up."

"I wasn't asking you to. I only wonder whether we might not finish our meal before being served the full particulars."

"Now, Roxie, darling, don't start reefing the sail just yet. I've got a savory yarn to spin."

Slicing off half the joint for himself, the rambling wanton then proceeded between noisy, spewing chews and long drafts of cold cider to relate news of the latest atrocity from the Kansas Territory: the shocking execution of an innocent Free Soiler name of R. P. Brown by a marauding gang of border ruffians pleased to dub themselves the Kickapoo Rangers. Seems the previous day a no-account puke called Cook had been found brutally murdered by a person or persons unknown. Inflamed with drink highly rectified and unquenchable fancies of revenge, the fun-loving Rangers waylaid the first misfortunate who happened along, in this case the hapless Brown, who was hauled into Dawson's grocery in Leavenworth prior to his trial for Cook's murder. Ticktock went the clock on the wall, ticktock. Nerves among the abductors, already strained, began in that drafty, oppressively cramped room to fray and part.

"Don't you leer at me with such an unfettered eye."

"Heap o' grit, ordering me around like that. Who was it pressed that ol' gray you now prance about upon in such princely style?"

"Speak one word more and I'll twist that bandanna around your pipe till the lamps pop out of your ugly mug," etc., etc., until attention turned inevitably to the bound prisoner.

"Gents, hold on now. Why try a guilty man? Was Cook tried? Has a single one of them eastern punkinheads ever come within hailing distance of the bar of justice?"

"But we got to try him," someone suggested, "so we can decide how to kill him."

"Arguing about how to kill a skunk?" replied another, running a filthy thumb along the bright bit of his hatchet. "You can't please a bastard." Rising almost reluctantly to his feet, he raised the hatchet and with one powerful swing planted the blade deep into Brown's cowering head.

The Rangers watched like spectators at a dance as the bleeding man writhed painfully about on the sawdust floor. After a while someone said, "Reckon we better take him home." So the groaning body was roughly tossed into a wagon bed and the Rangers, warming themselves on a demijohn of Old Monongahela, set off across ten frozen miles of the worst winter on record, when men went about draped in buffalo robes, their boots wrapped in burlap, and wild

---

turkeys were so numbed by the cold they could be shot like targets with a pistol.

"I am very cold," complained Brown.

"Here's some coffee for you," one of the boys declared, leaning over to deposit a fresh gob of tobacco juice into the open wound in Brown's skull. "Liniment for a damned amalgamator."

Yet drawing feeble breath, the body was rudely dumped at the door of the man's cabin with the cry to the horrified wife: "Here's Brown!"

Potter's dark dancing eyes had become as still as baked pebbles. He was staring not just at but directly into Liberty, searching the boy's gaping soul for points of recognition. "Those," he intoned gravely, "were pukes."

"Do what you will," Thatcher conceded. "The Territory is not Veracruz."

Roxana remained apart, seated at the table though out of the conversation, even perhaps out of hearing, her abtracted gaze fixed on a nearby window whose polished sash now framed in its glass a pale, distorted reflection of the lamp-lit dining parlor and its inhabitants floating in ghostly splendor within a rectangle of utter obsidian.

Over the years the westering impulse, as persistent and irresistible as sexual desire, had come to assume an almost physical presence, the neglected, unkempt urchin at Potter's side loyal as a favorite revolver, an ill-smelling snot-nosed kid ever tugging at his sleeve, pleading with eyes too enormous for such a small child, disturbingly blank, curiously cold, as if out in the providential lands just over the next rise, beyond the keeps and customs of the day, in the murk of the forest or the wail of the prairie, might be found the heedless parents who somehow lost track of their winsome boy.

So once again, heaving his not inconsiderable bulk into the saddle, Potter rode out over the mountains, down through the Pennsylvania woods and much of the same Ohio meadow country he had traversed nine years before, the beckoning sun declining each night between his piebald's twitchy ears, taking his meals, his sleep, in reasonable proportions at reasonable intervals, the reckless haste of his earlier aborted journey supplanted by a magnetic resolution that drew him deliberately, unswervingly, onward—to the landing at Weston and ferry passage across the Big Muddy and the novel sensation of actually leaving the states behind, entering K T, where the sky was so irredeemably vast, so *present*, a piece of it always seemed to be stuck in the corner of your eye, outdoors or in. From every vantage the land slid drunkenly away on high gentle swells of rippling, red-tasseled grass. Eventually, directed by an inner compass whose infallibility had withstood every extravagant test a life of apparent aimless vagabondage had been able to inflict upon it, Potter ambled out along the California Road past the burgeoning town of Lawrence, that impudent outpost of stiff-necked Yankee rectitude, the grand three-story brick hotel, the mobbed groggeries dispensing ten-cent whiskey by the barrelful, the sod huts and cottonwood cabins down on the Kaw, imported steam engines chugging day and night, reducing trunks of black walnut and hickory to hand-smooth planks of invaluable lumber, the call of one clanking machine—Home of the Free! Home of the Free!—answered instantly by another: Never a Slave State! Never a Slave State! and on between rustling walls of ripe sunflowers taller than a man in a tall hat, their mellow heads nodding inquisitively down, to find himself one somber midnight posted upon a windy plain amidst a company of armed Regulators, observing with an interest beyond the merely professional a dull forgelike glow fluttering unchecked off at the black edge of the world, too remote to distinguish the actual flames seesawing over the charred site of the former Goodin place.

"Wahl," drawled Furry Ike in the tenured voice of one who'd been in a tight corner before and was likely to be again, "reckon we're next."

"Never fear, lads," promised Captain Gracie, whose habitual promises, a salient element of his command style, had become understood by his men long ago to be aspects of the hollowness of a language they need no longer obey or even respect. "They're walking into a reception here warmer than any they ever bargained for."

"I'm not afraid, sir," Little Johnny Phelps piped up, words he had been repeating in one form or another since sunset several long hours ago.

Raising an unwashed finger to one nostril and bending slightly forward, Furry Ike abruptly expelled a projectile of heavy mucus that either hit or narrowly missed the upper of Potter's boot. In the dark it was hard to tell, and Potter wasn't about to reach down and feel with his hand.

"Sorry there, pardner," muttered Furry Ike through his tobacco-stained beard. "Misjudged my windage a mite."

"I ain't your damn pardner," growled Potter, rubbing his boot in the bunch grass, "and if you come against me one more time I'll thrash your hide five ways to kingdom come."

"Remark like that might cause a fellow to wonder just what you're doing here at all."

"I expect I'm here for the same reasons as anybody else, and if saving this country means having to save a flung-up yellow-bellied cuss like you, then so be it."

"Gentlemen," Captain Gracie cautioned, "save your vinegar for the foe."

Soberly then, and single file, persuaders of various makes and calibers clutched in each hardened fist, the Regulators trooped back into the solitary cabin, bolted and barred the timber door.

Dominating the one-room interior with implacable organic authority was a tree stump the diameter of a Conestoga wheel, of a magnitude so intractable the cabin had simply been erected around it, gnarled roots of an ancient complexity rising like a giant's petrified muscle out of the packed dirt floor, the stump's circular annulated top, planed and sanded, serving admirably as a low but permanently balanced table, now bearing half a dozen tin plates nailed into the wood to prevent theft and, seated at precarious angles in their own tallow, a pair of smoking candle ends.

On a pile of straw in the corner, visibly shivering beneath a sheet of tattered and begrimed tent canvas, lay the master of this homestead the Regulator boys had come tonight to help defend. His name was

E. F. G. Conklin and he'd been afflicted for more than a month with a case of the "shakes" seemingly impervious to all attention. Even in the warm candle glow, his face possessed a stark vegetative quality reminiscent of mushroom stems, the numerous hairs of his black beard stuck like so many random wires into the waxy flesh. His lips, swollen and flaking, parted slightly to release a rattle of syllables. "Yes," murmured his wife, Kate, "they're a-coming." Conklin's bituminous eyes remained fixed ceilingward. At his side his wife occupied the sole unbroken chair, a squirmy infant with the collywobbles wrapped in a crash towel sucking noisily at her breast, a shiny new Sharps carbine lying handily across her lap. She and her ailing husband, "rifle christians" from far-off New Haven, Connecticut, had endured unscrupulous road agents, broken axles, sick oxen, mud bogs, feuding families, lost children, petty theft, starvation, sunstroke, snakes, near drowning and all the trivial abrasions of the day along the emigrant trail for the promise of prime bottomland at $1.25 an acre, the fresh start guaranteed each dawn at the lofting of the American sun along with the opportunity to help dispatch as many godless Misery-ians as possible to the Happy Land of Canaan.

"He ain't got long anyway," Mrs. Conklin remarked, to no one in particular.

"Neither do them ruffians," replied Little Johnny Phelps, suddenly hopping like a bug from one foot to the other.

"Hold up, lad," advised Captain Gracie. "If you must piss yet again grab a tin or just let 'er rip in your linen 'cause this door is corked and will remain corked until further notice." Even in the wilting summer heat he was dressed in high stock and his best black broadcloth, as if prepared to officiate at a wedding or a funeral.

The Regulators had each taken up a position at one of the divers loopholes bored at shoulder level into the thick log walls, weapons cocked and at the ready, squinting in nervous anticipation down the length of their barrels into the perilous night, the watery eye of the moon.

The Conklins' daughter, Zillah, a solemn, barefoot girl of ten years, clothed in an unwashed man's tunic that fell voluminously to well below her soiled knees, had neither addressed nor even acknowledged in any manner this strange company of foul-smelling roughs who had infested her home several long hours earlier. Arms crossed behind her back, she leaned at rigid attention, as if lashed to a mast, against the cold bricks of the hearth, the magical agency of touch allowing her for a spell to partake of the stolid, unassailable properties of raw stone.

A prolonged, bovine groan escaped from beneath the trembling canvas, its rate of movement having noticeably quickened.

"Here, lass," Potter called as kindly as he could manage, his previous attempts at engaging the child having met with sullen silence, "why don't you fetch your pa a nice cup of water?"

The girl studied him with an amazingly adept impersonation of adult contempt. Then, after a defiant interval, she spoke. "That's not my pa."

Mrs. Conklin returned Potter's inquiring gaze exactly as given.

"Why sure it is," he said.

"No!" Zillah declared sharply, giving her head an emphatic twist.

"Then how came you to be quartered in such a close nook with an utter stranger for a father?"

Even as Potter watched, the focus went out of the girl's eyes like an exodus of blackbirds from each dilating pupil.

Mrs. Conklin yanked the squirming baby off her nipple and nonchalantly covered her breast. "The mister trained her to do that. Too many nosy outlandishers scratching at the door and pawing around into business that weren't no part of their business."

Her husband shifted around on the straw, the painful ratcheting of his breath virtually pleading for lubrication.

"All right," mumbled Potter in obvious irritation. Stooping to the bucket, he dipped out a tinful of water which he carefully conveyed to the suffering man and, raising up Conklin's clammy head, tilted the contents into his gaping mouth. It was like pouring water down a hole in the parched earth, and presently the tremors subsided somewhat. The wife observed without comment, her lips worn down from fretful years of unconscious compression into little more than a grim crease in the sallow flesh above her chin, her expression as unreadable as the weathered face of a rock.

Hardly daring to budge from their stations, the Regulators had by now achieved a pitch of vigilance where the menacing darkness outside began to shift and stir with every blink, assuming whatever shape for whatever duration that pleased the viewer, the general uneasiness of this phenomenon alleviated slightly this particular evening by the unabated force of an astonishing full moon.

"Doggone," blurted Harry Spelvins, "if that don't look just like fresh snow on the ground."

"Indeed," Captain Gracie noted, "the moon appears considerably larger here than home in Back Bay."

"Why is that, sir?" asked Little Johnny Phelps.

"Because we're nearer to God," snapped Mrs. Conklin.

The captain bowed graciously in the woman's direction. "Beacon Hill, I might remind you, madame, sits upon an elevation rather more pronounced than this griddle pan of bloody sod."

Before Mrs. Conklin could summon up a suitably annihilating retort, Furry Ike burst out excitedly. "I think I hear something. Yes, I think I certainly do."

All paused, attending warily to the dissonant strains of the unsleeping land.

"The wind, " asserted Mrs. Conklin. "That's all. Just the wind."

The afternoon's playful zephyrs had developed into a brutal, unremitting blast obviously escaped from some vast chamber deep underground, a roiling torrent of black air and tossed particles of a minuteness and granularity sufficient to sting the skin and easily lodge in any bodily crevice or portal, all the while accompanied by a prodigious shriek of such volume and monotony as to banish instantly any thoughts of relief.

"Never heard any wind carrying on like that back east," said Potter.

"No, sir," affirmed Mrs. Conklin. "You certainly have not. Nor have you sat out here in its uninterrupted path night and day around the hours of the seasons, plugs of beeswax, wads of flannel, a couple

dried beans or what-have-you stuffed in your ears in hopes of muf-
fling that bedlam scream just enough to postpone until tomorrow
putting the fatal ball into your head. One month on this ground is all
it takes, one month for that wind to slip inside your knowledge box,
where nothing you can do will ever get you shut of it. And then, after
a while, just when you think you've gotten used to the mindless
noise, it begins talking to you in your own voice, not your speaking
voice, mind you, but your thinking voice, the one you hear when
you're alone, whispering to you your own most private thoughts."
She glanced briefly at the rasping lump under the canvas. "When the
mister goes, I believe I'll load up the kids in the wagon and head on
out for Oregon."

"A long pull," said Potter.

"I do not fear distance," she declared, regarding Potter with an
unsparing eye. "Or death," she added.

"I've heard," offered Jack Stringfellow, "they grow cherries there
big as apples."

"Beavers, too," said Little Johnny Phelps.

"It's always springtime," Spelvins said. "No one ever gets sick."

"Hell with all that trash," Furry Ike declared. "It's the gold you go
for. Pardner of mine went out there about ten years ago when the
fever was on everybody, settled in that Willamette Valley and, after
about a year sent back a real nice picture of himself standing in front
of a hole in the ground and holding up a nugget big as your thumb.
Rest of the family left to join him the very next day."

"What became of that fellow?" asked Spelvins.

"Don't rightly know. Never heard a word about him ever again."

"No slaves," said Mrs. Conklin.

"Excuse me, ma'am?" asked Spelvins.

"No slaves," she repeated. "In Oregon. No slaves."

"I believe I heard something now," announced Furry Ike, cocking
his misshapen hat toward the outer wall.

"Kinder like a drumroll?" asked Stringfellow.

It was Potter's sharp blue eyes, long renowned throughout the
Mohawk Valley as possessed of an uncommon avian acuity, that first

descried the column of phantom riders, black figures mounted on black steeds, moving in stern orthodox procession against the moon-chastened sky. Then, with an almost diabolic celerity, the horsemen were swinging in off the road and clattering up into the yard.

"Douse the glim!" hissed Captain Gracie, and someone did. Lost in darkness, the baby began to howl. "Ma'am?" asked Gracie. A quick rustle, and the infant stopped.

Outside, the dark shapes were hurriedly dismounting, several loping around toward the rear of the cabin.

"I count twelve," Potter said.

"Steady, boys," cautioned Captain Gracie. "On my signal."

Coolly, without a word, Mrs. Conklin handed the baby to her daughter and, as if she'd been rehearsing for this moment over the span of a life, stepped adroitly atop a biscuit box, and, with practiced ease, slotted her carbine into a loophole and prepared to defend her property and her family from a pack of unholy, pilfering border bullies.

"Come on out of there now," demanded a voice from beyond the walls.

"Who says?" answered Captain Gracie.

"Friends of the white man. We're here for Conklin. Send the skunk out and we'll be on our way."

"The man's ailing. He's barely sensible."

"Who are you?"

"Stand a mite closer and I'll tell you."

There was a lengthy pause, then a different voice. "Are ye sound on the goose?"

"Can't hear you, friend. Step on up to the door."

"Sounds like there's a damned abolitionist in there just a-hankering to be hemped."

"More than one!" returned Potter.

"Happy to oblige all comers."

"They're fixing to rush the house," squeaked Little Johnny Phelps, his voice given to abrupt scale-runs even under the most ordinary circumstances and now losing its moorings completely.

"If I get any bead at all," Potter vowed softly, "I'm gonna blow one of them chawbacks clean through."

"Steady, boys," advised Captain Gracie. "Aim for the buttons on their breeches. Give a man time to prepare to meet his Maker."

Then, with a sudden whoosh, the night simply broke apart upon a rock of delirious flame that seemed to have plunged through this paper-thin partition of darkness from an alien realm beyond and, hovering mystically in midair, was now trundling full tilt on a wobbly course straight for the door. "My wagon!" shrieked Mrs. Conklin as every gun in the place discharged at once in a great flaring and cracking that set the baby off into a wail its tiny lungs couldn't possibly be producing, instantly filled the cramped room with choking clouds of sulfurous smoke and did absolutely nothing to deter the raging fireball from lumbering unsteadily onward as if drawn by a windlass, spitting and spewing a veritable Roman candle of sparks, ash and stems of burning hay until coming to a stop at last with a gentle bump against the Conklin cabin door. Foreheads dripping, eyes smarting, mouths cursing, the Regulators continued with undiminished vigor to pour forth their lesson in lead through an entire arsenal of exotic weaponry—Hawkin rifles and Western rifles and Sharps carbines, Hall's muskets and alligator guns—and, when ammunition ran out on the larger bores, shifting readily to Colt revolvers and Austin pistols as the baby screeched, gunsmoke suffocated their throats and enemy balls went plunk-plunk into the log walls.

"Blast ye demons!" cried Furry Ike and Captain Gracie: "Cut away at them, boys, cut away!" "I'm blind!" shrieked Little Johnny Phelps, stumbling backward in the dark and snatching at his face as he fell unattended into the dirt. Orange and yellow flame was now ominously visible, clawing frantically at the door, seeking entrance through the narrow cracks in the planking.

Potter hardly noticed the incessant clanging in his ears, so determined was he to plant some hard seed into one furrowed slavocrat carcass, firing with ruthless abandon at whatever appeared to move in all the surrounding confusion. He figured he had tallied maybe five, six hits, give or take a few when, with muffled shouts and a flurry of parting shots, the night riders sprang onto their mounts and abruptly galloped off into the western gloom.

Potter unbolted the latch and, with the aid of Captain Gracie and Furry Ike, pushed the flaming wagon away from the door. Too far gone into the world of fire to be saved, it was allowed to burn on, the remaining water buckets being used to quench the embers on the roof. Little Johnny Phelps, after rolling about on the ground in sightless panic, discovered that whatever particles had flown into his eyes during the course of the contest had flown back out on the stream of his tears and thankfully he could see again. Mrs. Conklin wiped her sooty cheeks on the hem of her dress, then bent down to attend to her husband's mumblings. "Yes," she was heard to say, "they're a-gone now." The baby was strangely silent, as if acknowledging that his own best protest had been humbled by the cry of gunpowder.

Henry Spelvins, wandering out to relieve himself, past the trampled flower beds, beyond the fitful glow cast by the still smoldering wagon, found the body, face blackened, sprawled whiskers up in the bugle brush north of the cabin, fancy hunting shirt with an eagle braided on the chest dark with blood from the nipples down, nearby a crumpled slouch hat, its band dressed with goose feathers and, a few yards off a fallen standard bearing the legend in ornate capitals, THE SUPREMACY OF THE WHITE RACE.

"Well, well," declared Captain Gracie, nudging the corpse with the sharp toe of his boot. "Let the Devil toast me on a spit if this isn't old S. G. Q. Jones himself. Doesn't look quite so puffed-up now. Whose is he?"

"Potter was firing from this side," offered Furry Ike, fairly dancing with glee over the very evidence that the night's work had not gone unrequited.

"Well, Potter, it appears you have sent one of the indisputable grandees of the Blue Lodge to his winter quarters. Scalp's yours if you want it."

"Thank you, sir. Don't mind if I do."

With beaming admiration, Furry Ike handed over his prized gold-plated Bowie knife. "Sharpened fresh this morning."

Weathered knees audibly complaining, Potter grunted down beside the tumbled body, seized a hank of greasy locks in his fist and began sawing clumsily away at the roots. In a moment the woman was at his elbow. "You're making a mess of that," she muttered, impatiently reaching for the slippery blade. "Let me." Potter eased himself aside as she bent deftly to her task as if peeling the leather from a human skull were little more than a common household chore simple as paring a potato. She worked with fierce concentration in the dying firelight, her awed onlookers straining to catch a glimpse of the technique until, with a sickening adhesive sound, the scalp was lifted away in one unbroken piece.

"Ma'am," Furry Ike said approvingly, "if you had a mind to, I believe you could butcher this gent clean by the board."

Framed in the low, now lighted, doorway of the cabin, scrawny arms still tightly wrapped about her baby brother, stood the Conklin daughter, Zillah, not a solitary dripping detail of this educational scene passing unregistered upon a gaze bland, defenseless, unfathomable as the night.

"So, where is it?" Liberty inquired eagerly, the baser facts of life on this planet where he happened to find himself holding a near insatiable fascination. Father, son and prodigal storyteller were gathered now in the front parlor a year later, all talk of the hemorrhaging of the body politic, whether in the airy abstract or the actual mortal flesh, having been banished permanently from the dining room.

"Danged if I know," answered Potter, scratching unconsciously at the dirt on his neck. "Pelt must've got lost or stolen somewhere between here and Springfield. I recall a bunch of boys in Lawrence wanted to swap for a barrel of choice corn, forty-jackass strength. And a funny old bushwhacker with a longhorn mustache in an emigrant-aid party east of Shawnee Mission took to admiring it so much he wanted to run that hair up a pole he'd fixed to his wagon, jettison the damned Jolly Roger he had flapping there. In Westport a bald-headed barber with a black eye showed me how to hitch my trophy to the bridle where it'd impress friend and foe alike and wouldn't nobody give me any trouble. So I just don't know. Maybe it fell off, maybe some rascal filched it, but either way it's gone now, gone for good, for sure."

"Is this the gun?"

"Aye, lad, the very one."

"Can I see?"

The rifle was heavier than any Liberty had ever handled. He hefted the scarred walnut stock to his shoulder and took deliberate aim toward the darkened window, sighting down the long, wavering barrel, in his mind, in the fullness of a pure unclouded day, a tangible image of the wild unadulterated item itself—a full-blooded puke at large in its preferred state of nature, barefoot, long-shanked, montrously gangly, more bone than meat—scampering through the brush on the far ridge like a flushed rodent, long black beard bisected by the wind streaming backward in separate scraggly halves over each shoulder, spindle legs pumping, rum-blossom nostrils flaring, beady black eyes converging on the appreciable cover of a colossal oak tree mere steps away as Liberty, expertly leading his prey, coolly squeezed the trigger and in an instant, the simple twitch of a finger, something was translated into nothing.

Pukes were not pards or pigs or pumas. Pukes were people.

Even at a distance, from the crest of the hill on Front Street, the packet boat lying moored down at the wharf between an inconspicuously dunnish pair of unlading bullheads resembled nothing so much as a circus wagon, its low roof, long hull and multiwindowed cabin and shutters all painted up in promiscuous shades of red, green, blue and yellow, a floating advertisement for the marvels of the watery way. Across the bow and stern, bold letters of flaking gilt announced the name *Croesus*, "the finest, fastest craft abroad in either direction upon the Grand Western, bar none, guaranteed," boasted the owner and captain, one Erastus Whelkington, a stubby, sun-toasted man finified to packet master nonpareil in a brass-button broadcoat, flowered sarsenet waistcoat with matching neckcloth, yellow small-clothes, prunella-topped morocco boots and a high, silky, gray castor with a picture of the *Croesus* itself passing through Lock 49 painted on the front. In appearance, a small rabbity creature of no discernible strength, his grip was sufficient to steer the tolerant father and his accompanying son deftly leeward of the increasingly frantic exhortations of a rival captain declaiming in a belligerent, high-pitched voice the manifold virtues of his own particular boat from the moment Thatcher and Liberty alighted, somewhat stupefied by the rollicking experience, from the Delphi–Schenectady omnibus.

"Pay no heed to the false appeals of that mud-chunking malefactor," advised Captain Whelkington, drawing Thatcher ever nearer the oriental fragrance of his breath. "His vessel leaks, his mules are lame, his old woman went mad—tossed her last two spratlings plunk into the canal the minute she was done with 'em. Told the sheriff their cries weren't quite human, said they put her in mind of rutting tabbies."

"Whelkington!" roared the man who had pursued the captain and his prospective passengers out into the middle of the bustling street where all were now engaged in dodging drays, runabouts, gigs, dog carts, coaches, carryalls and solitary mounted travelers from the staid to the picturesque, while trying also to avoid, not always successfully, the plentiful clumps, some still smoking, of horse manure. "You ingling son of a bitch! I'm about full up of your pestiferous lies, your gyppo shecooneries. You smell bad, and frankly, sir, I can no longer tolerate your brazen hooking of my rightful passengers."

Captain Whelkington halted midstride as if struck in the back with a brick. "Beg your pardon, gentlemen," he said, politely conducting Thatcher and Liberty to a spot in the shade of Corcoran's Saloon, whose veranda posts had been chewed halfway through by horses left tethered too long outside.

"Now," Whelkington exclaimed, turning on his competitor in a high choler, "this is the second occasion you have dared accost me in a public thoroughfare, not only embarrassing me personally but threatening my livelihood as well. I'll not brook your interference a day more. Let's settle this matter here and now." And he began unbuttoning his coat.

"I've whipped villains meaner than you from Troy to Buffalo, and it will certainly afford me much satisfaction to fix your flint, Captain Whelkington, once and for all." And he began to unbutton his coat.

Some people stopped to watch the trouble, some paused and moved on, but it wasn't long until a sizable crowd had collected and traffic in the street was calmly parting around the two enraged packet captains.

"By the way, Captain Mumford?" Whelkington had removed his fancy hat and was wiping his forehead with a yellow bandanna. "Reside in this fair city, do you not?"

"Yes, Captain Whelkington, you know I do." He folded his coat over a hitching rail and began rolling up his sleeves.

"Took a new missus recently, so I hear."

"Yes, sir, indeed I did."

"Comely woman, I expect."

"Yes, Captain Whelkington, she surely is. Why do you ask?"

"Because I aim to fuck her from stem to stern soon as I get done tanning your scrawny hide."

The punch would have caught a quick man square in the jaw, but Whelkington was even quicker, neatly sidestepping the blow and at the same time planting a hard fist dead into the middle of Mumford's ample belly, where it made a sound like a struck feed sack. The fat man grunted, staggered back a step, dropping his hands just enough for Whelkington's other fist to catch him on the point of his chin, and with a dry wooden crack his head snapped backward on a body already beginning to collapse into the hard pack of the road as Captain Whelkington walked contemptuously away, wiping his hands on his pants.

"Unfortunate you and your boy had to witness that whoobub, but actualities on this here canal tend now and again toward the sinfully impolite." Slipping back into his elaborately frogged coat, Captain Whelkington granted Liberty a sly, subversive smile whose vague complicities were obviously not meant to be shared by the father. Liberty stared impassively, blinking steadily back at him. In the street, wheels and hooves moved around the fallen man.

"I am quite familiar with the sordid side of life," answered Thatcher, "but I fail to see, in this particular instance, how such brutality was warranted."

"New to the Erie Water, sir?" the captain asked, gently guiding Thatcher by the arm. "Most likely be seeing worse than this 'fore we hit Syracuse. And tame times, these. Why, back in the raging heyday of the canal there was a murder a day along these fronts. Now we're lucky to see a body turn up every week or so." He paused for a moment. "And let me tell you, sir, you weren't acquainted with the good Captain Mumford and his bestial ways. Something in that man can't stop worrying at the natural goodness in others. Just the way some folks are, all twirly-headed from the git-go. Ain't a blamed thing you can do about it. Way the world was tossed together." He resumed walking. "Now, how far did you two gentlemen say you'd be traveling with us this trip?"

"We didn't," said Thatcher. "But now that you ask, the answer is Rochester."

"Rochester, eh?" Sizing up Thatcher as if he hadn't exactly looked at him yet. "Certainly hope it ain't to attend that damn abolitionist jubilee they're having over there. Won't have nigger lovers on my boat. Or preachers either, for that matter."

"I'd appreciate it, captain, if you'd rein in your language some."

Whelkington's thick black eyebrows began inching up his forehead. "You *are* one of them coon kissers, ain't you?"

Thatcher's gaze held true and steady. "I can remove my coat, too, Captain Whelkington. I am, sir, entirely at your disposal."

They walked on in silence, the private tussle between Whelkington's principles and his purse working itself out in the muscles of his face.

Liberty, whose habit on outings with his family was to dash on far up ahead or else lag well behind, roaming at will in the general vicinity of his parents, now took his father's hand. He kept glancing back over his shoulder, waiting for that heap of man lying facedown in the dirt to move, but it never did.

The sun, less than halfway to the meridian, had already begun to insinuate itself into the affairs of the day, the augmenting heat like syrup poured into the works of a clock, western windows and bricks all ablaze, the very air seeming to swell visibly. Down at the wharf, amidst a soft boiling cloud of pure white, a sweating and cursing crew of men, finely powdered from head hair to boot soles, was rolling barrels of flour onto one of the easting line boats. An old lumber wagon came clattering up piled high with freshly dug potatoes. Short-tempered clerks with pencils tucked behind their ears and garters on their sleeves scurried in and out of warehouse doors. In an open space near a pyramid of hogsheads labeled "NAILS," a brand-new printing press sat darkly shining and isolate at the center of all the dockside commotion, an object fabulous and inscrutable, like something dropped unbidden from the heights of another world.

Halting before the *Croesus*, Captain Whelkington held up his fist for Thatcher's inspection. "You see, I've already scraped my knuckles for the privilege of carrying you. You're my prize, and by God I won't give you up."

Thatcher offered a wry smile. "Now I suppose I'll have to fight you for the right not to be carried."

"If that's your style, I'm willing," said Whelkington, coolly looking him over. "But if it's not, all I seek is one favor."

"Yes, Captain Whelkington, and what would that be?"

"Shut pan on the boat. There's influential paying gentlemen of a sensitive nature who might take offense at the vinegar of your views. Do you reckon you can hold off on the nigger issue for the duration?"

"I can hold off if the others can. But I may as well admit to you, Captain, that I have found over the years that you can draw the shutters and bar the door and fire the hearth and yet somehow that darn topic will find a way in. And when that happens, I don't deny it a place at the table."

"Well, maybe what we need are stronger locks and thicker walls."

"Or a bigger house."

Whelkington's eyes flared with anger, then he looked across the canal and said, "Six miles an hour. You'll see. Ain't a quicker packet on the whole Grand Western."

Once under way, the *Croesus*'s smooth glide altered the immediate nature of the world, the tow line running out straight and taut to the trio of mules, their harnesses bedecked with fluttering plumes and jingling bells, plodding in synchronous step along the beaten towpath, the driver behind with reins wrapped about one gnarled fist and a long bull-snake whip in the other, the surrounding country dividing into perfect halves and passing—gable and brick, pond and paling, tree and meadow—like panels of painted scenery, in stately recessional. Arcs of water drew away from the bow of the boat in long, rippling wings carrying on their backs bits of broken light to a place far to the east where the sun would be eventually reassembled for tomorrow's appearance. There was a sweet animal pleasure to this gentle onward motion and it seemed to Liberty as if the canal he floated on was circulating up along his body, bubbling playfully through his bones. The heat and the slow, hypnotic rhythms of the ride induced in the drowsy boy a sumptuous dreaminess which might have opened into states of knowledge only a certain languor can provide but for the commotion erupting periodically on the bow when Captain Whelkington would come charging from his monastic-sized quarters like a man whose hat was too tight for his head to loose a barrage of invective and abuse upon the bald skull of his driver, a lean, leathery twist of a man known as Genesee Red, twenty years tending his long-eared robins from the Hudson to the Erie Lake, a route along which he was legendary for his ability to sleep while not only standing upright but even walking forward. At the first bark of Whelkington's voice, Red would come shuddering awake and instantly start lashing away in theatrical fashion at the poor mules' galled rumps, piling on his own distinctive curses, "Git up, God Almighty! Go on there, Jesus Christ! Lift a hoof, Judas Priest!"—delicate female passengers turning away and covering their ears until the pace quickened and the satisfied captain returned to whatever rare business so occupied him in his inner sanctum, when inevitably Red's gleaming head would begin to nod, the brisk beat of the hooves would slacken and out would rush the infuriated Whelkington like a frantic cuckoo in a capricious clock, the whole sorry episode repeating itself point for point, word for word, as if this were a crucial scene in a dreadful play requiring tireless rehearsal. After a couple reiterations, alert observers noted with amusement that the oaths "God Almighty!" "Jesus Christ!" and "Judas Priest!" were, in fact, the actual names of Red's animules.

At the stern of the boat, clutching the tiller as if it were the tail of a felled beast he dare not release, stood the steersman, a morose, phlegmatic individual who acknowledged no person but the captain and responded to no address of any sort, no matter how genial or well-meant. The storm perpetually brewing in his face abated only momentarily on those now increasingly frequent occasions when he lifted a small brass horn to his lips, sounded a piercing metallic note and cried, "Low bridge! Everybody down!" The subsequent scramble—as all who had flocked onto the deck to revel in the view endeavored to make themselves as small as possible by squatting, crouching or, better yet, flattening themselves in their finery against a rooftop ornamented with muddy footprints, bird droppings, peanut shells, apple cores and an astonishing number of tobacco juice puddles—kindled the vaguest suggestion of light in the old canaller's dark and pitted face.

Liberty, perched on the front edge of the roof, simply eased onto his back and let that narrow span of beams and planks slide wondrously over him, shadowed and cool in the underside where if bridges harbored secrets this was the seat in which they were lodged, the wooden corners soft and pale white with the shrouded nests of spiders, the keepers of the riddles.

Passengers aboard the *Croesus* this clear summer morning numbered about twenty-five, and a mixed lot they were. A party of young fashionables in full fig, displaying little interest in any aspects of the trip but one another. Several interchangeable families of German immigrants huddled together in refuge from the confusions of the English language; their baggage took up most of the space on the short rear deck, and they were referred to contemptuously as "those Dutch." A bunch of broad-brimmed farmers were embarked on a mysterious mission to Utica whose grave import they couldn't help alluding to in a veritable chorus of vague whispers that successfully alienated all within earshot. And, of course, the usual disposition of freely roving white males of dubious class and rank bound on errands no one dared question or, because of their gender and race, even think to.

One of these Lords of the Deck made his way, as if by chance, over to where Thatcher stood, gazing thoughtfully upstream, the canal winding like a shimmering snake through woodland and pasture.

"Quite a scorcher," commented the stranger, a prosperous-looking gentleman who held himself fully erect in a confident, dandyish sort of attitude. He resembled a drawing or a painting of a man, not a mark or smudge anywhere on his person, his fair skin or his tightly tailored black suit. Words slipped from his small mouth with a distinctly oleaginous quality, lending an air of disconcerting elusiveness to the most matter-of-fact statement.

"Yes, it surely is that," replied Thatcher.

"Traveling far?"

"Rochester."

"Business?"

"You might say."

"Yes, of course it's business. Business, business, business. Or it's politics. Politics, politics, politics. Or worse, a hideous amalgamation of the two. Now, as for me, I take no notice of either pursuit. Keep a clear head for the pressing concerns of the day."

"What is it you do?"

"Don't believe I can rightly say. This and that. Little of everything. Whatever it is that wants doing."

Then Thatcher noticed the stranger's feet, exceedingly small for a man of his size and shod in an elegant pair of brocaded carpet slippers.

"Sensitive hocks," confessed the stranger. "Cowhide rubs them absolutely raw. Is that your boy?" He pointed to where Liberty sat, legs dangling over the edge of the cabin roof.

"Yes, it is."

"Good-looking little man."

"We think so."

"Yes indeed. A finely molded form, well-digested in all parts, a guileless countenance of incontrovertible purity. Quite handsome, indeed."

Thatcher stared back at the man. "He's not for sale."

"Oh my no, you misunderstand me, sir," protested the stranger, his features undergoing a rapid revolution of effect, as of several contrary sentiments seeking simultaneous issue. "Certainly I was not implying anything of the kind. Sir, I am dumbfounded, so if you would graciously excuse me, I will be on my way." Hastily withdrawing, he descended the ladder into the cabin, casting a few furtive glances back at Thatcher before vanishing from sight.

"Liberty!" Thatcher called.

The boy turned halfway around. "Yes, Father?"

"I don't want you straying too far from my view."

"Yes, Father."

Vaguely annoyed at having been roused from his reverie, Liberty swung the hard blade of concentrated attention only children and certain privileged adults could authentically muster back to the oncoming flow of silken canal, of vaulting greenery, of streaming sky. He'd been imagining himself a sort of fleshy extension of the boat itself, a living figurehead, all eyes, ears, nose and mouth, but where did the senses end and nonsense begin? Obviously the water, no matter how greenly dank, scummed and dead it might appear to the corporeal eye, was insistently alive, and the boat, too, a dim pulse beating in every crucified board, chattel kin to the maples and ashes and cedars whose latticed canopies sometimes passed so closely overhead that Liberty could reach up and pluck a leaf or two. And it was then he understood, without the language to fully pronounce it, that the objects of the world, every blade of corn, every sullen rock, every clod of earth flicked into the air by a mule's hoof, was, in actuality, a disclosure of feeling, the physical elements of the visible world each marking a site where an emotion stopped, crystallized and was made manifest in three-dimensional form. Which meant that the code of the most obdurate thing, when confronted by a candid and inquiring heart, could be revealed in the current of feeling opened in the interrogator's breast.

It never occurred to Liberty to speak to anyone about such topics. He believed, in the blind innocence of his years, that everyone knew these things.

Ahead, a pair of white beams rose up out of the dark water and the steersman lifted his horn and sounded two long thrilling notes. They were approaching a lock! From out of a modest limestone house squatting on a knoll in the shade of a towering chestnut tree strolled the humped, gray-bearded locktender and his idiot son, arms thick and hairless and as long as his legs.

"Erastus, you old honey-fuggler," cried the tender, securing a line to the snubbing post and tossing the end to where Whelkington stood ready in the bow. "Looks like you've hooked another fine catch of pike for the blacklegs on Canal Street." The son stood there grinning.

"You know me, Luther, can't let a good one get away."

"Appears to me you should've thrown more than a couple back. Nothing but babies."

"I'm surprised at your ignorance, Luther. Don't you know them wee ones makes the best eating?"

Their loud laughter was taken up by the son, who continued on after both men had stopped.

Whelkington stepped off the slowing boat and onto the berm and, as Luther and son leaned into the balance beams to open the lock, he stood looking up at the house, where framed in the window, leaning carelessly upon the sill, sat a representative of that illustrious creature of fable and song, the locktender's daughter, this particular specimen perhaps not so well-favored as her mythical sisters, exhibiting poxy cheeks, a squinty eye and no more than four visible teeth in her head. She smiled and waved coquettishly to the captain and called out, "My pretty popkin." Someone laughed, then another, and Whelkington swung swiftly about, glaring at the offending passengers. Then he turned and mounted the narrow path to the door of the house, which he opened without knocking and went inside.

The *Croesus* was eased into the lock, bumping against the stone walls with sufficient force to cause several of the ladies to gasp and clutch at their companions. The lower gates were closed, the paddle-valve levers manned, and as the water rushed in the boat rose slowly, majestically, into the summer air. And when the lock was filled and the upper gates opened, the *Croesus* reemerged into the canal at a newer, more exalted altitude just as Captain Whelkington exited the tender's house, the customary stiffness of his face made somewhat more elastic. He conferred briefly with the old locktender, clapping him on the back as he handed over a palmful of coins. He presented a cherry sucket to the son, then stepped nimbly back onto the boat, and to Red's cries of "God Almighty!" "Jesus Christ!" and "Judas Priest!"—the whip cracking, the trace chains clinking—the harnessed mules moved off at a thoroughly healthy trot.

Utterly preoccupied by Liberty's obvious delight in the ongoing pageant that was life on the Grand Western, speculating on the nature of the memories taking shape in his young son's mind, Thatcher failed to mark the low burbling sound emanating from the quaint figure at his side. He didn't even realize he was being addressed until, at a rise in volume, he recognized in the faint incoherent noise various particles of speech and, bending politely forward, he inquired, "Excuse me?"

"Of course you understand, sir," his interlocutor replied promptly, as if Thatcher had been patiently heeding all along, "Providence has granted us an extraordinary privilege on this occasion."

His long white hair and beard were arctic bright, and he leaned upon an ivory cane, gazing out on the passing scene with the attitude of one who'd seen it all before, would see it all again and wasn't much impressed with the sight. In costume and demeanor he conveyed as prominently as possible his membership in that class known as gentlemen.

"Certes," Thatcher agreed. "We are alive, and it is a splendid day."

"I refer, of course, to the privilege of bearing witness to the end."

Thatcher allowed himself a modest smile. "The end? The end of what, precisely?"

"Why the country, sir, the whole living, breathing, scrapping country, at least such as we have known it heretofore."

"You are not the first to harbor fears for the future of our union. Parlous days we have entered on."

"I am not adverting to the tedious machinations of government, sir. Government is a touch and go affair. I neither take part in nor do I enjoy the least regard for its various storms and squalls. Those furies have ever accompanied us in the past and will continue to harry us

unto the shores of whatever trackless futurity we eventually find ourselves marooned upon. And I suspect that that sandy spot will not be
a kindly one for folks such as us."

"Us?"

"Why, of course. Those of mature years who came to manhood in
a now distant, now lost, age. We are superannuated, sir. We prefer
that the dust cling to our heels, that the mule shall not be whipped.
We were not built for haste. You recall the time when these packet
boats were first introduced? The consternation in certain circles,
some of them quite powerful, over the crews' improvident methods,
their untrammeled velocity? The damage caused to the banks by
their turbulent wakes? The bow-mounted scythes to cut the lines of
slow-moving barges? But to what avail? Haughty packet masters
paid and continue to pay their fines without complaint, proceeding
with impunity upon their reckless ways. And why? To ensure their ill-
turned profit. What is a modest forfeit compared to the monstrous
sums accrued by squeezing out two trips in the time it used to take to
complete one? Simple economics, sir. Speed equals specie. And there
you have it, the equation of the modern age." He thumped the tip of
his cane against the boards. "Might I inquire as to why you did not
choose to travel by rail?"

"Well, yes. Frankly, we are in no great hurry and—"

"Then I can assume you are not in business."

Thatcher smiled. "This makes the second instance this morning I
have been found out. The truth of the matter is that I wanted my boy
to experience the pleasure of a packet journey."

The gentleman nodded approvingly. "Before it is no more."

"Why yes, I guess you have me there."

The gentleman, still nodding, offered every appearance of a considered wisdom. "The rails are coming, sir. Indeed, the rails are here.
Running full chisel across the stones of every hearth, straight down
the center of every heart. We want proportion. The human ratio. A life
scaled to our organic needs. Where now is leisure? Where contempla-
tion? Where exists even a minikin measure of peace? We are become

slaves, sir, slaves to an extravagant precipitancy ruinous to body and soul." He paused and held up a finger. "Nevertheless, a remedy is at hand."

From the capacious pocket of his buff-colored coat he withdrew a small brown bottle, which he ceremoniously presented to Thatcher. The label, in florid capitals, read "COL. FOGGBOTTOM'S FLASH COMPOUND" and underneath, in smaller type: "Cures nettlerash, belly-bloat, vertigo and the Decline, and other subsidiary maladies induced by the Gallop of Modern Times."

"And you are?" commented Thatcher, remarking the prominent similarity between the engraved portrait on the label and the living gentleman standing before him.

The colonel rendered a slight bow. "Not my original moniker, but what's in a name? You appear to me, sir, to be a citizen of high intellect and penetrating probity. Would you be interested, perhaps, in purchasing a bottle of said stimulant?"

"What's in it?"

"A common, perfectly sensible request. However, I regret I am not at liberty to divulge the abundant array of beneficial herbs contained in this tincture other than to assure you and other sharp patrons that the wholesome derivatives of the poppy plant play a significant role and have been proven, scientifically, I remind you, to soothe the fractious symptoms of the go-ahead life. So, would you care to join the growing tribe of happy Foggbottom consumers? More than five thousand sold to date. A mere one dollar and twenty-five cents per bottle."

"I'm sure your nostrum is of a highly agreeable order, but as a matter of personal principle I refuse to ingest patent medicines of any stripe whatsoever."

"Perhaps your son, then. He seems rather an excitable lad."

Before Thatcher could summon up a remark withering enough to rebut this ridiculous characterization, a bell sounded and the colonel's polite formality evaporated like the morning mist. Snatching the bottle of compound from his hand, he lurched past Thatcher to join the stampeding throng racing for the stairs into the main cabin.

"What's happening?" Thatcher called, startled by this hasty abandonment of decorum among a listless group of loungers who, until now, had seemed to value little except breeding and good manners.

"Dinner, you damn fool!" the colonel shot back. "Last one there gets to lick out the bowls!"

Father and son watched in twinned amazement as the old gentleman, deploying his cane like a jousting lance, rudely wedged his way past several offended ladies and their irate escorts.

"Who was that man?" asked Liberty.

"A professional notion-higgler," replied Thatcher, quite unable to keep the trace of amused admiration out of his voice, "with as original and persuasive a line of palaver as I've ever heard."

By the time Thatcher and Liberty had made their prudent descent into what was optimistically termed "the dining salon," several male gourmands, having already downed their edibles, were vacating the room, faces flushed, lips greased, bellies amplified.

"Fourteen different dishes," declared one glutted diner, popping the top button on his breeches. "Two more than we were served on *Cleopatra's Barge.*"

"Four more than on the *Try and Beat It*," added another.

"What'd I tell you gents about ol' Captain Whelkington. Don't he treat his ruck right square?"

"Wonder if they'll feed us the same at supper," conjectured a third, picking at his nubby teeth with an unused lucifer.

The sated trio brushed past with barely a glance, stubby fingers extracting long nines from waistcoat pockets for a postprandial smoke and stroll about the deck.

Inside, where the ceiling was so low that even with his hat removed Thatcher had to stoop, reigned a bizarre but rigorous silence. Instead of conversation, the ceaseless scrape of cutlery upon crockery and enthusiastic chewing noises, as if the meal itself were a mammoth block of stone being chipped away at by a dedicated corps of inspired artisans. All bent upon the plate in the solemn task of consuming as much as possible, as quickly as possible.

Presiding over this enterprise was a large, testy woman with a wide, mustachioed face who claimed to be the captain's wife yet insisted on being addressed as Mrs. Callahan. She rushed to and from the galley, bearing great platters of steaming meats which were emptied the instant she set them down.

Captain Whelkington sat holding court at the head of a table, regaling a fawning mob of the "boys" with colorful tales of the canawling life: the great cholera epidemic of '32, tar smudges smoldering in every town square, chunks of skewered beef set out on poles to draw the toxins from the air; the drunken locktender who one night, deep into the corn, tried to light his pipe with a live coal and caught his beard on fire, and the next morning there was nothing left but a heap of char they sold to a local baker to burn in his kiln; the pathmaster's wife with the temptational eye who would lie down in the timothy with you for a mere pistareen; the terrible breaches that sometimes left the Croesus helplessly "mudlarked" for a whole day or more; and, of course, the rovers and the roughs who haunted the waterway like unappeased spirits, the soaplocks and the runagate apprentices, the gyppos and the swingkettles, the road men and the redemptioners, and the mighty brawls that ensued when this pot was stirred a bit too smartly.

"Then one night," Whelkington told his spellbound audience, "about an hour out of Rome, a norther blew down, shook the squirrels right out of the trees. The canal was boiling, you couldn't see to the end of the boat. Then an electron come down, knocked ol' Red senseless to the ground and I run out and—" He stopped, staring at the bewildered Fishes in the doorway as if he'd never seen them before and wouldn't want to ever again.

"Set yourselves down," snapped Mrs. Callahan, bustling by with an armload of dirty dishes, "or there'll be nothing to set down to."

As she spoke, the last slab of ham was speared away by a hard character in buckskin whose grizzled face seemed to pose the eternal question: What are you gonna do about it?

"That's quite all right," asserted a young woman sitting nearby with eyes so strikingly blue the pupils resembled black suns. She and the other members of her sex, all exhibiting the same grim countenance normally associated with cigar-store indians, were arranged in a row at a long table opposite the men, who, either too busy shoveling grub into their pieholes or too embarrassed by their perilous proximity to the better half, neither conversed with nor barely glanced at the ladies. "The boy is welcome to finish the remainder of my whatever-it-is," she said, pushing the plate distastefully away. "I'm thoroughly sated." Her smile, toothsome as it was, gave the appearance of a surface phenomenon only, suggesting that beneath the skin such smiles were rare, furtive things and much preyed upon.

Thatcher politely declined, adding, "We had a more than ample breakfast before setting out this morning."

"But I insist." She patted the empty seat beside her. "Breakfast must have been many long hours ago and, frankly, this boy looks as if he could lick the enamel off the plate."

Liberty looked at his father, then slid shyly into the chair as the young woman extended a slim, pale hand toward Thatcher. "Augusta Thorne," she announced boldly, and, indicating the older, portly woman to her immediate right, "my mother, Edith Thorne," who nodded sweetly, "and the naughty imp on the end is my baby sister, Rose, to whom no attention should be paid whatsoever or she'll be up on the table reciting, 'She walks in beauty like one so bright,' or however it goes, I have such a poor head for all that dreamy claptrap."

"'She walks in beauty like the night,'" corrected Rose, the blood rising in her downy cheeks to produce a tint that mimicked her name.

"Really," declared the elder Mrs. Thorne, aiming her lorgnette in Thatcher's direction, "I fail to see why these preposterous meals must be conducted like horse races. Are prizes awarded to the swiftest, or is it that everyone is concerned the fare will be depleted before all have had their fill?"

"A very real concern, I should think," remarked Rose, noting in wonder upon a sideboard the staggering pile of plundered serving platters.

The touchy Mrs. Callahan, passing within auditory range of these unpardonable criticisms, selected a particularly virulent sneer from her vast armamentarium of expressive hexes devised over the years to deal with just such ungrateful trash as these, though unfortunately no one noticed but the boy, whose strange colorless eyes seemed, for a brief, frightening instant, to penetrate directly into the deep private knowledge of exactly who she was.

"Do I detect a note of the old country in your speech?" asked Thatcher, after introducing himself and his son and settling into a chair across from the beaming Thornes.

"Yes, you do, Mr. Fish," replied Augusta. "Hampshire, to be exact. We're on holiday."

"We've come to see the Falls," Rose blurted out, almost lisping with excitement.

"Yes," declared Mrs. Thorne. "We've heard so much about the great Niagara our curiosity could no longer be politely restrained. We wish to experience sublimity and terror."

"Well," drawled Thatcher, "I'm sure you'll find America abounding in both qualities."

"Oh, we already have." Augusta took a sip of tea, looked into the cup and set it back down again. "We attended the most stimulating sermon by the Reverend Beecher in Brooklyn."

"Oh my," interrupted her mother. "I cannot recall precisely what the good man said, but I still get goosebumps just thinking about the sound of his voice."

"Then we witnessed a boiler explosion on a steamboat in New York harbor. More than twenty killed, I understand."

"But a gentleman we met at the hotel in Albany," Mrs. Thorne added breathlessly, "assured us that the consequence of the Falls would be to combine the effects of the two."

"Just what is it," mused Augusta, "about the sight of filthy water tumbling over a precipice that we find so positively thrilling?"

"Perhaps," conjectured Thatcher, "there is something in us that is eternally, noisily falling and we respond as magnets to the outward emblem of an inner descent."

Augusta's eyes narrowed, went rapidly in and out of focus, as if she were attempting to maintain a close watch on Thatcher while simultaneously concentrating furiously on something else. Then she blinked and said, "How absolutely transcendental."

"Your son," noted Mrs. Thorne, "does not appear to be so hungry as we thought."

Liberty had been silently studying the half-eaten contents of his plate as if contemplating a collection of dead oddities arranged under museum glass.

"Go ahead," Augusta urged. "You should understand that I'll not withdraw my attentions until you begin eating. And I must warn you, I can be a very stubborn woman. Ask my mother."

"The most willful child in the family," confirmed Mrs. Thorne, "perhaps in several generations. Even her dear brother Austin— admittedly, a boy of near pathological sensitivity, God protect his soul—would have nothing further to do with her after the age of eight, wouldn't even acknowledge her in public as his sister. Why, if she so much as lost at a game of croquet, she'd sit sulking under a mulberry tree until two in the morning, when Father would have to go out and carry her in to bed, the mallet still clenched in her hot little fist."

Hesitantly, Liberty turned a two-tined fork sideways as a sort of miniature trowel, then shoved onto the blade of his knife a slice of cold fowl which he lifted gravely to his mouth and gravely chewed and swallowed.

"Good," announced Augusta, patting his head approvingly.

Thatcher watched the tips of his son's ears grade into deep scarlet. "He won't complain or utter a sound," he said quietly, "but if you don't withdraw your hand, he just might try to take off a finger or two, as a warning."

Augusta's arm flew back in horror. "Why, how astonishing." She turned to study the docile lad at her side. "He doesn't appear to be that manner of boy."

Thatcher smiled blandly. "What boy does?"

Hunched now over his plate, Liberty consumed morsel after over-done morsel of various meats and sauce, boiled per Mrs. Callahan's strict instructions for a measured hour or more, effectively relieving flesh and plant of any taste, consistency or nutrition, the bony wings of his thin shoulders commencing to quake in gentle convulsions of secret glee.

"What's wrong with him now?" asked Augusta.

"He's happy," Thatcher explained. "He likes to eat."

Formally addressing the boy, she inquired softly, "What is your favorite food?"

Shaking and chewing, Liberty gave no response.

"He can't hear you," said Thatcher. "He's deaf."

"Oh my goodness!" Augusta covered her mouth with a dainty hand.

"What did he say?" asked Mrs. Thorne.

"He said the boy's deaf."

"Oh."

The Thorne family now shifted in their seats to contemplate the unfortunate child.

"He's adjusted to his condition marvelously well," said Thatcher. "Quite a quick study in the lipreading department."

"Can he hear music?" asked Rose, disturbed that the person at the table nearest to her in age should be so afflicted.

"No, but he can feel it."

Augusta bent down, positioning her face on a level with Liberty's, and spoke loudly, deliberately, spacing out the words like stones plummeting at uniform intervals into a dark pool. "What . . . is . . . your . . . favorite . . . food?"

Liberty regarded the woman with a look of complete vacancy, then abruptly dropped his jaw to reveal on his tongue a semimasticated mass of unidentifiable beige chunks to which he adverted with extended forefinger.

Augusta reeled back, gasping. "Why, that's the most disgusting sight I've seen since we left New York. I believe he certainly is capable of biting me, or worse. I beg your pardon, Mr. Fish, but your son's behavior doesn't appear much more advanced than that of an untamed beast." Unable, though, to turn herself entirely away, she continued to stare at the offending child as if expecting an apology or, at the least, an adequate excuse.

"I know you did not mean to insult my son," said Thatcher mildly, "nor he you, but I fear I must further inform you that, like certain creatures of the forest, he is also mute."

All the women exclaimed at once.

"Oh, Mr. Fish," declared Augusta, "I'm so terribly sorry. I had no idea."

"Doesn't seem to bother him much. He can satisfy most of his needs with a series of meaningful gestures."

Mrs. Thorne, settled on the edge of her chair like a nesting bird, absorbed this information with avid interest, then leaned giddily forward, jowls aquiver, to announce, "When I was a tender lass, younger than my own Rose here, our stableboy Edgar—you remember Old Budgie, don't you girls?—was kicked in the head by a rabid horse. Or, wait—perhaps it was that sick cow drove us mad always lowing down there by the gate, wouldn't come in, wouldn't go out, until one day Randolph simply walked up, shot it square between the ears with that antique musket Father used to kill Frenchmen with—well, it was all so long ago anyway, and afterward there was nothing they could do for the affected youth but prop him up in a corner and make sure his nappie got changed regularly. Poor dear couldn't speak, could barely lift a finger. Utterly unseated he was. And, curiously enough, as the years passed, he came to bear a remarkable likeness to the author Thomas Carlyle, although never having met the great man myself, I could not say for certain."

"Well," replied Thatcher, "I believe my son still retains enough sense than to lose himself in the writing line. He has, however, on a number of occasions, expressed an intense fascination with the role of riverboat captain."

Augusta's well-ministered facade had lapsed into an open gawk, thoughts, mostly dark, blowing cleanly as clouds across her powdery, unguarded face.

Having devoured every scrap of food on his plate, Liberty was diligently sopping up the last of the gravy with a ragged heel of wheat bread. When he was done, he pushed back his chair, stood and delivered a deep bow.

"You're welcome," replied Augusta, nodding courteously.

Thatcher, who had eaten almost nothing, also rose and excused himself, a tall man with large hands and a persistent light in his countenance whom Augusta found supremely intriguing because so fundamentally unreadable. "Pleasant meeting you ladies," he said, touching his hat. "My son and I both appreciated the enchantment of your company and the compass of your generosity."

"Thank you, Mr. Fish," responded Mrs. Thorne. "You've aided in transforming this horrid boat trip into a—how shall I say?—more *elevating* experience."

"At least he isn't blind, too," blurted Rose, quickly shushed by mother and sister.

Mounting the stairs, Liberty in front, Thatcher kept nudging sharply with a knee the back of his giggling son's leg until finally, Liberty, in some irritation, tried to look back to voice a complaint and his father simply seized the top of his head and turned it firmly forward again, as if the head were merely a finial atop a post, a wooden ball requiring minor adjustment.

Up on deck, Thatcher was immediately waylaid by yet another itinerant of disputable character who sought to engage him in a rambling "philosophical colloquy" on the subjects of table-rapping, animal husbandry and the verifiable demonstrations of the Devil in this, our fallen world—"cunningly constructed, sir, in such a style as to provide numerous nooks and crannies for the Great Tempter to dwell comfortably within."

His father thus diverted, Liberty took the opportunity to explore the limited deck space of the *Croesus*. Two circumambulations between bow and stern proving more than adequate to satisfy even a cat's curiosity, he settled once again upon the forward edge of the roof. Nearby, the party of young fashionables struck poses, flirted shamelessly and partook of the blessings of Nature with much bright chatter concerning ancient Phoebus, brindled kine, genial rustics, etc. A bored, pale woman, meditatively revolving a silk parasol above her lofty arrangement of coiled blond hair, turned to bestow on the boy a vague smile much as one deposits a coin into a beggar's cup— behavior Liberty had already endured enough times to understand that it might, and should, be safely ignored.

A stand of pine crowded the banks, draping the passing boat in a cool, medicinal shade, and a man laughed when a low branch almost reached out and plucked away his hat. A black cloud of gnats set passengers to coughing, windmilling their arms. Big green bullfrogs plopped into the water at the vessel's approach. A pair of dark, glittering eyes appeared at the roof's edge, peering intensely right at Liberty, no sooner noticed than their owner, in one dramatic bound, leaped high into the air and landed nimbly at his side.

"I'm the hoggee," announced the acrobat, thrusting out a soiled, well-callused hand. This was the fidgety, unattached boy Liberty had already observed skulking mysteriously about the boat or lying sprawled atop one of the mules whenever Red took one of his frequent breaks, retiring to the salon to share a tumbler of antifogmatic with the convivial Mrs. Callahan. He looked to be roughly Liberty's age and height, with skinny, bruised arms and bare, splayed feet missing nails on several toes, and he was dressed in a baggy, liberally patched man's shirt and a seedy pair of purple pantaloons. Every visible inch of skin was incrusted with dirt of sundry hues and layers. It was the hair, however, that was particularly noteworthy, each mousy strand cut to an identical length and then, apparently, dipped in molasses and brushed straight out from his scalp, giving him the appearance of a dandelion about to blow.

Liberty accepted the proffered hand, sticky though it was—the telltale star in this imp's pupil a beacon he would never be able to resist, vestige of the aurora that resided in all but was too often occluded by bad weather in the soul's outer provinces.

"I'm Stumpy, the hoggee," he declared proudly, emphasizing again the latter word as one would a title of no small distinction.

"Take a gander at the tile," indicating the high hat atop the man seated cross-legged on the foredeck below them reading a newspaper, Stumpy leaned over and from his puckered mouth let fall a juicy gob smack onto the center of the glossy crown. The man looked up, held out his hand as the boys scuttled back out of sight. "One of them fat Dutchmen," gurgled Stumpy, trying to check his giggles manually by pressing all ten smutty fingers against his lips. "I'd whang him in the eye with a fending pole if he so much as laid a single hand on me. See ol' Genesee Red over there?" He gestured toward the lanky somnambulent stumbling along behind the hayburners. "We're the ones make this boat go. I spell him in about another hour. Pretty whangdang, doncha think? Watch out for Captain Whelkington, though. Don't get in front of him. He'll knock you down quicker than billy-be-damned. Times he and Red get into it so bad they got to stop the boat and take it out on the towpath. Passengers always seem to enjoy it, though. Everyone loves a good knockabout. But like I say, you don't want to be in one yourself, so steer clear of the cap'n. He's notional, that one. Listen, want to see something bunkum?"

With a conspiratorial leer, he led Liberty down into the dining salon where, the tables cleared, the mop run once across the floor, Mrs. Callahan sat at the bar, sodden rag in one hand, cup of forty rod in the other. "What mischief you up to now?" she muttered.

"Cap'n business," mumbled Stumpy, moving on past the marathon whist game in the corner, serious men devoutly occupied, who hadn't stepped outside or glanced up at a window since boarding at Troy, and forward into the cuddy, where he carefully pushed the door open and, grinning wickedly, pointed upward. Liberty had no idea where he was or what he was supposed to be looking at. This cramped, murky space contained four bunks, one stool, and smelled of mold and sweat and mule dung. Overhead a betty lamp hung on a chain, and in the rough planks of the low ceiling he could see crudely carved initials and untutored words and symbols of enigmatic significance. Then he noticed, bored into the peeling and splintered wood, a configuration of auger holes, some bright as noon, some dark as a well bottom, others winking mystically on and off or hovering suspended in a dim twilight state in between.

Stumpy positioned the stool and motioned for Liberty to climb up and take a peek. His eyeball jammed up against the hole, gamely squinting into a grayish obscurity impossible to puzzle out, he was about to step down when the shadows shifted, the textured light, though still dampened, seeped in from another angle and into view materialized a comprehensible form, long and pale and shapely, a human leg, a woman's "limb" to be precise, revealed now in all its secret splendor beneath the protective tenting of ruffled silk.

Stumpy, tugging impatiently on Liberty's pants, informed him in a confidential whisper, "They don't wear no drawers under them petticoats," teeth gleaming even in this uncertain light.

Liberty's eye, traveling inquisitively up that turned column of tender muscle and opalescent skin, illumination steadily dwindling, endeavored to penetrate the beckoning mystery where leg met torso and it was very dark indeed. He was still seeking when the door crashed open, admitting Captain Whelkington and a couple of bachelors dressed like twins in matching cream linen suits and hats and brandishing identical segars of considerable heft and pungency.

"Piss in a bucket!" bellowed the captain. "What in the high holy hell are you two scrawns doing in here!"

Without awaiting a reply, he seized Stumpy by the ear and hauled him squealing through the door.

"And you, you little dawplucker!" he cried, advancing upon Liberty, who, having hastily jumped down from the stool, was feinting left, now right, striving to turn this lunatic's flank, but the room was too small, the captain's girth too wide. "I knew it were a monstrous misjudgement on my part to allow you and your nigger-loving father on my boat. Didn't know you were a damn pervert, too. Now get the fuck out of here"—cuffing Liberty hard enough on the head to send stars and bells reeling through space—"afore I tell your pa just what article of boy you truly are."

"Now hold on, Erastus," declaimed one of the creamy gentlemen in a hearty baritone. "Don't be too precipitate with your screed. Next thing you know, the old man'll be down here applying for a position."

"At which juncture," replied the quick-witted captain, "I'll be applying something firm of mine to something soft of his."

And the door slammed shut upon their coarse laughter.

His father still entangled in the coils of the same monotonous conversation as when he'd left, Liberty ignored Thatcher's concerned look and quietly reassumed his seat on the deck. Though it seemed to him as if he'd just been translated to another realm and back by means not yet officially recognized, scattered parts of him over there still trying to catch up, here topside, everything seemed exactly as before, the sky the same bleeding blue, the neighboring faces well padded and smug, all achingly familiar, the recurring vistas drab and undistinguished. He had the odd sensation he'd already been on board for several days. He was surreptitiously studying the women clustered unknowingly, like elegant and begowned dolls in the general vicinity of the tampered boards, attempting to determine which one it might have been whose veiled anatomy had been indiscreetly exposed to his aspiring gaze, and he'd just about decided on the pretty girl in the green dress with the high forehead and dimpled chin when abruptly she turned to look him full in the face, and all the skin from his neck up swelled with blood.

Mrs. Callahan came trudging up from the galley to toss a bucket of orts over the rail, cheese parings, potato skins, egg shells, animal bones, apple cores, congealed fat and the unidentifiable runoffs and leavings from the unsparing dinner meal to mingle with the other diverse ingredients of the canal this August day was industriously brewing into a memorably aromatic, rainbow-hued soup: traffic garbage and body waste, castoff clothes and discarded boots, missing traps and lost books, whiskey bottles and sheets of newspaper, hats and children's tops and a wooden leg or two, rusted pistols and lensless eyeglasses and untold gallons of tobacco juice, and playing cards and lamp oil, and all the dead: the mules, the horses, the cows, the dogs and cats, the muskrats and the snakes, the frogs, the fish and, of course, the humans. Liberty had overheard the affable bowman amusing a couple of Jonathans from the North Country with gruesome yarns of the stiffs he'd personally seen dragged from the water just this year—one, near Little Falls, a hairless giant who'd looked more like a bleached pig; the other, west of Ganajoharie, a faceless greenish thing half-nibbled by the carp and the turtles, its bones protruding from the spongy flesh like the ribs of a scuttled ship.

Stumpy had replaced Red out on the towpath and somehow gathered behind him a taunting gang of local children who mimicked his swaggering gait and chanted loudly in unison:

> *Hoggee on the towpath*
> *Five cents a day*
> *Picking up horseballs*
> *To eat along the way!*

Flashing Liberty a knowing grin, he cracked his whip with great authority.

Sometime in the blazing heart of the endless afternoon the *Croesus* arrived at the village of Sparta, and while the packet was being passed through the lock its bored and overheated passengers, having spied on the bank an animated crowd collected in the shade of an impressively developed chestnut tree and desperate for novelty of any stripe, rushed from the boat en masse in hopes of even a few brief minutes of entertainment.

Nailed to the ragged bole of the tree was a gaily executed sign proclaiming: "Dr. Wilbur Fitzgibbon, Esq. Extractions 50¢." And in the clearing at the center of the three-and-four-folk-deep throng of craning, clamorous spectators lined up like curiosities in a sideshow exhibit were the doctor, a lively, stout figure in a swallowtail coat and pipe hat; his assistant, short, bald and black and rigged out in a threadbare jester's costume and clutching in his left hand a hard-used banjo; and, seated between them rather tentatively on a bare wooden chair, an anxious white gentleman who responded to the shouted encouragements and drolleries of the crowd with a mirthless grin and the frequent mopping of his brow with a voluminous checkered kerchief.

"Quiet! Quiet, please!" called Dr. Fitzgibbon, removing his coat and stepping confidently forward. "Before we begin I would like to remind the assembly that what you are about to witness today is neither an idle stunt nor a theatrical performance, but an authentic dental procedure of paramount consequence, particularly to our suffering friend here."

"Bring on the fortifier, doc!" yelled a voice. "Calvin don't look so good."

Clapping a powerful hand upon the patient's shoulder and lifting a cautionary finger to his lips, Fitzgibbon went on, "I would therefore entreat each and every one of you attending this afternoon's operation to display an appropriate respect and consideration. Now, before we may properly proceed, we must verify the diseased tooth." Slipping from his waistcoat pocket a long, slim, glittering instrument that tapered down to a fiendishly fine point, he leaned over the seated gentleman, tilted his chin, and, requesting politely, "Open, please," began to probe the pink interior of the exposed mouth with an artistic delicacy.

The black man, his shining countenance a perfect blank, allowed his dark, impassive eyes to go roving among that encircling field of white faces, like upturned flowers really, basking in the unfailable light, his fingers idly plucking a few random notes from the banjo's taut wires.

Liberty, once more disregarding his father's injunctions, worked his way among a thicket of adult legs up to the front for a ringside seat on the grass amid an ungoverned pack of scruffy children, their synonymously narrow heads and vaguely fetal features testifying to communion at the the same polluted bloodline, as did their fondness for wrestling one another in preference to the big show the grownups were putting on.

Suddenly the patient let out a howl that sent sparrows wheeling from nearby trees and babies to crying and he bolted upright out of the chair as if his backside were on fire. A few nervous chuckles broke the awful silence that followed, but most of the crowd watched in mute apprehension.

"There, there," cooed Dr. Fitzgibbon, patting his patient consolingly upon the chest as he eased him gently back down into the chair. He glanced at the audience. "I believe we have located the offending molar."

General laughter of a relieved, temperate quality.

"Now," continued Dr. Fitzgibbon, "if I may, I require two volunteers, preferably male and of excellent strength. How about you, sir, and, yes, your friend, too," indicating a pair of brawny sunburnt youths who, though clearly embarrassed by the adverture, stepped dutifully forward.

"If one of you obliging gents would please position yourself behind the chair and firmly seize Mr. Turnbull's rather generous biceps"—more appreciative laughter—"and the other kindly come around and grasp the ankles securely like so. And do not be timid with your strength. It certainly would not do to have our friend coming up out of the chair in the middle of the actual operation."

"Now hold on a durn minute," protested Turnbull, vainly searching the mob for signs of moral support. "I reckon I just might have changed—"

"This ain't a hanging, Calvin," called a voice. "You're gonna walk away a better man."

"Or carried by the handles by six of your best friends," retorted a second.

"If you got any friends," added a third.

Again Turnbull made an effort to rise though, checked by the grips of four mighty hands, he could do no more than squirm feebly in his seat.

"Tut, tut," cautioned Dr. Fitzgibbon, wagging a horny finger in the man's blotched and sweating face. "Heed the worthy advice of your compatriots. 'Twill be over in an instant. The pangs of this trifling affair are as airy nothings to the unimaginable agonies to be endured should the festering pit in your splendid ivories be permitted to go untreated. Corruption black as the grave yet vital as a blooming organism continues to breed in wanton frenzy, partaking of whatever sustenance comes to hand, in this particular instance the nourishing fare of your own pearly whites, which, once devoured to the root, leaves our unwelcome guest free to move on to the second course, the succulent roulade of your gums, from the gums to the bone, from the bone to the brain. And once settled within the gleaming nobility of the skull, what does our mischievous interloper find being served in that grand chamber but a veritable foie gras of inexpressible delights whose consumption, regrettably, terminates in the irrevocable loss of sight, sound, touch, taste and, eventually, dear auditors, the toppling of the very throne of reason, reducing the unfortunate Mr. Turnbull to a mere drooling pantomine of his former hale and hearty self, bereft of family, friends, cash and cabin, resembling perhaps a figure much like this!"

Reaching over, he twisted his signboard to reveal on its backside a hideously detailed rendering of a bug-eyed, black-tongued idiot with writhing scarlet lips and chartreuse flesh who was tugging out great yellow handfuls of his own mangy hair.

A collective gasp rose from the crowd.

"You don't want to look like that, do you, Mr. Turnbull?"

The terrified man shook his head.

"Good," Dr. Fitzgibbon declared. "Now we may begin."

From a second waistcoat pocket he withdrew a pair of polished pliers he held aloft for public inspection. A hush had fallen over the mesmerized onlookers, the sole sound a mild breeze moving softly through the leaves.

"Gentlemen," the doctor addressed his volunteers, whose hold upon Mr. Turnbull's trembling limbs instantly tightened. "Open, please."

Then he inserted between the patient's gaping jaws a gnawed and discolored wedge of wood that had appeared in his hand from out of nowhere like a magical object. Grasping Mr. Turnbull by the shoulder and planting a knee in his lap, Dr. Fitzgibbon bent forward and commenced fumbling around inside his mouth with the pliers. "Very well," he announced momentarily. "I believe I have it. Are you ready,

Mr. Turnbull?" The man shook his head no, but too late, the evil pliers having already begun to twist and rock. Immediately, the black attendant, who had been accompanying these preliminaries with a delicately plunked interpretation of "Buffalo Gals," sprang madly into action, strumming away with a wild stereotypical abandon while shouting out lyrics of utter incomprehensibility. He had become a man transformed, limbs jerking in uncoordinated spasms, one leg bouncing frantically up and down in a demented parody of a performer trying in vain to keep time to the music, bloodshot eyes rolling in their sockets like loose marbles; and the louder Mr. Turnbull screamed, the faster he played, his hand a dark blur dancing over the stained vellum diaphragm. Dr. Fitzgibbon's face, red, wet, veins standing out in relief on both temples, seemed about to explode. All his wrenching and toiling had failed to dislodge a tooth whose roots appeared to reach down into the very earth itself. Immobilized by all these strange hands clutching at his body, Mr. Turnbull's efforts to fend off this assault left him thrashing about as limply as a galvanized fish. Then, just when it seemed that neither doctor nor patient nor onlooker could endure the excruciating spectacle one instant longer, Dr. Fitzgibbon staggered backward brandishing aloft the heroic pliers that held between their metallic jaws a barely discernible nubbin of such inconsequential size one could scarcely believe it could have put up such a fight. The crowd erupted into a pandemonium of hoots, cheers and rollicking applause as Dr. Fitzgibbon dropped the carious trophy into a fluid-filled vial he then fitted into a slot in a wooden case full of other slots, other vials.

The muscular youths escaped into the approving grins and hearty back claps of their friends while Mr. Turnbull, his complexion gone white as a sail, leaned meticulously forward and spat onto the grass a thick wad of bloody phlegm. And the banjo man, reverting instantly to his previous demeanor of unreadable stolidity, doffed his green cap and, costume bells jingling, passed silently among the dispersing throng, collecting what coins he could.

"Whopping show," someone exclaimed. "Why I'd pay fifty cents myself just to see it again."

The crowd drifted away, almost reluctantly, reliving in words what they'd just seen, anticipating the tale they would carry home, "Mother, we went to town and saw the extraction and you should have heard the poor fool howl," back to the farm, the dry goods store, the livery stable, the tannery and the bland succession of days so remarkable in their uniformity that existence itself could often seem to have taken on the guise of an elaborate practical joke in which the same day, with only trifling variations, was drawn round and round again like a wagonload of bricks, out the door at dawn, back in again at dusk, as there advanced over the unvarying seasons a surging sense of expectancy, a conviction profound and unshakable, that soon, *soon*, either now or tomorrow or the year after tomorrow (who could know when exactly?) something tremendous would arrive to redeem the quality of the day, and this belief, so indomitable, though typically half-conscious and inarticulate, was accompanied by an equally persuasive certainty that the waiting itself, the mystical devotion of attending, could serve to call forth the great something that perhaps you didn't even know you were waiting for.

"Well, son," commented Thatcher, who, along with the other delinquent passengers from the *Croesus*, all quite cognizant by now of the low boiling point of Captain Whelkington's many humors, was hurrying along at a noticeably brisker pace than the dawdling locals, "to quote the immortal Sam Patch, 'Some things can be done as well as others.'"

"I don't want my teeth yanked," said Liberty.

"I wouldn't fret unduly about it. We Fish have robust parts, running back to the Middle Ages. We've chomped and chewed our way through one tyrannical regime after another. Your grandfather Benton went to his grave at age ninety-two with a full set of perfect teeth. Fish teeth were made for biting and holding on. Have no fear."

Back at the boat, returning sightseers were presented with yet another memorable tableau to add to their unexpectedly rich store for the day. Out on the berm the excitable captain, having obviously worked himself into a fine pucker, had young Stumpy, pants at his ankles, prostrate over a barrel of pickled eels and was proceeding to lay siege to his shockingly white ass with a knotted ox-quirt while vigorously expostulating on certain obscure negligences in the performance of hoggee duties. At each blow a scarlet stripe appeared across those unblemished cheeks, as if Whelkington were wielding a stick dipped in paint. Stumpy kept eyes and mouth firmly locked, betraying nothing to this raving lunatic who happened to rule his life, at least this hopefully brief portion of it. Catching sight of his wayward passengers, the captain ceased in midstroke, allowing the corrected lad to hobble back to the boat as best he could, the black wind of his wrath sweeping down upon the thoughtless ingrates who'd dared to jeopardize packet schedules and the convenience of regulation-abiding travelers in order to indulge a taste for mindless frivolity which had no place on the illustrious Grand Western or anywhere else, for that matter, in these sober, hard-working States. He'd had a good mind to disembark and leave the stragglers to catch up how they might, suggesting that an energetic trot along the towpath would shake the tardiness out of the most cussed miscreant, even if he had paid full fare under the ridiculous presumption he was thereby guaranteed deck passage for the duration of the journey. The chastised party crept meekly back onto the boat, avoiding the captain's merciless eyes.

The female Thornes, who'd remained stoically aboard the Croesus, refusing to go dashing off on a whim simply because everyone else did, emerged from the cabin where they'd been forced to take refuge from Whelkington's vile language and more appalling behavior, all three visibly readjusting their lapsed facades to meet the obligations of public intercourse.

"So," inquired Augusta, gliding rapidly up to Thatcher, old acquaintances reunited after a long parting, "how did you enjoy the big dental harlequinade?"

"Quite well, Miss Thorne, though I must admit I have seen better."

"And your son?"

"He's not easily discomposed. He hopes there's a vagabond dentist in every town."

She was openly scrutinizing the boy with a constable's spiky gaze.

He and Rose had wandered a short distance off to study an old man in a bespoken deck chair with a truncated back, apparently whittling a firelog into a toothpick. The pile of shavings at his feet was ankle-high, and growing. Rose kept trying to communicate with Liberty through a series of improvised hand gestures. I like you, she mouthed, pointing back and forth with her finger. Can I be your friend?

Fire? mouthed Liberty, feigning confusion and indicating the man's yellowy heap of wooden curlicues. Fire?

"I believe he bears a most uncanny likeness to the Duke of Wellington, don't you think?" interjected the elder Mrs. Thorne. "The youthful duke, of course, before he became a duke, though never having met the great man myself, I couldn't say for certain, but the resemblance, nevertheless, is strikingly present."

"Oh, Mother, you promised this morning to refrain from prating for the remainder of the trip."

"But I'm not prating, daughter, I am merely giving voice to an observation I thought might be of some interest."

"Well, it isn't."

The dusted veneer of Mrs. Thorne's face collapsed like the crust of a cooling pie, and without a word she retired to the dining salon and the reliable hospitality of complete strangers.

"Will she be all right?" asked a concerned Thatcher. "Does she require attendance of any kind?"

"Heavens no," snapped Augusta, impatiently. "'Tis only her manner to which, over the years, I've become tediously accustomed. But tell me, do all you impetuous Americans go at each endeavor with the same unbridled enthusiasm? I mean, you all rushed out higgledy-piggledy to gulp down that dental disaster as if it were a fabulous picnic being served up on the banks of the canal."

"Yes," Thatcher admitted, "we are the great devourers. We devour experience, we devour geography, we devour time, we devour each other. A nation of unrestrained appetites, no question of that."

"And yet you proclaim the value of individuality as of the highest worth, above all others, while chasing your so-called happiness in a ragtag mob."

Thatcher was unable to suppress a smile. "I'm afraid, ma'am, you have unwittingly penetrated the recesses of Independence Hall. Yes, we are all proud, self-sufficient individualists, but we prefer to pursue our separate interests in a group."

"Well, I fail to see how a society based upon such pronounced contrarieties can ever possibly work out in the end."

"Neither do many of us."

"Low bridge!" bellowed the helmsman.

As they squatted there, a breath apart on the humped deck, her questing blue eyes happened to brush across his pleasant but guarded browns. "I must also inform you, Mr. Fish—if that is indeed your proper name—that English though I may be, a fool I am not. I believe I possess adequate intelligence and sensitivity to comprehend when I am, in the quaint parlance of your countrymen, being diddled."

"Why, Miss Thorne, I regret I haven't the vaguest clue as to what you are referring."

"I won't protest, Mr. Fish. Not another word on this matter. I do, however, wish to confess to you that wherever I may go, whatever implausible sights I may witness or fantastic characters I might encounter, you and your 'afflicted'"—the shifting tone of her voice emphatically installing the talons of quote marks about the adjective—"son shall no doubt remain the most singular creatures I've ever been introduced to in this preposterous land. Good day to you, sir." After calling sharply for Rose, she took her younger sister's hand and retreated briskly below.

That evening, at the first tinkle of the supper bell Liberty leaped up, raced down the stairs ahead of the stampeding adults and threw himself bodily across two empty chairs, determined that, for one meal at least, he and his father would receive their proper comfort and their proper share.

A garrulous judge from Lockport, long retired and newly widowed, charging his impoverished days with weekly packet excursions, a different destination each trip, drew the table into a theoretical consideration of the comparative intellectual abilities of the horse, the mule and the ass—the judge arguing that the horse's willingness to drink freely from a bucket of polluted canal water leveled a decided stroke against that creature's mental capacities, while the mule's refusal to touch so much as a drop of the vile liquid, no matter how thirsty, gave proof of a superior discernment, but the stupidest, of course, had to be the ass, the two-legged beast trudging insensate to the hairy rear of his betters, downwind, downstream, downsoil, subsisting entirely on stale oaths and tainted brainpop.

In the ensuing discussion Thatcher happened to mark Augusta's shrewd eye observing them from across the room, trickster father and "dumb" son chatting volubly with one another, and he acknowledged her discovery, over the monkishly bowed heads of their fellow diners, with a look that admitted clearly, Yes, madam, all apologies, no pardon too sincere, but we simply got caught up in—what shall I say?—an irresistible turn of good ol' one hundred percent American fun.

Around nine that evening, as Mrs. Callahan and off-duty crew members set about converting the dining salon into a sleeping chamber, pushing the tables into the center of the room, fitting the narrow bunks into the walls at a width hardly greater than that of bookshelves, drawing an illusive red curtain of privacy between the men forward and the women aft, though every groan, whisper, snore, fart and dream-cry would be readily apprehended by all, and while seasoned travelers were already drawing lots for the beds and arguing over precedence in the use of the communal toothbrush, Liberty and his father settled themselves on the roof deck to observe the advent of night. The sun flamed and swelled and slowly sank, burnishing the curve of the sky, the undersides of drifting clouds, tinting the air itself a soft salmon pink. Swallows flitted about in the approaching darkness, feeding on the gallinippers that even now were swarming over the boat, where a basket of pennyroyal leaves was being distributed to rub as a repellant on exposed hands and faces. Someone had produced a fiddle around which soon congregated a makeshift chorus of willing singers, obscure figures in black cutout against the last fading light, and then the familiar strains of "Old Folks at Home" rose up against the night in fluidly adroit, unforgettable harmony and it was possible to believe that the world and the things of the world were connected by a melody of their own, persistent though often indistinct, traces of which could be heard lurking even beneath the sentimental cadences of a popular tune of the day, and as the final note dissolved into a pure sustained silence, all noise and motion beyond the boat, the toiling mules, seemed to cease—even inanimate objects held their breaths—and into that becalmed interval glided, silent as a shade, the long, graceful packet and its entranced human cargo, as through a mystic cavern hewn from nature's own stuff, and then the bow hit the strings (the opening bars to "Turkey in the Straw") and the spell was broken, and time fell back onto the travelers' shoulders like a cloak spun of material so gorgeously fine you didn't even realize it was wearing you until it had been briefly whisked away. Above the clustering treetops the scythelike smile of a crescent moon came sailing radiantly in, spilling cold fire in its wake. Stars began to punch their way through the black sky-fabric, each hard prickly point only the tip of a longing without stricture. In the levels Liberty could see far up the great, glimmering waterway where ranged in near faultless symmetry the tenderly glowing lamps of the preceding boats dwindled off into the western distance, a floating panorama matched by the approaching headlights of the boats behind, emerging in unnumbered stateliness, one after another, from the darkness aft to move surely on into the obliterating darkness ahead, and for a drawn moment he understood absolutely, as only the heart can be convinced, that here, at the best end to the best day of his life (so far), he was joined in a grand procession of enigmatic intent that had been launched upon the tide untold centuries past and would assuredly continue on in the same wondrous and determined manner to the edge of doom, and Liberty, young as he was, felt quite fortunate he had been able to obtain a ticket.

His mother. Liberty never tired of looking into her face, the weather there ever changing, moods and expressions passing over it like clouds, temporarily altering her appearance but not the permanent geography underneath formed in comfort and kindness and love, features abiding though sometimes obscured by fronts, squalls, persistent fogs, low-hanging overcast that disturbed and puzzled him. She seemed to him on those occasions to be somewhat absent, the parts of her that made her his mother having departed for some other realm. She'd be rocking on the porch, Liberty reading a book at her feet, when abruptly she'd blurt out in a bright, unnatural voice, "My, the daisies are so forward today." In time Liberty came to understand that in such moments she was back in Carolina again. He came to dread the periodic arrival in the mail of those envelopes with the spidery handwriting in lavender ink that would sometimes sit untouched for days on the table by the door until impulsively, in passing, Roxana would snatch the letter up into her hands, tear open the envelope, hastily read the contents, burst into tears and rush upstairs to her bedroom, leaving behind a confused, frightened son. If Thatcher were home, he'd go upstairs, too, and what transpired behind the closed door of their bedroom, from which Liberty could hear the unrestrained sobbing of his mother, was a profound and disturbing mystery.

"What's wrong with Mother?" he'd once asked in a trembling voice when Thatcher had emerged, grim faced, from the bedroom.

"Come with me," his father said, guiding him into his study and closing the door, the two of them in facing chairs only a few feet apart, Liberty's short legs dangling well above the burgundy carpet.

"Your mother," he began, "many years ago was forced through difficult circumstances to leave her own mother and father and come to live up here in New York. This was a terrible event. No one likes to have to run away from their family. Sometimes it makes people cry."

"Why doesn't Mother go back then?"

Thatcher sighed. "She can't," he managed, then seemed unable to continue.

"Why?"

"Because she's been hurt. She doesn't want to see her parents, and they don't want to see her."

Liberty's face exhibited the effort of trying to digest this curious information. "I would always want to see you."

Thatcher smiled. "I know. And your mother and I would always want to see you, too, but sometimes, Liberty, differences come up between members of the same family and sometimes those differences get so big it's hard for people to even see or talk to each other across them. Do you understand?"

"Does Mother's mother love her?"

"Yes, of course she does, but love, unfortunately, does not always protect people from misunderstanding each other or from disagreeing. Then, sometimes, things are said or done which can be hard to forgive."

Liberty pondered these words for a moment. "Is this about the slavocracy?" he asked.

Thatcher's expression was serious. "Yes," he said.

Thereafter, whenever Liberty glimpsed one of those ominous letters with the lavender writing lying on the sideboard, he would stuff it under his shirt, hurry up to his room and hide it beneath his mattress.

Then, one afternoon Roxana summoned her son into the parlor, ordered him to take a seat and produced a handful of these envelopes. "What is the meaning of this?" she demanded.

Liberty shrugged. "I don't know," he replied, preferring to study the pattern in the carpet rather than his mother's penetrating eyes.

"What do you mean, you don't know? They were secreted in your bed. Are these letters yours? Are they addressed to you?"

"No."

"Then what were they doing in your possession?"

"I don't know," he replied, and despite his most heroic efforts to stop them, tears began to roll down his cheeks.

Roxana rushed to her son, gathered him in her arms and began to cry, too. "It's all right," she said, stroking Liberty's head. "I understand."

Liberty pushed himself away to peer directly into her brimming eyes. "I won't do it again. I promise."

"I'm sorry, Liberty," she said, wiping his face with her handkerchief. "I suppose I haven't been paying sufficient attention to you lately. It seems certain you have reached an age where you are ready to hear the story of your family."

So from that day on, whenever Roxana deemed it appropriate, she would tell her son tales from when she was a girl and lived on a great plantation with her mother and father and sister and brothers on the banks of the Stono River in South Carolina, surrounded by dogs and cats and horses and chickens and everywhere you looked, near and far, against the distant horizon, under your very feet, a sullen horde of negro slaves.

Her favorite view of the big house was from the boat coming upriver from Charleston and how, on rounding the final bend, the great bare columns of the cypress trees shifted magically about to reveal the matching columns of the veranda and the curtained window on the second floor that opened into her bedroom. There was a grand mystery and haunting romance to the setting which she experienced viscerally like a sweet breath drawn throughout the length of her small, thin body. Home. She simply could not imagine living anywhere else. She had been born in her parents' bedroom mere steps down the hall from the room she now occupied and fully expected, some far distant day, to die in. And to glimpse again, after an absence of even the shortest duration, the familiar grounds and comforting lineaments of the family estate was a pleasure not to be exceeded in a whole life of pleasures great and trifling.

Gathered at the wharf was the usual welcoming throng of excited servants, who upon sighting the approaching boat began to shriek, whoop, cry, moan, hop up and down, break out into ecstatic dance, clap their hands and generally conduct themselves like a tribe of unruly children awaiting the arrival of a cargo of candy. As Roxana and her mother stepped ashore they were immediately engulfed in this crush of bodies, fingers reaching out to touch their arms, their faces, Old House Sally, the cook, seizing Roxana about the neck and planting a hard wet kiss upon her blushing cheek as Cripple Tom, the carpenter's son, his frail form twisted by rheumatism, accident and sundry unknown ailments that had rendered him hardly fit to crawl, wrapped his misshapen arms around Roxana's legs so she could not move. She and her mother had been away for less than a full day.

Mother Maury raised her hands above her, brought them together with a sharp slap and in her imperious mistress voice which had been known to carry distinctly across the river, commanded, "Enough now! Back to work, all of you!"

The smiles a shade too broad, the shuffles a bit too comic, the whole exaggerated party atmosphere vanished instantly, and, as the sobered crowd reluctantly dispersed one young girl with clay-streaked skin and a hideous scar across her forehead lingered on.

"What do you want?" snapped Mother, her eyes like blue fire.

The girl studied her dirty bare feet.

"Well, out with it. You may be free to laze away your day, but some of us in this family have duties to perform."

Mustering her courage, the girl asked, "Did Missus bring me a pretty ribbon from town?"

Mother expelled a long, impatient breath. "No, I didn't bring you any damn ribbon from town, and how you ever got the notion into your skull that I would is as mysterious as all the other ridiculous notions you've no doubt got stored up there, too."

"But Missus promised."

"I certainly did no such thing."

"Yes, Mother, you did," said Roxana. "You offered her a ribbon for helping Lucy polish the silverware."

"I have no recollection of that whatsoever. Is my own daughter now correcting me? Are you suggesting that I'm losing my mind?"

Roxana turned to the girl. "Come see me after supper." The girl smiled shyly, did a slight bow and disappeared running around the corner of the house.

"Honestly, Roxana, you're going to get these niggers so spoiled that one day they'll be lounging about in the parlor while we work the fields."

Brother Val was seated on the steps of the gallery between two of his hunting dogs, meticulously cleaning his gun. A pair of dead grouse lay on the step at his feet, limp necks dangling over the edge, dripping blood onto the step below. He barely glanced at his mother and sister, sliding a piece of cloth up and down the barrel. "You remember to get that tack?" he asked.

"Yes," replied Mother. "I got the tack and the currycomb. I expect Nicodemus has already taken them up to the stable. And why you should send an old, ignorant woman on such a mission is a riddle only the Good Lord could solve."

Val pulled the cleaning rod from the barrel. "God's eye is upon you, Mother," he said, winking at his sister. "He knows to choose the proper person for each task."

"Now look what you've done," declared Mother as she carefully removed her hat from the complicated arrangement of hair on her head. "Blood all over the front steps and Dr. Quake coming to call this afternoon. Samson!" she shouted at the house, rapping her cane against the planks of the gallery. "Samson! Get out here at once! Where is that doddering fool?" The cane beat louder and louder. Finally the front door opened a crack, revealing a grizzled head that peered impassively out at them.

"Get out here," demanded Mother. "Didn't you hear me calling you?"

Samson hobbled onto the gallery. He was dressed in a threadbare butler's jacket with raveled sleeves and holes at the elbows. "I was in the back parlor, Missus, dusting the lamps."

Mother snorted derisively. "You haven't dusted a lamp or anything else, for that matter, in months. I want you to clean up the mess Val's made before the wood gets permanently stained. I want this done immediately."

Samson crept to the edge of the gallery and looked, shaking his head regretfully. "I ain't touching no blood. That's bad business."

"My God," Mother exclaimed, "what does one have to do around here to get a single lick of work out of any of you good-for-nothings?

Val, dear, could you please find someone to attend promptly to this muddle?" She sighed. "This day has drained me utterly. I'm going to my room to take my medicine and rest."

"That's fine, Mother," answered Val, again smirking at his sister, "you need your medicine. You need your rest."

"And I expect to see these steps washed off by the time I come down for supper," she said, leaning against her cane and laboring up onto the gallery.

"Yes, Mother," answered Val. "Tabula rasa it shall be."

At the door Mrs. Maury paused to inquire, "Where's your father?"

"In the office listening to grievances. I heard some yelling coming from there a while ago. I wouldn't go in if I were you."

"And Roxana," said Mother. "I don't want to hear that piano until I come back down, do you understand?"

"Yes, Mother."

The door banged shut.

"Enjoy your outing?" asked Val. There was something in his clear green eyes that always seemed to be moving, some mischievous thing trapped in there and constantly shuttling back and forth, seeking an escape.

"Out in the harbor a drunk man fell off the boat and drowned," said Roxana. "Then his dog jumped in after him and swam round and round, barking and whimpering. And they couldn't get the dog back into the boat even with ropes and hooks. Then a man dived in to save it, but the dog tried to bite him. So finally old Mr. Trotter pulled out his pistol and shot the dog dead and it sank beneath the waves as everyone at the rail stood and applauded. I hope never to witness such a ghastly spectacle again."

"And Mother?"

"She helped direct the rescue effort. Then she told Mr. Trotter to shoot. She said, 'A dog without his master is a useless thing.'"

"But not old Paddy here." Val stroked the head of the dog on his right. "Or Luke, either." He stroked the head of the dog on his left, then allowed each animal in turn to greedily lick at his own mouth.

"You're so coarse," observed Roxana. "You'll certainly never win a belle with that behavior. Who's going to want to kiss lips wet with dog slobber?"

Val raised an eyebrow. "There's some who already have."

"You're not going to start boring me with that awful Abigail Moses again? I hate her. I don't even wish to hear her dreadful name."

"Well, dear sister, you may not only have to become accustomed to hearing her name, I'm afraid you're going to also have to bear with seeing her often—and quite soon."

It took a moment for his words to register, and then Roxana's pale young face attained further degrees of paleness normally possible only through the application of fine cosmetics. "You're not—" she blurted.

Val smiled indulgently. "I love her."

"But she's a feather-headed flirt who's already rejected at least a dozen suitors this year alone."

"But not me."

She studied him curiously, then all at once glimpsed what he'd been hiding for so long in his expression. "Oh brother!" she exclaimed, hugging him tightly to her. "Please forgive me. I didn't know. I wish you all the happiness in the world, you know that."

"I know, and I'll always wish the same for you." He stared down at the puddles of blood between his feet. "Now who in all this pleasant land am I going to convince it's worth their while to wipe up this sticky mess?"

"Ask Milla. She'll do it for you."

Val laughed. "Indeed she might. She might, that is, if she were still here. Ran off sometime last night, I believe."

"Again?" asked Roxana, astonished as much by the persistent courage as by the frequency of her flights.

"No one's even bothered to go out hunting for her this time. She'll be back by sundown, said Father, and I suppose he's probably right."

"Where do you think she goes?" She couldn't begin to imagine setting off at night into the swamp country with just the clothes on her back. What would one eat? Where would one sleep? A deeply inscrutable, troubling act.

"Ah, who knows?" said Val. "She's probably got a beau over to Pettigrew's Landing."

The thought startled Roxana. At once she could see Milla stealing through the darkness, listening for the hounds, watching for snakes and gators, all to be near a man she must love immensely. What was his name? What did he look like? Did he ever come sneaking over here? The risks taken, the dangers challenged, under the spell of love. A force stronger than iron shackles. She wondered if her own sheltered life would ever be visited by such an experience. She wondered how long it would be until it arrived.

Val was scrutinizing the pattern of blood drops on the step as if, through augury, he might read there the name of the person willing to make it disappear. He glanced up at his sister. "Sall?" he asked.

Roxana shook her head. "I don't know if she can bend down far enough with the rheumatism she's got. No, dear brother, looks like this is one mess you're going to have to clean up all by yourself."

"Go get me a rag."

"I certainly will not. Go get your own rag. I'm going out back to look at the garden."

Rounding the house, she passed beneath the window of her father's office and into the agitating sound of voices raised in disputation. She stopped and heard her father say in the cold tone she hated, "I'll tell you who you're married to and who you're not married to, and I don't care what Mama Jo said. Is she running this plantation or am I? Frankly, I've had a hard bellyful of you people telling me how to conduct my business. And as long as you are here, you are my property and my business. Do you understand?"

There was a mumbling she couldn't comprehend.

"Now get the hell off my carpet and get out of my sight before I have to fetch the crop."

Roxana heard nothing, then the sound of a door closing, and she continued on to the back of the house. The flowers she had planted only a few months before were blooming magnificently, heads buzzing with color. A black woman in a gunnysack shift was seated on the ground in the shade, leaning up against the trunk of the chinaberry tree, hands curled palms up in her lap. She gave Roxana a long bleak look. "I'm so tired, Missus," she said. "I'd get up but I'm so tired."

"That's quite all right, Chloe," said Roxana. "Stay where you are. I've just come back for a minute to look at the garden."

"They sure are pretty, Missus."

"Yes, they are." Simply gazing upon the plants seemed to open up a plot of color inside Roxana, a soft, cozy place where she, too, could curl up and rest. "Chloe, how would you like a nice bouquet of flowers for yourself?"

"Why, yes, Missus, I sure would. I'd like some pretty in my house." And with enormous effort and wheezing she began to rise.

"No, Chloe, stay right where you are. I'll go inside and get the cutting shears."

As Roxana approached the back gallery, she saw her mother standing regally in the doorway, a scented handkerchief tied over her nose and mouth. "Roxana," she said, "we have servants in order that we might be waited on, not the other way around. What do you think you are doing? I forbid you to give flowers to Chloe as if you were her fawning paramour. These people are spoiled enough without my own children presenting them with romantic gifts."

Roxana squeezed past her mother, saying, "I thought you were upstairs lying down."

"Who can get any rest in this house what with all the shouting going on down here? Field hands traipsing in and out. The smell alone is sufficient to lay us low with God knows what wretched diseases."

"Well, maybe if you'd encourage them to bathe more often you wouldn't have such a problem."

"An exercise in futility, child. They're like cats when it comes to water."

Roxana heard the purposeful thud-thud-thud of her father's boots coming down the hallway. "My baby," he declared, throwing wide his arms and enveloping his daughter in a mammoth hug. "Why didn't you come greet your papa when you got back? I've missed you."

"I thought you were busy. I didn't want to disturb you."

"You can't disturb me, Roxana, you know that. Did you have a good time in town?"

"No," interrupted Mother, "we certainly did not. Everywhere we went people were talking about that terrible Middleton affair. It brought on one of my headaches from which I have yet to recover."

"A sorry business," said Father. "And now the people are restless all through the country. I'm afraid we're going to have to be even more vigilant in the coming weeks. Mr. Dray just informed me that Nicodemus threatened him twice yesterday and once this morning, even after receiving thirty-nine stripes."

"Perhaps," observed Roxana, "if Mr. Dray weren't so free with the whip, he wouldn't get threatened."

Asa Maury patted his daughter tolerantly on the head. "It's Mr. Dray's job to supervise the hands and administer discipline as he sees fit. Believe me, child, he knows what he's doing."

"I'm going upstairs," announced Mother. "I do not wish to be called until supper." She moved off down the hall like a statue being drawn forward on little wheels. Then they could hear her ponderous feet mounting the stairs step by careful step.

"She'll be better once she takes her medicine," noted Father. "These trips, even the brief ones, are becoming such a burden to her."

"She seemed fine the whole time we were gone," said Roxana, who had observed this same maternal phenomenon countless times before. And already had learned it was prudent and realistic to ignore much of her mother's behavior, particularly the complaints.

"Cooper called while you were away."

"Yes," Roxana replied wearily.

"He's a very nice young man."

"He is at that." She began fidgeting with her hands.

"He said he'd call again tomorrow at three."

"Yes."

"I want you to receive him. I want you to be polite. I want you to consider his feelings."

She looked her father directly in the eyes. "Has anyone considered mine?"

"Oh," said Asa dismissively, "you're too young to know what your feelings even are."

"Then I doubt I can progress much beyond this point while surrounded by people who hold to such patronizing views."

"Don't take that tone with me, Miss Roxana. I simply will not tolerate it."

"And what will you do," she answered sharply, "have me whipped?"

Without thought or hesitation Asa reached out and slapped his daughter across the cheek. "No one speaks to me in that manner, not even my own flesh and blood."

Roxana stared at her father in mute shock, tears rolling down her face like drops of oil. Her body began to tremble. "I hate you," she declared. "I hate you with all my heart." Then she turned, bolted down the hall, her father calling after her, "Roxana! Roxana!" and up the stairs to her room, where she found Ditey curled up asleep on her bed. "Get out!" she shrieked. "Get out of here right now!" It was all she could do not to strike her. The frightened girl jumped up, crying, "I'm sorry, Missus, I was only resting for a minute." "Get out!" Roxana screamed again, and Ditey rushed past her and out into the hallway. Roxana slammed the door shut, drew the bolt and threw herself across the bed, sobbing uncontrollably. She couldn't think. All she could feel was a dark pain that plunged right through the center of her like a vein of throbbing sorrow. Then she heard her mother's voice from beyond the door. "What on earth is going on now? Roxana, answer me this instant. I demand to know what is the meaning of this commotion." "Go away," Roxana moaned, weeping into her pillow. "Please." There was a pause and then her mother said, almost wistfully, "Why is there no peace in this household?"

After crying herself out, empty as a hollow gourd, Roxana lay quietly on her back, chest occasionally heaving, and contemplated the network of cracks in the ceiling, a system of imagined roads or rivers she had been studying her entire conscious life as, over time, the fissures developed and lengthened. One day the whole ceiling would probably collapse in chunks and fragments, burying her alive in her own bed.

After a while she got up and went to sit in the window. She looked out at the sky and the trees and the river winding slowly seaward and she thought about running away. But where would she go? How far would she get? Her fear and her sense of incompetence at pursuing such a course only made her angry. If she were a boy, she imagined, she'd already be gone like her brother Winchester had done years ago. They'd heard he was somewhere out in the West, picking his way through a mountain for gold.

As she watched, a decrepit black sulky came rattling up the road and turned in at the gate. That insufferable ass, Dr. Quake. Come to make eyes at Mother and inflict his boring, self-satisfied conversation on all ears within reach. She'd never been able to understand why her parents even continued to receive him. He'd been discouraged (but oh so politely) from calling at most of the great homes in the county when, after receiving medical attention and advice, the residents would discover he desired further claims on their social regard than most were willing to give. She could hear him now, standing outside in the dust, calling for Hokie to come tend to his horse. Well, the way things had been going on this magnificent estate lately, he would still be out there at midnight, holding the bridle and waiting.

She sat in the window, watching the water running between the trees until she managed to bring on a vague self-induced trance (a trick she had begun to master as a very young girl, when she fell down the stairs and broke her arm and the pain made her almost crazy) in which her brain seemed to hold itself within her head in a frozen suspension, not a single thought traversing the horizon of her mind. She didn't know how long she had remained so transfixed when a sudden peremptory knocking sounded on her door.

"Roxana!" her father demanded.

She turned lethargically toward the door and spoke to the dead panel of wood, not the living being standing beyond it. "Yes," she answered dully.

"We have a visitor. I want you to come down and at least put on a show of civility."

There was no reply.

"Roxana."

"I don't want to," she said at last.

"I don't want you hiding in your room like this. It doesn't look proper."

"Maybe you should have thought of that before striking me like a common house servant."

"Open the door." He rattled the knob impatiently. "Open the door. I want to speak with you."

The bolt scraped back, and Asa gently pushed his way in. Roxana was standing stiffly in the middle of the room, staring at the window. He closed the door behind him.

"Roxana," he said simply. "I'm sorry. I lost my temper. It's a shameful thing, and I don't feel right about it. You know you are my sweetheart, my only treasure in the world. I wouldn't want any harm to come to you, ever."

She remained still, her head turned away.

"Come here, darling, come to your papa." He held out his arms.

At last she turned and came to him and fell against his chest, weeping. He held her until the convulsive sobbing stopped. Then he said, smiling to himself, "You know you have quite a tongue on you. Take after your mother, I suppose."

Roxana pushed herself away and began wiping at her face with her hands.

"Dr. Quake has asked after you. You will come down and at least greet the poor man, won't you?"

She nodded.

"Good. We'll be out on the gallery taking some refreshment." And he left.

Alone, she sat on the edge of the bed and looked at her hands.

They were such pale, soft things. What would they do with her life, what shape would they give to it? Perhaps handwork would be preferable to headwork. She thought that probably she thought too much about too many things, things that girls and women should not trouble themselves about. She resolved from this moment on not to think, or at least to think less. The idea calmed her. She could dress now and prepare to face company.

When she was ready she studied herself in the mirror. All in perfect place except for her expression. She tried out a variety of smiles until she succeeded in finding one suitable for the good doctor.

Quake and her father were seated comfortably on plush armchairs that been carried out from the parlor. Their legs were stretched out on the rail. Each man held a cigar in one hand and a glass of whiskey in the other.

"Why here she is," declared Dr. Quake, leaping to his feet, taking Roxana's hand and kissing it. "I had so hoped you might find the time to join us."

"You know I can't keep away whenever you come to visit, Dr. Quake," she responded, producing the smile and staring past the doctor's shoulder at her father.

"It is always a pleasure, a distinct pleasure, to share a portion of a superb day with such a delightful presence as yourself, Miss Roxana."

"But it's my pleasure also, Doctor. I learn so much from listening to your conversation."

"Please, sit down," said Quake, offering her his chair.

"But where will you sit, Dr. Quake?" she inquired, settling herself down.

"My God," exclaimed Father. "We are not destitute. I think we can summon up a stray piece of furniture. Samson!" he called. "Samson, get out here!" He addressed the doctor. "This will require a minute or two."

"I don't mind standing," answered Quake, who was leaning against one of the columns. "It affords me a clearer view of your lovely daughter," he added, beaming intently at Roxana who, ignoring his gaze, was noting with silent amusement the untouched blood-stains on the steps.

"Samson! Where the deuce is that useless rascal? If I have to get up and go in there . . ." Asa had placed his hands on the armrests of the chair and was preparing to rise when Samson's head came peering around the edge of the doorway. "Yes, Master."

"Where the hell have you been? Didn't you hear me calling?"

"Yes, Master, and I came soon as I heard you. I been dusting the lamps in the back parlor."

"And I'm sure by now they're clean enough to eat off of. Bring another chair out here for Dr. Quake."

"One chair or two?"

"How, may I ask, is Dr. Quake going to sit in two chairs at the same time?"

"I didn't say he could, Master. I just thought maybe you might be expecting some more company."

"I'll tell you what to think," said Asa curtly. "Now go get that chair and get it out here damn quick. Dr. Quake's tired and needs to rest his feet. Show some hospitality, some due respect."

"Yes, Master," replied Samson and, leaving, muttered under his breath, "I'm too old for all this cussed shecoonery."

"What's that, Samson?"

"Nothing, Master," came the fading voice as he shuffled off down the hall.

"I've a good mind," said Asa, "to order up a sound whipping for every soul on this—" And, catching his daughter's eye, he stopped.

"Full moon tonight," observed Dr. Quake. "Always makes them fidgety, prone to sauciness and the like." His voice possessed a flagrantly knowing manner that irritated Roxana tremendously. "And then, of course, there is this Middleton business, riled up the whole country. White man, too. I can never understand that."

"Some folks," pronounced Asa, "are too dumb or too ornery to comprehend just where their best interests might lie. And all this abolition devilment has a pernicious effect on weak minds."

"You mean like women?" asked Roxana, smiling sweetly.

Undeterred, her father went on. "There's no denying women's sympathy with those in want or need, or their natural tendency to ally themselves with the more tender affections."

"And what's wrong with that?" asked Roxana.

"Not a thing. That is woman's proper sphere. She should follow her inclinations and do that which is proper to her estate."

"An estate located in a backwater region well off the main routes on which the world as a whole travels."

"My, my," commented Quake, regarding in new wonder this beautiful, clever girl with such outrageous opinions.

"You exhaust me, Roxana," admitted her father. "I cannot dispute each and every syllable with you."

"I do believe, Asa, you have the makings of a fine lawyer in that girl."

"And a difficult wife," Mr. Maury added.

"Not if the husband is an agreeable, generous, open-minded young gentleman," offered Roxana.

Quake burst into toothy laughter. "Where, indeed, are you going to find one of those?"

"One never gives up hope, Dr. Quake."

A commotion of banging and scraping erupted from the interior of the house, began advancing slowly, achingly slowly down the hallway toward the door.

"Pick it up, Samson!" yelled Father. "I don't want that floor scratched all to hell."

The noise subsided somewhat into an occasional bump and at last Samson, hunched over and wheezing, rounded the corner, a huge wooden chair teetering unsteadily in his arms. He let it drop onto the gallery boards with a loud bang.

"Took your sweet time about it," Father snapped. "What'd you do, hammer a chair together in the backyard?"

"No, Master, I had to find the chair first."

"And where would the chair have gone to?" Father wondered.

"Next thing you know we'll be having to put leg irons on the furniture to keep it from running off."

"Yes, Master." Samson's rheumy eyes hopped skittishly from one of these buckra faces to the next, unable to linger long beneath the scrutiny of any white gaze.

"Go tell Sally that Dr. Quake will be staying for supper."

"Yes, Master."

"And Samson?"

"Yes, Master."

"Don't let me catch you out back chasing a footstool around the barn."

"Yes, Master." He retreated back inside, mumbling unintelligibly as he went.

"That boy's quite a character," said Dr. Quake.

"Yes," agreed Asa, "and we've got a houseful of characters here. Suppose I could rent them out as a traveling show and retire on the proceeds."

"I wish you wouldn't treat Samson so," said Roxana.

"Why not, Daughter, look how he treats me. If I stopped to worry about the sensibilities of every one of these niggers, nothing would get done and we'd be bankrupt in a month. We'd lose the house, the land, the crops and the stock, and there'd be no place for anybody to live, white or black."

"Mother talks constantly of selling the plantation," said Roxana, "and moving to Cuba."

Father laughed. "Your mother is a prime talker. She hasn't quit to take a breath since the first day I met her. She doesn't know a damn thing about Cuba, or any other place for that matter. She knows the Hall, that's what she knows, and *all* she will know until the day she is laid to rest in its hallowed soil."

"Cuba," mused Dr. Quake. "Heard some fine things about that country. Wouldn't mind sailing down there one day to see for myself."

"Oh, nonsense," said Father. "What could they have down there that we don't have right here?"

"Peace of mind?" suggested Roxana.

Father snorted derisively. "You think you can escape slavery by going into the Caribbean? Why, they practically invented the institution. I've heard how they work the niggers on those big sugar plantations. Don't believe one of ours would last half a day down there. No, you can't get free of slavery, and even if you could you'd be back living in barbarity. Can't have civilization without slavery. Read your history. That's a fact."

"Well," replied Roxana, "maybe this 'civilization' isn't the grand thing everyone likes to pretend it is."

"Why, Miss Roxana," declared Dr. Quake, "wherever do you get these bizarre ideas?"

"Her mother and I," Asa explained, "have meditated over this question many a night through the years. She seemed to arrive in this world with a contrary disposition and it's only grown worse with age. All we can figure is Grandma Nannie on her mother's side was arrested several times for uttering public and seditious remarks against the king. They threw her out of the colony and, story was, she ended up in Rhode Island living in sin with a defrocked preacher. We think Roxana has more than a few drops of Nannie's blood coursing through her veins."

"And every drop is precious," said Roxana, "and nothing to be ashamed of."

"I didn't say it should be. I am merely attempting to offer up a plausible theory for the origin of some of your strange beliefs."

"Is it not possible that I could have arrived at these 'strange beliefs' through the operations of my own mind and without a whisper of assistance from ghostly ancestors? I have a fairly decent pair of clear eyes and a working brain, and I really don't think anything more is required. In fact, I don't understand why more people don't subscribe to similar views."

Father turned to Dr. Quake. "Once her sister was gone, she was left surrounded by brothers. She's always somewhat seen herself as a boy, arrogant, tenacious, brave and foolhardy, and frankly, at this point, there appears to be damn little we can do about it."

"But why would you want to?"

"Because," explained Father, his voice steadily rising, "I don't want to see my sole surviving daughter ostracized by society, shunned by men, condemned to a solitary, lonely, bitter existence as a spinster."

"There are men, I'm sure," interjected Roxana, "who would find my ideas invigorating, madly inspiring perhaps."

"The best of luck," said Father, "in locating one."

"You remember that Hampton boy from years back?" asked Dr. Quake.

"Indeed I do," said Father. "The one they called Reed. A wastrel, a renegade and, ultimately, a traitor. Arming the negroes? What could possibly have gotten into that head of his?"

"I recollect hearing that the father was quite the tyrant."

"Then deal directly with the man, sir, don't go turning the country upside down over a quarrel with your parent. Old Win Spencer died of heart failure just hearing about the crushed rebellion."

"And now there's Middleton."

"Middleton, yes, and northern agitators and abolitionist propaganda and too many damn foreigners running down here nosing around in matters they know nothing about and are none of their concern."

"I should think injustice to be a matter of everyone's concern," said Roxana.

"Yes," agreed Father, "when there is a legitimate injustice for people to trouble themselves about."

"Know it all around," said Dr. Quake kindly, directing his remarks to Roxana, "it's a murky world for all of us to see clearly in."

At that instant a huge black figure in a woman's bright calico dress came bounding out of the fields through the trees, making terrific speed toward the river. The front of the dress was spattered with what appeared to be an excessive quantity of fresh blood.

"What was that?" exclaimed Dr. Quake.

"Why I believe it's Nicodemus," said Roxana, voice quavering with alarm.

Father was on his feet at once, leaning out over the rail and calling,

"Nicodemus! Nicodemus, stop!" to no effect as the retreating figure disappeared into the row of trees lining the riverbank. It all happened so quickly no one was certain what they'd seen.

Father descended the steps, walked out into the yard and looked back toward the fields. There was no one in pursuit. He stood looking and waiting. "I reckon I'd best go and see what this is all about." He started out through the grass.

"I don't believe I've ever seen a boy run so fast," declared Dr. Quake.

"He's a full-grown man," replied Roxana tartly. "I'm afraid something awful has happened."

Both looked up at the keening sound of a frantic woman struggling in from the field, arms flapping above her head, stumbling, falling to her knees, rising again, struggling on, all the while crying out breathlessly, "Master Maury! Master Maury!"

Roxana and Dr. Quake hurried out to join Father, gathered round the woman who was down wailing into the dirt.

"What is it, Patsy?" demanded Father. "What's happened?"

"Terrible, Master," she gasped out between breaths, "terrible thing. Nicodemus, he's killed Mr. Dray dead. Planted that hoe right in his chest. Then he commenced cutting and chopping, hoed a furrow right through Mr. Dray's body. Worst thing I've ever seen, buckets of blood everywhere, you wouldn't even think it was once a man."

Father's face had swelled up into a shade of purple Roxana had never seen there before. "And what prompted this murderous act?" he asked coldly.

"It was Mr. Dray, Master. He been pounding on Nicodemus all week now and today when Nicodemus said his back still hurt from the beating the day before and he couldn't do no hoeing, Mr. Dray called him a little old lady and made Jenny go get a dress from the cabin and stripped him naked out in the field and made him step into that dress and threw a hoe at him and told him to get back to work and Nicodemus, he looked Mr. Dray right back in the eye and said no, he wouldn't and Mr. Dray started whipping at him and Nicodemus grabbed that hoe and drove the blade plunk into Mr. Dray's heart and

126

he was stone dead before he hit the ground and he lay there still as a rock with that hoe handle sticking up out of him like a crooked fence pole." And she ceased, staring up at the trio of white faces encircling her in masks of shock and outrage, and she thought now that she, too, might be punished simply for telling what she saw. There were more people now running in out of the field, several hands and Tom, the driver.

"Well," said Father flatly, glancing up into the sky as if searching for a spot he could put his eyes on that wouldn't remind him of what he'd just been told. "Well," he said again.

"Are you all right?" asked Roxana, reaching down to feel Patsy's sweating forehead.

"Yes, Missus, drawing breath a mite easier, but I don't believe I can get up just yet."

"That's fine, Patsy, you stay right where you are."

"Want me to go call out the patrol?" asked Dr. Quake.

"Yes," said Father, "you go do that, but tell everyone I want him first and I don't want him banged up any more than is necessary to take him. The punishment is something I want to handle personally."

Quake ran back to his sulky, which remained where he had left it, vaulted up onto the seat and, whipping away at the horse, clattered down the lane and out onto the road as though pursued by a tunnel of dust.

Roxana looked up at her father. His face seemed as if it had been cast in bronze for a likeness to be made after his death. "What are you going to do?" she asked.

"That's none of your concern," he replied. "I don't want you involved in this business. I don't want you to know what happens. But you must understand, we cannot permit an act of such wanton savagery to go unpunished."

"Will Val be riding with you?"

"I expect so."

"Then I want to go, too."

"No."

"Why not? This is as much my home as Val's."

"No. And I'm not discussing it any further."

"Asa!" came a cry from across the Bermuda grass flowing in the mild breeze like hair being stroked. "Asa!" Mother stood alone on the gallery, at this distance a small figure clothed in black and posed stiffly there, hands gripping the rail, leaning forward anxiously, almost heroically, as if bearing herself against an invisible wind, fierce, implacable, ruthless. "Asa!" she continued to call. "Asa!"

The remaining events of the day and the oncoming night took place, as events of any consequence tended to do in her sequestered life, at somewhat of a remove from Roxana's awareness. Once Mother had been informed of the situation, she unlocked the case herself and brought Father's guns out to where he sat waiting atop his horse. Several of the men from neighboring plantations had already arrived and grimly touched their hats in mute greeting to the mistress of Redemption Hall, each expression holding the burden of the moment. Father leaned down to kiss Mother on the forehead, then swung the head of his horse around and, attended by several riders, trotted out to the gate where another group of horsemen waited with the same somber expression on their faces. Then all, with barely a word to one another, went galloping together down the road, surrounded by a pack of yelping hounds.

The sun set and quiet settled over the house but for the ticking of the parlor clock and the occasional sigh escaping Mother's compressed lips as she bent in tense concentration over her sewing. Roxana sat in the chair opposite, the book in her lap open to pages she had read and reread without comprehension or memory, each thinking the same thoughts they did not permit themselves to voice. Finally, Mother's hands stopped moving and she leaned back and sighed again. She glanced over at the clock. "After eleven," she said.

"Yes," said Roxana. "It's getting late."

"I believe I'll be going up to bed."

"Yes. I probably should, too."

They gathered up their belongings and left the parlor and

mounted the stairs together, pausing to wish each other a good night before retiring to their rooms. Roxana undressed and slipped into her nightclothes and lay in her bed wide awake, thinking, then trying not to think, watching the shadows of the branches and leaves from the tree outside cast by the moon (Dr. Quake had been correct) across the wall and ceiling. Then, without awareness of the transition, she was in a dream, one with the vivid light and color of day, strolling alone down a street in Charleston when she is approached by a stranger dressed in black with a bushy black moustache. Removing his hat, he bows courteously before her and she begins to feel a telltale blush moving across her cheeks which only deepens as he straightens up and gazes directly into her unguarded eyes, his eyes are black, too, globes of rich black fire like musket balls fired point-blank into the center of her heart, and she feels herself start to swoon as the stranger's lips draw slowly back in a smile that reveals his bright, shining teeth, teeth horribly shaped and sharp as a dog's canines, and then she awoke to terror and the clattering sound of hooves advancing toward the house.

Roxana scrambled out of bed barefoot and in her nightclothes to rush downstairs, arriving in the hallway just as Father stepped through the front door, his face the same stolid mask he was wearing when he departed hours before. "It's all right," he assured her. "We got him."

"What happened?" she asked, fearful of the answer.

"Never mind," Father said, hanging his hat up on the rack. "It's been taken care of."

"What's been taken care of?"

"I said, never mind. This is no business for young girls. You should be upstairs in bed."

"But I want to know."

"Go to bed. I'll tell you about it in the morning."

"Is Nicodemus all right?"

He took her by the shoulders. "Yes, everything's been properly taken care of. Now you, child, should get some sleep."

Back up in bed she found neither rest nor comfort, and at dawn she got up, put on a dress and, in a sort of languid trance, made her way downstairs.

Sally was in the kitchen making breakfast. "What happened to you, Missy?" she asked. "Your eyes are all red and black. You don't look like you slept a wink all night."

"I'm afraid I didn't," said Roxana. "Where's Nicodemus? What did they do with him?"

"Now don't trouble yourself about that. You need some breakfast and then you'll be feeling better."

"But I want to know," said Roxana angrily. "Why won't anyone tell me? Is he dead?"

"You better sit yourself down, Miss Roxana. Sit in this chair here. I'll make you a nice plate of eggs."

"I don't want eggs. I want to know what happened last night."

Sally's hand went faster and faster, beating the eggs in a bowl. "Why do I always have to be the one telling everybody what's going on in this place?"

"Because you know, Sally, you always know. You know the truth and you aren't afraid to speak it. Remember, the truth shall set you free."

Sally stopped, staring in astonishment at the young white mistress. Then she threw back her head and laughed so hard she had to wipe her eyes with her apron. "Good Lord, child, the stuff that comes out of your mouth sometimes. The truth never set nobody free on this plantation and isn't never likely to, neither. Only things that could set anyone free are money and death. Nobody got any cash, but we got plenty of death, yes, more than enough of that to go around for everybody."

Roxana sat silently, staring at the floor.

"Oh, come now, Miss Roxana, don't be putting on such a down look. Don't work so good on you. You were born to be happier than that. All right then, I'll tell about last night if you promise me you won't tell a soul where you heard it from."

Roxana confronted Sally, eye to eye. "I promise."

"Well, you know that Nicodemus is a powerful runner. Couldn't nobody catch him. So he got down to the river way ahead of anybody else and swum clean across before even them dogs could get down there. So Master Asa and the rest of them paddyrollers got to go galloping down to the bridge and try to pick up his trail on the other side, but it takes them a real long time, maybe the water washed away all of Nicodemus's scent or maybe he had some special powder on him but they got to spend more than an hour or two running them damn dogs back and forth through the bushes till finally they all begun tearing off and howling in a heap and all of them go riding after through most of the night, yelling and shooting their guns and waving their lanterns around till sometime in the deepest middle of darkness all the dogs go sniffing around a tree and yapping and jumping up 'cause way up in the teeniest branches was ol' Nicodemus himself. 'Come down from there!' they yelled, but he wouldn't, even when they shook that tree. He wouldn't move, no matter what they did. Then one of the men took out his gun and shot and he come tumbling down, but he was still alive so they got a rope and hung him up and while he was hanging there they shot him some more. So ol' Nicodemus, he ain't coming home no more. And that's the God's truth." She turned back to her pots and skillets. "Now, how do you want them eggs?"

Roxana didn't answer. She sat there watching Sally's hands lifting lids and stirring things with a big spoon. Then abruptly she leaped up and ran back into the hallway past her mother, who called out her name, and up into her room, where again she bolted the door and collapsed on her bed and again cried until there were no more tears. She stayed in her room for two days, ignoring all entreaties to come out, the trays of food set dutifully outside the door at mealtimes carried away untouched. She hated her father, she hated her mother, she hated this awful house, she hated the slaves, too, and the dogs and the cats and the chickens. She got out Grandma's old valise and packed it and placed it carefully by the door. She plotted in her head a dozen different journeys to a dozen different destinations, but each time her imagination failed her, trailing off into a vacuity of impossible futures. How would she live? What would she do to support herself?

By the third day she felt incapable of feeling anything at all. She left her room and rejoined her family, but rarely spoke. Her mother fretted, her brother teased her. "Leave her alone," advised Father. "This shall pass."

Then, during one of Mother's weekly charity days when she would appear on the back gallery with a bucketful of dimes and the children would be summoned from the quarters so she could toss handfuls of the coins to her frolicsome "pickaninnies," Roxana lost her temper, grabbed the bucket and dumped the dimes down the well. And when her mother attempted to berate her, she refused to listen, saying, "Where's Eben? I want to go for a ride."

"And where do you think you're going?" asked Mother.

"Out," replied Roxana. "Away from here, away from you."

"I'll not be spoken to in that manner," said Mother as Roxana turned and walked from the house. She found Eben in the stable, dozing on a bale of hay. He was delighted to hitch up the carriage and take sweet Miss Roxana for a ride. As they came around the house, Mother was standing on the gallery rigid as a post, mouth tight, eyes cold, not uttering a word as they passed.

"Missus look to be having a hard day," observed Eben, turning out through the gate.

"Yes, Eben," said Roxana, "but what day around here is not hard?"

"That's the sure spoken truth," commented Eben, snapping the reins, urging the horses into a trot. "That it surely is."

Off to the right the hands were out working the fields, most of them half-naked, and Roxana averted her gaze. The sky was high and streaked with thin white clouds that obscured the sun, giving the landscape a melancholy shadowed quality. It was strange how altered all the old familiar scenes seemed to her, as if a film had been washed from the lenses of her eyes, or the very eyes themselves exchanged for a fresher, cleaner pair.

"And how are you today, Eben?" asked Roxana.

"Oh, Missus, I expect as poorly as ever. I got the aches and I got the pains and they don't seem to ever want to go away."

"I believe, Eben, I know exactly what you mean."

"You do, Missus?"

"Yes."

"Well, I hope you never has to feel the same ones I got 'cause they are a powerful lot to bear."

"Eben, I sincerely wish you did not have to feel them either."

"Well, I appreciate that, Miss Roxana, I truly do."

As they approached the crossroads, Eben slowed the team and suddenly blurted out, "Don't look at that, Missus, don't look."

"Don't look at what?"

"The pole there, Missus, I'm awfully sorry, I forgot for a minute there where we were going."

Then she saw it, the pole planted in the ground where the roads came together so that travelers arriving from four points of the compass might pause to reflect upon its lesson, for mounted at the top, like a gaudy finial carved on a post, was a human head, exposure having already so altered its appearance Roxana did not at first recognize that this ghastly object with pecked-out eyes and nose, its peeling skin in places revealing patches of white bone, its mouth agape and lips drawn back in a hideously toothy grin, was, in fact, Nicodemus, the man who taught her to play the fiddle, who laughed at her silly jokes, who, when the river topped its banks and flooded the house and grounds, had carried her to safety on his shoulders, and as Eben hastily turned the carriage out onto the Boynton Road the head seemed to turn, too, watching her from its vacant sockets, and Roxana began to scream and there was nothing Eben could do about it, there was nothing anyone could do, this was the world, her world, and her cries the sound of Roxana being born, however belatedly, into it.

Roxana took to carrying wherever she went a Bible that Grandma Octavia had brought back from Europe years ago, big and thick and gilt-edged and bound in tooled leather, and at the dinner table it occupied an extraordinary amount of space next to Roxana's plate as it sat throughout the meal like some menacing foreign object no one dared comment upon or even look at. But when her older brother Saxby, whose relationship with Roxana had from infancy consisted largely of good-natured teasing, returned home from school, his normal disposition was not one to be readily stifled.

"So, Roxana," he began, with the look of a man who had spent much time studying himself in the mirror, "I understand you've become quite the student of religion since I've been away."

"A practice I sincerely commend to you, dear brother," she replied.

"I haven't opened a Bible since I was twelve," boasted Saxby. "Or any other book for that matter." He leaned forward, looked around the table and burst into raucous laughter.

"Honestly, Saxby," commented Mother, "I do wish you would learn to contain yourself. These intemperate outbursts of yours too often give the wrong impression."

"To whom?" Saxby asked. "You? Father? My brothers and sister? Or is it the servants who are not to be offended? Is that it? Are we all expected to put on a show for the servants so as not to give them the wrong idea? Seems to me like this whole plantation's run backward. They're the ones who should be putting on a show for us."

"But they do," interrupted Roxana.

"Roxana," warned Mother, "if you're going to start in lecturing us all again, you can just take your plate up to your room."

"Well, maybe I just will." And she pushed back her chair with a dramatic squeak.

"Stay where you are," commanded Father. "I'll not have one of my own children gobbling down her food in private like a prisoner in a cell."

"Why not?" asked Roxana. "It's what I feel like, what I've always felt like around here."

"Goodness," declared Saxby, the smile still in place, though not as bright. "What has happened while I've been away?"

"Roxana's become an abolitionist," explained Val, who had been steadily chewing at his meal as the conversation rolled and swelled about him.

"She has not!" snapped Mother.

"I won't have that word spoken in my house," said Father.

"Why not?" asked Roxana. "I've heard much worse at this table, every vile word the language has ever produced."

"It will not be spoken," explained Father, "because I forbid it."

"You've forbidden many things that continue to go on nevertheless. Tell Saxby about Nicodemus and Mr. Dray."

"No," said Mother. "That is not a fit subject for the table."

"I wish," declared Roxana, "someone would inform me one day just what is a fit subject for the table."

Sally entered, set down a bowl of boiled potatoes and left without looking at anybody. Immediately Mother reached in, felt each steaming tuber with her fingers, then abruptly picked up the bowl and hurled it against the wall, the porcelain shattering and potato chunks flying. "Sally, you black bitch!" Mother shrieked. "Get in here and clean up this mess!"

After a long moment during which no one spoke, the door again opened and Sally entered with a shredded broom and a greasy rag and bucket and again without looking at anyone or speaking a word went to work scrubbing at the stain on the wall, which only seemed to increase in size with her efforts.

"Sally," Mother declared, without even bothering to turn in her seat, "those potatoes were half raw. I want another bowl brought in here immediately and I want them properly cooked. Do you understand?"

Sally was sweeping the gummy pile toward the door. "Yes, Missus," she replied, pushing the refuse out before her.

"You needn't have bothered on my account," said Roxana. "I've quite lost my appetite."

"Young lady, I know it may come as a surprise to you but there are more people in this family than just yourself."

"How could I possibly forget? You remind me of it daily."

Suddenly Father brought his fist crashing down upon the table, rattling the dishes. "That's quite enough. From everybody. When we gather together here at dinner, this should be a time of peace and thanksgiving, not an incitement to general indigestion."

"Well then, you shall have it," Roxana declared, rising from her chair. "It's time for meeting."

"Oh, Lord," groaned Mother.

Roxana picked up her Bible, clutching it snugly to her bosom with both arms.

"Sure you've got the strength to carry that book all by yourself?" asked Saxby, again directing his remarks as much to the family as his sister.

"Saxby, it appears to me that the only thing you've learned in that fancy school of yours is how to wax your mustache." Then Roxana turned around and marched briskly from the room.

"What meeting?" she could hear her brother asking as she passed down the hallway. "What's this meeting about?"

Roxana left the house and moved out into the night. The sky was clear, alive with the vivid spots of a million stars. She could hear the raised voices of the crickets and the tree frogs and off in the distance a dog howling and every sound seemed to possess its rightful place in an order at once mysterious and correct. Guided by the light of the moon, she made her way down to the quarters. From steps and shadowy doorways she occasionally heard voices soft and pleasant, "Evening, Miss Roxana." By now she had made this walk so often she could have picked her path in perfect darkness, through the quarters, around the north corner of a plowed field, through the thickets and down the slope to the praying ground. A crowd had already gathered there, kneeling in a hushed, expectant circle. Again she was greeted kindly and politely and a place was made for her to kneel down on the ground with the others. Soon a lane opened in the press of people, admitting a tall, intense man with a high forehead and quick bright eyes and dressed in a clean frock coat and store-bought shoes—Uncle Dan, the preacher man. He acknowledged no one, though he knew all and all knew him, but glancing neither left nor right he advanced confidently forward, as if sheltered within an invisible bubble of his own personal force and the gravity of his mission. He settled on his knees in the center of the circle, paused for a moment, then tilted back his head and stared up through the trees at the night sky, at the drops of light sprinkled benevolently across it. Then, bending his head down toward the ground, he opened his mouth and began to speak in a gruff voice that was almost a whisper:

"Come unto me all ye that labor and are heavy laden and I will give you rest. This is the province of the Lord and the truth of God who made all the people out of one ball of clay and made them all to sit upon the same bench, shoulder to shoulder, eye to eye. He has spoken the words stronger than any chain and He will not be denied, He will not be mocked. I have seen these things that He has shown me and I have felt His power pressing down upon my own shoulders, I tried to rise up but I could not. I tried to see but He took away this terrible world and showed me another. I saw the throne and it was of a gold so shiny it seared my sight. And I saw a throne placed there for me and I saw a throne for each one of you, arrayed in the glory of heaven and fixed so as to spell out a word. You know I cannot read, but I have The Book in me, warming my heart, and when I saw that multitude of empty thrones just a-waiting to be claimed by their rightful masters something inside me read the word clear as the rising sun and I knew that word was 'FREEDOM.'

"Then, quick as I was taken up to that place, I was brought back down again and I saw my body stretched out on the ground before me and it was dead and lying there upon the very doorstep to hell and I began to tremble and shake, but God leaned down and spoke to me, saying, 'That is the body of sin which I have cast off from you. I am with you now from this day forth, and from this moment on each step you take will bring you nearer to deliverance out of the torment and wickedness of the house of bondage. This is My promise to you and as you bring the Word to your brothers and sisters, so shall it be My promise to them. Faith shall be your strength. Do not despair. The day of judgement is at hand, when those who are first shall be last and those who are last shall be first, all united in the power and glory forever, amen.'"

"Amen," cried out a voice.

"Hush," responded other voices. "Hush up there."

Sweat streamed down Uncle Dan's face. Solemnly, he looked in turn at each member of his woodland congregation yet did not seem to be actually seeing any one of them. He's seeing past us, thought Roxana, her own eyes brimming with tears, he's seeing into our spiritual bodies. A woman fell moaning onto the sandy ground. A few cries were heard, then instantly muffled. Uncle Dan closed his eyes and seemed to be in prayer. When he opened them again, he said, "Our Divine Master is a kind and just god. We have not suffered in vain. The sins of a people in bondage are as a mote in the eye of God to the sins of those who hold them in bondage. But the end is near, my brethren. The Lord has shown me that this is so. The day when the shackles melt in the fire, when the whip falls from the hand, is fast approaching. I have seen this and it is so. And to hasten that glorious time, to help bring on the jubilee, all that is required is that we love God and love one another. Do you hear? Love God and love one another. Do you believe the Gospel? Love God and love one another. Do you feel the truth in your heart? Love God and love one another. Amen and a-men."

There was a silence then, an absolute stillness in which all that was human seemed to have withdrawn from the planet, and leaf and stone and creatures furred and feathered held reign and the world was as it appeared in the beginning and how it would appear at the end with all mankind taken up into the spirit and allowed to brood upon the consequences of their travail on earth. Then an owl hooted and the spell was broken and all was as it had been before.

Uncle Dan's eyes found those of Roxana's and something within each broke free of confinement and glided out to touch the other and Uncle Dan said, "I believe we have a visitor among us this evening who wishes to speak."

And without compulsion or volition Roxana began to shake her head slowly, almost imperceptibly, from side to side. No, she could not, no, please do not make me do this. But Uncle Dan's eyes never left her, never strayed for an instant to break the bond that connected them there in that place. Then he reached out his hands and she could not restrain herself; she simply rose from her knees as if obeying an irresistible command and drifted out into the center of the circle where she knelt obediently in the dust beside Uncle Dan. She could feel a company of eyes focused squarely upon her and her mind simply went out like a candle extinguished by the wind and when at last she was finally capable of daring to meet even a few of those not unfriendly gazes all she could say was, "I'm sorry," the words no sooner taken shape than she was up and stumbling through the silently parting crowd and then running and then she was back safe in her room, and though she lighted one lamp, then another, this familiar place of hers, usually so comforting, seemed sunk in shadows as if she had carried some of the night back inside with her and if she slept at all she did not remember doing so and all the following day she wandered about like the subject of a mesmeric experiment or one who is about to come down with a serious illness. Her complexion was pale and she did not speak.

Father sent word to the quarters that henceforth all prayer meetings were forbidden. Mother decided that she and Roxana would depart earlier than usual on the family's annual trip to Saratoga, where the change of scenery and atmosphere would no doubt do her daughter a world of good. Roxana acquiesced without complaint, seeming not to really care where she was.

Even before mother and daughter left the following week on the packet from Charleston to New York, Roxana experienced two more memorable visions. In one she saw herself costumed in white linen and gliding in a decorous manner over a lawn of deep green grass. She felt as if she were performing before an audience of thousands, though she saw no one. She had somewhere urgent to get to, but she had either forgotten her destination or had never known it to begin with. Then, abruptly, the ground beneath her feet began to soften and, as she went on, her shoes began to sink deeper and deeper into what was now a sea of viscous mud until finally she reached a place from which she could no longer advance nor could she retreat, but, remaining upright, while steadily floundering, trying to free herself but unable to, hopelessly stuck in this noxious mire, she opened her mouth to scream and though her tongue and throat seemed capable of movement, and the air rushed out of her windpipe, she could make no sound, not even the whisper of a noise.

In the second vision she saw herself collecting eggs from the coop, carrying them in a woven basket back to the house, and when she broke the eggs into a bowl on the kitchen table each separate egg released a torrent of blood, the rich private scent filling her nostrils and turning her stomach.

By dawn she had hardly slept at all, the skin under her eyes pouchy and dark as the lowering sky. Their luggage was loaded into the carriage and Eben drove them down to the landing. Roxana would remember little of their journey, neither the voyage down to Charleston nor the long Atlantic passage to New York, only the rocking of the water and the incessant noise of her mother's voice, beating upon her ear like the incoming surf. She still carried her unwieldy Bible, clutched to her breast like a shield, and when she wasn't staring vacantly off into the horizon she read from it, sometimes aloud.

When one of the gentlemen passengers aboard the packet *Creole* asked politely if she might refrain from quoting from Scripture during dinner, she glanced up briefly at him and replied, equally politely, "No." No one would talk to her for the remainder of the trip. Her mother occasionally broke into tears, wiping at her eyes with a silk handkerchief she kept up her sleeve. "I never believed that God would ever see fit to curse me with a daughter like you," she remarked coolly one afternoon as they sat together on the deck, watching the gulls diving for scraps from the bucket one of the mates was emptying over the rail.

"Perhaps it was part of His plan," Roxana replied. "To awaken the conscience in you."

"I don't believe I'm required to take lessons in morality from my own child," answered Mother, drawing herself up in her seat. "I talk to God daily and that is more than sufficient."

"And what does He say to you?" inquired Roxana with a note of genuine interest.

"He gives me guidance." Her mother spoke with an air of self-satisfied finality. "He directs my mind and my heart."

"He directs you to keep slaves?"

Mother stared coldly at her daughter, her lips thin and firm. "Yes," she replied.

They sat there for a moment, turned toward each other like figures molded from the same block of wood. Then Roxana looked away. "That isn't God you're listening to."

"I'll not have my personal relationship with the Lord questioned by anyone."

Roxana did not reply. She stared at the sea swelling and subsiding like the breast of a breathing creature.

For the duration of the voyage they spoke civilly but avoided discussions of any kind on topics any weightier than the dinner menu, the day's clothing, the passing sights, etc. In New York they transferred to the boat to Albany, cruising up the Hudson among a group of northern merchants who talked monomaniacally of money, and Mother remarked it was like listening to a pen filled with hogs rooting for grub. The coach from Albany to Saratoga was overpacked with all male passengers, each of whom was either smoking or chewing tobacco, filling the interior with clouds of repulsive vapors, the floor with an inch of brown spittle that rolled back and forth with the movement of the coach, staining their shoes and the hems of their dresses. By the time they arrived at the Congress Hotel in Saratoga, Mother was so thoroughly depleted from the ardors of the journey that she had to immediately retire to her room for her medicine and a nap. She told Roxana she didn't care what she did, but that men, particularly Yankee men, must always be regarded with grave suspicion.

Roxana found an unoccupied plush chair in the lobby where she could sit, Bible in her lap, and entertain herself with the prodigious spectacle of guests in transit. When anyone inquired whether she needed assistance, she merely replied, no, she was fine, she was simply waiting for her mother. Though the hotel seemed smaller to her than it had in previous years, the clientele seemed much the same: the well-to-do of both North and South. She was personally greeted by several Charlestonians and recognized many others passing through the great lobby, their servants trailing dutifully behind and often outfitted in clothes as fine as those of their masters. The absolute strangeness of the system of slavery, of one man literally owning another as if he were a mere yard dog or a soulless inanimate object like a chair perhaps, seemed up here in Yankeeland to be even more peculiar. How could this have happened? How could people in every other way kind and decent tolerate this cruelty and barbarousness in their midst? She didn't know and just thinking about the subject, if it failed to ignite her anger, had a tendency to collapse her body and her will. What could she, a plain girl, do to help drive this injustice from the world when she could not even influence the opinion of a single family member?

She was sitting there reflecting upon such pressing issues when she noticed a young man in a chair across the lobby who appeared to be aiming his rather magnetic smile precisely at her. Quickly she looked away, pretending she had not noticed his attention, but each time she happened to glance surreptitiously back she saw the same dazzling smile attached to the same handsome face which at the moment seemed to be the only face in the vast milling lobby. She could feel the blood coming up into her cheeks like a draft of warm air blowing across her skin. She pretended to study the people at the desk as if the person she waited for was finishing up his business there and would return momentarily and then she would leave with this person and just before passing out the door she would turn for one last brief glimpse of this silly young man.

Then, after an eternity of not looking, she allowed herself one tiny glance, and there he was, still staring quite openly at her, only now no longer smiling, and even as she watched he rose and began striding purposely toward her. Refusing to be embarrassed or intimidated any further, she remained frozen in her chair, face set, shoulders squared, and awaited his approach.

"Excuse me," he said, removing his hat and bowing slightly. "I've come to tender my apologies. I hope you'll forgive me for staring so openly, so impolitely, but I simply found myself quite unable to do otherwise. I know that's no excuse for such rude behavior, but it is the truth. At first, you see, I thought you were someone else, someone I knew back in the city, but then I realized my error, though now, interestingly enough, standing here before you, I can see that, yes, perhaps I do know you." And the smile appeared again. Then, noticing the oddly fixed expression on her face, he stopped talking. "There, I'm sorry again. You must think me an absolute madman, accosting you here in public, babbling on like an idiot, and we haven't been introduced." He extended his hand. "Thatcher Fish," he said. "Yes, I know it's an odd name. Some people mishear it and think I'm referring to a business—hatch fish—but it is a name people remember."

Roxana waited a moment just in case there was more, and when convinced he was finally done, she smiled up at him and said, "Pleased to meet you, Mr. Fish. I'm Roxana Maury."

"Not the Maurys of Charleston?"

"Why, yes," she answered, brows lifting in surprise.

"I believe my father does business with your father. Textiles," he said. "Fish and Sons Textiles."

"Perhaps he does, but I wouldn't know," replied Roxana, not unkindly. "I'm not permitted to know. I'm a girl, you see."

Thatcher flashed that smile again which, appearing now up close, forced her to look away. "I do see," he said. "Do you mind?" he asked, indicating a nearby chair.

"Oh no, not at all. Please do."

"I assume you are here with your family," he asked, seating himself. "A vacation?"

"Yes," Roxana replied. "We've been coming every year since before I can remember. At the moment, though, it's just my mother and I."

"I'm here with my family, too. My father is sick. He comes for the water."

"I'm sorry to hear that."

Thatcher brushed the comment aside with his hand. "It's nothing, really. He's always sickly. Digestive problems. He needs to get away from the business more often."

"I understand. But up here at least you don't have to contend with the summer sicknesses we are subject to."

"You know," said Thatcher, "and please do not think me too forward, but I must say you have the most beautiful voice. I've never heard anything quite like it before."

"Thank you," said Roxana, unable to think of a single additional word to say.

"So," asked Thatcher, "what's it like growing up on one of those big old southern plantations?"

"Quite pleasant," she said. "As long as you don't mind keeping your eyes strictly closed." She couldn't understand what was happening to her. In the presence of this stranger the internal barriers that usually moved into place in the company of eligible men had seemingly dissolved away, leaving her feeling disturbingly open—a sensation she didn't believe she had ever experienced before.

"I imagine you must have witnessed some terrible events."

This is a rather bold gentleman, she thought, but just as she could not look too long directly into his face neither could she refrain from answering whatever question he posed. "Yes," she said simply. "I've witnessed."

"I'm sorry. I didn't mean to pry. It's just that up here we hear so many shocking stories you can't help but wonder how true they are. I've often thought about one day taking a trip down there. See for myself."

"Then you should."

"Yes, and the notion is even more inviting now that I know someone who actually lives there, someone I might possibly visit."

"Mr. Fish, you are always welcome to pay a call at Redemption Hall. I think you'll find our hospitality as satisfactory as any."

They sat quietly then, side by side, gazing off in opposite directions. Finally, Thatcher turned to her and asked, "How long do you and your mother plan on staying in Saratoga?"

"I don't know," replied Roxana. "And, frankly, I don't much care. We are here, you see, for my health."

"Are you ill?" asked Thatcher, obviously alarmed.

"No, not really, only insomuch as morally objecting to a brutal system of involuntary servitude is an illness."

"Give me your hand," said Thatcher, and cradling it in his palm he gently kissed the back.

"Mr. Fish—" she began.

"No, no," he answered. "It's all right." As their eyes met Roxana found herself gazing into something so alive, so astonishingly real, she momentarily forgot where she was.

They spent the rest of the afternoon in the lobby conversing upon the fateful "subject." Thatcher, too, had alienated himself from the affections of his family through a too vigorous questioning of the issue of human bondage and his father's financial implication in it. Some years before, Thatcher had met a young Quaker girl who had attended many meetings devoted to the cause, seen Garrison himself dragged through the street with a rope around his neck, the remandment of Anthony Burns, and she began to educate Thatcher on the scourge of slavery. They became engaged to be married but several months before the ceremony she contracted cholera and after much painful suffering she died.

"I'm sorry," said Roxana, tears gathering in her own eyes.

"No," said Thatcher. "I'm the one who should apologize yet again. I should not have burdened you with my past."

"But we all have pasts. That's who we are."

They saw each other every day after that, meeting first in the lobby, then taking long strolls through the town. All these hours spent in the company of a strange man, a strange northerner at that, quite alarmed Mother.

"Who is this person?" she demanded to know, unconsciously pleased that she and her daughter now had a topic other than politics or religion to discuss.

"His name is Thatcher Fish. He's studying to be an attorney. His family are merchants. They're all rich. And he's a staunch abolitionist." The word fell between them like a bloody knife and Roxana waited, unblinking.

The reaction, however, was not what she expected. "Sit down," said Mother calmly. "I want to talk to you."

They sat facing one another, Roxana's countenance grim and implacable.

"Roxana," her mother began. "You know your father and I both love you dearly. Since your sister died you have become even more precious to us. So we've been most concerned with this recent behavior of yours. It seems your intention is to deliberately provoke as much dissension as possible within the family. You seem to wish to separate yourself from the care of your father, your brothers and myself. Unhappiness roosts in our house and you have called it in. And I want to tell you that personally I do respect your beliefs. All I ask is that you also respect mine."

Before Mother could continue, Roxana broke in with, "But I cannot. Does it not say in Psalms 2:3 'Let us break their bonds asunder and cast away their chains.'"

"Don't start quoting Scripture at me," said Mother angrily. "I can quote passages right back at you."

"Slavery is wrong," argued Roxana, her own voice matching her mother's in emotion. "It is not only wrong, it is evil, and to participate in it, to profit from its fruits, is to make one an accomplice in evil."

Mother sighed. "Are you suggesting to my face that I and your father and brothers are evil?"

Roxana didn't answer.

"Are you also suggesting that you, too, are evil. Because this trip and this room we're sitting in have been paid for with money earned from the products of our fields, of our hands. So, too, has the food you've eaten, the clothes you've worn, the clothes you're now wearing."

Without a word Roxana rose in fury from her chair and, seizing her dress at the collar with both hands, began to pull frantically at the cloth until it started to tear. Then, her hands working now in a frenzy, she yanked at the material, opening the tear down to the hem, and, pulling her arms from the sleeves, she stepped out of her dress and stood before her mother in white undergarments that, after a pause, she began to pull from her body.

"Roxana!" her mother shouted. "Stop! Stop this instant!"

Glaring fiercely back, she refused to stop until she was completely naked and her mother, in a single swift motion, rose up and slapped her across the cheek and, as though it were all part of one continuous movement, Roxana's hand flew up and slapped her mother across her cheek.

"How dare you?" Mother asked coldly, her eyes searching the room.

"What are you looking for? Your cane?"

"One more word from you and—"

"And what?"

"Put on some clothes. We're leaving this wretched place today."

Roxana pulled a sheet from the bed. "Considering where we are I suppose this is somewhat less sinful to wear since it was probably woven by free labor, even if the bolls it was made from were probably splashed with blood." She wrapped the sheet around her body and walked out the door.

"Roxana!" called her mother. "Roxana!"

Not until she had closed the door behind her did she allow the sobs to come, but she kept moving, her bare feet marching down the carpeted corridor, hair askew and cheeks wet. She could feel the eyes upon her, hear the gasps, the startled whispers, but she stared straight ahead and kept on down the hall, then down the stairs to the next floor and the door whose number she had involuntarily memorized after hearing it spoken just once, and she rapped timidly, once, twice, and when the door was opened and she saw Thatcher she felt herself begin to fall and it was not entirely unpleasant, this falling, as she gave herself up to the sensation and thinking before thought ended that she didn't care where she landed.

She never saw her mother or her father or her brothers or Ditey or Sally or Eben or Redemption Hall ever again.

Once, after an absence of some three days, Liberty returned home with a blackened eye and a cut across his chin. He refused to admit where he had been or to explain how he had received his injuries. He went up to his room while the family sat in the parlor, discussing their wayward son.

"I told you," declared Aunt Aroline. "I've told the both of you for years and no one paid any heed. I said the boy lacks discipline, he wants the correcting hand, but no one listened, no one minded what poor old Aroline had to say."

"That's not true," argued Thatcher. "Your contributions to this household are received with gratitude and respect and I will not have you going on like this."

"All I've ever asked," said Aroline, "is that I be shown the scantiest hint of appreciation for what I do to help hold this fragile house together. God knows we've had enough strife in this family and I simply don't know if I can endure watching this precious branch of it falling into splinters." She extracted a flowery handkerchief from her apron pocket and held it firmly clenched in her fist as she gazed dolefully around the room, daring the others to just try to make her cry.

"Honestly," said Roxana, impatience harshening her voice, "you act as if the issue before us today is you. The issue is not you, Aroline, and I would take it kindly if you did not always carry on as though it were."

"I have as much right to an opinion as anyone else in this room."

"Certainly you do," said Thatcher, "but we seem to be straying from the topic at hand."

"I was not the one who strayed," said Aroline firmly.

"I never suggested you did," said Thatcher.

"She appears to have difficulty hearing clearly what anyone says," offered Roxana.

"I heard that clear enough," snapped Aroline, "and I don't like it."

"That's quite all right. Is it absolutely necessary that you personally approve every word spoken under this roof?"

"If we could get back to the question of Liberty," interjected Thatcher.

From the refuge of the sofa where he had been half-reclining with his brandy and his cigar and listening with detached amusement to this charming family colloquy, Uncle Potter cleared his throat, waited until he had gained everyone's attention and said, "Give the boy over to me for a few days. I can show him what he wants."

"Nonsense," said Aroline.

"Thinking of taking a jaunt down to the big city," Potter continued. "Boy's got the wanderlust, same as his old uncle. He might enjoy the sights, get his eyes filled up good."

"I wouldn't trust you to walk that child into the next room," Aroline announced.

"He's no longer exactly a child," Thatcher reminded her.

"Child or no, any soul delivered to the custody of this reprobate is certain to be placed in jeopardy."

Thatcher eyed his wife, who had remained strangely silent. "What do you think, dear?"

"I trust Potter," said Roxana. "I'd prefer he accompany him than run about the countryside alone."

"Capital," said Potter, taking a huge gulp directly from the bottle. "We depart on the morrow."

"Please, Potter," asked Roxana, "keep a close eye on him. I wouldn't want—"

"Tut-tut," declared Potter, waving his cigar dismissively. "I'll cleave him to me as if he were my very own."

"God help us," commented Aroline.

Mother and Father exchanged a look, and though she managed to produce a smile it was an expression that seemed to have been laboriously constructed from the flimsiest of materials. Roxana had always known a day like this would eventually come, but not so soon. Nevertheless, she had promised herself long ago that she would be strong, she would not protest, she would not cry. She was determined that the circumstances of her own traumatic departure from home would not be repeated in any family of her own. She couldn't bear to think that her own child might feel imprisoned within the walls of his natural home. So however much the decision pained her, she believed that allowing Liberty the freedom to go when he wished might assure that he would also come back when he wished.

New York. A fanciful realm where all the noise and heat and general untidiness of desire unfettered was allowed full and natural exhibit in a daily frenzy of banknotes. People were different here, Potter had instructed his young nephew, money was as an elixir to them, their health, their mental harmony dependent upon a vigorous regimen of the stuff. So should you happen to spy a nearby chap suddenly erupt into a sweat, eyeballs a-dancing, limbs a-twitching, quickly stand aside 'cause likely you've come unknowingly between the slathering habitué and his dose of corrective tender. And never look a stranger in the eye, as he will believe you might be preparing to rub him down with a knuckle towel. Don't talk to anyone, Jack or Jill, for they ever seek to pick your heart's pocket. Keep your own coin in your boot, along with a well-whetted sticker. These metropolitans were a cagey lot.

As the packet from Albany approached the unimaginably crowded docks, ships from all nations moored nearly hull to hull into the receding distance, an excited Liberty strained to catch a glimpse of the notorious city through the intervening leafless forest of masts, spars and rigging, and his initial impression was this: bricks and people in equally astonishing numbers and though the masonry was more or less uniform in size and color, the circulating citizens were not. Here seemed to be contained every shape and hue the human animal was capable of attaining and, apparently, dressed in every costume the human brain was capable of devising.

A brief rainstorm had moved off shortly before they disembarked, leaving the gutters running with a thick black gruel of garbage and bodily waste, and the odor was, as Potter grimly remarked, "absolutely tremendous." Gulls cried, dogs barked, goats bleated, herds of insolent pigs rooted boldly through the congested streets. The rattle of wagon and carriage wheels, the clopping of hooves, the tramping of uncountable feet was near deafening. Liberty felt thrillingly disoriented. A scarlet and yellow omnibus clattered dangerously by, heads poking animatedly from every window, passengers hanging precariously from the sides. A small girl in layers of calico rags, pushing a steaming cart before her, chanted in high singsong, "Hot corn! Hot corn here!" A gang of filthy urchins dashed deliriously through the crowds, bumping aggressively into startled pedestrians. Around the corner a fat man in a stained butcher's smock and brandishing a long carving knife chased another man into a saloon. Impudent women, young and old, in various states of dishabille, lounged in doorways and windows, calling out to passing gentlemen, one even addressing Potter by name. "Not today, Pearl," replied his uncle good-naturedly, "I've got my nephew with me." The woman looked Liberty over in a manner he had never known before. "Bring him up, too," she said. "He looks plenty old enough to me." Potter laughed and they walked on.

"So, Liberty," inquired Potter, "what think you of our fair city here?"

"It caps the climax," he replied, eyes glittering.

Potter squeezed the boy in a suffocating hug, then led him on through the tumult that was New York to a mammoth building on lower Broadway with architecture so fantastic, columns and gargoyles, towers and turrets and domes, even gilt-framed portraits, it resembled the most elaborate wedding cake Liberty had ever seen. Streams of people were entering, streams of people were exiting. A huge sign the length of the front façade announced that this establishment was the famous P. T. Barnum Museum and Hall of Wonders and Oddities from around the world.

Potter, who announced proudly that he had visited this grand edifice several times before, bought tickets from a woman in a caged booth at the entrance. She was wearing a turban on her head and jeweled rings on her fingers and she barely glanced at either of them, ignoring Potter's comment about the natural loveliness of her face.

Inside, wide hallways stretched in every direction, leading to room after room stuffed to the rafters with bizarre exhibits. Liberty and his uncle spent three hours wandering the corridors, gazing in admiration and awe at two-headed chickens, three-legged ducks, monstrous human fetuses with webbed feet and clawed hands and twisted features, a bearded lady who replied sharply to all hecklers, a man who caught hot pennies in his mouth, strolling magicians who pulled crisp banknotes from the air, a dwarf with his head on backward and so much more that Liberty would still be recollecting the pageant days afterward.

But what fascinated him most was the exhibit displaying a deformed black man in the apparently spontaneous process of turning white. His arms and legs had already made the transition into a sort of ashen pallor while the rest of his body, including his glum face, manifested an arresting mottled appearance, as if the black skin were being progressively invaded by patches of dim white flesh. The strident barker in a bowler hat, gesticulating with a malacca cane, explained that herein lay the solution to the troubled nation's political problems, Liberty came back twice to stare at this poor soul who lay on a straw pallet, a rag covering his loins, barely stirring, not speaking, refusing to respond even to a direct question, the huge, somber eyes occasionally fixing on one of the more vociferous spectators and reducing him to silence, too. As he stared, along with the others, Liberty experienced a confusion of emotion he found unpleasant but fascinating and difficult to understand.

For Potter one glance was sufficient. "Lead oxide," he pronounced emphatically. "Seen a whole troupe of banjo players over in Buffalo once, all painted up like that."

Liberty was dubious. To him the skin appeared genuine, unretouched.

"Lead oxide," repeated Potter, nodding knowingly and leading his nephew into the next room, where he proceeded to "explain" all the mysteries housed there. It was, in fact, Potter's delight to debunk every single exhibit in the museum, and with Liberty as captive audience his enthusiasm reached a level that began to draw a modest crowd. All, in his view, could be easily duplicated by the skillful application of theatrical costume and cosmetics. Nonfunctional extra limbs, tails or heads had been merely sewn on the animals. Several of his auditors began to challenge his opinions and then his physical person, and Potter grew perilously heated. A policeman was summoned, whereupon Potter and Liberty were escorted from the premises with a stern warning never to return.

"People like to be fooled," declared Potter out on the street. "It is the national pastime."

"I think they like to argue, too," offered Liberty.

"Ah, no doubt, my boy, no doubt of that at all." He stood on the sidewalk looking quickly in every direction, then suddenly strode off through the crowd, Liberty struggling to keep up. As they went, Potter dispensed more advice for survival in the urban wilderness. "Let none see your money, ever. Miscreants abound. Saw a huckleberry in a checked suit flash his roll one night in Mother Polly's doggery and before he got it back in his pocket a gang of b'hoys at the next table left him dirked and bleeding on the sawdust right there in the middle of the floor. Seen it happen other times, too, but that one there was some pumpkins."

"Can we go to Mother Polly's?" asked Liberty.

"Up for it already, are you, boy? Well, we shall see, we shall see. Let us first procure ourselves lodging for the night. Don't want to have to sleep out here on the stones with the pigs."

The name of the hotel, situated on a back street off Broadway, was Ye Old Oaken Home, walls and foundation of rusty brick, floors of unvarnished pine and roof of crumbling slate. The rooms themselves were the size of a jail cell and stifling hot. An aged black attendant with white hair whom the sallow, sunken-cheeked woman at the desk addressed brusquely as Ned shuffled into the room and with much show of physical labor and heavy grunting attempted to open the window, then turned to face them. "Can't do nothing about that," he said, and departed. Later, in the middle of the night, sweating and cursing, Potter would get out of bed and break the window with the butt of his pistol, though even then no air would stir within these oppressive quarters.

They ate supper at a loud, smoky saloon filled mostly with men and scantily dressed women who strolled from table to table, draping themselves over the men's shoulders and whispering in their ears until the men laughed and then rose to accompany these fascinating women into small boxlike compartments lining the far wall. A woman sauntered over to their table but Potter told her to go away. "I know of a much better place for that than here," he said meaningfully to Liberty, who nodded silently as if he knew more of what his uncle was talking about than he actually did. They drank some beer and ate two plates of oysters each, which Potter emphatically declared "the best in the city, the best on the whole eastern shore."

At the distant end of the room was a raised stage and, as Potter and Liberty were finishing their meal, the tattered red curtain parted to reveal a line of chorus girls arrayed in bits of clothing that concealed only their secret parts. To the ragged accompaniment of a five-piece band seated below and to the left of the stage, the girls kicked into a graceless but enthusiastic dance. The audience hooted and hollered and clapped and offered verbal suggestions for the next dance and the faster the girls bounced and the higher went their legs, the louder and rowdier the men became. Potter climbed onto his chair for a better view and so did Liberty. There was a wild feeling in the room of something tremendous either happening right now or about to happen momentarily. Then, abruptly, the music ceased, the dancing stopped and the curtain closed. The disappointed audience began shouting even louder, banging their mugs against the tables, but the curtain remained closed and gradually the noise in the saloon subsided to its normal shrieking roar.

"What do you think?" asked Potter.

"Do they come back with their clothes off?" asked Liberty, at which Potter erupted into laughter and clapped his nephew on the back. "I like you, Liberty," he yelled, "I always have."

Then, with a tinny fanfare from the band, the curtain parted again, disclosing the stage now set with a row of empty wooden chairs in front of which posed a tall, lean man in a black frock coat, blue satin vest and black pantaloons. Tacked to the rear stage wall was an enormous banner announcing Professor Winslow McGurk's Laughing Gas Exhibition. The tall man stepped to the edge of the stage and raised his hands for quiet.

"Good evening, gentlemen," he began. "I am Professor McGurk." From scattered points of the room, great cheers at this information. "I have recently returned from a grand tour of Europe in which many of the more notable crowned heads sampled the demonstration which you are about to witness. What I will show you this evening are the entertaining effects of an exhilarating chemical compound upon the human brain. You will observe your fellows altered and positively transformed and transported beyond the mundane concerns of our dull daily life. This is a metamorphosis perfectly natural, perfectly safe.

"Now, I am going to require some six or seven adventurous souls willing to risk passage through that delicate veil that obscures us from the numerous delights beyond and who also possess a mere twenty-five cents as the price of admission, Don't be shy, step forward, everyone who desires to partake of the gas will be accommodated. This, I need not remind you, is the experience of a lifetime. You will not want to miss it."

There was a shuffling of chairs as several men rose and advanced toward the stage.

"I want to do it," Liberty said suddenly, standing and fumbling in his pocket for a coin.

"If you go crazy," declared Potter, obviously amused, "it ain't my funeral."

"Never said it would be," answered Liberty, heading for the stage.

"Here's a bold lad," said Professor McGurk, reaching down to help him up. "Perhaps he'd like to go first."

"Sure."

"What's your name, son?"

"Liberty."

"Liberty, eh. Well, I guarantee you are about to be liberated." He handed the boy a rubber mask attached to a length of tubing whose other end was fitted into the stopper of a large glass jar. "Place the mask over your mouth and nose, and when I give the signal I want you to breathe in as deeply as you can. Do you understand?"

"Yes."

"You'll be sorry," called a voice from the crowd.

McGurk fiddled around with the jar, released a metal clamp on the tubing and, nodding his head, said, "Now."

Liberty inhaled. He felt something cool and sweet rush headlong into his lungs and even when he stopped inhaling, pulling the mask away from his face, the inward rushing kept on, filling not just his lungs but all the organs of his body. His arms and legs, seemingly emptied of all bone and tissue, were also filling with this most peculiar vapor. Then a most terrific rushing, as loud and rapid as a train, went shooting up his spine into his head and exploded against the roof of his skull, pretty flecks of colored light cascading warmly, gently over the rolling meadows of his brain—all these weird sensations occupying no more than a brief moment, but Liberty seemed to have found himself in a new place where "moments" were not only meaningless, they did not even exist. No longer securely lodged in his mind, he was swelling into a pleasant space vaguely bodylike in form that seemed to act as a strange prism upon the world, sharpening its colors, amplifying its sound.

When the professor asked if he would care to imbibe a second time, Liberty reached into his pocket for another coin. His attention was shifting constantly and haphazardly from the sensations within to the phantasmagoria without, where events occurred in a perpetual past as if he were actually remembering what he was witnessing. It appeared that one of his fellows onstage was engaged in standing on his head while another scurried about on all fours barking like a dog, and at some point he seemed to join in with all for a rousing chorus of "Oh Susannah." After some unknown passage of time, he discovered himself back at his table, where he quickly downed two beers and informed his uncle that he looked like a lobster.

Then Liberty was moving through a fog where each flame of each gas lamp stood, haloed, separate, distinct, eyes of fire guiding one on to a catastrophe unforeseen. Faces loomed in and out of the mist like clouds with human features and all the speech around him sounded like Chinese, though he had never heard that language spoken before. It felt like an infinite rain was falling inside his head.

Then they were seated in a red parlor surrounded by women in silken robes, a sweaty man with a moustache pounding away at a piano and singing in a harsh voice a tuneless version of "Jimmy Crack Corn," each of the lamp flames swaying in rhythm and singing along in harmony. He realized he had never hated a particular song with such venom. Now his uncle's face looked swollen and about to explode.

Then he was in a room with papered walls and on the paper were pictures of birds in flight and he could hear them crying as they passed in ranked formation. Somehow his pants were off and he was seated on the edge of a bed, a girl kneeling between his knees and washing with a warm rag his awakened privates and suddenly it was like he was sneezing at the wrong end of his body.

Then, the girl was gone, and miraculously, without benefit of balloon and basket, he was ascending upright through a sun-splashed sky; below, the isle of Manhattan, as vivid and unreal as a fairy tale dragon bathing its battered flanks in the cooling confluence of waters; every rooftop a shiny scale; every plume of chimney smoke a dark venting of noxious vapors from the creature's infernal interior; and the hectic inhabitants of the city itself a plague of mites infesting the great slumbering body. From the dizzying heights he now occupied it was impossible to discern whether such a visitation was salutary or malign, distinctions growing more and more obscure with each elevating second. Imagine then the view from the Maker's porch. Who to receive the favor of His munificent eye? Host? Parasite? Both? Through the lens of eternity was the difference of any consequence whatsoever? Did He care? The questions themselves seemed trivial. Perhaps these mundane discriminations were symptoms of a profound error, a fruitless sorting of beans with faulty equipment. Even at an angelic altitude, vexatious thoughts. New York.

When news of Sumter arrived, Roxana promptly took to her room. For five days no one saw her but Thatcher, who carried the meal trays up the stairs and carried them back down again, largely untouched. "Fine," he'd reply to all inquiries, "she's just fine." But his manner grew uncharacteristically abrupt, his temper short, and he seemed increasingly prone to periodic intervals of arrested motion when his body simply ceased to function, the eyes turned inward, and he'd stand fixed as a hunter in a painting straining to hear over the next ridge the awful baying of the hounds.

Lying alone in his garret in the comfortless dead reaches of the night, anxieties about both parents dancing like devils about his bed, Liberty would listen to his mother crying, sometimes for hours, and pray to a dubious God he could neither fully believe in (behold the gifts He had showered upon this particular family) nor fully reject (matters could be worse, much worse) that whatever obstacles impeding the Fishes' natural migration be speedily removed so that happiness might be more fairly pursued. Of course it would be Carolina who commenced the big ball, and though Liberty had never met his maternal grandfather or even glimpsed his likeness, he could not help but imagine a pop-eyed, sunken-cheeked Grandpa Asa yanking the lanyard on the inaugural cannon.

In the morning after the first night of what would be years of perpetual night, a rueful Thatcher studied his son across the neglected breakfast table for some interminable minutes before remarking, "I suspect I know how you may be feeling on this dreaded occasion, but I want to emphasize to you that your mother and I do not wish to see you, despite the understandable pressure of your convictions, stealing off to a recruiting office. I know that halfwits on both sides have been claiming rather vociferously that if the worst did come, the worst would be over in a handful of weeks, so there will no doubt be a terrific rush among certain impetuous hotheads to enter the fray before it abruptly concludes. But I ask you, as your father, to please refrain from such rashness. You are too young."

"I'll be seventeen in a few months."

"A foal who's barely strayed from the barn. Please do not burden your mother with more cares than she already has. You realize how frightfully difficult this time is for her."

"As if I would ever require even a gentle reminder. Every tear is a drop of scalding oil upon my own skin, and . . . and . . ." He faltered for a moment and had to glance hurriedly away. Outside the half-open window the sun shone idiotically on, the proud maples waved their soft fresh leaves at him and somewhere a dog was barking with great urgency, as if the production of that one grating sound was absolutely vital to the execution of the day's business. "The situation," he resumed, "is no less intricate for me."

"I understand, and I sympathize thoroughly, but I must ask you now to promise me that you will not even attempt to enlist without the specific permission of your mother and myself."

Liberty's gaze went skittering about the room in a vain attempt at avoiding his father's steady, unblinking stare. "I'm sorry," he admitted quietly. "I don't believe I can, in all conscience, do as you ask."

Thatcher gave a brief nod, rose heavily from his chair and left the room.

Liberty remained at the table, scrupulously warding off any thought whatsoever, and calmly finished his coffee. Then, wandering out into the hallway, he paused at the parlor door from behind which could be discerned a low murmuring and the rustle of quick rodent-like footsteps—Aunt Aroline pacing nervously to and fro and muttering to herself. From upstairs came only a profound silence. Once the sobbing commenced again, he didn't know if he could restrain himself from fleeing the house. On the front porch he found Euclid planted in Roxana's chair and rocking to a firm genteel beat, a country squire contemplating the compass of his property on out to the distant hills where the green mottling of spring was well under way. Without turning his head to see who had approached, Euclid simply opened his mouth and began to speak: "I saw the dawning of this day long, long ago. I been praying for it nightly since I was a little chap buried in darkness down in Mississip, brushing flies off Master John's babies. Be patient, says the Lord, a mighty house requires a mighty foundation. But now the good work has finally begun, only there will be storms, Liberty, blows to shake the spirit of the sinners as well as the saints, angry thunders, trickster lightnings and infinite seas of infinite blood all boiling and heaving. I saw all these afflictions as a muffin back on the Twelve Trees."

"But they're saying six weeks, Euclid, ninety days at the most."

"That's man talking and man is nothing but air and noise and the sound he makes never did nobody any damn bit of good. Should hush up now and listen to the Lord. He's the Grand Projector and His business ain't necessarily our business. This here is going to be the knockdown of all knockdowns. You say ninety days. Try nine hundred. Try nine hundred and more."

"I'm thinking about signing up."

Euclid rocked rhythmically on. "Beautiful sky today," he observed. "Hunter's sky. That's the Lord's Traveling Exhibition up there, Liberty, and oftentimes those passing shows can lay such a powerful peace upon your soul you think you just might drop from the plumb pleasure of it." He stopped rocking. "What does the voice say?"

Liberty smiled. "Which one?"

"Your true voice, baby doll, the one in your heart."

"Euclid," confessed Liberty shyly, "I honestly do not know."

"Then you have a confusion upon you. Go out into the woods and set the issue before the rocks and the trees. The leaves will tell you what to do."

An hour later, seated on a moss-padded boulder shaped remarkably like a monarch's throne, Liberty pondered his destiny, much, so he imagined, like an ancient troubled king, before him an almost perfect circle of dead earth in which no living thing grew or trespassed, and apparently never had, this tranquil glade neatly scooped out of the traceless depths of the forest always for him a supremely magical place where it was said witches once capered and primeval tribes performed elaborate rituals of a thrillingly hideous nature, and whatever presences had been invoked by those pagan mystics must linger still else why did the soil remain so indelibly poisoned? Once he thought he had even glimpsed the spade-tipped tail of some green leathery creature slipping deftly behind a large stump at his approach. And once he had heard voices conversing in a guttural foreign tongue right out of the unbodied air before him and, as he attended to their intriguing confabulation, he discovered, after a mysterious auditory adjustment, he could actually comprehend their gibberish, his mind translating the nonsensical sounds into recognizable English that instructed him where to find a birthday coin given him by Aunt Aroline that he, careless boy, had promptly lost. The coin glittered in the exact center of the contaminated circle. Euclid was right. Solutions to the important riddles of this rough-and-tumble world could only be discovered through an appeal to the sphere unseen. But now, though, as he debated the question of the hour, taking up both sides in equal turn, the woods and stones remained frustratingly mute. Eventually, the words in his head trailed away and, entering a region where, language and logic spent, he simply surrendered the struggle and in that very instant it was not a voice but the silence that spoke clearly to him, and at once he stood and went down out of the forest to a road on the edge of town and a sad, saddle-backed cottage of cracked boards and crazed windows where a one-wheeled buggy stood tilted on its axle in the dried mud before the door. Loud, persistent knocking finally summoned a female voice from within. "Who's there?" it cried.

"Liberty," he announced softly, and in reply the bolt was instantly drawn and the heavy oaken door opened on a tiny woman no larger than a ten-year-old child. She was wearing a peruke and a soiled and torn ruby gown.

"Liberty!" she exclaimed, hugging him warmly about the waist. "I've just been thinking about you. Come in, come in," she commanded, pulling him roughly into a dim cluttered space fragrant with pine smoke, stale grease and the distinctive effluvium of human bodies, numerous and unwashed, at close quarters.

"I knew," declared Mrs. Fowler with a twittering enthusiasm one hinge removed from outright mania, "the moment I woke this morning that the sun would not set without an appearance of your face at my door, so I immediately decided that today's pie, in your honor, would be rhubarb. And so it is, my special rhubarb pie for Liberty." And she produced from a sideboard in a shadowy corner he could barely perceive a heavy platter whose circular cap of crust he did recognize once it had been shoved up under his flaring nostrils.

"Excellent!" he pronounced, frankly unable to distinguish the singular scent of that tart vegetable from the sundry robust odors clamoring for olfactory attention.

"It has a secret ingredient," Mrs. Fowler confided in a coquettish aside, "I cannot divulge to the others but which I can reveal to you, Liberty." She leaned forward, her voice dropping into stage whisper. "Gunpowder," she murmured confidentially.

"Gunpowder?"

"It adds a certain tonic charm to any dish."

"In which case I may require an extra slice," he submitted politely.

"Gobble up what you will, Liberty. My family mislikes plant pie."

In the gloom to which his eyes had gradually become accustomed, Liberty discovered baby Lucius teetering stark naked in the middle of the floor, sucking industriously on his thumb and clutching in his other chubby fist what appeared to be a dead mouse. From obscure corners came the rustlings of other creeping things, bestial or mortal or both. Despite having known the family since the advent of memory, Liberty had never been able to ascertain with any surety the precise number of Fowler children nor had he ever been informed of Mrs. Fowler's Christian name.

"I had to send Phineas to town," she explained, "simply to clear some space around me. You know what he can be like once something momentous settles over his brain, up and down, in and out, it's enough to put a parson into a pucker. I do hope you're not vexing your own mother unnecessarily."

"No, ma'am, she's taken to her room."

Mrs. Fowler gave him a curt nod of approval. "Exactly where I would be if I had a room to take to. But what are we doing standing about in the dark and jawing like a couple of damn fools? Lucius!" she called out sharply as she began leading Liberty back into the well-lit kitchen, "what the devil do you have in your mouth? Drop the thingum on the floor, baby, that's right, on the floor. That child," she uttered, shaking her head in exasperated wonder.

Settled before a relatively clean table in a relatively filthy kitchen, Liberty stared almost uncomprehendingly at the mammoth slice of pie Mrs. Fowler had set out for him. The filling oozing threateningly from between the crusts was of a suspicious tinge and consistency. When he finally dared a bite, employing one of Mrs. Fowler's prize possessions, a recent gift from a dotty Boston aunt, a pronged silver utensil she called a "forp," he encountered a taste best described as sweetened saddle soap. In fact, he was so absorbed in exploring the bracing novelty of this flavor that he failed to notice at first that Mrs. Fowler had quit her anxious puttering about and was now leaning precariously upon the back of a chair and emitting a stuttering series of distressing noises.

"Mrs. Fowler?" he inquired tentatively.

She turned around to reveal to him her flooded eyes, her hot red cheeks. "Don't think I am ignorant of what you boys are secretly planning. I have been dreading this day ever since that awful man was elected president. I've been young, I know what youth is like, an occasion for folly and artlessness unbounded, deaf ears to elders all around, I understand, but I will not permit my oldest boy to throw himself convulsively upon the pyre, and, if Mr. Fowler had not gone to Canada to seek his fortune in pelts, he would be here at my side blocking the door against the both of you. Mr. Fowler, as do I, abhors violence. He believes all disputes can be readily settled with a shot of old orchard and a deck of cards. If Mr. Fowler were here he would deal out a hand of faro and nobody would be going anywhere. Mr. Fowler understands the proper conduct in life and Mr. Fowler is never wrong."

"Yes, ma'am" was all Liberty could offer in reply to such fervent reasoning, though he had never seen a Mr. Fowler or any other man about the place and lately had begun to wonder where all the fresh babies kept coming from.

"I always knew you possessed more than a single grain of sense, which is more than I can say of my Phineas. You've always been death on a speech, Liberty, ever your parents' child, I suppose, and Phineas listens to you with far greater attentiveness than he does his own mother, so I ask you, please, try to talk some reason into that cast-iron noggin of his, would you?"

"I'm not so sure, Mrs. Fowler, that he really listens all that well to anybody," replied Liberty, recollecting the time young Phinny, eager to sample the rumored delights of erotic bliss, dropped his pants and despite repeated warnings stuck his erect penis into the presumably honey-slick knothole of a dead tree containing what he swore was an abandoned beehive only to painfully learn that numerous angry tenants remained in residence, and as he ran howling across an open field, his unmentionables aflame, toward the relief of Wilson's Creek, onlookers in a passing coach, namely his sweetheart Elmina Carlisle and her stuffy mother, were treated to an unobstructed view of his predicament, their combined shrieks adding to the general effect of wanton mayhem and causing the horses to bolt.

"I have faith in you, Liberty," she said, patting him affectionately on the head. "You could coax snakes out of the ground with the music of your voice."

"Mrs. Fowler, I really must object—"

"Ssssh," she cautioned hastily, finger to her lips, "hush now, here he comes."

A door slapped shut, clumsy footsteps approached and into the kitchen stumbled a tall, freckled, cream-faced boy about Liberty's age bearing upon his shoulder a sack of ground flour which he unceremoniously dumped to the floor, causing a puff of white powder to explode gently upward.

"Phineas!" exclaimed Mrs. Fowler. "Burst that bag and you'll work it off shoveling shit in the barn for a month."

"But I already shovel shit nearly every day," her son quickly replied, rolling an eye for Liberty's benefit.

"Don't you dare direct such profane language my way. I'll not tolerate such disrespect under my roof."

"Why should you when you can go to town and get freely insulted any damn time you please."

The slap she attempted to administer across his cheek was easily dodged and as Phineas headed out the door, he grabbed Liberty by the shoulder, saying, "Meet me by the woodpile."

"I'll meet you by the woodpile," promised Mrs. Fowler heatedly, "birch rod in hand."

Phineas raised a threatening fist, turned his back and departed.

"It's a disjointed world, Liberty," remarked a melancholic Mrs. Fowler, touching her hair as if it had just been mussed. "No snug fit to the parts anymore. We are tumbling and tumbling into a great abyss, I fear, perhaps one with no bottom. Go out and speak with him, Liberty. Tell him there's rhubarb pie."

He found Phineas seated on a fence post, studying his fingernails with grim intensity. "I've been to the rally," he announced flatly. "The whole town's in a positive jimjam." The mayor had orated in his usual florid manner for more than an hour and then read a telegram from the governor promising that the state would chaw up all other states in the contest for duty and honor and glory. The band played, miserably, not a tune anyone in the crowd could recognize. Dogs scampered wildly about. Girls granted boys knowing smiles never revealed before. Then Wilbur Jenkins, rigged up in a fancy captain's uniform, displayed the regimental flag his wife had stayed up all night sewing and asked for volunteers to step forward and take the oath. "And every man in the square but for me, Pegleg Tom and Ben Brown, that thieving coward, dashed cheering up to the table as if someone had just shouted 'Free beer!' I felt so bad I had to come right home. I don't know what to do. She don't want me to go."

"Neither do mine."

"Well, we could just desert the old homestead, march off like brave Greeks and let the old folks know by mail once we're there."

"Where? The battlefield?"

"No," Phineas replied, eyes alight at the prospect of the stirring drama before them. "Richmond."

"Got this dust-up won already, have you?"

"Do you think it'll be over before we get our chance?"

"No, I reckon there'll be more than enough killing and dying to go around. My father's always said that breaking up chains requires a bigger, hotter fire than the one to forge them in the first place."

"Perhaps there's time then to lay seige to the mothers."

"As a rehearsal for the rebs?"

"We'll dazzle 'em with elocutionary rockets, Liberty, we'll invest 'em with inductions, divert 'em with apostrophes, we'll bombard 'em with a prioris, and if all else fails, we'll simply outflank 'em and head smartly on out."

Unlike most military campaigns, which rarely proceed as intended, Liberty's crucial scene with his mother turned out to be not at all the lachrymose ordeal he had feared. She received him cordially in her bedroom, costumed in no mask of pale grief but appearing as herself, in the role he had largely known her by, eyes unringed, the whites startlingly pure and bloodless, complexion fair as a country milk-maid's, her silvery black hair freshly washed and brushed. To her son she looked like a perfectly healthy adult woman who had decided, for understandable reasons, to simply remain beneath the shelter of the covers for a few days. He hesitated just inside the door.

"I've been expecting you," she said, carefully closing the well-thumbed copy of the Bible she had been idly leafing through, a book to which she maintained a long, difficult, ambiguous relationship but one she could not, at least as yet, entirely abandon.

"It took a certain amount of time to accumulate the required courage."

"I was expecting that, too. Come, sit beside me," she urged, patting the blanket. "I want to feel your weight on the bed."

As he settled into the soft knolls and hollows of the feather mattress, he noticed now, up close, a disturbing vagueness to his mother's presence, a slight truancy around which attention skirted.

"Have you been eating properly?" she asked, then, feeling his forehead, "Do you have a fever?"

"No greater than the country's."

She sighed. "I don't suppose there's anything I could say which would matter at this point. I couldn't keep you from wandering as a child, I certainly cannot lock you up in your room now."

"And there's always the window."

"I've known all these turbulent years that one day the turbulence would certainly invade our home, but I think I willfully refused to admit just how frightfully personal it might be."

"But I'll be back before summer," he argued, the promise sounding ridiculously hollow even to him.

"Don't, Liberty. Please stop. I have found that the unpleasant episodes of a life are more fruitfully endured when regarded through the strong lens of truth. All I ask is that you write regularly and that you try to refrain from imprudence. Don't play the hero for anyone. There will be more than enough fools scrambling for that position and you will, no doubt, witness what becomes of them. The satisfactory fulfillment of one's duty is heroism enough for anybody. Remember: the successful transit of even a single day is heroic beyond measure."

"You understand this is an obligation I cannot shirk."

"Yes. And you understand that I am a mother."

"A grade that outranks the highest general."

"Good, now give me a kiss."

She smelled of soap and hyacinth and her own particular Roxana scent, somewhat vanillalike, ever allied in his mind with sentiments of safety and love, and as he paused in the doorway to say good-bye (for the last time as it turned out; he would never see her again) he was presented with a privileged glimpse into the nature of nature when for one eternal aching instant he beheld his mother as a complete discrete being, entirely isolate from himself, with a history his knowledge of which would remain forever spotty and elusive, and a present he could never fully inhabit, and he figured his own uncertain passage into muddling maturity had already begun.

The army was settling into uneasy bivouac when sometime after dusk it began to rain, an omen some claimed, though whether for good or ill was not altogether clear. In the dark, men tripped over objects that weren't there, dogs barked for no discernible cause. Even the battle-tested horses seemed spooked, whinnying without provocation, snapping occasionally at passing humans. "There's a higher officer than Little Mac or Bobby Lee directing the course of this campaign," claimed Sergeant Wickersham, attempting to calm the "strawfeet." "On this field we're all outranked, private and general alike. And that commander ain't going to let the Union go down. He ain't going to let you boys go down." Corporal Albion Franks, a veteran of Bull Run and the Peninsula who'd been listening nearby, averted his face and spat carefully into the dirt.

And all through that long rainy night the remaining regiments came straggling into camp, spectral beings from realms underground gathered out of the fog, the silence of their grand procession broken only by the jingle of metal and the steady monotonous hissing sound of their feet upon the road.

Liberty and Phineas Fowler sat huddled cold, wet and miserable inside their tent, munching on handfuls of dry coffee mixed with the last of their sugar. No fires, the general had ordered, no talking either. The opposing armies now lay as close to one another as weary travelers sharing a narrow bed, their restless shifting throughout the night setting off periodic flurries of picket fire, the muzzle flashes darting like bright reptilian tongues through the drizzle and thickening fog, attempting to sense within this tense obscurity the adversary's precise location. Sleep would be a rare commodity tonight on either side—especially for Liberty, who the previous day had discovered gunpowder in his canteen and, this morning, that his ramrod had gone missing. "Once the ball's in motion," Sergeant Wickersham had assured him, "you'll be able to fetch another easy enough. The field'll be scattered with them."

"I didn't like the sound of that," complained Fowler, wiping the grime from the metalwork of his Enfield. "How many of us do you reckon are going to end the day no longer in need of muskets or anything else for that matter?"

"Ill reflections, Phinny. Lieutenant Quincy says it's such thoughts that help draw the minies."

"But how do you know I'm not having thoughts like this because I'm already sensing the balls coming toward me?"

"They're coming for all of us, Phinny, and I would suggest the best remedy is whatever rest we can pinch from this grudging night." He rolled over onto his dry side, which became immediately wet.

"I'm scared, Liberty. I don't know if my soul is adequately prepared."

"Go talk to the chaplain." He could feel the leading edge of a cold taking up residence in the back of his throat.

"Chaplain Poague doesn't like me. He believes redheads are all bound for perdition."

"Yes," said Liberty, trying to determine if that was a rock or a root pressing so insistently against his hip, "and all southpaws are thieves. I've heard the speech."

"You'd think they would provide us with spiritual counsel of a loftier quality, especially on the eve of battle."

"Well, what do you expect? Look at our officers."

Fowler examined this sobering opinion for a full silent minute or two before remarking, "We are indeed commanded by a most peculiar tribe of gentlemen, that's for certain. Why just the other day I saw

Captain Dougherty kissing that damn fool dog of his right on its slobbering lips. 'He's my sweetheart,' he said. What do you make of that?"

"I try not to find fault with expressions of true love wherever they might appear." Liberty had shifted his body into a relatively comfortable position and if, as he suspected, sleep should prove elusive, at least he could provide some relief for his aching limbs. So, arm for a pillow, he lay there on the dank ground shivering like a drenched puppy, but was it the cold, the ague or these pesky studies on death that seemed to have arrived unbidden for not just a visit but an extended residence? Death appeared to him to be the natural hollowness about which all life was uneasily constructed. And perhaps its distance to you varied considerably over the years, a black planet inexorably orbiting your being, near, then far, but eventually, over time, moving closer and closer. It was now quite apparent to Liberty that your own personal demise differed dramatically in color and tone from the shocking yet still vaguely remote passing of friends and even family. Liberty wondered how he would behave tomorrow at death's nearest approach thus far. Would he be brave, would he flee, and if his hours, in all their novelty and consuming intrigue, should actually come to an end, what would that be like, to be transformed from a warm, upright breathing creature of passion and hope into one of those discarded sacks of decaying meat he had glimpsed just yesterday coming up the mountain, mules and men tossed carelessly by the roadside in a tangled heap of aborted life? His imagination stopped, paralyzed before the prospect of eternity, in whose features he could discern only a yawning pitch darkness and an icy wind. His nerves seemed as taut as fiddle strings, helpless before whatever grim invisible hand chose to play them. But consolation of the sort available in such a desperate emotional situation was found at last, however momentarily, in a variation of Father's favorite injunction: your grandfather Azariah didn't help Colonel Knox haul sixty tons of artillery three hundred miles over the Berkshires in the dead of winter for you, at the crossroads of honor, glory and all that is right and moral in the universe, to torment yourself with oppressive speculations, let alone cut and run before the foe. The notion of the Union and his family's long, intimate and convoluted relationship with its history seemed to call him back to himself. His mood actually brightened. Thoughts were weapons, too, as his mother had repeatedly instructed. Duty, then, duty and a resignation to the hazards of fate, would carry him, safely he prayed, through the perils of the advancing day, which by the time he had finally managed to soothe somewhat his anxious heart was already beginning to reveal itself faintly against the eastern sky. Now the four batteries of twenty-pound Parrott rifles perched on the hills behind opened up with a startling roar that once begun seemed to go on without cease until the reluctant sun itself died into the west. The ground heaved, the air shook. By the time Sergeant Wickersham arrived, most of his men were up, gathered in a ragged group, every eye searching Wickersham's face and gestures for signs of confidence.

"Easy, my boys, easy. Remember the Lord and you'll all be fine."

"No coffee?" asked Private Haskell, an inveterate guzzler of even the stingiest, meanest brew to qualify for the name, but the sergeant was already gone, his progress down the row of laggards' tents marked by a fading refrain of grunts and oaths.

"Well, at least the infernal rain has stopped," remarked Private Goodspeed. "I didn't sign up to fight the weather, too."

"Considering your valorous achievements so far," answered Corporal Bell, "you didn't sign up to do much of anything else, either," which ignited an explosion of laughter and left Goodspeed, always too slow with a witty response, staring dolefully at the ground.

"I'd take on the rebs any day compared to these goddamn gray-backs," complained Private Coxe, popping a pair of newly discovered lice between his thumb and forefinger. "I can't seem to outrun the little buggers."

"They like you, Thaddeus," joked Bell. "They smell fresh linen and good grub in your pantry."

"The only fresh linen in this man's army," said Private Bromfield, an attorney's son from Albany, "is the hankie in General Hooker's breast pocket."

"And we're not too sure about that," added Bell.

A white-bearded private, eyes rolling loosely around in his head, came stumbling past shouting, "It's a-coming, it's a-coming, all out it's a-coming."

"What's that you say?" yelled Fowler. "What's coming?"

"Oh, you'll see, young duck, you and all your green comrades will see soon enough." And he vanished into the mist, his monitory cry trailing eerily behind him.

"Who in the hell was that?" asked Liberty. His boots were wet, his clothes clammy and a decidedly unpleasant ache had sprouted up behind his right eye.

"Oh, that's just Old Man Perkins," explained Corporal Bell. "Pay him no mind. He gets quite exercised before every engagement, and then, when it begins a-coming, you'll see him a-going quick enough."

A Confederate shell, then another and another, came crashing into the trees overhead, producing an immediate shower of shredded leaves, twigs, bark and splinters, then an entire branch big as a railroad tie and complete with an abandoned bird nest plummeted down directly onto Private Goodspeed's head, knocking him senseless to the ground.

"Quite a novel effect, don't you think?" asked Lieutenant Rice, a grocery clerk from Elmira who had decided to attend the war in what he apparently deemed the protective guise of a fop, hands adorned with frayed kidskin gloves and knotted around his scrawny neck a bright red silk scarf which Sergeant Wickersham kept cautioning would make him an extra fine target for the secesh. "Rather like trying to conduct a dance in a collapsing saw mill."

Fowler's eyes were jerking frantically about, as if searching for the door out of this place.

"Not exactly what we expected, is it?" remarked Liberty, picking the wood chips out of his teeth, and before Fowler could reply all the Federal cannons went off at once and the artillery battle had begun. The noise was so tremendous the troops could barely hear Sergeant Wickersham ordering them into line. On Liberty's left Private Alvah Huff, a lover of cards and money in that order, began to repeat aloud The Lord's Prayer, mouthing the words so rapidly they lost all sense, blurring into one long indistinguishable sound. Without losing a beat in his chant, he removed from his coat pocket a deck of playing cards he then scattered carelessly at his feet.

Suddenly, amidst the din, Liberty heard a voice clear and calm, "I'm right behind you, amalgamator." He swiveled around to confront the leering eyes of Private Arthur McGee, former horse thief, company bully and small-town racist. "Welcome to your last day on earth."

"Well," drawled Liberty, "I shall try not to leave it as I found it."

"Listen to me, you little nigger lover, by the time the sun sets on this day you're going to be dancing with your Ethiopian pals around a campfire in hell."

"That so? Then I'll be sure to save a place for you."

Instantly, Liberty's jacket just below the collar was seized in a huge meaty fist.

"Seems like you want to get rowed up Salt River before this here ball has even begun," McGee hissed, spraying Liberty's face with a liberal quantity of spit.

"Hold!" declared Sergeant Wickersham, stepping between the two. "Save it for the johnnies."

"McGee don't lie," growled McGee, wagging a nailless forefinger under Liberty's nose. "McGee don't play no jokes. Unlike people, McGee means what he says."

"Unlike people," responded Liberty, "I forgive you."

McGee glared back, his face the color of raw beef.

"Get in line, you two," ordered Sergeant Wickersham, "we're moving up."

"I thought the bumpkins," commented Fowler, leaning in toward Liberty's ear, "were all collected on the other side."

"America," replied Liberty. "We spread the bumpkins around evenly."

The company was guided through a continual cascade of tree parts to the southern edge of the woods, where they were positioned with the rest of their regiment behind a freshly formed unit from Wisconsin, farm boys mostly, who were gravely studying in a murky dawn-light the sobering vista spread before them. Beyond a worn fence there was a wide rolling pasture, fog in the hollows, then another fence and a field of maturing corn and on a small knoll in the far distance stood a modest white one-room building surrounded by Confederate batteries which, even as they watched, were sending an impossible barrage of metal and explosives in their direction. One shell, dropping short, hit a rock outcropping in the pasture and, fuse still sputtering, bounced clean over Liberty's entire regiment, detonating somewhere in the foliage behind them. Then Liberty noticed blooming upright among the tall stalks of tasseling corn blades of polished metal glinting in the early light—bayonets, hundreds of them, the rebs were in the corn. Liberty's own rifle kept slipping through his sweaty hands, and each time he swallowed it felt as if a pebble was in his throat.

Then, with a flurry of shouted commands, Wisconsin began climbing the fence and moving across the open pasture, flags fluttering, swords waving, bugles crying. "Grand, ain't it?" shouted Corporal Franks, a huge grin plastered across the face of a man who had never been celebrated for his smile. "Have you ever known such bliss?" Liberty stared back in open-mouthed astonishment.

Wisconsin was about halfway across the pasture when out of the hollows rose a line of Confederate infantry, muskets blazing, as simultaneously the artillery on the hill let loose a thundering salvo and Wisconsin disappeared in an angry cloud of fog and powder smoke. Through the shifting haze all that could be seen was a handful of men running back toward the rear and a pleasant green meadow littered with hundreds of blue-coated bodies.

"We're next!" cried Sergeant Wickersham. "Guide on that schoolhouse over there. We're going to take out those damn guns!"

Liberty was experiencing the oddest sensation: that he was no longer properly situated inside his body, that the thinking, feeling portion of himself was now hovering mysteriously ghostlike above the physical self. His hands, wrapped clumsily about his rifle, seemed miles away. Last night Private Todd had informed him, with a certain resigned conviction, that today he would be killed and asked Liberty if he would be so kind as to make sure his effects were returned home to his family in Buffalo. Liberty had scoffed at this grim premonition, but now wondered if he might not be undergoing a similar apprehension. "Think of the bondsmen," his mother had exhorted him in a recent letter on how best to get through this terrible war. "Think of their stooped toil, their martyred agony." The words, in his mother's own fair hand, appeared at the moment cold and distant. All the sermons and arguments he had heard throughout his short life on the wickedness of chained servitude had, for him, come down to this: a mad charge through clouds of dense, choking smoke into the very barrels of the slavocracy. And when at last the dread order to advance was given, his body seemed light, almost weightless, and he floated over the ground like a spirit.

Though there was nothing to see, no clear target to fire at, men began toppling out of the ranks like broken dolls, falling soundlessly to the earth. A riderless horse came charging out of the smoke, a booted human leg dangling from the stirrup. Major Hays, their company commander, who had not been seen all morning, rushed unexpectedly past brandishing his saber in one hand, a bottle of whiskey in the other, and muttering a stream of unintelligible gibberish. "Looks like Ole Pricklylegs has called it a day," yelled Fowler before exclaiming "Ow!" and, with a surprised look on his flushed face, falling backward into the dirt. "Phinny!" cried Liberty, kneeling beside his friend. "Are you all right?" Fowler replied, managing a tight smile, "Sure, Liberty, just got the wind knocked out of me. I'll be up in a second." Then Liberty noticed the hole in Fowler's chest. There was froth around the edges, as if his friend had miraculously grown a new mouth outside his ribs. "You'll be fine," Liberty said, patting his hand. "I never thought this would happen to me," Fowler said, voice already reduced to a low rasp. "Kill a johnny for me, Liberty, I'm going to miss you." "Keep moving!" shouted Sergeant Wickersham, abruptly materializing out of nowhere. "Fowler will be taken care of. Keep moving!" Reluctantly, Liberty retrieved his rifle and, with one last look back at his dying friend, stumbled on ahead to rejoin the line. He could hardly advance a rod without stepping on a body or a part of one. Heads were lying about like an unharvested crop of grotesque pumpkins. In many places the ground was surprisingly soft, soggy with blood. The wounded groaned and writhed about with an aching slowness, like strange marine animals trapped on the ocean floor. The frequent calls for "Mother!" near and far were almost unendurable. A hand reached up, grabbing Liberty by the pant leg. "Help me!" pleaded the man whose features were obscured in blood, his right eye missing. Liberty shook his leg free and moved on. Up ahead he finally spotted a familiar face, that of Private Amor Dibble, a farmer's son from Lake Placid who had apparently never been around many people in his young secluded life and had hardly spoken a word to anyone since joining the company back in June and who now, observing an evidently spent cannonball rolling lazily across the grass, stuck out his foot to stop it and in an instant his entire right leg was torn from its socket and Dibble thrown screaming to the ground.

"Lord have mercy!" exclaimed Corporal Bell, rushing to Liberty's side. "Why aren't you firing, man? You want to end up like him?" gesturing toward what remained of Private Dibble. He tore a paper cartridge open with his teeth and poured the powder down the barrel of his Enfield. "And look at poor Huff there." He pointed to a body a couple yards away, where one neat bullet hole decorated the man's left breast. "Guess he shouldn't have tossed away those cards, might've saved his life. Now get yourself together and start taking part in this scuffle. You can see we need every man we've got." He lifted his musket to his shoulder and fired off into the murk, then took off running after the bullet as if eager to see if his blind shot had happened to bring down any quarry.

It was then that Liberty became aware for the first time that morning of what had been a constant accompaniment to his every move, the phenomenon veterans joked about, the nettlesome sound of bumblebees buzzing incessantly about one's head. He also noticed in every direction small geysers of dirt were spraying into the air as if the bubbling ground itself were being cooked over a slow, mammoth fire. Men on all sides of him were screaming, cursing and, like frantic automatons, loading and firing, loading and firing, the ten-step procedure necessary to shoot the standard musket keeping even the quickest and most skilled down to about two rounds a minute. Liberty had never felt so alone. Though the sun seemed to have hardly budged a degree since first breaking through the overcast, it seemed this battle had already lasted a full day, and he had yet to fire a shot. As the good sergeant predicted, there were discarded ramrods aplenty littering the field. He gathered up several just to be safe. Then, hurrying as quickly as he could, he clumsily loaded his own rifle—at his best he was fortunate to get off one round a minute—and aimed and fired in the same direction as his fellows into an advancing wall of acrid smoke. And again and again and again until he lost all sense of himself and the failing world around him except for the monstrous, demanding rifle, which actually seemed to him to be alive, a vast, imperious host, which for a spell was permitting his pathetic, parasitic self to serve its divine needs. A sliver of pride was starting to edge into awareness—he hadn't bolted, he was doing his duty—when a sharp blow to his buttocks sent him sprawling onto someone's sticky body. He twisted around to see Sergeant Wickersham towering over him like an enraged giant.

"Forward, you coward, keep moving forward."

"I was," Liberty replied, climbing unsteadily to his feet. "I was shooting."

"With that?" Wickersham gestured contemptuously toward Liberty's rifle, out of whose barrel protruded at least three twisted and bent ramrods. "Take this." He reached down to yank the rifle from Huff's dead hands. "He don't need it anymore. And all you're gonna need in about half a minute is the bayonet. Now, come on, get up there with the boys and drive these johnnies back into the Potomac."

Advancing now out of the smoke and fog came a whooping horde of demonic rebs who were upon the Federals in an instant. Men slashed at each other with bayonets and knives. Others, weaponless, squared off to beat on their opponents' skulls with bare fists. Fallen to the ground, pairs grappled furiously, fingers seeking to close windpipes or gouge out eyes. With a sudden, inhuman roar a section of the fence surrounding the cornfield simply blew up into a hail of needle-like splinters, blood and bits of pink flesh. A dazed Captain Dougherty staggered past, clutching at the gaping wound in his shoulder where a limb had once been attached.

"Sir!" cried Liberty. "Your arm!"

The captain glanced wanly at his injury. "I am aware, private, of my unfortunate condition. Let's see if you can attend properly to yours." And he went on rearward.

Someone bumped into Liberty, almost knocking him down, and he turned to see Cub O'Toole, a formerly meek professor's son from Rochester, swinging the butt of his musket hard into the surprised face of a teenaged reb. There was a sickening crunch and the boy went down as if all his leg strings had been simultaneously cut. "Liberty!" cried O'Toole. "Where you been? You're missing the dance!" But before Liberty could reply, O'Toole's eyes rolled abruptly upward as he seized his own neck in both hands, blood gushing between his fingers in an obscene torrent.

Then through the sulfurous haze, came a man running directly at Liberty. He was yelling something unintelligible and seemed quite angry, almost as if he'd taken a personal dislike to Liberty's appearance. His maddened features were smeared black with gunpowder and in his right hand he waved a big gleaming Bowie knife. As he leaped screaming upon Liberty with a strength and weight unimaginable, Liberty managed to grasp the man's knife hand with both of his and the two tumbled backward onto the slippery ground where they rolled around like dogs in the dirt, grunting, cursing, each grappling for control of the knife. "I'm going to kill you, Yank!" howled the reb, his hot, foul breath in Liberty's nostrils. He was attempting to force the sharp edge of the blade up against Liberty's larynx. "No you aren't!" countered Liberty, drawing on muscles he didn't know he had to push the knife at least a couple inches back from his pulsing skin.

They were frozen in a stilled moment of maximum tension, and Liberty didn't know how much longer he could fend off this man's determined desire to murder him when he heard a loud, commanding voice and looked up into the grim countenance of Arthur McGee. "Turn your head!" he ordered, and when Liberty obeyed he placed the end of his musket barrel against the back of the reb's head and coolly pulled the trigger. A warm stew of wet organic matter went spraying across Liberty's squinched face. McGee kicked the heavy body off of Liberty and graciously helped him to his feet. "Hate to see some damn secesh finish a job I aimed to complete." He flashed Liberty a tight, significant smile and then vanished into the fray.

Heart audibly racing, emotions as diverse and confused as the battle itself, Liberty instinctively understood that in his present, desperate situation the one thing he must not do is think. Thought tended to dice a moment, particularly a crucial one, into too many puzzling and disconnected fragments. He wiped his face on a trembling sleeve, retrieved his weapon and hastened on.

Bodies were piled up along the base of the cornfield fence like rejected sacks of spoiled potatoes. Astraddle the top rail was perched a dead man, hands still locked around the wood, feet twisted about the bottom bar. He appeared to be studying the far horizon with intent interest as if hopeful of assistance from that quarter. Liberty had lifted himself over the fence, careful not to dislodge this silent sentinel, when a major with a blood-soaked bandanna wrapped around his head dashed up and demanded, "What unit, boy?"

"Eighty-ninth New York, sir."

"Well, where the hell are they?"

"I don't know, sir."

"Jesus Christ Almighty. What a way to conduct a war. Move on up there, then. Close up that gap." And he slapped Liberty across the back with the flat of his sword.

Liberty took half a dozen steps before being accosted by the hideous shrieks of a wounded soldier who looked to be no more than twelve years old. He was missing both legs at the hips. Liberty paused to offer him a sip of water from his canteen, but the boy couldn't seem to keep the liquid down and his incessant screams prompted the thought that if the very walls of hell were cracked open with a chisel this was the noise the fiery rock itself would emit. He moved on.

In addition to the perpetual storm of nasty minies, shell and canister were repeatedly plowing the teeming field, filling the humid air with cobs, leaves, stalks and a goodly portion of mangled arms and legs.

"Devilish hot work, eh?" cried a Federal Liberty did not recognize, and who insisted on giving him a curiously demented wink. He was loading and firing his weapon without even bothering to take aim. "I've been back and forth over this same ground three times already!"

"Well," replied Liberty, "looks like you're about to do it again."

Despite the energetic efforts of a capless colonel to stem the retreat, the Union line suddenly broke in the face of yet another Confederate charge. Men simply dropped their rifles and ran for their lives. Before Liberty could even react he was clobbered in the left temple by a scrawny, toothless johnny whose only weapon was the rock he wielded in his filthy fist. The sky turned black, the stars jiggled in their courses and when full vision was finally restored, Liberty found himself prone amid the multitude of fallen soldiers in varying states of consciousness and, of course, most numerous, the ones possessing no consciousness whatsoever. The battle, apparently, had pressed on without him. His head, throbbing like the inside of a bell upon which the midnight had just been struck, felt huge and red, and before he could even struggle gamely to his feet he was surrounded by a raggedy-looking pack of unwashed johnnies whose rifles, he couldn't help noting, were all directed straight at him.

"That's one angry knot you got there, son," observed a tall man with eyes so arrestingly blue they seemed like clear pieces of summer sky.

Everyone ducked for a moment as a shell went sputtering a bit too low overhead.

"Rufus!" called the tall man.

"Yes, sir." Rufus was hardly more than a small freckled boy with thatch hair and bare feet and outfitted in what appeared to be a random sampling of soiled rags. The rifle he clutched in such ungainly fashion was twice as tall as he.

"Conduct this prisoner to the rear immediately."

"Why?"

"Because I said so, that's why."

"Sir," observed one soldier, anxiously scanning the far tree line. "Looks like they might be fixing to attack again."

"I thought we didn't take any prisoners," Rufus persisted.

"We're taking this one. Now go on, skedaddle."

"Fucking hell," the boy muttered, nudging Liberty in the back with his barrel. "Step lively, Yank. Ain't killed one of you birds yet and my finger's gettin' awful itchy."

"I'm in a poor way," Liberty complained. "How far do we have to go?"

"Shut your mouth, you stinking bluebelly. Now move your shanks." The barrel poked Liberty in the ribs.

"Aren't you a mite young for soldiering?"

"I'm older than I look."

"And what age is that, exactly?"

"None of your damn business."

"Quite a mouth on such an innocent tyke."

"It's all you Yankees' fault. Before this war a curse word never passed my lips. Now I swear like a Spanish trooper without even knowing I'm doing it. Seems to rile some folks sometimes."

"Why don't you stop?"

"Can't. Got the habit." A stray bullet lifted the cap right off Rufus's head without touching a hair.

"Holy shit!" cried Rufus. "Let's hoof it, Yank, 'fore you get killed by your own side."

In a half crouch they dashed through the dense choking smoke, stopped, turned, ran on again. All around them, now visible, now obscured, masses of howling men—from which army who knew?— shifted to and fro in clamorous confusion.

"Do you even know where the rear is in this mess?" yelled Liberty.

"No Yankee's gonna tell me I'm lost. You just head away from the noise."

"But the noise is all around us."

"I told you once to shut your pan." He raised his rifle threateningly. "Want a taste of the stock?"

Suddenly the air around them began to sing rather persistently and they found modest cover huddling together in a disappointingly shallow depression in the ground.

"This is the goddamndest thing I've ever seen," announced Rufus, "and I'm missing out on all the fun."

"We seem to be experiencing our fair share." Liberty could actually hear the bullets hitting the earth around them like one shovelful after another of tossed pebbles.

"Know why the old man ordered me back with you? He's sweet on my ma and don't want nothing to happen to me. I can't seem to ever get into the scrap. There's always some excuse for sending poor Rufus to the rear."

"What if I just up and bolted?"

A slow smile spread across Rufus's babyish features. "Well then, I reckon I'd have to pop you."

"Maybe you'd miss."

"I come from Alabamy, Yank, and you ain't ever seen any real dead-eyes if you've never been to our county's turkey shoot."

"I'm not a turkey."

"No," agreed Rufus, "but you'll do."

At a momentary lull in the metal storm overhead, they rose up cautiously from their hiding place and had barely taken a step when they were engulfed in a sea of blue uniforms.

"Well, lookee here," declared a big, bearded sergeant. "Drop the piece, reb."

Rufus's musket clattered to the ground as he obediently raised his hands.

"Glad to see you boys," said Liberty.

"Our pleasure," replied the sergeant. "Looks like you've been officially emancipated."

"What regiment?" asked a lieutenant.

"Eighty-ninth New York, sir."

"Don't believe there's many of them left. Heard they're out of it for the day. But as you can see, we need every body we can get. Sergeant Trask, find this man a musket and get the prisoner to the rear."

"I hope," Liberty couldn't help saying, "he has better luck finding it than Rufus here did."

The boy glared savagely back at him. "You best hope we never meet again, Yank. I owe you one."

"Yes, I know," answered Liberty. "Gobble, gobble, bang, bang."

Rufus, cursing furiously, was led roughly away.

"What was that all about?" asked the lieutenant.

"I think he was eying to put me on his dinner table."

"Them rebs," offered the sergeant. "They'll eat anything."

A rifle was abruptly thrust into Liberty's unwilling hands and he was placed in line between one private visibly trembling from "the cold" and another flushed and sweat-soaked from the heat.

"I wish," said the first, "that darn sun would get down out of the sky."

"Hell," replied the other. "It ain't even noon yet. You still got plenty of time to get killed in, don't you worry."

They both ignored Liberty, who was frankly somewhat stunned by the growing enormity of his situation, that fate had apparently decided, for whatever cryptic reasons, to send him waltzing through the hail yet one more time.

"Why are you always so blamed nice to me?"

The sweating private spat a stream of tobacco juice on the grass. "'Cause I love you so much, Huntzinger, can't you tell?"

Huntzinger, refusing to respond, turned away in disgust.

Orders were barked out and the line stepped bravely off, bodies slightly stiffened, heads bent, as if advancing into a bracing wind. Not twenty yards had been crossed when men began to topple like bowling pins. The balls whistled all around, the cannons continued to thunder, the combination as deafening as if a universe of boulders had gone rolling eternally down a great mountain. Before Liberty's astonished eyes Huntzinger's entire right shoulder and arm were torn away, and as the man fell Liberty could clearly see the exposed heart still throbbing in Huntzinger's crimsoning chest. Men emitted strange, harrowing cries one wouldn't have thought even a tortured animal capable of producing. Liberty felt one round pierce the sleeve of his jacket, another drill a hole in his canteen, sending a stream of water pouring down his leg. Regimental flags of both sides, all in a tangle, swayed wildly above the smoke as if these tattered pieces of gayly colored cloth themselves were principals in a contest to which humans were merely incidental. A man came crawling on all fours over the broken cornstalks, dragging his entrails behind him. "It's all right," he kept chanting, "it's all right."

The Confederate army loomed out of the haze ahead, and the line was halted. "Make leather out of 'em, boys!" shouted the lieutenant, and everyone bent to the repetitive task of loading and firing. The measured hysteria of their actions was accompanied by a mystical sense that the faster one worked, the more shots one fired, the safer one would be. They seemed now to be no longer men but transformed by the forge of battle into mechanical parts, identical cogs whirring inside some infernal engine whose demonic maker had not only fabricated but also personally selected each and every individual to serve his frankly evil needs.

Then, in the midst of this enveloping hell, Liberty spied a Confederate not thirty yards away leveling his rifle and taking dead aim at him, and he thought, I cannot believe this is happening to me, as all noise and fury fell away, faded into a nebulous cloud at the center of which vision concentrated solely on the enormous barrel and the hot-beaded squint behind it and time stopped as if the eye of a great tornado of iron were passing overhead and in that eerie interval of calm and silence he heard himself say, Now I am dead. He saw the muzzle flash and then nothing.

When he awoke he found himself seated on a hard, rather uncomfortable chair in a pleasantly furnished but foreign parlor. Across from him in a periwinkle blue rocking chair sat his mother or a woman who resembled Roxana in every significant detail from the creases on her face to the scattering of freckles across her nose and cheeks, but his sense of her, of her inner being, seemed of an order he had never experienced before. She had changed or perhaps he had changed, for she was now radiating a certain candlelike mellowness that had eluded her all her life.

"You look tired," she said in that instantly familiar, soothing, softly accented voice. "Have you been ill?"

"No," he answered, smiling slightly. He had never felt so happy. "It's been a long journey."

She nodded. "I know now the answer to your question."

"What question is that?"

"The one that so perplexed your boyhood. 'What color is the soul?' you kept asking. Well, I now know that it is the color of no-color."

"White?"

Her faint, wistful smile spoke of the traversal of vast distances, the abridgment of organic time. "There is no word adequate to describe the properties of the human soul. Its peculiar tincture can only be apprehended through the visionary optic." Her own magnetic eyes seemed to have grown larger, brighter. "Now, come here," she said, holding out her arms.

He went to her, and in her warm embrace, enfolded in the natural fragrance of her hair and skin, he rested in the peace that was the rock-solid core of a frantic world, and in the dozing tranquillity of that enchanted space he knew with absolute certainty that his mother was dead.

"Hey, pard," came the voice, at first faint and distant, but increasing rapidly in nearness and volume. "Are you all right?"

Liberty blinked and discovered himself staring up into the not unkindly face of a portly, blue-coated, tawny-bearded angel whose eyes possessed whites so pure, so amazingly uncontaminated, they seemed the cleanest spots on his essentially grimy person. "We thought you had pegged out for sure."

"Yeah," added the shorter man beside him, "we was about to dump you in the hole."

"Creased you good, didn't it?"

Liberty reached up to trace gingerly the extent of the burning furrow opened, interestingly enough, on the side of his head opposite to his previous wound. When he looked at his fingers they were coated in blood, as was, he now realized, the entire right half of his face.

"Guess it wasn't your turn yet. Reckon you can stand?"

Light was draining steadily from the sky and the dissonant decibels of war had been replaced by the subdued complaints of the injured and the melancholy scrape and clink of shovel and pick. Liberty studied the beaming countenances of his saviors, members obviously of a burial party, and asked, "Who won?"

The shorter man let out a contemptuous snort. "The Reaper," he replied.

Somehow, with the gentle assistance of his new friends Sergeant Weeks and Private Klinefelter, Liberty managed to stand erect and, between their arms, hobble painfully off the field.

In a barn filled from stalls to loft with the wounded, their laments, their effluvia, Liberty's head was cleaned and dressed. Laid out on a makeshift operating table—a door placed between a pair of sawhorses—one unfortunate casualty was undergoing the unanesthetized ordeal of having his left leg amputated. Ignoring the man's anguished but inventive oaths, the surgeon worked quickly, slicing away the meat in one continuous cut, then sawing through the bone, the entire procedure completed in less than a minute. "Hey, Fish!" cried the man as his stump was being sewn and bandaged. Amazingly, it was Private McGee. "Searched for you the rest of the day and look what happens to me."

"I'm sorry," said Liberty.

"Don't think for a second this little setback changes anything between us. No matter where you go, no matter what you do, ol' Pegleg McGee'll be right behind you. Watch your back."

"Good-bye, Mr. McGee," said Liberty. "I wish you well."

He went outside and sat on a bench in a kind of whirring stupor that was interrupted when the man beside him opened his mouth and, staring straight ahead, began to speak aloud to no one in particular. "I've not only seen the elephant, I've fed it, I've watered it, polished its tusks, swept up its droppings, and still, despite all my sweet attentions, the moment my back is turned, the damn beast tries to step on me, squash me flat." He raised the short wing that was all that remained of his left arm.

"Maybe now, after all this bloodletting," said Liberty hopefully, "it will finally end."

"And maybe I'll grow a new limb."

Then a passing doctor, noting Liberty's relatively functional condition, brusquely ordered him back to his regiment.

"Where is it?" Liberty asked.

"How the hell should I know? That's your lookout."

Reluctantly, he got to his feet and, carrying his pounding head as if it were a basket of rare delicacies, his vision still somewhat blurred, he wandered through the night until the futility of attempting to locate his unit in this utterly disorganized darkness overcame him entirely and he slumped to earth beneath a ragged apple tree, its crop picked clean by iron hands.

At daybreak he roamed, for as long as he could bear it, across the desolated field. In hours this once pastoral landscape had been translated into the interior of a butcher shop after the fall slaughter. Bodies were already beginning to bloat and blacken in the rising sun. A hatless major sat on the ground weeping, "My boys, my beautiful boys." Liberty thought of the thousands of souls, most of them probably still undeveloped, who had departed the planet forever from this now haunted and sacred place, and then wondered if God were actually as deaf and dumb as He often seemed. In a corner of the field a spotted pig was energetically rooting beneath the exposed rib cage of a fallen soldier, the bloody remains shaking like a husk in the animal's stained jaws.

One week later, the army still encamped in a massive sprawl along the banks of the Potomac, the letter from home arrived. Liberty would always remember, until the day he, too, died, the smell of frying bacon, the laughter from the boys playing cards, the sight of his scarred and dirty hands clutching the paper, the shadow of his head falling across the sheet as he read:

My Dear Son,

This is the most difficult letter it has ever been
my painful duty to compose. I scarcely know
where or how to begin....

Then his eye went leaping rapidly ahead, consuming the news in
phrases that entered him like a barber's razor: "mother's distresses
growing progressively worse . . . a communication from Carolina
blaming her for the war . . . traitor to the country, traitor to the
family . . . disinherited forever . . . distraught, your mother went
for a ride . . . the carriage found below the upper bridge . . . broken
neck . . . death instantaneous . . ."

Liberty sat on the biscuit box outside his tent until the sun sank
and was sitting there still when it rose again the following morning.
All around him, as the army awakened to another dull round of
drilling and loafing, life, oddly enough, continued on, but he was no
longer a part of it. He drifted through the days like an automaton,
performing his duties without awareness or reflection.

The following week he asked Major Hudson, the cartographer, for
a map of South Carolina.

The road was red and the sky was blue and they'd been hours on the march, toiling through the empty Georgia countryside, the billowing clouds of fine coppery dust that stung their eyes and choked their throats and gilded their sweaty faces giving them the appearance of exhausted, ill-tempered devils. At rest halts they would collapse on the needle-carpeted ground in the mentholated shade of the thick pine and lie there gasping like beached fish until the order came to rise and move on. A trio of mounted officers came galloping down the line, stirring up more dust, the flanks of the horses coated with the dry red powder. "Look," declared one of the reclining men, "it's Uncle Billy." "Who gives a rat's ass?" asked another, not even bothering to open his eyes. "I'll give all my worldly goods to buy his horse," submitted a third, an offer whose innate preposterousness occasioned a few mild chuckles. "I'll give my left ball," said another, "to be home lying in my own cool bed." Then Sergeant Ainsworth began passing among them, kicking at their feet, and they struggled up and started down the road again. The dust rising from the long column appeared, even from miles away, like a lowering cloud of red smoke.

Late in the afternoon the rain began and fell all night and into the following day. The road dissolved into a buttery paste that buried wagon wheels up to the hubs and clutched at their heavy feet and legs. By the time they arrived at the river it was swollen enough to be threatening its banks. The bridge was still passable and the army narrowed into one thin file picking its slow, careful way over the wet, slippery planks. Halfway across Major Pickles's personal wagon slipped a wheel over the edge and the metal coffin in the bed started sliding out. Several men leaped forward and, cursing and groaning, heaved the entire wagon back onto the bridge and the stalled column moved on. Finally the rain stopped and they were settling into camp for the night when the major called for his men to gather round.

"I appreciate your efforts, boys," he said, patting the metal lid of the casket. "You know how much this box means to me. I understand it's been a godawful trial for the whole regiment carrying this clumsy thing along with us, but me and my family will be forever grateful for your assistance. So as the merest token of my gratitude, I'd like you all to fetch your canteens, your cups, your hats, and everybody take a dip." He unscrewed the lid of the coffin, all-aluminum, rustproof, waterproof, eternity-guaranteed, which he had brought with him from home, dragged through five major campaigns, in the event he was called to glory and his earthly remains could be shipped back to Elmira in as sweet a condition as possible, but until that tragic day serving admirably as a first-rate barrel for the major's private stock of fine whiskey his men were now scooping out so enthusiastically.

"Hurry, boys," cautioned the major. "Exposure to the elements dilutes the quality."

So there was much drunkenness in camp that night. A fight broke out among the cooks over frying rights to a stray chicken and in the ensuing melee a stove was overturned and a large pot of soup was lost to the porous sandy soil. Men could be heard singing tunes sentimental or bawdy well into the gray dawn. In the morning Private Duffie was found drowned, lying facedown in a puddle of rusty water two inches deep.

Liberty lay awake most of the night listening to the water dripping off the trees onto the tent canvas. He thought of his childhood nights in bed under the eaves and the comforting sound of the rain on the roof and thought about his father and his aunt and Euclid and how they were and what they could be doing. Then he started thinking about that other home, the one he'd never seen or visited but in his imagination. Georgia, he thought, I'm in Georgia. He was as close to that other place as he'd ever been in his life. He took out his own set of maps, kept in a waterproof pack in his pocket, and marked off with a pencil the miles traversed today. His map of South Carolina was pristine but for a small black X denoting a spot on the Stono River. He folded up the maps and put them and the pencil back in his pocket.

Otis Dodds, an amiable lad also from the North Country, was stretched out next to him reading a yellow-jacketed dime novel entitled *The Gold Fiend*, pausing periodically to read aloud his favorite parts. He'd read the book twice before and was fond of recommending its myriad pleasures to all who would listen. "'I advanced with great stealth toward the locked door,'" he began, "'and bending forward applied my curious eye to the keyhole and what I saw in the adjoining room beggars—'"

"Otis," drawled Liberty, "if you read to me one more time from that wretched novel, I'm gonna rip up the pages and toss 'em into the fire."

"Easy there, Liberty, go easy, boy. It's too wet and I'm too tired to have to get up and give you another good licking."

"Since when did you ever give me a good licking?"

"You don't remember? A year ago I believe it was. Back in Pennsylvania, or maybe it was Virginia. I get all these damned states mixed up by now. I reckon it was the day of the big regimental rough-and-tumble. You hit me in the head with a rock."

"It was a mistake. I was aiming at Beetclaw."

"Well, so you say."

"Yes, and I'll say it again if you want."

"Don't get touchy with me or we'll have to commence another go-round right here in this damn tent."

"Suits me," said Liberty, rolling over and turning his back on his friend.

Eventually, without speaking, they drifted off separately into sleep. Liberty's dreams, at least the one he remembered since joining the army, always seemed to be the same. He is walking down a deserted country road, rolling green fields on either hand, a modest farmhouse, a clump of trees in the distance. A pretty young woman in the doorway beckons to him. But when he arrives at the house, she has disappeared and all the rooms are empty. A table has been set, though, for one place, a platter piled high with chicken and ham and turkey and boiled potatoes and a tall glass of cold milk, but once he sits down to eat the meal has vanished. Suddenly he is upstairs in a bedroom, a mild breeze blowing at the white lace curtains. He feels unaccountably sad and quite tired, so he stretches out on the big clean bed and falls asleep and dreams he is awake and his still body covered entirely with reptiles.

"Hey, doghead, wake up!" It was Sergeant Ainsworth's bewhiskered face peering into the tent. "Cap'n wants to see you two buzzards right away."

They struggled up out of their bedding and stood blinking groggily in the foggy dawn, warily eying each other and deciding, no, not yet, too early to speak.

Captain Roe was seated on a barrel under a dripping oak tree. Gathered around him were Lieutenant Wills and privates Strickling and Vail. The captain glanced up, arching an eyebrow. "Glad to see you gentlemen could join us for breakfast." Liberty and Otis remained silent. "Actually, there is no breakfast, which is what I wish to speak to you about. The general has issued orders giving us permission to send out foraging parties and since none of you, with the possible exception of Wills here, has shown much aptitude for the various other aspects of soldiering, I thought I'd give you all a chance to try your hand at officially sanctioned thievery. How does that square with you?"

A mumbled chorus of vague assent.

"I thought this task might meet with your approval. I'm sure I don't have to tell you what we need. Lieutenant Wills will supervise the operation. Don't take more than you can carry, and civilians and private property are to remain untouched. Understand?"

More mumbles.

"I'm looking forward to a grand supper, boys. Don't disappoint me. And, boys, keep a weather eye out for Wheeler's cavalry. Don't want to find any of you lying in a ditch with your throats slit."

They all agreed they would do what they could to forestall that particular fate.

The day was cool and pleasant and they followed the road out of camp. The land flat, empty and eerily quiet.

The first farmhouse they came to was deserted. A dead dog was sprawled in the yard, the gaping wound in its side black with flies. A silver tray and bowl had been nailed to a tree and riddled with bullets. Inside, the rooms had been ransacked, the furniture broken up, holes punched in the walls.

"Nothing for us here," observed Wills, a short skinny man who wore a pair of hexagonal spectacles and possessed the abstracted look of an overworked scholar. The men called him Professor.

"I ain't giving up so easy," said Strickling and ran upstairs where the others could hear his boots tramping about the floor and the sound of objects being hurled about.

"This place has been licked clean," said Vail, rooting through a pile of torn clothing in the corner, "unless you're in the market for a spanking new blue baby bonnet." And he clapped said article atop his shaggy head.

On the mantelpiece in a broken frame was a daguerreotype of a young woman with ringleted hair and intelligent eyes and a serious mouth. Liberty, wondering who she was and where she could be or whether she was even alive, removed the picture from the frame and shoved it into his pocket.

"Got yourself a girlfriend?" asked Otis.

Liberty didn't answer.

"Probably a cousin," joked Vail. "Ain't you got rebel kin all over the damn South?"

"Enough to teach you some manners before you go skedaddling back to Buffalo."

"Save your powder," suggested Wills. "Lord knows what we'll be needing 'fore the sun sets on this day."

"It's all right," said Vail, exhibiting his toothless smile. "I like this little secesh, always will."

"I like you, too," said Liberty, "you knock-kneed cross-eyed son of a bitch."

Vail beamed. He seemed to enjoy being insulted, and a good gibe at his expense was for him as good a way as any of ending a disagreement.

Strickling came stumbling down the stairs with a peacock feather in his hat. "Someone poured molasses on the bed up there," he reported.

"Are you sure that's molasses?" asked Otis.

"Hell," declared Vail, "this sucker's all played out."

"Yes," agreed Wills. "Let's move on."

As they ambled away from the house, Strickling turned and fired his revolver, shooting out the glass in an upstairs window. He laughed. The others looked at him, but no one said a word.

A mile or so down the road they encountered an aged black man with white hair in a tattered coat and pants, wrapped rags for shoes. He was hurrying briskly along and singing in a booming voice. As soon as he spied the Union soldiers, he grinned and waved his hand.

"One of your friends, Liberty?" asked Vail.

"Uncle!" Wills called out. "Any johnnies about?"

"No, Master!" the man declared emphatically. "They lit out soon's we heard you was coming." He couldn't stop grinning. "Yankees," he said, and let out a laugh, as if the very word tickled his mouth. "Never thought these old eyes would live to get filled with the sight of you people."

"Any big plantations out this way?" asked Wills.

"Oh, yes, Master. You just keep on and you'll come right up to Missus Sarah's."

"Any bluecoats been there yet?"

"No, Master, but the missus, she and the children, they're back there expecting you all."

"She got any food for us?"

"Oh, yes, Master, got it all buried under the trees out back. Made up to look like a grave, but that's where the food is hid."

"You don't have to call anyone 'master' anymore," said Liberty.

"Why, yes sir, you are powerful right about that, but I expect that's gonna be a tight tooth to pull out of my head."

"What are you doing out here all alone?" asked Otis.

"Why looking for you people, sir. I'm looking to join up; I'm in it for the duration."

"We don't need your help," snapped Vail. "None of this is any of your business."

"Oh, Master, I expect it surely is."

"We're fighting to save the Union," said Strickling, "not your scrawny ass."

"Yes, Master, but I've been pondering a long spell and I expect this here war has something to do with slavery."

"Bullcrap," said Vail. "You darkies seem to think everything in the whole damn country is about you."

"It is," said Liberty.

"By God," exclaimed Vail, raising his rifle. "Don't start up with me again or I'll bust your crust, send you both to hell in each other's arms. You'd probably like that, wouldn't you, you goddamn nigger lover."

Liberty leaped at Vail, thrusting the rifle aside, and managed to get both hands around his neck as they fell back into the dirt. As Liberty squeezed, Vail's head reddened and swelled. "Get off him," said Otis, pulling Liberty away by the shoulders. Vail sat up gasping and coughing. "You ever touch me again," he warned, "and I'll open you up, you little shit, from your chops to your balls."

"Mind your language and your manners," answered Liberty, "and you won't have cause."

"Either of you try that again and I'll finish it for you," promised Wills. "We've got enough enemy in front of us without turning on one another."

In the distance the old man could be seen hobbling frantically away, toward the Union lines and his hope of becoming a soldier.

The foraging party moved on in the opposite direction in a tense silence, Vail rubbing repeatedly at his neck.

"Want my bandanna for a bandage?" cracked Strickling. He seemed to regard the entire fracas as a hilarious joke.

"You're next, you shit-filled louse," growled Vail.

Three miles on they came to a fine-looking two-story white house set amid a grove of oak and magnolia trees. A gaunt woman with stern, pale features stood on the veranda flanked by several children of various genders and ages, all gazing upon the approaching foe with countenances suitable to a bereaved family waiting on a station platform for an overdue train. A pair of female slaves hovered anxiously in the doorway.

Wills advanced and, tipping his hat, said, "Missus Sarah, I presume?"

Nothing moved on the veranda but the woman's lips. "Yes," she said. "I would expect nothing less of a boorish Yankee than to boldly address a lady to whom he has never been properly introduced by her Christian name. It is indeed the height of presumption."

"Then I apologize, ma'am. You see, we met a black man down the road a ways and that was the only name he gave us."

"White hair, filthy coat, half an ear missing?"

"I believe that would serve as an adequate description."

"Hiram, that black bastard. If you had searched his person you would have found most of my fine silverware tied in bags beneath his clothing."

"Damn!" Strickling blurted. "I thought I heard something jingling as he trotted off."

"Yes," the woman said. "You Yankees are all in for a great surprise once you free all these people and have them living and working among you. Good, I say. It's what you deserve."

"Might I inquire," ventured Wills politely, "as to whom I have the honor of addressing?"

"I am Mrs. Sarah Popper and these are my children, Brett, Wade, Thomas and Liza." Again, no one stirred. The children looked like painted statues assembled on the veranda for decorative purposes.

"Pleased to make your acquaintance, Mrs. Popper. I am Lieutenant Wills, and me and my boys have come to respectfully ask what food-stuffs you have readily available on the property here. We have been authorized to requisition whatever eatables we deem appropriate. We've come a long way, you see, and we're mighty hungry."

"And who granted this authorization?"

"General Sherman, ma'am."

"I recognize neither the man nor his authority and would like for you all to depart at once."

"Sorry you feel that way, Mrs. Popper, because frankly, ma'am, your opinion on this issue is irrelevant."

"If I were a man you wouldn't dare speak to me like this."

"No, ma'am, I wouldn't, because if you were a man I probably would've shot you stone dead by now." He turned around. "Boys, search the property."

Vail and Strickling started immediately for the house while Liberty and Otis headed for the barn and outbuildings.

"Are you currently married, Mrs. Popper?" Wills asked as Vail and Strickling pounded up the front steps, shouldering past the frightened slaves huddled in the doorway, Vail muttering, "Out of the way, you black bitch," as he brushed by.

"Yes, Lieutenant Wills, I am married," admitted Mrs. Popper, hugging her teary-eyed daughter to her side.

"Where is your husband?"

"He's away, proudly fighting for his country."

"Any other men about?"

"Only the servants, those that are left, and right now I don't know how many that could be. Hush now," she said to her daughter, patting the child tenderly on the back. "I suppose you have accomplished your aim, Lieutenant Wills, of frightening defenseless women and making little children cry. We always knew this is what we could expect from you soulless Yankees."

"Oh now, don't be so modest. I'm sure there's much more you could expect from us, but let's hope everybody stays good and chirky so you won't have to witness it. Good day, ma'am," he said, and touching his cap he moved past her into the house.

Out in the barn Liberty and Otis discovered a sick cow with slatted ribs and a large festering sore on its belly.

"I don't know if I'd even want to eat that beef," said Otis, "no matter how hungry I was."

"I'm sure we've chewed on worse," said Liberty.

"But I don't suppose this is what the captain had in mind when he spoke of a 'grand supper.'"

"No, and it appears to be all these poor folks have left. Good excuse to just move on and leave 'em alone."

At the sound of rustling behind a pile of hay Otis swiveled about, his rifle raised. "All right now," he called, "come on out of there now." A pair of black children emerged blinking into the light, stems of hay stuck in their hair, grain sacks with holes cut out for the head and arms serving for clothing.

"Well, well," declared Otis, "what have we here? Rebel spies?"

The children's eyes grew larger.

"What are your names?" asked Liberty.

"Posey," answered the taller of the two. "This is my baby sister, Bowzer."

"What kind of name is that for a little girl? Who gave your sister such a name?"

"Why, Master did, sir. He gives out all the names."

"Where is Master now?"

"Off killing them Yankees. He been killing 'em for near three years now."

Otis laughed. "Well, I guess he hasn't got all of 'em yet."

"Are you all Yankees?"

"We were when we woke up this morning. Who'd you think we were?"

"You going to cook and eat us?"

"No, certainly not," said Liberty. "Who filled your head with such nonsense?"

"Missus Sarah said you folks liked black meat 'cause it was nice and tender from being raised up so good."

"Sounds like the missus needs a hard lesson or two of Yankee schooling," said Otis.

"None of you is going to be harmed," Liberty assured the children. "We've come to free you, not hurt you."

"Are we free?" asked Posey.

"Yes."

The girls stared in disbelief at each other. "Let's go tell Mama," said Posey, and both went scampering barefoot out the barn door.

When Liberty and Otis emerged they saw clouds of dark smoke boiling out of the rear windows of the house, Mrs. Popper and her children silently watching the destruction of their home at a distance, Vail and Strickling off in a grove of trees jabbing their bayonets repeatedly into the ground and Lieutenant Wills seated calmly in a chair in the yard, observing the flames and gnawing on a hock of ham. "Over here, boys," he called. "Requisitioned some fresh rations from the larder." On the ground at his feet were a dead turkey, a bag of dried peaches, a bunch of carrots, a couple onions, a jar of honey and a bottle of peach brandy from which he imbibed freely. "Ain't much," he confessed, "but Vail and Strickling are out prospecting for the rest of it. After a bit of coaxing, Mrs. Popper here kindly offered to share her bounty with us. Anything out in the barn?"

"Nothing but a peaked cow," said Otis.

"That's okay. I expect Vail and Strickling are about to strike the main lode any minute now." He held out the bottle. "Care for a tasty slug of Georgia juice?"

"No thanks, sir," said Liberty.

"Don't mind if I do," Otis said, stepping forward.

"Why has the house been fired?" Liberty asked. "I thought we were under orders to respect all civilian property."

"Well, Private Fish, ordinarily that would be the case, but this Mrs. Popper, you see, is something of an unregenerate secesh prone to a powerful lot of disrespect toward uniformed representatives of the government of the United States. In all the commotion someone accidently dropped a match. Wasn't nothing of any value in that cracker-box, anyway. These dirt-eaters put on a fine show, but once you get inside you discover it's all bluff and fudge and the whole damn operation's made out of sand and hot air. We've been bamboozled, gentlemen, and nothing for it now but to sit down and enjoy the show."

"Lieutenant Wills," called Mrs. Popper, clutching her frightened children about her, as if posing for a portrait of motherhood besieged, "where do you propose I and my family spend the night?"

"Try the slave quarters," cracked Wills. "Haven't touched a single one of those cabins and don't plan to. Don't know how you feel about sharing a bed with Sambo and Dinah, but I reckon your husband was quite accustomed to it, so I believe you could make the necessary adjustments, too." He laughed and pulled at the bottle of brandy.

"I hope you, Lieutenant Wills," said Mrs. Popper, "and your minions end up burning in hell where you belong."

"I don't dispute you, Mrs. Popper, but wherever I may end up the fire's going to be of a cooler temperature than the one you'll eventually find yourself in."

The house, a mere skeletal frame within the shifting body of flame, seemed about to take a step forward when suddenly the entire structure simply collapsed in a great sigh and an eruption of sparks. All the Popper children were huddled protectively around their mother and all were in tears.

A whoop went up from the grove of pecan trees and Vail called out that he had indeed struck paydirt: a brace of fat porkers, a turkey, a couple chickens, a case of whiskey, a barrel of molasses, a peck of potatoes, a sack of meal and, lordy be, a bag of gold coin.

"Grand dining tonight, eh, gentlemen?"

"I beg you, Lieutenant," asked Mrs. Popper, "to please leave us something to eat. That's the only food left on the plantation."

"Should have thought of that before you seceded," said Wills.

"Have you Yankees no heart at all?"

"Hardened, ma'am, in the forge of war. And if you think this is bad, wait till you see what happens when we get to Carolina."

Liberty walked over to where Mrs. Popper stood trembling in rage

and grief, leaned down, kissed her on the forehead and without looking back, kept on walking out to the road.

"Private Fish," called Wills, "where in holy damnation do you
think you're going?"

There was no reply.

"Dodds," asked the lieutenant, "where is Private Fish going?"

"I don't know," said Otis.

"Well, don't that beat all."

They watched Liberty moving steadily up the road until finally he
was lost in the drifting clouds of smoke from the burning house.

It was strange after years of tramping through the countryside in the company of a vast horde of armed and boisterous men for Liberty to find himself alone on an empty road rambling through a landscape from which all living presence had apparently fled. No cows in the pasture, no chickens in the yard, no pigs at the trough, not even a single insect chirping in the grass. Ragged columns of black smoke stood at random intervals on the far horizon, and once he thought he saw a party of mounted riders racing across a distant meadow—or were they merely the shadows of passing clouds, movement of any kind in this time and place readily assuming the appearance of war? He possessed no food, no water, and clad in the blue uniform of his army he was solitarily adrift in the territory of what? The enemy? The adversary? The disowned cousin? There was no adequate language. Because deep down abided a preternatural conviction he could not be harmed on this ground. He was not an invader, he wasn't even a trespasser, he was a son of the soil returning home on a singular odyssey that seemed to have been prepared for him long before his birth.

He rested for a while in the shade of a dry creek bed beneath a decrepit wooden bridge, carefully unfolding and reexamining his tattered map. He was tending, as he knew, in the proper general direction, but had no idea how long the journey would take. He had no plan. He would allow what was going to happen to simply happen. In his mind he viewed this excursion—which he realized could be regarded as desertion, a capital offense—as only a temporary detour from military duty, though, of course, other deserters had their reasons, too.

Back in the spring outside Chattanooga he and his brigade had been turned out in the rain to witness the execution of another such individual thinker, a boy even younger than himself who, discovering war not to his liking, had decided independently to give up his place in the ranks and head back up north where trees didn't explode and no metal fell from the sky. He had kept so to himself that few even knew his name, much less that his father, without consulting the rest of the family, had summarily signed him up for a soldier despite the boy's bad eyesight, clumsy hands and skin so pale that, refusing to tan, it turned painfully redder and redder throughout the long last summer. He was the lad who cried himself to sleep every night, his muffled sobs audible to those lying awake in their tents several company streets away. Under his first fire, a brief skirmish prior to the lead storm of Chickamauga, the boy dropped to the ground behind a fallen log, body curled tight as a doodlebug, and refused to budge—a position he immediately assumed whenever shots were fired, lightning cracked, or even at the sudden utterance of a loud oath during a heated faro game. And then one bright cold morning he was gone, having slipped away unnoticed during the night. A patrol of Kilpatrick's cavalry discovered him later that same day, soaking his naked body in a secluded mill pond. Coming upon a hive of bees and hungry for honey, he had attempted to help himself over the swarm's angry protests. When the troopers brought him back into camp, tied to a saddle, his face was swollen up big as a melon and he could see out of only one eye. They held a court-martial the following day and shot him the next.

At the report of the executioners' rifles, Liberty had closed his eyes. And he kept his gaze averted during a pensive meal around the fire with his glum comrades, this rather emphatic demonstration of military justice having blackened the mood for days to come. What Liberty's fate would be for a similar transgression he could not even begin to guess. All he did know, and this with a granite certainty, was that this mad course which now placed his own life in positive jeopardy seemed a divine necessity because finally what choice did he have but to follow the trail of his mother's tears.

He came then to what could only be characterized as a shell of a town, grocery and groggery, church and cooper, all yet untouched by the vandal's hand, standing mute and abandoned in the hazy Georgia sun, Liberty sat slumped in a chair before the saloon (F. T. Wade & Son, Whiskey 5¢ A Glass) musing upon the sad desolation of the place. Devoid of their usual human traffic, the buildings seemed to have naturally lapsed back into their original being, as if they had been constructed for some other purposes entirely and were now patiently awaiting their rightful inhabitants. Even as a child Liberty had known—though he couldn't begin to say how—that this world was not what it seemed, that closely hidden behind the mundane affairs of the day lurked layer upon unexamined layer of outright strangeness, of which what passed for ordinary was merely the protective outer covering, the skin, so to speak, of a beast so huge, so vital, it could never be discerned whole in all its proportions. This vacant town was permitting him a modest peek.

As he brooded, a mangy, emaciated dog with patchwork fur slunk out from beneath the boards of the dry goods store opposite (T. Worth, Ladies Finery, Linen, Bijoux), gave Liberty a sidelong glance and tottered off on spindly drunken legs. Aroused by this first sign of life, Liberty heaved himself out of his chair, crossed the deserted street and entered the store. Inside, the shelves were stripped, rolls of cloth unfurled across the floor and the great brass cash register tipped upside down in a spreading pool of dark molasses. In the back office he discovered a forgotten half jug of peach brandy at whose mouth he sniffed cautiously—his nose after months of field experience having developed a fine sensitivity to questionable food and drink. Successfully passing the olfactory test, the sour liquid was poured without stop down Liberty's parched, bobbing throat. When he was finished, he coughed once and spit on the floor. Outside the grimy window he noticed a dark figure scuttling across the back lot into the yawning doorway of a disheveled barn, and then came another loping close to the ground, but by the time Liberty went creeping out to the barn to investigate, rifle at the ready, the men, if such they were, had disappeared. Was he already, lonely castaway in this wide and lonesome country, beginning to lose his faculties, glimpse things that weren't there, like Crenshaw had after gobbling down a tin of bad oysters?

He wandered on to the edge of town, where on a well-tended plot of ground stood a large, pleasant-looking white frame house with a neatly painted sign affixed to the rail of the veranda: Mrs. Porter's Rooming House, All Boarders Welcome. He climbed the worn wooden steps and discreetly approached the front door, which swung easily open at his touch. The interior was dim and lavishly appointed, and not a single vase, painting or fringed pillow seemed to have been disturbed. A vague smell of, oddly enough, gingerbread hung like a kind of aromatic bunting over the silent shadows of each room. On a polished mahogany table in the hallway rested an exotic potted plant of a species he had never encountered before, its thick, hairy stalk drooping over in a sad, upside-down U. Floorboards creaking softly beneath his heavy army brogans, he explored the house, expecting nothing, finding nothing, until upstairs, behind a half-open door, he discovered an elderly man stretched out upon a narrow unmade bed and wrapped in a bloodied Stars and Bars, his face gone from the white beard up, a shotgun lying carelessly across his stilled chest. A busy host of wasps and flies moved in and out of the dark cavity in his skull, greedily feeding upon the sweet treasures within.

"Rest easy, Pop," muttered Liberty, softly closing the door.

The other chambers were empty, the beds, too, and somewhat apprehensive about lying down in a house where death was already taking a nap he spent the night on a pile of malodorous straw in an abandoned livery stable, the doors wide open at both ends. If it was sleep that visited him on that ammoniac nest it came in the shape of a ragged spirit with coals for eyes and a hot, foul breath that whispered into the snarled labyrinth of his soul the singsong lessons of an infernal primer he was failing repeatedly to memorize: *A is for Abolition, Fiery tracks to perdition, B is for Black, Drowned white cats in a sack.*

At first light he rose up, muscles and joints stiff and weary, and staggered out into the morning mist in which no sun could be discerned, no bird heard to call, the country shrouded in fog and bleak silence, as if he had awakened upon a featureless plateau high up in the clouds. Around him the visible universe was reduced to a shifting circle no more than twenty feet in diameter. The road came toward him, magically materializing out of the gauze ahead, fading away into the gauze behind. He felt diminished in size, as though he were a simple weevil boring determinedly through the largest boll in all creation. Sounds periodically assailed him from off in the murky distance, the rattle of metal on metal, the leathery creak of tack and saddle, a muffled cough—noises without origin or consequence.

When, several hours later, the enveloping obscurity burned away, Liberty found himself strolling between the sturdy columns of a vast pine forest, its scented shade shielding him momentarily from the augmenting heat of the day. Then, as if by chance, he happened to glimpse deep in the shadowy tangle of these woods the unmistakable man-made geometry of a human dwelling. Cautiously, rifle raised, he approached what appeared to be, beneath an awkwardly arranged camouflage of leaves and branches, a tiny cabin, its roof listing precariously to one side as if leaned upon by a giant hand.

"Hold," commanded a reedy voice at his back. "Throw down your arm and come about so I can take a gander at ye."

Liberty let his rifle clatter to the ground, raised his hands and slowly turned around. From behind a mossy boulder some twenty yards away stepped a red-whiskered man no bigger than a boy. He was wearing a crumpled cap, a flannel shirt and pants that stopped halfway down his hairless calves, his skin an unwholesome yellowy tinge and his eyes as pale as wood chips. The battered Enfield he held in his childish hands was aimed directly at Liberty's chest.

"Well, Lord skin a goat," he declared, animated points of light suddenly rising in the moons of his eyes, "if you ain't a genuine Yankee after all. Say something to me, I want to hear what a real one sounds like."

"Put down your piece," replied Liberty in a voice so unexpectedly calm he hardly recognized it as his own. "There's a whole army behind me, so you'll hear soon enough what Yankees sound like."

"Is that Boston or New York?" asked the stranger, the barrel of his rifle still dead level.

"It's Fish," answered Liberty. "Might you please put down your weapon?"

"Never heard of no city called Fish. Where's Fish at?"

"It's my name."

"That so? Knew a Fish over at Atkins Bend. Hung himself with a shackle chain when his wife run off with a pedlar's son. You any kin to him?"

Liberty shrugged. "Fishes seem to be quite common in every part of the sea."

"That's a good one, young fellow," replied the stranger, chuckling dryly into his beard. "Always knew you Yankees was sharp." He lowered his gun and stepped forward, hand extended. "Ellsberry Simms, at your service."

"Liberty Fish." The man's grip was surprisingly strong and vigorous.

"Now there's a moniker to choke a tyrant on. Come on inside. I got something to show ye."

"May I be permitted to retrieve my rifle?"

"Leave it be. Ain't nobody gonna disturb it out here."

Liberty looked skeptical. "That's property of the United States government. I'm responsible for it."

"Well," said Simms, stooping to pick up the gun, "certainly don't want you getting into any trouble with General Sherman, now do we? Appears you're probably in enough trouble already. Follow me." Then he disappeared through an exceedingly low doorway into the curious interior of his rude cabin.

The single room, not much wider than the span of one man's outstretched arms, was a space of astonishing cleanliness, the walls whitewashed to a blinding sheen, the plank floor swept and polished, and hanging above the scrubbed hearth a pristine Stars and Stripes and a framed lithograph of President Lincoln. In the center of the room was a bare table and a pair of chairs in which they sat formally facing one another.

"Got any coffee?" asked Simms.

Liberty shook his head. "Sorry."

"Didn't think you would, but no harm in asking, is there?"

"Last true coffee I tasted was a couple weeks ago."

"Thought you Yankees came equipped with everything from sacks of fresh beans to the mill to grind them with, but you, Mr. Fish, don't look like you even got a crust of bread hidden in your hat."

"I'm afraid you've been slightly misinformed as to the bounty we travel with. Actually, none of us in this army is carrying much more than our personals. We are expected to live off the land as per General Sherman's instructions."

Simms arched an eyebrow. "That so? Well, I imagine you've found precious little to graze upon in this desolate country."

"You'd be surprised."

"So I would. I've tried for four long years and more to suck sustenance out of this bitter soil, and you behold before you the fruits of such futile endeavor." From a nearby sideboard he produced a tin box which he opened and offered in Liberty's direction. "Care for a hush puppy?"

Liberty held one of the doughy balls to his nose and sniffed.

"Perfectly fine," said Simms. "Daughter brings 'em by once a week or so. Doesn't want the old man starving to death out here in his hovel in the wilderness."

"What are you doing alone in the woods anyway, if I might ask?"

Simms couldn't help but smile. "Sometimes ask myself the very same question. Truth of the matter is, I've seceded."

"Seceded?"

"Yes sir, seceded from the secession. Back in '60 when we went out of the Union, I decided to go out of Georgia. Couldn't stomach the whole business. Made me sick to think about it then, makes me sicker today. But this scant little plot of earth you occupy at present I have reclaimed in the name of the Republic and the Union forever. You stand on free soil here and it will remain free as long as I am capable of drawing an honest breath."

"Must have been a hard judgement to come to."

"Terrible hard. Lost my family, lost my farm. They run me off of it, sir, run me off my own property."

"How could they do that?"

"With guns and torches, my friend, that's how. Suspected me of arming the niggers. Lucky to have escaped with my life."

"What an incredible tale."

"Oh, there's plenty of folks like me from one end of the state to the other. Most of 'em learned right quick to keep their chawholes shut. Me? Never was much good at holding my tongue. Couldn't abide the silence." Suddenly he raised a hand and cocked his head. "Hush, hush now," he cautioned, listening intently. "Horses on the way. You best get on down in here." Hastily he pushed the table to one side, pulled up a trap in the floor and motioned for Liberty to jump in the hole. Then the door dropped and Liberty was plunged into a darkness so complete it mattered not whether his startled eyes were open or closed. He seemed to hear, as if from a great distance, the rumble of male voices, their sound baffled, their import indecipherable. Time passed. He speculated on the quantity of air available to him in this tomb and how long he could bear squatting here in gloomy dampness before his thriving sense of suffocation and claustrophobia caused him to leap franticallly free like a lunatic from his cell. Gently raising a shoulder, he tried the door. It was locked. Now what? He decided to wait another five minutes or so before attempting a more rigorous escape. Mentally counting off the seconds, he began to notice that the surrounding darkness was not the dense, solid block of obsidian it had originally appeared to be but was, in fact, a shifting panorama of shapes and shades of diverse complexity and depth, and that within these murky subtleties swam forms of a creepily animated character. Curiously, shutting his eyes produced no variation whatsoever in the effect, outer and inner natures absolutely indistinguishable, while consciousness, that dim instrument, seemed for the moment little more than a tenuous fulcrum precariously balanced between two equally disturbing worlds. As hordes of terrible white bugs went swirling about him, he started to entertain the notion that perhaps it might be prudent to cut short this subterranean sequestration, a bullet in the sun now seeming urgently preferable to this hideous confrontation with the nameless, numberless plutonian beings of madness. In his sudden panic he imagined he heard a cry, most likely his own, but when it was repeated, then followed rapidly by the sharp crackle of gunfire, he decided to linger yet a few moments longer. After a decent interval in which the only detectable sound was the caninelike panting of his own breath, he rose, setting his back against the hard wooden door, and after a few determined shoves the trap abruptly flew open and he was free, climbing up into the muted light of the empty cabin.

Outside he discovered his samaritan lying face up in the ruddy dust of the deserted road. There was blood on Simms's shirt and hands, but the bellows of his chest continued to work, trying, however futilely, to keep alive the fire within. Red saliva was bubbling from his mouth, trickling down his hairy cheeks. When Liberty attempted to open Simms's wounds, the man pushed him roughly away, hands flailing awkwardly.

"Now, now," said Liberty, patting Simms on the shoulder. "It's a friend."

Simms's eyes slid briefly into focus. "I'm a dead man," he muttered. "I'm gone."

"I don't know about that," answered Liberty. "If you'll just permit me to examine—" He leaned forward and again was pushed impatiently away.

"No, no, I can spy already the far shore."

"What do you see?" asked Liberty, figuring it not only beneficial to keep the man talking, but also frankly curious about the nature of his vision.

"Nothing much, my friend. Rocks, trees, piles of sand. Looks desperately lonely. Not what I expected."

"Nor I," said Liberty, checking the road east and west for signs of armed riders.

Simms coughed, wincing in pain, producing an explosion of bright blood that settled thickly across his beard. "No," he managed to say, "this is not at all what I had imagined." He tried to rise but could barely lift his head. "Give me a grip, son," he said, seizing Liberty's hand and clutching it tightly to his heaving chest. "If you continue along the road here for some six, seven miles you should come to a farmhouse in a grove of oak where you will find my daughter. Her name is Olivia. Would you please inform her that her father died defending the Union he loved?"

"Yes," promised Liberty. "I will."

"Those sons of bitches been lying in wait all these years. Smelled the end coming and—" Though the fierceness of his grip did not slacken, Simms let out a deep sigh and his eyes ceased their blinking, turning motionless as wet marbles. Gently, Liberty pried loose his hand and for a moment stood there gazing mindlessly down at this newly stilled body, an object ordinarily conducive to elemental reflections had not his previous encounters sorely diminished his capacity for speculative thought. He considered leaving the body where it lay but reckoned he would not wish his remains to be so carelessly abandoned in the dirt of a public road, so, gathering up Simms by the ankles he dragged the corpse off into the shade behind the lonely cabin, where he covered it as best he could with handfuls of fresh pine needles.

Simms's daughter, to Liberty's mild surprise, turned out to be not the sallow-skinned, pipe-smoking, hard-used country woman he expected but an educated, well-mannered wife and mother over-burdened with the care of her father's failing farm and a kaleidoscopic brood of small children so numerous, noisy and restless that he could barely tell one from the other or even how many nimble rascals there actually were. Olivia Simms received the news of her father's demise with an equanimity born of hope-famished years in which the worst arrived with such alarming regularity, sense had become dulled to the blows. She simply slumped silently into a chair, still clutching the long squirrel rifle with which she'd greeted Liberty at the door. Then, without a sound, tears slowly filled her eyes, brimmed and over-flowed in crooked trickles down her cheeks. Liberty remained stand-ing in the middle of the room, shifting uncomfortably from leg to leg, kneading his cap in sweaty hands and trying to avoid stepping on one of the babies crawling around his feet. When one of the toddlers began tugging on her dress, Olivia pulled the child up onto her lap, opened her blouse and guided the nipple of her breast into the child's pursed mouth.

"Maybe," said Liberty, clearing his throat, "maybe I'd best be mov-ing on."

She turned and stared out the window for a long while. Then she said, in a clear, firm voice, "All my life I've always wondered why the sky was so blue, but never could find a soul who could answer the question. Can you?"

"No, ma'am," replied Liberty, trying to avoid the scrutiny of her sharp black eyes. "Afraid I can't either."

"Just as well," she said. "Probably we're not supposed to know." She slapped the nursing child lightly across the cheek. "No biting, honey, please. So," she addressed Liberty, "is it your Mr. Lincoln then who decided to costume you boys all in blue and frighten us southern folk into thinking you were as big and powerful as all heaven?" The child paused in eager sucking as if it, too, awaited Liberty's reply.

Liberty, attempting as best he could to keep his unruly eyes from straying in the direction they seemed determined to go, managed to stutter out, "My, what curious thoughts you must entertain out here all alone on the farm."

"No more curious, I suspect, than the ones that must plague you while out fighting this great big war."

"I think you learn not to think so much," he replied, uncertain now how to proceed, overwhelmed by regret that he had been forced by chance or whatever mysterious force governed such matters to be the messenger of grief in a scene even now being reenacted in homes innumerable north and south, no boundary of sufficient temper or dimension to hold at bay the Masked Player who now dominated the American boards.

"I'd offer you coffee, if I had any," she said, her disconsolate stare roving aimlessly about the barren room. "Would you care for some acorn tea?"

"That'd be fine."

He watched as she placed the baby back down on the floor where he or she was instantly set upon by another he or she, producing a series of cries almost unendurable in volume and duration. "Children, hush!" she shouted, setting the kettle on the stove. "Not in front of company." Though not a single one of the bawling, laughing, singing imps seemed to have taken any notice whatsoever of this stranger in their midst.

When the tea was brewed, she presented a steaming tin cup to Liberty, warning, "Mind yourself, it's hot."

He sipped carefully at the vile decoction which tasted remarkably like boiled swamp water. "Excellent," he declared. "Better than anything Dog robber John ever served out of the mess tent." Her rough red hands, he noticed, had trembled slightly when passing him the cup. The enemy in her house? A man in her house? Both? He waited, studying his own dirty hands, the cup trembling now between his fingers, as the woman settled back into her creaking chair.

"Are you all right, ma'am?" he asked, detecting the trace of a sigh.

She leaned forward, touching him lightly upon the knee. "Please, don't call me 'ma'am.' My name is Olivia." Her large brown eyes seemed to have increased in size and brightness.

"Yes, uh, Olivia. Is there anything I can do?"

She turned and looked directly into him. "You're waiting for me to shed more tears. Well, I can't. I'm all dried up inside. Like the land." Again she sighed. "Of course, I suspect you wish to know more." Her white-knuckled fist clutched at the harsh material of her shift, her fingers clenching and unclenching as if kneading dough. "Certainly I warned him until my voice was hoarse. I knew this would happen one day and so, I think, did he, but the days passed, the months and the years, and when it still hadn't happened I guess both of us started thinking that maybe it wasn't ever going to. I guess we were wrong." Raising her head, she directed toward him the bleakest expression he had ever seen. "This war," she went on, "this horrible, evil war, it's never going to end. You do understand that, don't you? Even after it's over it will continue to go on without the flags and the trumpets and the armies, do you understand?"

"Yes," said Liberty softly. "My mother believed such."

"Well, I'm glad to know there's folks up north who understand."

"She was a southern woman."

"Well."

"Yes, born on Redemption Hall plantation over in South Carolina." Her penetrating gaze bored directly into his eyes, as if searching for something she wasn't hopeful of finding. "I'll never understand this world," she said.

"Maybe it's like the sky," Liberty offered. "We're not supposed to understand it."

"Then what's the good of any of it!" she suddenly shouted, rushing from the room and slamming the door behind her.

Liberty found her out back plucking savagely at the carcass of a dead chicken, the bird's severed head and a bloody hatchet lying atop the tree stump before her.

"I was saving this hen for a special occasion or until I couldn't stand not to kill it. I reckon that time has come. You partial to fried chicken?"

"Of course," said Liberty, "but, ma'am, you don't have to cook for me."

"I know I don't, but maybe I might just want to."

Oddly affected by the sight of her bloodied hands and a sacrifice, so she claimed, made solely for him, Liberty, although anxious to move on, found himself warming to this obviously strong and self-sufficient woman who also, at the moment, was in terrible need of adult companionship. "You sure, ma'am, I shouldn't just be heading out?"

She stopped her work and brushed the feathers from her face. "What'd I tell you about that 'ma'am' nonsense, and you're not going anywhere until your belly's been loaded to the rim."

"Whatever you say"—he paused—"Olivia."

They sat together at a wobbly pine table, Liberty chewing industriously on the remarkably tough fowl and nibbling at the gray crumbs of a withered potato she'd managed to produce. Her portion she cut into minute pieces which she dropped one by one into the gaping mouths of the children who'd begun gathering around the table at the first scent of cooked meat. Halfway through the meal, an ancient black man with a stooped back shuffled up to the open doorway and stood boldly staring in at them as they ate.

Liberty, uncomfortable at such scrutiny, finally asked, "Aren't you going to see what he wants?"

"I know what he wants," Olivia replied. "Jasper," she called rather sharply, "go away from here. You know better than to stand out there like that."

The man remained as he was, his soft brown eyes betraying not a hint of what might be going on behind them.

"Now git, shoo, skedaddle back on home."

"Missus."

"I'm not talking to you, Jasper. Say what you will, I ain't answering. I ain't even listening."

And when Liberty looked again, the empty doorway framed only a patch of sandy soil in forlorn sunlight.

"Man's got a nose like a bloodhound," said Olivia. "Hobbled over here to see what he could cadge. Some of these people, I swear, could smell an uncooked egg in a pile of manure." She slowly licked at her greasy fingers. "I don't know, I no longer have the will or the patience to look after them. They're free now, free to starve along with the rest of us." Then, noticing the expression on Liberty's face, she added, "I'll send the remains around to the cabins. You can boil up a fine soup from these bones."

Afterward, they sat out on the gallery watching the children wrestle with one another. Olivia offered Liberty a pipe packed with a harsh but not wholly disagreeable tobacco of sufficient potency to send his brain into a pleasant reel.

"Peyton Camp brings me by a plug or two every so often. He lives up the road five, six miles from here. Expect you'll pass by there on this interesting journey of yours," she concluded, glancing sideways at her young visitor.

Liberty laughed. "I appreciate your discretion in not mentioning it sooner."

"Well, I'm only a country woman and certainly no expert in military matters, but I do know enough to recognize that a detached soldier such as yourself, wandering alone over dangerous ground, is not someone to be questioned too closely about his motives or destination."

Liberty nodded slightly. "Again, I appreciate your politeness."

"But that's not to say I am not highly curious in a purely personal way as to the nature of your mission in our beautiful state."

"Ma'am, my mission, at the moment, is to depart your beautiful state at the earliest opportunity. Am I headed, I wonder, in the proper direction?"

"Any road traveled far enough will lead you successfully out of Georgia."

"I should have known better than to even try to be coy with a woman such as yourself."

"One who sits all by herself, daring to summon up a brazen thought or two?"

"You know how to fasten onto a wooden mind quick as a wood-chuck."

"Don't the ladies up north have any thoughts?"

Liberty smiled. "Oh yes, plenty of 'em. Many, many thoughts by many, many women."

"And I'll bet you know more than a few of 'em."

"Not so many," he replied, feeling the blood rushing to his cheeks, thinking yet again that it was his mother foremost in his mind; then he dangled for a moment on the precipice of confessing all to this relative stranger, but something kept him from falling headlong into the arms of her sympathy.

"Why so eager to get on into Carolina ahead of the rest of the boys? Planning on liberating the whole state by yourself?"

And so, following a nervous bout of preparatory throat-clearing—his being seemingly wholly transparent before her keen gaze—he recounted the pertinent facts of the picturesque Fish family history, providing examples enough of the tangled skein of misfortune and accident that had led him from bucolic upstate New York to the threshold of her hospitable door, yet withholding from her the one crucial event that had set him on his odyssey toward the ancient maternal homestead in the Carolina marshes, saying no more than that he wished to meet the grandparents he had never known.

"I hope you find them well," said Olivia, obviously thinking of something else.

"Yes" was all he could summon up in response.

There then ensued an awkward and protracted silence, broken eventually by Liberty. "I'm sorry about your father."

Olivia rubbed her hands across her weary face. "I am, too. But what's a body to do, particularly a worn-out female one like mine." She seemed then to leave herself for a minute. When she spoke again, it was in a voice so soft he had to lean forward to hear. "I'm going to miss him," she said.

"He appeared to be quite a remarkable man," Liberty observed, shifting uncomfortably in his seat.

"He loved cake," Olivia said through a small, sad smile. "Peaches, too. He loved to eat and he loved to argue. Sometimes we couldn't help but wonder if much of his contrariness was but a mummer's role designed to entertain—himself most of all. Sun's sinking," she noted, the trace of a dark stain spreading over the eastern sky. "You're welcome to stay the night if you wish."

"Well—"

"Better than a mud wallow by the side of the road."

"Quite true, ma'am—I mean Olivia."

"You need some clothes, too. You can't go traipsing about the country in that damn Yankee suit."

"But traveling in civilian clothes, I could be shot as a spy."

"As you are, you'll be shot for certain as an enemy soldier."

She found him some old clothes of her husband's, a patched shirt several sizes too large and a pair of pantaloons he would need a length of twine to hold up, and then told him about how her dear Peter had run off at the first bugle call and his letters had stopped arriving months ago, whether due to understandable disruptions in wartime mail service or something worse she did not know. The vast and relentless uncertainty of the age had whittled her heart to a mere nubbin. The last time she actually laid eyes on the man had been more than two years ago, and now she feared the details of his features were fading from memory. They were standing in an upstairs bedroom, the cries and laughter of the children pouring through the open windows and rising up through the floorboards. It was apparent Olivia wished to ask him something but momentarily lacked the nerve or the proper words, and Liberty waited expectantly until she spoke. "Mr. Fish," she began, "I propose this request to you with great hesitancy, but I find, nevertheless, that I am compelled to do so: might I be permitted a glimpse, however brief, of your naked maleness?" Ignoring the sudden look of modest astonishment upon his face, she went on. "I say this not out of any pressing desire to actually touch it, I believe I'm done with all that"—she swept her arm toward the window, the screams, the shouts, the squabbling—"but simply because it has been so very long since I have gazed upon such an organ and I find to my embarassment I am troubled by a need to do so once again." She regarded Liberty with a perfectly sober, almost clinical expression, its severity abridged slightly by the faint tint coloring her expectant face.

"Is that all?" asked Liberty. "I thought you were about to ask me to kill somebody. I might have minded before joining this crazy campaign, but, frankly, everywhere we've gone, north and south, whenever we halted to bathe in a river or pond the banks would fill up mighty quick with crowds of young ladies for pretty much the same reason as yours. No different from what the boys would do if it was an army of girls taking a dip. I guess we like to look at each other. Now, where is it exactly you want to do this looking?"

She crossed the room and quietly shut the door. "Right here would be fine," she said, a nervous haste and tremor in her voice.

"This is as strange a request as has ever been put to me," said Liberty, fumbling with the buttons on his drawers. The pants fell to his ankles and he stood there fully exposed from the waist down. Olivia said not a word, she simply looked, and Liberty felt that never before in his life had he been so thoroughly looked at by anyone, imagining himself visibly shrinking beneath her stringent scrutiny.

When she finished, she nodded curtly, her countenance as blank and unreadable as a masque at a ball. "Thank you," she said. "It's not everyone who would provide such a service for a lonely plantation wife."

"Well I thank you, ma'am, for being so appreciative."

"You may as well put on my husband's things now," she said.

"You're already half-undressed." And she turned and left the room, closing the door behind her.

That night, alone in the room she insisted he occupy while she slept with one of the older daughters, tossing fretfully in the very bed lately shared by Olivia and her departed husband, Liberty was visited by unbidden fantasies of a decidedly salacious nature until hours into the struggle, he heard, filtering through the thin walls, the distinct sounds of a woman sobbing and, as long as he was awake, the sound did not stop.

In the morning she thanked Liberty for his kindness, saying she expected she would ask Jasper and his son to bring around the wagon and help her go retrieve the body of her father, firmly rebuffing Liberty's offers of assistance, saying he had cares enough to attend to and she wished him well. She kissed him once on the cheek, they exchanged good-byes, and Liberty marched off down the road. When he paused to look back, she had vanished.

Child and adolescent, Liberty had so often visited the old homestead in his mind—inspecting the spacious grounds, greeting the hands, drifting down the long carpeted corridors, caressing furniture worn into intimate family contours, sampling the distinct atmosphere of each individual room—he was sometimes surprised by the stark realization he had yet to set foot in the actual house, having perhaps forgotten that the entire grand edifice had been fabricated for him solely out of words, the bright lumber of a mother's recollections.

Now, hiking up the sandy road along a river winding sluggishly through this exotic low country, swollen feet blistered and sore in ill-fitting boots, numerous bug bites of an exceeding itchiness appearing mysteriously on skin exposed or not, he was struck by the unimaginable (at least to him) quality of the place. He could never have foreseen the brooding impenetrability of the encompassing forest, the alligator dozing here and there in the pungent mud, the gaudy eye of a blue heron fixed resolutely upon him from the clattering reeds or the bony old white man in a lopsided wagon some miles back who was proud to inform Liberty he'd lost his right blinker in an eye-gouging contest back in Old Hickory times when this country'd still amounted to something. Deep inside the cratered socket, the collapsed skin was all puckered up like a little shrunken mouth. Trotting along behind the wagon on a length of frayed rope fastened around his neck was a black boy of about ten.

"Ever hear tell of the Emancipation Proclamation?" inquired Liberty.

No, the driver allowed, he had not.

Liberty explained.

"Don't recognize Black Republicans in this state," muttered the driver. "Jeff Davis is president of this here country and he ain't freed any niggers I ever heard of. And he ain't about to, neither."

"Federals might have a say in that."

"Let 'em come. I'm too nigh the grave to be afeared of any Yankees."

The driver then went on to declare that though he'd been born and bred in the county, never passing the line more than once or twice throughout his mortal existence, he thought he might have heard of that Redemption Hall but couldn't rightly say if Liberty was headed in the proper direction or not or even what the proper direction might be. Liberty left him scolding the boy for having dared to wet, as he stood there in the dust, "his one good pair of breeches"— a ridiculously outsized meal sack clumsily cinched about the boy's skinny waist.

An hour later, rounding a graceful bend in the river (he'd been on the right road after all), Liberty was abruptly presented with an initial revelatory view of the ancestral homestead as it appeared not in fancy but in harsh, implacable fact. First he spied the landing, or what remained of it, a sad asymmetry of tilted piles, precarious roosts for adventurous gulls, one of which was topped by a carved wooden pineapple, symbol of hospitality, and then, in a rapid series of irrevocable glimpses, between thick columns of peeling live oak, the Big House itself—in size physically imposing, though the bleak, unpainted façade certainly offered no intimidating vision of unspeakable opulence and romantic ease. Perched on four sturdy corner posts in order to encourage air circulation and inhibit insect traffic, the "mansion" also provided sheltering shade for a family of dozing hogs and a brace of scraggly chickens pecking furiously away at several small heaps of unidentifiable trash. There was a shabby, secondhand tone to the place, as if the entire hall had been hastily hammered together out of discarded boards and logs. Even the surrounding vegetation seemed utterly used up, the leaves of the myrtle bushes hanging dull and listless, the brittle branches of the nearby oak, magnolia and cypress trimmed in ill-fitting wigs of crinkly Spanish moss, nature itself a haphazard construct of cast-off material.

A dilapidated fence, fallen altogether away in some sections, enclosed the grounds, and out front, lounging against the top rail in attitudes of studied insouciance, were two black men of medium build and indeterminate age, one of whom was outfitted in a suit of striking design, shirt and pants fashioned entirely of mismatched patches of diverse cloth, patches sewn atop patches. His companion, bearded, with bright brown eyes, was dressed in ordinary homespun, and both men displayed upon their hands and faces a mottled network of strange, open sores Liberty had never encountered before.

"How dee-dee, Master," called the patched man in a genial, insinuating tone.

"Good day, gentlemen," responded Liberty, which greeting occasioned an outburst of raucous laughter from the two men. Amused himself, Liberty stepped forward to formally shake each man's roughly callused hand. "How goes it?" he asked.

"Well, sir," Patches replied, "take it all around, could be better, could be worse, but, tell you true, that there sun's"—squinting meaningfully skyward—"growing brighter by the day."

"Lighting up the country like God's own lantern," seconded the bearded one. "I'm seeing things now ain't never been seen before."

"Glad to hear it. Guess, on this farm, the jubilee has already arrived?"

"Not quite, Master," said Patches, "but it sure is drawing mighty close."

"Please," requested Liberty, "if you would, please refrain from addressing me as 'master.' I am master of no one. I am hardly even master of myself."

The two black men exchanged a significant look. "Sir," questioned Patches, now boldly eying Liberty up and down, "you ain't a Carolinies man, are you?"

"Surely not," agreed the bearded one.

"Fact, you must be from somewheres so far off they ain't never even heard the word 'slavery.'"

"No doubt," seconded the bearded one.

"Well, I'm sure I wouldn't know where that mythical land could possibly be, but yes," Liberty admitted, "I have dared a treacherous distance to arrive finally at the fallen gates of the fabled Redemption Hall, if that is indeed where I now find myself."

"Oh," declared Patches, "this is Redemption Hall all right, but like the rest of us, it ain't what it used to be."

"'Grass in the cotton,'" crooned the bearded one, "'weeds in the corn.'"

"Is Mr. Maury about?" inquired Liberty.

"Oh yes, he's about," Patches replied, "but about what we surely do not know." A second round of outrageous laughter.

"What, may I ask, are those terrible sores on your bodies?"

"These?" asked Patches, indicating the raw, weeping ulcers on his forearm. "Well now, these here are not sores, they're speculating spots."

"Speculating spots?"

"Yes," explained the bearded man, "some more of Master Asa's demon witchery. Always bragging he could raise up the dead, bring down the moon, change the leopard's hide, but nothing come of it I could see but this here pox."

"Do they hurt?" Liberty asked, appalled by the angry toxic appearance of their many and variously sized blemishes.

"Not so much," answered Patches. "Itches like hell sometimes just before a big blow, but never bothered me much except when the master first put that damn medicine on. Bad as bee stings then."

"And what, pray tell, was the purpose of applying this so-called medicine?"

"Why, to make us white, of course. Master been trying to turn everything white around here since back around the time Mistis Roxy run off."

"Where's Mr. Maury now?"

"Reckon he's where he always is, up in the speculating shed back of the big house."

"Will you show me?"

"Reckon not. Master don't like to be disturbed when he's in there conjuring."

"I guess I can manage to find it by myself."

"Then good luck to you, sir," cautioned Patches. "Just don't let him spill nothing on you. Under all that dirt and sunburn you already look whiter than a pot of boiled milk."

Boot soles slipping and squeaking, Liberty followed the long sloping path of crushed oyster shells up to the waiting house, where he recognized immediately the scrawny orange tree from whose upper branches his mother, leaning out her bedroom window, had often plucked her morning fruit. Her warped sill, her very hand. Was it possible, he wondered, to be visited for even a mercifully brief instant by a piercing nostalgia for a past one had never personally experienced? In some form or another he had passed this way before. Of that he was quite certain.

The gallery was deserted but for a sleeping dog, a sea green broken-backed rocking chair, its loosened sticks held precariously upright with crudely knotted twine, and on the boards nearby a heavy earthenware mug which, when raised to Liberty's alert nostrils, revealed itself as having been the recent container of an intoxicating spirit of some considerable force. Cautiously, he approached the strangely inert animal. Detecting a slight but rhythmic heaving of the ribs, he touched the toe of his boot to the red-furred hound's bony back. "Hey," he called softly. "Hey, pooch." The dog lifted his head, granted Liberty one extended doleful stare before nuzzling its gray-whiskered snout back between balding paws.

An open window offered a conveniently framed view of the front parlor, a spartan room spartanly furnished, the centerpiece a sprung horsehair couch propped up on one end by a stack of yellowing law books, on the floor a faded rug, on one of the otherwise bare walls a series of six curiously murky paintings, each no more than six inches square, each progressively darker than the last, all devoid of even the faintest outline of a discernible image. Stepping to the door, which was also open, he rapped softly on the jamb and when there was no reply, called out a few tentative hellos. He entered the house, passing through the deserted rooms like a bewildered apparition abruptly returned to a world forgotten yet oddly familiar. These the walls upon which were once projected the pure dreams of youth, this the favorite chair in whose unyielding embrace resided the comforting notion of home, that the very cup of buttermilk pleasures, its rim memorized by corporeal lips. Cherish the past, no matter how bitter, he remembered hearing his mother declaim, therein lies the gate to future freedom.

From the back door he could see a tattered strand of gray smoke lazily unwinding from the chimney of the kitchen outbuilding, and within a sense of shadowy movement that drew Liberty to investigate. There he found an elderly woman with no teeth and big bony hands who seemed not at all surprised by the sudden appearance of a strange man in her kitchen. She was standing at a table and shaving a monkey in a bowl.

"Who are you?" she asked, barely glancing in Liberty's direction.

"A friend."

Up went a skeptical eyebrow. "We don't have any friends here," she replied tartly, lifting this amazingly docile monkey's right arm and expertly drawing a straight razor down across his lathered armpit.

"I'm not from here."

"Didn't think you were." She had now begun shaving the belly, and Liberty was intrigued to note how white the animal's skin actually was.

"Is Mr. Maury in?"

"Well, that depends which Mr. Maury you're asking about."

"Asa," he replied, nimbly gliding over a slight hesitation, the spoken name tasting oddly gamy upon his tongue.

"Oh, him. Yes, he's here all right."

Liberty waited, the pause lengthened, scrape, scrape, went the blade, I have endured much said the monkey's doleful brown eyes, and when it became plainly apparent no further information was forthcoming, he inquired politely, "And where might I find this Mr. Maury?"

The woman let out a protracted sigh. "Expect the doctor's where he always is, out back taking care of business."

"Doctor?" blurted Liberty, surprised by a title previously unknown to any member of his branch of the family as far as he could recollect. "Doctor of what, I ask you?"

The question met by an incoherent tumble of dark chuckling and garbled syllables.

"I'm sorry, I didn't catch—"

"I say, you'd best go and quiz him yourself and see if he don't allow he's the beatingest Professor of Niggerology in all creation."

"There are actual degrees granted in such a preposterous subject?"

"So white folks say. And they ain't shy about professing, neither. They got a right smart chance of 'em, too. They got a professor of sunshine, a professor of cats, a professor of misery, they got a mess of fancy professors and not a one knows a damn thing."

She directed Liberty to follow the trace from the vegetable garden past the stand of wilted pear trees, between the smokehouse and the fowl coop, along the row of cabins, the boneyard and straight on down into the hollow and the isolated wooden shack she grandly referred to as "Dr. Maury's office," further advising him to raise a sufficient ruckus when approaching since the doctor did not take kindly to unexpected interruptions of his work.

"What work is that, exactly?"

"Nothing I want to know anything about," muttered the woman, wiping the blade with a soiled towel. "And if you're as smart as you look, you wouldn't want to know anything about that business, either."

"I'm a curious fellow," explained Liberty, offering up a helpless, apologetic smile.

She turned on him a searching gaze of well-practiced pity, the knowledge in her rheumy eyes reducing him for an instant to the green boy he thought he'd long outgrown, and in that distracting interval the woman's hand slipped, the monkey screamed and, trailing bright gobbets of blood from the fresh cut on his thigh, leaped from his mistress's flailing arms to clamber adroitly atop a nearby cabinet from which vantage he glared furiously down upon the two hapless humans, canines bared.

"Sharp razor," observed Liberty.

The instrument went clattering into the china bowl and the bowl went sailing through the open door as the woman unleashed a torrent of colorful blasphemies such as Liberty had rarely heard even from the tobacco-stained lips of the most grizzled veteran. From the relative safety of his perch the monkey now commenced to emit a series of chattering sounds in which an element of mockery was plainly present, the insults seasoned with a goodly rain of primate spittle. The enraged woman, all but consumed in a mindless frenzy, responded with a lively barrage of whatever was at hand, flinging pots, pans, plates, cups, assorted vegetables, a wooden mallet, even one of her shoes, a heavy man's brogan, at the nimbly dodging beast.

"Well, ma'am," Liberty said, touching his cap, "good luck to you."

"Luck?" cried the woman, preparing to scale the cabinet herself. "Better plague me with curses from hell than bless me with any of your damn luck."

Outside, Liberty was at once confronted by a matching pair of massive hounds, no relation, obviously, to the mangy animal dozing on the gallery. They sat like lifeless statues in the middle of the path, their cold olive eyes studying him as if he were a rabbit about to bolt. "Easy there, boys," he said in as genial a tone as he could muster, holding out his hand in a gesture of peace. Then, abruptly and without ceremony, as if this had been in the plan all along, one of the dogs simply got up, trotted over and licked the back of Liberty's quivering hand. Family, he thought, they smell family on me.

Off in the haze in a freshly harrowed field, a solitary man was beating on a mule with a stick, flailing energetically away as if the animal's flank were an anvil and the length of wood a smith's heavy hammer. Noticing Liberty, he paused in his labors to shout out something unintelligible. Liberty waved and went on. The mischievous sun, having consumed the morning in a spirited game of hide-and-seek with thickly passing clouds, broke briefly free, flooding the somber plantation with a light so sudden and pure it seemed positively benedictory. But then a cloud intervened, the sun went out and all was returned to its naturally fallen state.

The path, as promised, guided him past the cabins (from open doorways the round, omniscient eyes of half-naked children marking his progress), the well-populated cemetery graves were decorated with bottles, gourds, pieces of colored glass, and on down into an unexpectedly cozy little dell where, nestled in the comforting shade, stood a nondescript shack of rusted tin and moldering wood. Applying a hearty knock to the weathered door, Liberty stepped back and waited. He was about to try again when a voice that seemed to emanate from a cavern deep underground gruffly called out a word that sounded something like "Yare!" Then, a moment later, "Well, open the damn door if you want to come in!" Liberty did as he was told, entering a cramped, musky pitch-black interior. "And who in the freezing hell might you be?" came the same voice out of the gloom.

"My name, sir, is Liberty Fish," he replied, advancing uncertainly into the shadows.

"Hold!" the voice commanded, as a match was struck and applied to the wick of a lantern, raising out of the pungent murk the shape of a room, a cluttered desk and, behind it, seemingly suspended in midair, a great wrinkled head wreathed in an untidy mass of luminous white hair, and, in place of eyes, stones of polished obsidian in which a full heaven's worth of night was fiercely gathered. And as Liberty's vision adjusted to the low flickering flame, he also noted that the head was connected to a rather youthfully lean body and the body to a muscled arm and the arm to an imposing-looking regulation U.S. Navy revolver. "I can glim you fine from here. The lamp's for your benefit. I could see you without it."

"Exceptional sight."

"Nonsense. Any fool could do the same. Just practice, that's all." He leaned forward into the light, his features rearranging themselves into a passable picture of elderly kindliness. "You ever enjoy sitting alone in a room in the dark, ruminating?"

"Ruminating?"

"There's no dearth of topics on this confounding, disjointed planet that couldn't be measurably enlarged by the application of superior mental leverage."

"I think I prefer a bright, warm fire and good company."

"Figured as much. Noticed your bumps, your cranial organs. Rather pronounced for amativeness and vitativeness. Have a seat," he added, wiggling the barrel of the gun toward a chair piled high with thick old books. "Just toss that trash on the floor. Done with that business anyhow. As you may have observed, my quarters, though necessarily secluded, are a trifle confined, quite in contrast to the magnitude of the work performed herein, but then original minds have often wanted for proper lodgings and equipment."

Liberty lifted the heavy stack into his arms, curious titles swimming dizzily before his perplexed gaze: *The Eastern Origin of the Celtic Nations, History of the Anglo-Saxons, Northern Antiquities, Dissertation on the Origin and Progress of the Scythians or Goths, The Genuine Principles of the Ancient Saxon or English Constitution, An Account of the Regular Gradation in Man.*

"Follow the Teutonic line, son, that's my advice to you. There's your progress, there's your evolution."

Once settled into the chair, Liberty found himself on a bit too intimate a plane with the pointed revolver. "Excuse me, but is the weapon quite necessary?"

"Probably not." He placed the gun on the desk with exaggerated delicacy. "Due to diminished contact with the moderating influences of society, my manners seem to have undergone an unfortunate degeneration, but let me also inform you that I have walked about in this world for some seven decades and I have learned, through hard necessity, that this superb example of the metallurgical arts"—indicating the Colt—"is more dependable, more worthy of trust than your nearest kin."

"Are you Asa Maury?"

"What's in a name?" He regarded his visitor with detached bemusement. On a shelf above his head, ranked according to size, stood an orderly row of gleaming skulls of various species and dimensions, in silent contrast to the persistent activity taking place within the numerous wire cages scattered haphazardly about this cramped den, where growled, cried, scuttled and scampered an extraordinary collection of exotic creatures feathered, furred and scaled.

"Have I actually traveled these hundreds of miles, risking injury, imprisonment or worse to engage in a mere verbal joust?"

"Supposing I were the gentleman you take me for, what would you want of me?"

"I thought, unwisely perhaps, that simple courtesy required this visit, just as simple human curiosity and the unsparing needs of the soul to comprehend its own origins demanded it. I expected, after absorbing a lifetime of tales about the prodigious man, to meet finally face-to-face the legend himself, my maternal grandfather. And frankly, sir, I presumed the reception would be somewhat more enthusiastic than that provided."

"You speak quite eloquently for one of such meager years."

Liberty permitted himself a slight smile. "I descend from a long line of acclaimed talkers."

"Ah," he mused, the chair creaking as he shifted about, "a gathering of the clan then, a union of the severed branches north and south. An early peace." He glanced inquisitively at Liberty.

"So I had hoped."

"Hope, a rare and precious commodity. Difficult to bear the demands of the day without it." He pawed through the fermenting mass of books, journals, pamphlets and loose papers heaped helter-skelter on the desk before him. "Have you perhaps had an opportunity to peruse Morton's *Crania Americana*, an essential monograph on an endlessly fascinating subject? I commend it to you with the heartiest of endorsements." Thrusting into Liberty's outstretched hand a warped volume exuding a distinctly fusty odor, he went on affably, "Tell me, have you in your admittedly brief existence given any con-

sideration to the topic of race? I mean, of course, serious consideration, not the frivolous prattle of politicos and grubby newspapermen.
I have devoted a lifetime of toil to this vexing issue, and as a consequence I have arrived at some rather shocking conclusions." From
somewhere out of the desktop chaos he produced a tooled moroccan
leather box. "Care for a cigar?"

Liberty declined. At this precise moment feeling neither particularly genial and not at all gentlemanly, he had no desire to relax into
the sort of clubby, postprandial chat his "grandfather"—for who else
could this silly old man be?—was attempting so anxiously to weave.

"Difficult to obtain in these pinched times," he said, inhaling the
scent of a long, bulky cheroot. "Cuban, of course. You'd be surprised
at what gets through the blockade. If you don't mind," he leaned into
the lamp to ignite the tobacco, his sidelong glances silently appraising
Liberty through the resulting clouds of smoke that added yet another
noxious note to the cacophony of offensive aromas already assailing
his nose.

"As I was saying," the old man went on, "from scholarly endeavors both profound and exhaustive I have concluded, with great reluc-
tance, I might add, that the so-called negro race is in fact a distinct
and separate limb of the evolutionary tree—a limb untended,
unpruned, thoroughly blighted. But what of Genesis, you might well
ask, and the rather authoritative account of the Adamic origin of all
humanity? Again, along with several other eminences in the field,
I have determined—sorrowfully, sir, sorrowfully—that the biblical
depiction is simply false. Study the Gospel closely and you will discover a text riddled with disturbing anomalies. Quick, name me the
daughters of Adam and Eve. No? You cannot? Of course not. No such
daughters are ever mentioned; yet they had to exist. And, similarly,
when Cain is banished, he takes a wife by whom he begets a son.
Who is this mysterious woman, and whence did she come? The scrip-
tures remain strangely silent. The obvious solution to these thorny
problems is that there were indeed other peoples formed at the creation. They go unremarked because the Good Book is a chronicle of
the superior types. Now, the next question, of course, and a most

troublesome one at that, is why the Divine would even bother to fashion a dusky tribe so innately dull, so barbaric in custom, so wanting in physical beauty, so incapable of even the most trifling improvement. Can you reply?" He spoke with a pronounced animation of speech and eye Liberty had previously encountered only in an unfortunate victim of "camp fever" shortly before he died.

"Enlighten me."

"Is that a smirk of sarcasm I detect leering so disingenuously through that silky, ingratiating voice of yours?"

"Oh no. No, I certainly didn't mean to suggest—"

The old man raised a mollifying palm. "Please, go right ahead, assault me with your skepticism, wallop me with ridicule, give me a good flogging. I'm quite accustomed to defending myself against honest objections in whatever spurious guise they might appear."

"Kind of touchy about these notions of yours."

"Science, young man, not baseless conjecture. What do you know of natural history, of comparative anatomy, cranial capacities, facial angles?"

"I'm sure not as much as I should."

"You never responded to my question."

"Which one was that?"

"Why the black race?"

"Because they were the ones on the bottom of the pot who got scorched?" replied Liberty promptly, conscious now of the sound of tiny claws scratching at the dark edges of the room.

"Because the Infinite, in His all-encompassing wisdom, chose to bless us with a great gift. The Ethiop is the shadow laid across our path, a perplexing obstacle to the soul's attainment of the harmonious and the good. We need such a trial in order to develop our faculties to the utmost. But the way, of course, is stubbornly difficult and fraught with peril of the gravest sort, and I fear we may have lost our direction. The outcome is in doubt, as surely it must be, or the tribulation would not be worth enduring. Luckily, the remedy to our ordeal occurred to me one evening many years ago, long before the dawning of this terrible war, after a particularly grueling day in the field when

I had to personally oversee the hanging of Proud Jed, one of my most dependable hands, for a demonstration of insolence I simply could not abide and needn't bother elaborating on now. It was a perfectly clear night. I was relaxing on the gallery, meditating on the cold, stately wonderment of the heavens, all that indissoluble darkness, so little light, when the stars spoke to me. They provided the receipt to all our ills."

"Which is?"

"Why, the transformation of black into white, of course."

"And this deliverance to be achieved by . . . ?"

"A subtle chemical process too intricate for lay understanding."

"I believe I've already happened upon some of the fruits of your handicraft," said Liberty dryly. "Two gentlemen out by the fence, horribly disfigured."

The old man brushed aside the comment with a dismissive wave. "A mere biological sport. Of no lasting consequence really. Those blemishes should heal fully in no time. The march of knowledge, you know. Always a few casualties left hobbling about in the rear."

"Why not the transformation of white into black?"

"Impossible. A gross violation of natural law. You might as well command the leopard to change into a snail. Can't be done. Our ebony friends, you see, are an intermediary species, the bar Our Father has placed between man and beast, beneath which humanity cannot fall. All aspires upward, into the light. We of the present generation shall be the first in recorded time to witness the grand metamorphosis, the final defeat of pigmentation."

"From what evidence I've seen I would expect the wait to be a tad lengthier."

"Those were primitive efforts I have advanced far beyond. But also, over the years, I have been developing a parallel, nonmedicinal method which, as the Good Lord no doubt intended, has proven to be most profitable. Would you care to see?"

"I certainly wouldn't want to miss a single exhibit on the tour."

"And so you shan't." He rose grunting from behind his desk, addressing Liberty for the first time in a measured, placid tone that seemed almost reasonable, even confiding. "I seem to have attained an age when I must keep moving fairly regularly or the various parts start to stiffen. One of these days, I'm afraid, I'm going to doze off in a chair and they'll have to bury me upright in it. Your arm, please."

Liberty hastened to offer his assistance, guiding the shambling man around the desk and out the door, each tentative step surprisingly firmer than the last, until by the time they stood blinking together in the harsh afternoon sun all the man's previous vigor seemed to have been regained. He led Liberty around back to another shack no larger than an outhouse, its flimsy door secured by an enormous iron lock into which the old man inserted an equally enormous key from the heavy brass ring of keys jingling incessantly at his waist.

The interior smelled worse than any stable, as if once living matter had been left to fester and grow, intermittent illumination provided by the thin bars of light slanting in between the boards. Once Liberty's eyes had adjusted to the gloom, he was able to make out a vaguely human form collapsed on a pile of straw in the corner.

"This is Bridget," the old man announced.

"Hello," Liberty said softly.

There was no response.

"And how you doing today, Bridget?" the old man boomed out, as if greeting a business colleague on a city street.

Silence.

"I asked you a question, child, and expect a prompt answer."

Silence.

"Well?"

The woman rustled about in the straw. "Don't expect I have an answer," she said at last.

"Are you hungry? Did you get your edibles this noon?"

Silence.

"Where's that damn plate? I tell you, if Luther forgot again today . . ."

"There," said Liberty, pointing to a metal bowl on the dirt floor in which a heel of uneaten bread sat amidst a puddle of uneaten beans.

"Bridget, Bridget honey," lamented the old man, "this will not do, this will not do at all. What have I told you, over and over again? You have to eat, have to stay healthy, produce good milk for that new suckling of yours." He turned to Liberty. "You see firsthand what we're up against here. Even the adults are little more than overgrown children. Bridget, step on over for a moment so that our visitor may see what a fine specimen you are."

After a protracted pause, the woman roused herself from her squalid bedding and shuffled toward them, chains clanking between her bare feet. The old man gripped her by the chin and forcibly twisted her head into a knothole-sized beam of light. "Look," he exclaimed, "at this remarkable ivory skin. Delicious, isn't it?"

"Albino?" To Liberty, from the dimmed presence in her fragile brown eyes, it appeared this woman had long ago vacated the moment, probably permanently, to reside in a separate place private and remote.

"No, not at all. Examine the features closely, observe the virtual absence of negroid characteristics." He was stroking her trembling cheek with his knuckles. "No, what you see standing before you is no freak of nature but a different type of mulatto altogether. And the color, isn't it extraordinary? Fresh cream with a splash of coffee. But wait till you see the baby. Bridget, where's Wellington?"

Stooping down, the woman retrieved from her foul nest a bundle of rags which she passed without comment to her master.

"Now, prepare to gaze upon absolute astonishment," he boasted, carefully unwrapping the wad of soiled linen to reveal a weak, dwarfish face, chalky in hue, purplish eyelids glued firmly shut, minute fingers curled into translucent balls like grotesque fetuses prematurely hatched from a shell. "Wait, what's this?" Pinching each of the infant's pallid, sunken jowls in rapid succession. "This child is no longer breathing." He glared furiously at the woman who was attentively studying her fidgety feet. "Don't give me any of your down looks, you insolent wretch. What have you done to your baby?" He flung the swaddled thing against the wall, where it made a plopping sound and then dropped like a spent ball to the earthen floor. "Answer me! Now!"

She looked up at him, a latticework of tears already streaming down her stricken face. "Nothing, Master," she stammered hastily, "didn't do nothing. That babe was poorly from the start."

His hand lashed out quick as a moccasin's strike, the sudden slap catching her full across the left side of her head and pitching her backward to the hard ground, the crack of the blow echoing in the close air like a lingering odor.

"Are you a doctor?" he cried, looming over her cowering body. "Are you qualified to make such a diagnosis? Why didn't you seek help? You must have known the infant was ill." He stared coldly down upon her helplessly heaving back. "Yes, yes, go on, water the soil with your sobs. Maybe what I should do during the next drought is line you people up at field's edge and drive you all boo-hooing between the rows. Probably double my yield. Nothing the land appreciates more than a good penitential rain."

Then a relative calm descended over him as abruptly as his temper had flared. "Sorry you had to witness such an unpleasant scene," he apologized to Liberty, "but perhaps you have gained a clearer under-standing of my chronic dilemma. The obstacles in my path have been nearly insurmountable. How I have managed to achieve even a few modest successes is a miracle only Divinity comprehends."

"You are mad."

He responded with laughter of unembarrassed abandon. "Of course I'm mad. Everyone's mad, the country is mad. What is war but public madness, the outward manifestation of an unplumbed and tenacious disturbance? And now the disease of racial differentiation, which has infected us all for generations unnumbered is running its inexorable course. Time is short. I fear for the outcome because it is very likely, in my estimation, that even all this dreadful bloodletting will ultimately do little to drain the insidious pus from our core. That in the aftermath this illness will persist, under newfangled labels of course, cunningly rigged out in fancy masquerade, but beneath the surface persisting nonetheless. No, our social ailment will not be cured by iron and gunpowder. What we require are physics of a boldly imaginative bent. As I have been trying so patiently to explain—have you been attending to my words at all, dear boy?—we can end the curse of color by eliminating color entirely. This unfortunate babe was the most triumphant realization of that happy goal to date. Speaking of which, I really hesitate to ask, Mr. Fish, but would you mind terribly fetching Wellington for me. My lumbago, you know. I can barely lean down of a morning to pull my own boots on. Not too squeamish, are you? I'm sure you've handled worse articles on the field of battle. That is the bloody arena from which you have lately retired, is it not?"

"Yes," Liberty replied coolly, "and may I remind you that those 'articles' were once human beings."

"'Were,' my boy, 'were'—the operative word here. Once you've been physically and permanently entered into the past tense, does it really matter what is said of you?"

"Most folks would say yes."

"Most folks are fools. Thank you," he said, accepting the diminutive corpse into his arms. "I'll dissect the little chap up in my office. See what went wrong. And you," he added, shifting his attention and his mood onto the weeping mother writhing about in the dirt, "I want you to contemplate the enormity of your crime and how you could've been so bad, and I want you to decide on your own just what your punishment should be. I'll be back later to administer whatever judgment you have chosen. Come, lad, this stifling place oppresses me."

Back in his own disheveled den he dropped the dead baby on the desk and began rooting about in the encompassing mess. "There's a splendid article on the diversity of origin by the great Louis Agassiz you absolutely must acquaint yourself with. Professor of zoology at Harvard, no less. I had the honor, many years ago, of attending his lecture series at the Charleston Literary Club. What a stir in the audience as one hot nugget of wisdom after another was tossed into our laps. A revelatory experience during which one's intellectual firmament was altered forever. Did you know, for example, that the brain of the grown Negro is equal to that of a seven-month-old fetus in the womb of a white? Or that each of the species, animal and human alike, is the manifestation of a specific thought in the mind of the Creator? Imagine the melancholy state He must have been languishing in the day the Negro race popped into being." A precarious stack of papers went sliding to the floor and he threw up his hands in defeat. "Well, it'll turn up eventually and I shall immediately pass it along. Anyway, you must be burning with questions after our eventful call on the charming Miss Bridget. Please, indulge yourself, I shall be delighted to entertain all inquiries."

"Where's Grandmother?"

"I suppose," he pretended to go on, pointedly ignoring that particular query, "you must find yourself in a perfect perplexity as to who the father might be. Well, I'll tell you. It was I. And a frightful chore it was, lying down with that cold woman. She lacked—how shall I put it?—the appropriate scientific spirit for the job. But I knew what had to be done, and I did it.

"Now, you might further wonder, who exactly is Bridget's sire? And I would be forced to reply in precisely the same manner. What say you to that?" The gleam in his eye had become so alarmingly pronounced it threatened to escape the gravitational field of the ocular globe altogether.

"I say your soul is in extravagant peril. Probably the mortal coil along with it."

"On what basis?"

"Surely you joke. I'm no theologian, but numerous sins appear to be involved here, incest being the most prominent among them, not to mention whatever civil and criminal statutes have also been transgressed."

The old man grunted contemptuously. "I leap over laws as if they were broomsticks."

"Obviously."

"The work is much too important to be fettered by the trifling orthodoxies of small-minded authority. I'm not certain you have fully grasped the historic, nay, epic significance of what you have witnessed today. Had this pathetic suckling survived and grown to a suitable breeding age, I would have been the author of her offspring also. Can you even dare to contemplate the tone, the texture, of those children's skin?" His voice drifted off into a seductive reverie only he was privy to, posed in statesmanlike attitude atop a bracing mountain peak, the lucent sapphire sky behind him streaming dramatically with clouds of a blazing, uncontested purity. "The iniquities of the world," he mused softly, "washed away in the blood of my flesh. Can you conceive of such a welcome boon?"

"But the infant died."

"Regrettably, yes. A minor setback that will not deter me from my ordained course."

"But isn't Wellington a boy's name? How could you proceed with your plan if the child was male?"

"I'll baptize the bastards however I damn please. Now let us adjourn to the house and rest in the shade of the gallery. It's been a trying day."

The long trudge up the hill in company was no less dismaying to Liberty than the earlier solitary descent. The old man kept rattling on in his excitable, scattered way about how the rate of insanity among the Negro increased progressively from Pennsylvania to Maine but dropped by half in Delaware and continued declining steadily on down into Florida—the Mason-Dixon line itself drawing a virtual boundary between dementia and reason. An extraordinary statistic! Did you know that seventeen sacred cubic centimeters of cranial volume constitute a permanent intellectual Grand Canyon impossible for our prognathic inferiors ever to bridge? Blessed be the name of the Lord! Or that it was not a snake but Nachash, a Negro gardener dwelling in the Land of Nod with his sooty brethren, who tempted Eve with the apple? His wonders to behold!

This vicious farrago of humbug, deluded fancy and crackpot ethnology was delivered in a rather genial humor, as if sharing only the most innocuous of local gossip. Liberty, depressed, depleted, the works of his brain ensnared in a kind of all-enveloping mucilaginous fog, kept mum—what possible rejoinder to such raving conviction?—his widening amazement directed not at his mother's daring rebellion and eventual flight but at how she'd endured life under this lunatic's roof for as long as she had. And he couldn't help but loiter for a pensive moment or two about the plausible conjecture of precisely what size portion of ancestral madness, so far as he knew still untasted, had been fated for his plate.

Still jabbering away like a distracted parrot, the old man led him through the back door of the house, down the main hallway he had already explored, up an imposing staircase of polished mahogany beneath the accusing gazes of a remarkably stolid-looking portrait gallery of male Maurys to a closed door at the far end of a long, unornamented corridor. All was dark, all eerily silent. He tapped tentatively with his knuckle, then cocked his head as if listening for sounds from the bottom of a mine. Then tapped and listened again. "Stay here," he commanded, cautiously opening the door and slipping inside. Presently Liberty became aware of a rapid exchange of silibants, then a muffled cry, then nothing. The door creaked open. "You may enter," the old man declared.

The room had been essentially sealed, windows shuttered and thoroughly obscured by several layers of thick green drapes, the fetid air exceedingly warm. On a nearby nightstand stood a solitary candle, its sputtering flame gasping for oxygen, the uncertain light still sufficient, however, to reveal a mammoth four-poster bed curtained on all sides but one, in which, under an impressive mound of heavy blankets, lay a tiny old woman, her tiny gray head propped upon a pile of feather pillows. She might have been dead but for her eyes, hard, blue, strikingly alert and animated, so radiant they appeared preternaturally lit from within. "Is this he?" she inquired in an equally incongruous voice of surprising clarity and vigor. "Come closer, that I might see." Warily, Liberty approached the bed. "You do look young," she pronounced, "quite young," and, addressing the older man, "You see, he's got the Maury brow and the cleft chin. Lord, I never thought I'd live long enough to see one of ours come home a Yankee. Of course never thought I'd live to see my own daughter . . ." The singular voice trailed off into a tremendous stillness.

"Favors Langdon a mite, don't you think?" offered the old man, hastening to mend the pause.

"Touch around the eyes, maybe the nose," she replied, scrutinizing Liberty's features as if he were a commissioned portrait. "You don't suppose he has any nigger blood in him? Something suspicious about the mouth, don't you agree?"

"She wrote that the husband was a New Yorker."

"Well," declared the woman, as if that fact were explanation enough. "But never mind. All my life I've struggled to embrace white and black alike. Come here, boy, let Grandma give you a kiss."

Liberty edged closer.

"Well, bend down, for Christ's sake," she commanded sharply. "You expect an old shriveled-up woman like me to lift herself up out of her deathbed for you?"

Liberty leaned over, inclining his face to within what he hoped was respectful range, and was abruptly startled by the unexpected sensation of her thin, papery lips pressing somewhat indecorously against his. There was no suitable comparison. It was like sparking with your own granny.

"He smells," she announced decisively.

"Oh, oh," stammered Liberty, still slightly distracted by the intimate matriarchal touch. "Terribly sorry, I've been traveling through open country for some weeks now, occasions for refreshing oneself being understandably rare."

"I didn't say I minded. God knows the promiscuous bouquet of man and beast I've had to endure on this forsaken farm. Yours is rather pleasant, actually, puts me in mind of black pepper." Turning to her husband: "Remember Aunty Dell's rabbit stew? How it smelled after sitting overnight in the pot?"

"Because once we were done, you spit in it to keep her and her brood from sampling any."

The woman snorted contemptuously. "They were all such unregenerate thieves. What could I do?"

"Now, now," he soothed, "those times are long past."

"Yes," she snapped, "to be replaced by worse ones."

"Now don't go riling yourself up again. You know what can happen."

Her pale, bony fingers had begun plucking restlessly at the covers. "Goodness," she exclaimed, noticing Liberty still standing politely before her, "this boy must be famished. Take him down to the kitchen and have Nicey fix him some supper. "

The old man sighed. "You know Nicey's been missing for two days now."

"I know no such thing."

"We discussed the matter only this morning."

"I have no recollection of any fugitive being reported to me since Horace run off for the swamp with a side of bacon."

"Horace?" repeated Maury patiently. "That was over twenty-five years ago."

"What ridiculous nonsense. You were always no-account on dates, anyway. If Nicey's gone, who's been cooking my food?"

"Old Portia."

"Old Portia?" she shrieked in alarm. "You permit a crazy woman to prepare our meals? What careless stupidity! It's a wonder we're not all poisoned. Remove her from the kitchen immediately, and I want her replacement to be personally witnessed by you tasting each portion on my plate before it is served to me. Do you understand?"

"Yes, dear."

"And I should think you would do well to have your own dishes tasted, also. I've never been able to fathom why I wasn't laid out in my grave decades ago, brought low by the cruel burden of managing this absurd jamboree all by myself."

"Now, Ida, I believe there you are exaggerating again."

"How dare you? I never exaggerate. If you hadn't wasted your life puttering about in that damn shack teaching a monkey how to hold a pencil or whatever profitless folly you're engaged in out there, you'd know I speak the truth. Conditions on this property have been so monstrous, even from the moment I said 'I do,' that a simple recitation of the plain facts sounds like a ten-cent melodrama."

"I will not have you blackening the value of my work."

"Show me a result and I won't."

"I'm not going to argue with you, Ida."

"Then don't." She settled back regally into the immaculate plumpness of her pillows and, through emphatically shut eyes, instructed, "Now go. Get that boy fed. When everything else has gone up the flue, we can yet demonstrate to the world that southern hospitality still prevails through the smoke and the dust."

"Nicely put."

"Write it down for me so I can read it later."

As they hastily withdrew, Liberty thought his ears must be mistaken on hearing Grandmother mumble drowsily, as if already adrift in sleep, a single indelible word—and that word was "Shit."

Out in the hallway, as his grandfather fiddled with the latch, a flimsy contrivance of bent nails and string, Liberty was finding himself somewhat disconcerted by the wild fantasy of bringing both fists crashing down onto the back of this stooped old man's white, white head when Maury shot him an amused glance and said, "She'll outlive all of us."

That night, after a distinctly satisfying platter of dodgers and chicken fixin's concocted seemingly out of thin air by the moody monkey woman, who apparently was not the dreaded Old Portia, and a julep-fueled rehash of Maury's rigidly selective views on history, nature, politics and religion—an arrogant amalgam of fact, fancy and folly that would have been outright laughable if it weren't so potentially lethal—Liberty was shown by his grandfather without comment to a second-floor room he guessed at once must have been that of his mother. He felt as if he'd been conducted into the private sanctum of a great museum where were stored priceless rarities the public was never permitted to see. But after a long, deliberate, respectful exploration of the room he could find little that was demonstrably hers. The bureau, the trunk at the foot of the bed were both disappointingly empty, as was the closet, though he did manage to locate there the loose floorboard under which she had secreted her precious diary. All that remained now were some dried mouse droppings. It was a chamber from which all evidence of previous occupation had been thoroughly expunged.

Then there was the bed, the one dominating article of furniture.

He walked around it a few times, actually contemplated curling up on the hardwood floor, but finally plain weariness of bone and heart nudged him mattressward where he lay like a painted figure atop a sarcophagus, pondering the imponderable mysteries of time and family. The smoldering fantasies of revenge, the grand schemes for personally administering a sublime brand of exquisitely calibrated justice usually found only in the wishful pages of airy romance or in visions of afterlife proceedings before the bar of God, now seemed hopelessly childish and futile. These ghastly people who had, over years of reiterated tales of their fabulous exploits, assumed in youthful reverie ogreish proporions of utter invincibility appeared in their furrowed flesh to be little more than puny, imprisoned creatures, old, deranged, lost. And what could one do about that?

If he slept at all during his first fervid night on ancestral ground, it was a slumber hardly worthy of the name, an anxious roll between the sheets, endeavoring in vain to elude unwelcome visitations from the ever-present past, memories of his mother mostly, but her memories, not his, yet somehow through a kind of occult agency transmitted clearly and abundantly, scenes from a young girl's passage through the privileged world of the southern landed gentry and, strangely enough, the heart's most piercing intensities fully refracted through the implacably commonplace: the emblazoned side of the gin house at dawn; the spooky intelligence in her spaniel's wet brown eyes; Mother Maury at the piano at candle lighting, each distinct note as pure, as melancholy, as transient as the fading western sky; the thrill of Baylor's lips behind a peeling oak tree at the Charleston cotillion; a rusted shackle lying untouched for months in the shade of the big house—a shifting cargo of perilous remembrances sufficient at times to scuttle even the sturdiest ship of being, often resulting in such convulsive episodes as "the month of tears," so termed by a sardonic Thatcher, when Mother (his mother) rarely left her New York room, seemingly unable to keep from bawling for hours at a time, and Liberty, a frightened and helpless son, resolving then with all the fierce determination of a half-formed eight-year-old mind that once grown up he would find and punish terribly the fiends responsible, whoever they were.

Now, as he thrashed about in the lair of the beast, so to speak, mulling obsessively over the unforeseen intricacies of his visit, ruefully concluding that he, too, was as trapped as his forebears in the venomous nettles of the overarching family tree, he became aware of a disturbance in the atmosphere, faintly at first, then swelling swiftly in volume, the sound of querulous voices raised in contention and though muffled by the intervening walls, still capable of conveying to his attentive ears an audible quality of daggers slashing at the air. It's me they're arguing about, he understood at once, a visible embodiment of their once beloved daughter's unforgivable treachery, the insidious canker in the genealogy, a corruption to be coldly felled, sectioned and kindled into fine powder. It is Grandmother, Liberty surmised, who wishes him gone, returned to a banishment too good for him and his kind. But perhaps Grandfather, amused by his youthful audacity, had begun warming to him and might, after a probationary day or two, take Liberty aside for a private palaver on the hypocritical paradoxes of life above the Mason-Dixon line, then attempt to satisfy what must be a natural parental curiosity about the fate of his daughter, a woman he last glimpsed in the flesh more than two decades ago. And, if Grandfather asked, how would Liberty reply? She is dead, sir, he might explain, first driven to distraction, then harried to her grave by Furies you and Grandmother incubated and nourished to exact petty vengeance for a courageous assumption of moral duty you people, in your mutual blindness, could not perceive as anything other than willful disobedience, Furies I recognize even now leering from the wallpaper, decorating the trees, perching atop each and every fence post, Furies gathering themselves, I fear, for the final hunt, and this time, Grandfather, the quarry will be you and your invalid wife. Could he actually dare utter such damning language to a man who was still as much a stranger as he was kin? Well, Liberty was a pirate, remember; he knew how to bide his time until the moment was ripe for running up the black flag.

Maury came for him at dawn with a steaming cup of what passed for coffee in those straitened parts, a groggy Liberty startled at his window by the postdiluvian spectacle of flattened grass, dripping leaves and countless metallic-bright puddles of water standing about in the yard, as if the land itself had broken out into weepy eruptions.

"Rheumatoid's acting up in all this dampness," complained Maury, clutching his grandson's shoulder as they laboriously descended the gallery steps. "Sleep well?"

"Apparently so," admitted Liberty, not having heard a single drop.

"Rain on the roof, a soothing elixir vitae to the weary wayfarer. How many times, frazzled and sore, have I found myself, even in woefully inadequate foreign quarters, nodding plumb off to the gentle lullaby of an evening drizzle in my ear? Suppose it reminds us of the womb or some such truck."

"How's Grandmother today?"

"Wouldn't know. Elsie does a bang-up job of tending to her. I haven't slept in the same room with the woman since Nullification. Watch your step there"—brusquely yanking him around an impressive pile of dog manure. "A good soaking turns this place into one big crap farm. All varieties and shapes, too. There's a cash crop for you." He laughed mirthlessly. "Probably make a better job of it than with this cussed cotton. Got bad rust in that field there," he noted, pointing through the trees. "And a plague of caterpillars in the one yonder. And I've just received word another of the gins has seized up, so we're only working two today. If I weren't already crazy the futile attempt to coax a marginal profit out of these shiftless people and this played-out land would've brought the asylum cart to our door years ago. See those banks?" He indicated several distant acres of cleared ground laid out in ridged rows of soil and straw. "Those are my eating potatoes. Finest leatherjackets in the state. As you shall soon discover later at table. Ah, here we are." He had led Liberty through the mud and the mist to a long, narrow, weatherbeaten shack from whose malodorous interior seemingly emanated every unbearable sound of which human beings in distress are capable. "The sickhouse," he announced, in grand butlerian tones.

"What's all this commotion in here?" demanded Maury, stepping through a filthy curtain of frayed linen.

An overwrought woman with a milky eye and the letters *A M* branded on her cheek rushed forward. "It's Goldie, Master, she got a griping in the bowels and it pains her terrible."

"Well, what do you expect me to do about it? Brew up some of that cross root or fence grass and pour it down her whining throat."

"Already did, Master, and she's worse than ever."

"Well, we shall see about that. Goldie, where are you? Goldie!" Out of the clustering mob of howling, wailing, women, children and babies, all uniformly plastered from sole to crown in such a baked-on crust of matter biological and mineral it was obvious no bar of soap had approached anywhere near skin in weeks, if not months, came a timid young woman in a stained calico gown split up the back.

"Now then," asked Maury not unkindly, "where do you hurt?"

She pointed shyly to her belly.

"Lift up your dress."

Removing the ring from his belt, Maury chose one of the longer keys and began insistently pressing the business end into various spots on her stomach and abdomen while inquiring, "Does this hurt? Or that?" and the girl repeatedly shook her head no.

"There's nothing wrong with her," he declared. "Have her back in the fields by noon."

"But Master," pleaded the ward mistress, "she can barely walk."

"Are you deaf? Did you hear what I said? Maybe what I should do is send for Doctor Cooper, eh? Get ol' Doc Coop over to examine all of you malingerers. How'd you like that?"

"Now, now, Master, we don't need that old fool mucking about in here. My medicine's as good as his. Maybe I'll make up one of my turpentine and chestnut seed poultices for Goldie. Haven't tried that yet."

"Oh, really? Thought that peanut brain of yours might be able to come up with something. I'm sure, Goldie, that shortly all this nonsense will pass away and you'll be out there in the bottom pulling bolls like a machine."

Several small children who had attached themselves to Liberty almost immediately remained fast at his side, clutching tenaciously at his trouser legs. He felt immobilized in body and mind.

"How's Bridget?" asked Maury. "She's the one I've come to see."

Glancing away, the ward mistress pointed mutely to a lump under a ratty blanket. Nearby, two naked women struggled together on the dirt floor, apparently in the final stages of childbirth.

"Dead, eh?"

"She tried, Master, she tried awful hard not to fail you, but them galls was just too much for her little body."

"Well, get her buried then, and I don't want you to be carrying on all day about it either, understand? Plant her and get back to work. And by tomorrow I want at least half these shamming wretches cleared out of here. I got more people in this sickhouse than I do in the damn quarters. Come," he said to Liberty, who was daintily prying each child's hand, a grimy finger at a time, from his pants. "If I have to swallow one more breath of this deplorable air, I'll need one of Aunty's bark concoctions myself."

They trudged up the muddy lane toward the Big House in thoughtful silence. The clouds had broken up into ragged pieces a mild west wind was tidily dispersing. Sky's the same wherever you go, mused Liberty. Comforting notion to carry with you on your transit through life.

On the front gallery, awaiting their return, stood the overseer, Clement C. Malone, a transplanted northerner who had wandered into Dixie before the war in search of a job suitable to his talents and temperament. Apparently he had found it.

"My grandson," asserted Maury, admitting, to Liberty's astonishment, the blood relation for the first time. "Come all the way from New York state."

Malone cocked an interested eye, examining Liberty as if he'd never before beheld a living human of this particular age or sex. "That so? I hail from Brattleboro, Vermont, myself. Used to teach school up there." His grip felt like a clutchful of twigs wrapped in an old glove.

"Passed through the place once," Liberty remarked.

"Business? Pleasure?"

"Believe I was running away from home at the time."

The overseer glanced at Maury and chuckled dryly. "Itchy feet seem to run in the family. Contagious too—most of the servants being likewise affected."

"Easy now," cautioned Maury. "I don't pay you to strew insults upon my name."

"Or to do anything else, for that matter," Malone replied, avoiding eye contact by fumbling around in his pockets for something he couldn't find.

"Now, Clement, I don't notice you wanting for food, shelter or clothing."

"There are other wants."

"Yes, but none you really need filled. As I have previously explained, with great forbearance I might add, this plantation is a joint-stock enterprise. We rise and we fall as one. When I have money, you shall have money. If everyone had grasped this simple principle from the start, had pulled together as a team, perhaps we wouldn't find ourselves in our present predicament."

"With all due respect, sir, I would venture to suggest that with the unforeseen, catastrophic events now ruling us it wouldn't have mattered how hard we pulled, we would not have been able to outpace the bluebellied tide. In fact," he added, with a sly gaze in Liberty's direction, "looks like the advance guard has already arrived."

"Mr. Malone, the entire country can go down for all I care, but here at Redemption Hall we are staying up, do you understand? We are not going down."

"Tell that to the hands. Two more bolted this morning."

"Who?"

"Moses and Ella."

"Perfidious bastards. Well, let them go. I want only the faithful around me. In the pattyroller times we would have treed 'em and hung 'em from same. I should have whipped the pair of them more often when they were younger. That's where you take your durable lessons in love and devotion—at the tip of the lash."

"Horace quit hoeing again today after about an hour and says tomorrow he might not do any hoeing at all."

"Well, then, lay into him, man, lay into him good."

"Be happy to, Mr. Maury, but I wanted to check with you because, as you know, the administration of discipline in our current circumstance can provoke some additional, rather inexpedient problems."

"You provide the correction and I'll worry about the consequences."

"Very well, sir." And, with a tip of his hat, he abruptly departed.

"The bottom's dropped out of that imbecile's gut," Maury muttered, and then, as if struck by some untoward occurrence, invisible to Liberty, sullying the immutable perfection of the clear horizon, he froze completely for a spell, studying the empty distance as if positively entranced, his expressionless face dominated by what Liberty remembered his mother describing as "faraway eyes," that invariable precursor to a day spent brooding in his office or, worse, striding around the property in full possession of what the intimidated family termed his "manwrath," harassing dependencies and kinfolk alike. But the mood seemed to pass off quickly enough, and a minute later he was civilly, even cordially inviting Liberty to wash up for the noon dinner, an occasion of occasions, since on this very special day Grandmother had decided, against Maury's better judgement, to venture forth from her sick room in order to take her meal with her only surviving grandchild.

Aided by two wheezing, hopelessly inept servants, one on each frail arm, the old white lady was clumsily maneuvered out of her bed, down the creaking staircase and across the barren hall to the dining room, all the while as if wrestling with a sack of dry sticks, where the infirm, impossible woman was unceremoniously deposited in her bespoken padded wheel chair. Once seated, she waved her skeletal fingers in a gesture of impatient dismissal and addressed the waiting room. "I swear, I'll never become accustomed to those unscrupulous black hands touching me where no proper lady should ever be touched." She glared accusingly at the slaves now arranged in a respectful rank against the wall, arms decorously folded in attitudes of patient attendance.

"Now, now," soothed her husband.

"Are you daring to imply, Mr. Maury, that I am imagining such improprieties?"

"I didn't say that, Ida."

"I know you tend to regard me as hardly more than an antiquated fool, so bereft of her senses she cannot distinguish between assistance and assault."

"When you're crazy, Mrs. Maury, I shall be the first to inform you."

"Yes, and how would you know, dawdling about in that precious hideaway of yours like a feeble-minded recluse, and what, I'd like to know, has all this blasphemous projecting gotten us but fresh graves in the yard and a mess of crippled niggers?"

Ignoring the question, Maury leaned back in his chair and called out sharply through the open doorway, "Ditey! We're ready for the potatoes now!"

"Jonah," said Mrs. Maury to one of the ministering domestics as she continued to fuss ceaselessly with her silverware, "you and the others wait outside until requested. I can't bear to eat with all those devil eyes boring into me."

"Nerves bad today?" asked her husband. "We could increase the drops this evening."

"At this point, Asa, what does it matter? Awake or asleep, it's the same accursed life I'm passing through, the same death. And you, boy." She rotated her chair in Liberty's direction. "Excuse me for not addressing you by your Christian name, but I find my tongue simply refuses to pronounce the word. You bring a green perspective to all this moth and mildew. What is your opinion of our Redemption Hall?"

"With due respect," replied Liberty, "it's a bit more than I can adequately absorb in a single day."

Her nose made a horrid snorting noise that could almost have been the beginning of a laugh, but wasn't. "I've been here half a century, and I haven't absorbed a single thing."

"Ditey!" Maury shouted again. "Where are those potatoes? I promised the lad potatoes!"

"I do have a question," submitted Liberty, somewhat hesitantly. "Redemption Hall. What is it exactly you seek to be redeemed from?"

"Ourselves," cracked Grandmother.

"There may be more truth in that remark than you intend," Maury observed with a grimly indulgent smile. "My own grandfather, Samuel Maury, cleared the land and named the plantation. An enthusiast of the most dangerous stripe, a bit too enchanted by moonbeams, if you know what I mean, he envisioned the Hall as a sort of school for the natural man where souls were to be educated in the ways of God and, through a magical metamorphosis I've never been able to fully comprehend, attain to a paradise, not only spiritual but material as well. You sit at the very heart of what was designed to be a new Eden on earth."

"What happened?"

"What do you think happened? He went bankrupt. If it weren't for Whitney and his gin—and who's to say the Lord was not working mightily through the inspirations of the inventor—the entire estate might have passed out of family hands. As it was, once seeds could be separated from fiber quickly and efficiently, rational Maurys could reestablish the enterprise on a healthy cash basis."

"Whose abundant rewards we reap today," interrupted Grandmother.

"Too many folks lost in spiritual error," Maury continued. "We would not find ourselves in the midst of war and desolation had we not strayed so far from the teachings of the Testament, where the prescriptions for the good life are laid out clearly and precisely. This confusion over the issue of bondage is absolutely baseless. Servitude exists as the foundation for every great civilization from the ancients on. It's the axis of the divine plan. Read Genesis 9:25–27, Genesis 24:35–36, Leviticus 25:44–46, among others."

"What about Hebrews 13:3?" interjected Liberty. "'Remember them that are in bonds as bound with them.'"

"I'll admit Satan can be found here and there peeking through the bars of sacred verse, but we should bear in mind that he is indeed caged."

Grandmother responded with another dismissive snort. "Why I ever even agreed to marry you and settle down on this exhausted patch of nothing is a mystery known only to the angels. Or perhaps the demons," she added. Her small round head with its wispy halo of thinning gray hair swiveled about to address Liberty. "I've wasted my life shackled to an idiot, and I pray to God you should possess better sense. Your mother was the smartest of the brood, and you can only hope you've inherited a portion of her brains, which, of course, she must have gotten from me since, well, you've just heard a sanitized version of the lunacy that resides on the other side. And to think I could have eloped with that young Franklin boy and run off to Europe and spent my declining years in a Roman villa well out of all this consternation." She looked to Liberty for signs of sympathy and, when none were forthcoming, quickly averted her head with a theatrical sigh.

"Ditey!" bellowed Grandfather with genuine heat. "Bring the fucking potatoes! Now!"

"Your mother," Mrs. Maury went obliviously on. "Such a beauty, too."

"Not as beautiful as Aurore," commented Grandfather.

"No, not as beautiful, but she could have had any man in the state. We were so sorry when we heard about the accident. We even gave the niggers the day off to mourn. Honestly, I don't believe Redemption Hall has ever been the same since."

"No," Maury agreed, gazing somberly down at his own reflection in his empty plate, "none of us have."

"Even though, of course, we had always regarded her as dead long before the actual event, the news of its terrible reality came as quite a shock."

"We made a mistake with her," interposed Maury in an uncharacteristically chastened tone.

"We made a mistake with all of 'em," she snapped back. "That's what happens. What are we supposed to do about it now? Five of 'em gone already, and the other might as well be for all we know. Chasing after glory and a storybook life that never could be, never was for anybody. Just a silly, destructive dream, that's all. A dream that's failed, as we have failed as a family. And now it's our turn to go, and frankly I'm looking forward to it. The fire and ice of hell couldn't be much worse than what I've been privileged to endure as a dragooned member of this dissolute clan."

"Stop this nonsense at once," ordered Maury angrily. "You're tired and hungry and don't know what you're saying."

"The boy knows. He understands. I can see it in his eyes." She reached over to pat the back of Liberty's hand. "I'm so glad you were able to make this visit. You can tell the others what became of us. The world blew up and took Ida and Asa with it. Tell them that. That's what I want them to hear."

At the sound of approaching footsteps, as arrhythmic and heavy as bricks being dropped singly onto the floorboards, the dinner party turned as one to observe an ancient woman dressed in a parti-colored frock bearing a huge chipped bowl of steaming vegetables. Her crooked nose had obviously been broken sometime in the distant past and never correctly reset, and her left ear reduced to a twisted knot of cartilege stuck to the side of her balding gray head.

"What in the name of weeping Jesus is this?" demanded Mrs. Maury, indignantly examining the dish placed on the table before her. "These aren't potatoes, they're goddamn turnips!"

"There ain't any more potatoes," replied Ditey, wringing her hands, wiping them on her dress. "This here is all we got."

"There were potatoes yesterday," insisted Mrs. Maury, stabbing a turnip with her fork. "What happened to 'em?"

"All et up, I expect."

"Yes, and I'm sure all you thieving ingrates made a fine meal of it too, leaving us to dine on this miserable hog food. And they aren't even properly cooked. These things are as hard as stones."

"I did the best I could, Missus."

"Well it wasn't good enough, and it's never been good enough, you worthless bitch." Grandmother lifted her knife as if preparing to carve some fowl. "Hold out your hand." And with a single swift movement she opened the cringing woman's palm to the bone. In an instant, with a savage cry, Ditey was upon her, the chair overturning, both women toppling to the carpet, Ditey's hands, blood spilling from the one in shocking amounts, locked tight as iron collars about her mistress's scrawny neck, a stunned Liberty only half-risen from his seat as Grandfather, with astonishing celerity, charged around the table, seized a chair and brought it crashing down upon Ditey's head in a dreadful splintering of wood and skull. Then, yanking the unconscious cook from atop his wife's body, Maury knelt down beside her, wiping the blood off her neck and face with the napkin Liberty, at a loss to do anything else, had handed him. "Get some water," he ordered.

Out in the kitchen, the other servants having briskly fled, Liberty found only a distraught young girl crouching under a table. "What's going to happen?" she cried frantically. "What's going to happen now?"

"I don't know," he replied calmly, grabbing a half bucket of water from the counter. "You'd best get out of here."

Back in the dining room Maury had managed to prop his semiconscious wife into a sitting position against the wall where he now knelt, dabbing tenderly at her ashen cheeks.

The moan issuing from her tiny, fishlike mouth was of such an unusually low pitch and impossibly long duration that it seemed to be emanating from beneath the floor.

"You're all right," Maury kept repeating. "You're going to be all right."

Grandmother's eyes fluttered open. "No," she whispered in a faint, diminished voice, "I'm not all right."

"There's not even a bruise," Maury observed, carefully inspecting her neck.

"Is she dead?" came the voice, ever more feeble.

Maury glanced over at where Ditey lay facedown in a widening puddle of her own blood. She appeared to be still breathing. "I believe so."

"Good." The eyes closed again. "Isn't anyone going to give me a drink of water?"

At a nod from his grandfather, Liberty dipped a cup into the bucket and held it to his grandmother's trembling lips.

"Are you able to walk?" Maury inquired.

Impatiently, she pushed away Liberty's hand. "No, I'm not able to walk. How can you ask such a ridiculous question? I've just been almost murdered."

"I think you'll feel better upstairs in your bed."

"Apparently I have no choice in the matter."

"We'll help you." Then he and Liberty lifted her unsteadily to her feet and, without much more grace or skill than the servants who had originally brought her down, half carried and half dragged the querulous old woman back into the hallway, up the rackety stairs, down the musty corridor and into her bed where, her little girl's body decorously arranged beneath the covers, her exposed head rested on the pillow like a sculpted bust of rare worth, eyes as black and resolute as stones.

"This is the end," she muttered. "The absolute end."

"Goodnight, Ida."

"Goodnight," seconded Liberty, the unspoken "Grandma" practically audible in his ears.

"Goodnight?" she sneered. "It's two in the afternoon."

"Once your lids are shut," noted Maury, "what difference does it make?"

"Get out," she commanded wearily, "the both of you."

As they descended the stairs, Maury's face assuming an additional stratum of petrification at each step, Liberty found himself increasingly distracted by the alarmingly high proportion of familiar features—his own, largely—he could detect in the ancestors' likenesses arrayed so symmetrically down the wall. As if the unholy mess of one family's problematical past could be subverted or even ignored by a simple touch of ornamental harmony.

At the foot of the stairs Maury paused. "As you might have reckoned," he informed Liberty, "I have some further business with the dependents which requires my immediate attention. The library's in there. Help yourself. I'll be back for you later this evening. I have a special treat prepared."

"I want to come with you."

"No, you needn't trouble yourself. I've been handling such matters since before you were born, and I expect I can make a fist of this one just fine. In the meantime, read a book, take a nap." And he departed through the back door, leaving Liberty alone in the hallway to absorb the private sounds of the house. It was so quiet he could discern even the faint metallic cadences of the clock in Grandfather's office, each separate, steady tick as sharp and harsh as the scraping of a cold chisel on marble.

The library was a modest room with one chair, one hopelessly abraded red velvet sofa and one bookcase, most of the shelves half-empty, most of the remaining volumes mildewed and insect-ridden, and, except for a forlorn cultural outpost of about a dozen novels by Scott and Dickens, all the titles chanted the same dreary singsong he'd already heard down in the "office," of skulls and saxons, genesis and genealogy. He grabbed a copy of *Great Expectations*, its first twenty pages mysteriously missing, and retired to his room.

Stretched out on the bed, unable to read or think, he allowed himself to subside gratefully into the all-enveloping cloudiness of a deep feather mattress, into nothingness.

He came awake to disorienting darkness and a knocking so forcefully insistent—the door rattling in the jamb at each blow—it seemed like something begun in a dream and then willed into existence by its own brute necessity. Liberty managed to pull himself up in bed and croak out a feeble "Yes?"

"It's Asa."

"Come in." He realized he was still lying atop the sheets in all his clothes and muddy boots. "If you would, sir, please excuse me. In my fatigue I seem to have inadvertently soiled the linen."

"Don't trouble yourself with such trash," Maury responded. "Earlier today I promised you a surprise, and now I've come to make good."

Liberty swung his legs out onto the floor. "How's Ditey?"

"Neither more, nor less, than she should be. Now hush, and follow me."

He led Liberty to a plain, unmarked door at the far end of the hallway from Grandmother's, a door bolted on the outside. "Valuable contents within," he revealed in an alcohol-scented stage whisper, genuine excitement infecting his manner for the first time since his infatuated lectures on the human brain pan. Pushing back the door, he presented Liberty with a theatrical bow, insisting, "After you."

The entire chamber had been dramatically transformed into a dazzling cube of pure white, every exposed surface, floor to ceiling, wall to wall, liberally coated in several layers of untinted wash, the startling effect heightened by the dozens of candles scattered haphazardly about the floor but for the orderly double row at Liberty's feet that formed an illuminated path to the bed, the sole article of furniture in the room, freshly sheeted and from its mahogany posts draped in endless yards of billowing muslin. Posed before this monstrous object—despite appearances, a ship whose dream weather would no doubt always be inclement—was a young girl, younger even than Liberty, and also wrapped in immaculate muslin, though of insufficient quantity to obscure wholly the naked body beneath. On her head she wore a makeshift crown of cotton bolls and in her right hand she gripped a rusty hoe. Her smooth, glowing face was a perfect blank, her eyes inaccessible voids.

"Liberty," Grandfather announced with a certain degree of apprehensive ceremony, addressing his grandson by name for the first time, "I would like to introduce you to Slavery." He made a petulant gesture with his hand, to which the girl responded immediately with a slight curtsy, the hoe, however, in the process, tumbling to the floor and knocking over several candles.

"Christ on a stick!" shouted Maury, springing forward to correct the damage. "Have you any wits about you at all, you stupid cunt. Burning down the house, screwing on the parlor rug, crapping down the well, it's all the same to you, isn't it? Why, I ought to—" The girl cowered before him, anticipating the blow. "You'd like me to hit you, wouldn't you? Show the stranger here just what a terrible ogre your master truly is. Well, the stranger already knows, and he certainly doesn't require any instruction from—"

"Please," Liberty interrupted. "Would you please stop badgering this girl?"

"She's my daughter," Maury proclaimed blandly. "I'll do with her as I see fit. There, the secret of the evening revealed, and not exactly the stirring climax I had so tantalizingly envisioned."

"Would you please tell me," Liberty asked, exasperated, "what all this tedious grotesquery is about?"

"Isn't it obvious? I want you to plant a sucker in her."

"So you can examine the result?"

"Yes, so I can examine the result. I've already been granted a glimpse, you know, in my mind's eye, of the fruit of such a noble union. I foresee a favored issue, impeccable in proportion, sound of judgment, exemplary in character and, need I add, unblemished in complexion—the inheritor of our future, the final yield of my dreams, the glory of a nation."

"Your lunacy exceeds the bounds of definition."

"But I have freely, even cheerfully confessed to you my own spectacular derangement. And, on the cosmic scale, what is the eternal value of such a bold admission? I'll tell you. A bungtown copper, that's what. Because it may very well be that the universe itself is what we call crazed and the appearance of such a condition in an ordinary human implies that the individual has only adjusted himself as he would to a suit of ill-fitting clothes, for the commendable purpose of attaining a more accurate alignment with the stars."

"Well, that beats my flush."

"Good. Now, enjoy yourself. I shall see you again at breakfast." He headed toward the door.

"Hold on. I feel obliged to point out the curious irony that you, an unapologetic, antiabolitionist soul stealer, working alone in secret, have surpassed every other member of this tormented family, including us northern agitators, in the pursuit of amalgamation. You not only promote intimate relations between the races, you actively practice it."

"Prophetic vision is a merciless gift."

"And mercy itself a greater dispensation."

"I shan't bandy words with you on this topic any longer. You have a pressing duty to perform, and I would suggest you not waste time. Remember, I have a parson's faith in you and despite the evident distastefulness of the deed, you're a Maury, you'll find a way through." The door closed behind him, the bolt slammed pointedly shut.

By the time Liberty turned around, the girl had somehow freed herself from her muslin cocoon and now stood revealed before him in all her youthful nubility, any seductive appeal altogether dampened by an expression of such abject submissiveness on her face that he could only look away.

"Have you any real clothing?" Liberty asked, noting the pile of gauzy material at her feet.

"No, sir," she replied. "Most of the time Master keeps me penned up in here with nothing but a handful of frill to cover my quim."

"Well, here," he said, yanking a sheet from the bed. "Wrap this around you. I'm not the master."

"Aren't you going to make a baby with me?" she asked, obviously quite surprised.

"No," returned Liberty promptly, "there'll be no baby making tonight. Given the genealogical anarchy that prevails in this house, by my calculations I do believe, and I think correctly, that you are my aunt." He tried the door with his shoulder; it refused to budge. "What's your name?" he asked, stepping between the candles to the open window.

"Slavery," she insisted.

"I mean your real name, your Christian name." Outside the window were no conveniently located trees to shimmy down. The drop was straight to the ground.

"Slavery is my real name."

"You've never been called anything else since your birth?" he asked, incredulous.

"You mean my buckra name or my nigger name?"

"Please, don't use that word. It makes my ears twitch. Tell me, what did your mother call you?"

"I don't remember."

"Yes you do. What did she call you?"

The innocent question plunging the girl into a quandary of no minor scale, the internal contest writ plain across her countenance, she must have finally concluded that this was one white boy for whom the rules of the place were mere signs, erected to be transgressed. "Tempie," she answered shyly.

"Tempie? Good. Now was that so hard?"

"Master spoke about you all the time," she dared to go on, "ever since I was a wee babe. He always said you'd show up here one day."

"He did, eh?" The bleached, featureless claustrophobia of the room was starting to oppress him. He felt as if he were trapped inside a snowbank.

"Master said there was a powerful calling on you that you'd try to throw off, but it stuck to you like tar."

"That's Grandfather for you, ever the sly divinator. Listen, I think we could fashion a fairly sturdy rope out of these remaining sheets and slide out the window in relative safety."

The girl regarded him with a detached stare. "Why?" she asked flatly.

"Why? Why, to escape, of course."

"Escape where?"

"Anywhere you please. The days of whips and chains are over."

"Master says the whole world's a slave ship on its passage out, bound for the fiery fields of Satan's plantation."

"Yes, he certainly would know. Tell me, how long have you been locked up like this?"

"Since before the war come."

"Well, Tempie, I'm here to inform you that the house of bondage is thoroughly ablaze from cellar to ridgepole. The old haunted manse is coming down at last." He caught her glancing anxiously upward, scanning the ceiling for tendrils of flame. "No, no," he tried to explain, "not this house. The one I was referring to is more of a verbal representation really, a sort of mental picture made up of words, which aren't real but which stand for something that is real, in this case the entire institution of slavery which, of course, is not exactly a house, either, but"—this rather clumsy and long-winded descent into the maze of metaphor thankfully interrupted by a wild clatter of hooves up the lane and into the yard where, as Liberty watched from his second-story vantage, the riders, perhaps a dozen of them, hatted, cloaked and armed, milled about in confused excitement, everyone speaking loudly, incoherently, and at once, Grandfather suddenly appearing in their midst, his great white head glowing eerily in the humid darkness. There was a minute or two of frenzied conference, then the horsemen swiveled around and went galloping away, one intelligible word still ringing magically in Liberty's ears: "Yankees!"

"The war," he declared to Tempie, who continued to sit, almost demurely, on the edge of the bed, firmly moored to some durable sense of inner constancy utterly indifferent to, and totally immune from, public event, "come in the true flesh to free you from this damn room."

Hardly had the words left Liberty's mouth than the bolt was drawn and in charged Maury, looking grimmer than ever, the navy revolver strapped imposingly to his waist. "Still got your clothes on, I see," he observed contemptuously.

"What's happening?"

"Federal patrol. Just crossed the county line with, I reckon, all hell and damnation fast behind. Here to fetch you, eh?" he asked tartly, though Liberty remained diplomatically silent. "Well," he went on, "we sure ain't waiting around to sound the welcoming horn. We're clearing out tonight." He tossed a wadded-up shift in Tempie's general direction and ordered her brusquely to get dressed. "You," he said to Liberty, "I want to help me get Ida down to the wagon."

Grandmother, however, from behind her fortress of quilts and blankets would not be moved. She appeared, in fact, not to have budged an inch. Hands folded like molded curios across her abdomen, she listened without comment to her husband's persuasive assessment of the situation and his strongly considered judgement that all should now hastily flee the property in prudent advance of the approaching Union tide.

"No," she responded bluntly.

"Ida," he pleaded.

"You heard me, so don't ask again."

"But you always claimed you'd rather die first before witnessing a single Yankee set foot in this house."

"One already has," she replied, refusing to grant Liberty so much as a glance. "Now, bring me my pistols. I should be able to manage quite well by myself. I came into this forsaken world alone, and I do believe I'm more than capable of passing out of it equally unencumbered."

"If you think for one instant that I would even consider abandoning my own wife to the foul depredations of—"

"Oh, Asa, please. Just stop."

"Monday's preparing a bed in the wagon I trust will be comfortable. The road is good, the journey brief, and I'll tolerate no further objections, do you understand?"

"Bring me my pistols."

"I'm not going to argue with you, Ida."

"Nor I with you." She held out her hand. "The pistols."

"You try me, Ida, you try me terribly." Maury stepped to the bureau and from the top drawer removed a polished red mahogany box he carried dutifully over to the bed. Opening the box, his wife removed one of the pair of small silver pistols encased within and brandished it about, remarking to no one in particular, "My father killed a man in a duel with these. Pretty, aren't they?" She arranged the pistols on the blanket, one on either side of her, within easy reach. "No damn abolitionist would dare to lay a finger on a sick old woman like me." Then, noting the uncommon look of momentary distress passing over her husband's face, she allowed her own expression to soften slightly.

"I'm sorry, Asa, I simply cannot go with you, but I'm tired, so very tired. What a precious blessing it will be to arrive finally in the place where 'the wicked cease from troubling and the weary be at rest.'"

"You don't weigh any more than a child. I could pick you up and carry you bodily from this room."

"Don't." A fluttering hand strayed to touch one of the pistols. "Please don't."

"I'm through contending with you, woman. Fifty years of ache and fret and strife repudiated on a ridiculous whim."

"Blackberry jam," she muttered. "I could sure use a taste of sweet blackberry jam."

"Enough!" Maury cried, then curtly addressing Liberty: "Say goodbye to your grandmother. I'll meet you outside."

"Come," she beckoned, raising up her withered arms. "Come closer." Bending over, Liberty was abruptly seized in a grip of unexpected ferocity which drew him insistently downward toward her ancient, creased face. At such intimate proximity she smelled of camphor and powder and carious teeth. She breathed then into his waiting ear, "I always loved Roxana best," and kissed him delicately on the cheek.

"Good-bye, Grandmother," he returned, hugging the dry bones of her body. "You know, we Yankees are not the lecherous, baby-eating fiends we're reputed to be."

"Yes, yes, I know, I'll be fine," she asserted, "but you watch out for Asa. He's not as young as he thinks he is."

The last view he had of her was of a disembodied, pillowed head, her dark eyes furiously alight, as if consumed forever in infernal flames of black fire.

Down in the yard the wagon stood ready, Monday, an elderly gentleman of questionable competence but iron loyalty, or so Maury claimed, perched anxiously up on the seat, reins in hand, Tempie crouched on a straw mattress in back like a feral cat amid a chaos of trunks, bags, boxes, loose stacks of books, skulls, wire cages and dozens of thick manuscripts wrapped in protective linen. Mounted on a large, handsome bay, Maury gripped the halter of a second, decidedly less handsome animal. "Last able-bodied mare in the county," he bragged. "Kept her hidden out in the swamp for just such an eventuality."

"I think I should stay," insisted Liberty. "Watch over Grandmother until the boys arrive, maybe have the surgeon take a look at her."

"Out of the question, lad. You know as well as I do she's practically impervious to harm, no cause for concern there. But you I need. Our project remains woefully incomplete. You're now a crucial wheel in the on-rolling advance of science, and, frankly, as I well know, any knowledge worth possessing requires a certain degree of sacrifice. Get on the horse."

"I reckon I'll stay."

Reluctantly, Maury pulled the revolver from his holster and leveled it in his grandson's face. "Get on the horse."

"Everyone in this family seems awfully handy with a gun," remarked Liberty dryly, stepping up into the saddle.

"Self-protection," answered Maury, with a rare snicker of amusement. "From each other."

"Where exactly are we going?"

"Where a man's rights are still respected and the people understand that the God-ordained, necessary and sacred institution of human bondage is not to be trampled upon."

"And where would this blessed paradise be?"

"Brazil," Grandfather replied, swinging the bay roughly about and leading wagon and rider down the lane and into the cumbrous night.

The tide was high, the sky low, the wind a mere whisper, when Asa Maury and his sullen party—not a word exchanged among them during the whole spine-rattling journey—arrived flushed and exhausted before the strangely derelict geometry of the Charleston docks. "Runner's weather," noted Maury approvingly, eying the silent, oil-dark water, the dim, turbid clouds.

"Stuff and nonsense," countered Liberty, eager for any quarrel he could muster. "Even without a moon, what vessel, no matter how skillfully piloted, would dare the blockading squadron at this late date? The harbor's been corked tight as French grape since the fall of Morris Island."

"Quite correct," replied Maury with a wry smile. "I see you northern lads, in addition to your marvelous attainments in art and industry, also possess the ability to absorb a newspaper or two. But hear me: 'impossible' is the credo of the multitude. I am interested in the 'one,' because there is always a singular 'one,' one who says no to no, one for whom the great, giddy game of hares and hounds with the Federal fleet is far from concluded. That is the one I seek and the one I shall find. There, look there, conjured out of my very thought!" He pointed a bony finger toward a wharf some several hundred feet distant, where shifting glints of lantern light revealed the long, low lines of a narrow knifelike steamer and a shadowy bustling about the mooring uncommon at this hour. "The signs magnify and bear fruit.

What says the skeptic in you now, young whelp? Fathom how Providence ever eases my way. This silvery head of mine is a crown anointed. Come, let us search out the captain."

Leaving their mounts and plunder in Monday's charge, Maury led his grandson and his grandson's presumptive bride down to the ship, the CSS *Cavalier* according to the ornately carved plaque on her bow, every deck inch already piled high with three-hundred-pound bales of crop cotton, and brazenly past the glum, sweating crew of half-naked slaves wrestling even more bales up the creaking gangway but pausing in their labor to behold the curious spectacle of a queer old white man escorting aboard a surly white youth and a sorrowful black girl with all the imperious assurance of a company owner conducting a surprise inspection.

Directed by a churlish mate with one eye and one tooth who, the strangers no sooner departed, leaned over, deliberately spat upon the very place where Maury had stood and then proceeded to rub the warm spittle into the wood, they found the captain, one Wilbur Wallace, alone in the pilothouse, chewing on an unlit cigar and reading a month-old edition of the *London Times*. "Looking dire for our side, gentlemen," he announced brightly, folding the paper and tossing it carelessly onto the chart table. "In fact, we probably surrendered last week." His laughter was like an explosion of champagne bottles. There was, in the infectious sound of it, the promise of merriment everlasting.

After a perfunctory round of introductions and handshakes, Wallace's sharp gaze lingering briefly on the shy Tempie, whose attention remained fixed, as ever, on her bare feet, Maury got promptly down to business. "I require, sir, immediate passage for four to whatever port of call you happen to be bound."

"That so?" Wallace's eyebrows, like the rest of his extraordinarily mobile features, seemed to have been fabricated to produce the most theatrical effects possible, sliding abruptly upward, then down again with an almost audible click.

"I am willing to pay, and pay dearly, for the privilege. I have money. Greenbacks. Carpetbags full of them."

———

"As do I, Mr. Maury, as do I."

"Who doesn't need more?"

"Mr. Maury, please allow me to make one crucial fact perfectly comprehensible. This scruffy little spat of yours between the states has been for me, as well as for a distressingly sized host of the unscrupulous, what your bluenoses like to call a 'High Daddy.' Ministering to privation has made me a wealthy man many times over. I have no need of your greenbacks, and no need, I'm afraid, of you." He turned his attention to the young people. "Motley company you've assembled here. This your son?"

"My grandson."

"Remarkable. These two might even be brother and sister if it weren't for the obvious difference in, um, skin color, of course."

"Name your fee."

"The *Cavalier*, Mr. Maury, as I would expect you have already noted, is decidedly not a pleasure boat. In a matter of hours we lay our head for Nassau, under the most deplorable conditions imaginable, with probably the last lading of the long staple to depart this wretched city. Why is this poor girl trembling so?"

"She's of a fretful nature. Look, Captain Wallace, if space is indeed the issue, I will be delighted to pay whatever amount you think fair to occupy even a few feet of open deck, but it is imperative that I and my party leave Charleston as soon as possible."

Wallace's glance, bold and intense, even as he addressed Maury, flitted about the room like a trapped bird, apparently unable to locate any more suitable resting place than Tempie's thinly clad person, which object it explored in all its fine particulars. Sensing the girl's discomfort, Liberty stepped forward, shielding her with his body. The spell broken, Wallace once again took up Maury's request. "Imperatives, these days," he replied, "are about as abundant as palmettos in the marsh. And about as useful. But as it happens, there does remain available a single stateroom which, I regret to say, had been reserved for a certain young lady. Only a lunatic or a lover would try these heavily patrolled waters, and I fear I partake much of both qualities. It was she who beckoned, she who drew me in under the guns. And a close shave we had of it, too. Lucky shot from a Yankee cruiser carried off the supercargo and five barrels of coffin nails, of which our embattled Confederacy is, at the present moment, I am led to understand, in desperate need." He seemed to be winking perpetually, even when he wasn't.

"What might 'supercargo' be?" asked Liberty.

"Not a 'what,' a 'who.' Mr. Perkins was Fraser, Trenholm's man, company representative on board. Fussy, pedantic sort, though there was no questioning his bravery. He'd survived a dozen runs, including two sinkings and a capture which culminated in a brief but pleasant sojourn within the confines of the Ludlow Street Jail up New York way. Still, I never could warm up to him much. A thoroughly sour gent from the rind to the pulp. Disapproved of the ladies, too. Couldn't see any profit there. We nearly came to blows over this trip, I tell you. But perhaps he sensed his doom, caught a premonition or some such. We veteran webfeet are quite prone to divine messages, angelic visitations, prophetic dreams and the like."

"Soldiers, too," interjected Liberty.

"Aye, soldiers, too. Stand upon the precipice long enough and even a blind man will be granted a few squints into that far horizon. Maybe Perky glimpsed from a bed in Liverpool the ball coming for him. I don't know. Bad business, very bad. Frightful losses all around. At least my Ellen still tarries among the living, though not, I admit, in my latitudes."

"Captain, if I may," broke in Maury impatiently. "My majordomo awaits, and the docks are not safe at this hour."

"Have you a single good ear, my man? I've promised you the berth, but interrupt me once more and you may find yourself dog-paddling to the Bahamas. I am relating a tale of considerable gravity upon the subject of love and its sweet conundrums. As I was explaining, in the course of my frequent and lengthy absences, my dear Ellen met and lost her affections to another whose own absences, while numerous, were neither as frequent nor as lengthy as my own. A young captain of the cavalry, she informs me, who even now buzzes about the flanks of Grant's army at Petersburg in the manner, I suppose, of a gnat pestering the ass of an elephant. I am no longer of any use to her. She awaits the return of her hero."

"Yes, yes, the heart's inconstancy," proclaimed Maury in his grandest style. "Theme of the ages, yes, yes. The cheap mania of every scribbler who's ever been given the mitten."

"I should prefer, I think, to compose odes in tranquillity upon the topic than suffer its singular enjoyments in the actual harrowed flesh. But enough of my complaints," Wallace added brusquely, waving an irritated hand before his face as if to shoo away that selfsame gnat. "Mine is a dreary old story being reenacted even as we speak, no doubt, by different players in different homes all across this splintered continent. A regrettable denouement for me is, however, an unexpected boon for you gentlemen, and lady"—bowing deeply in Tempie's direction. "I detect a destiny at work in this encounter. Perhaps you all have been directed here to instruct me in some matter of which I am blithely unaware. Or perhaps you bring luck, a blessing of good fortune to this voyage. But at the least we shall have the pleasure of your company, and that may be luck enough. Interesting issues we shall have ample opportunity to investigate further. For now, we embark within the hour. I want you and your goods securely stowed away by then. Flynn!" he called out, prompting the instant appearance in the doorway of a remarkably young, remarkably clean-cut sailor but for the crude tattoo of an upside-down anchor inscribed upon his left cheek. "Mister Flynn here will assist with your baggage and show you to your quarters. You will find our accommodations tight but tolerable. Welcome aboard the *Cavalier*," he said briskly, shaking the hand of each man in turn before pausing to grant Tempie yet another elaborate bow. Then, taking her small, slender hand in his own, he gently, politely, offered her a delicate kiss.

At the appointed hour, having turned loose the horses, Maury lifting his arms in mad benediction as the frightened animals went clattering away over the dark stones and crying out, "Let them find service in the Cause, wherever the Cause may find them," and, having hauled Maury's assorted books, boxes, cages and equipment onto the ship, down along narrow passageways made even narrower by the bales of cotton stacked against the bulkheads and into a modest compartment whose cramped oppressiveness was further heightened by a conveniently wrapped stateroom-sized bale occupying most of the available floor space, the frazzled travelers found themselves seated in utter darkness under strict injunction by Captain Wallace to neither speak nor move about until sent for. The hatches had been covered in tarp, the lanterns and candles extinguished, when the *Cavalier* slipped quietly away from the pier, the only sounds the deep dull throb of the engines, the soft rhythmic plop of the paddles, the sense of motion conveyed through their bodies in a steady series of vibratory waves. It was as if they were a set of rare figurines encased in a block of darkness and being discreetly transported from one secret location to another. The heat was stifling, the tension near unendurable. It was Maury who broke first.

"Kissing a nigger like that," he hissed savagely. "As if she were goddamn royalty."

"Please," requested Liberty, in an access of emotion that startled him, so much unsaid and undone for so long, "I ask you never to employ that loathsome word in my presence ever again. It stains the very air around us."

"May I remind you, young Mr. Fish, that I still possess a weapon which even now is aimed squarely at your heart."

"You wouldn't kill me even if you could see your target."

"And why, pray tell, not?"

"It would ruin your grand experiment in human husbandry."

"But I may not be of sound mind, as you yourself have suggested more than once, and a certain flooding of the heart could conceivably topple what few paltry pillars of reason remain, in which case the actions of my finger could take place in total isolation from the monitor of my brain."

"Then you'd better pray you are a good shot."

Maury's stifled laughter sounded through the closed cabin like a bad case of the hiccups. "I'm only doodling you, lad. I wouldn't harm a hair on that precious amalgamator head of yours. Besides, you've got good bumps. But please, try to refrain from talking back to me. Insolence doesn't become you, and it agitates my blood."

"Well, you might give a tad more consideration to the sensitivities of those in your company."

"Feisty as your mother indeed."

The floor shuddered, the ship moved on, the muffled strain of broken sobs began to emanate from the corner where Tempie sat huddled.

"What the hell's wrong with her now?" hissed Maury.

"She misses her mama," replied Monday in a low, mournful voice.

"We all miss our mama," Maury whispered contemptuously. "Life's a damn trial."

"With you as presiding judge," added Liberty.

"Well, there are not many in this confounding existence who truly understand the difference between right and wrong."

"You understand nothing."

"And a green cob like you presumes to educate me in the just ways of the world?"

"Your world, thankfully, is defunct."

"Hush!" Maury cautioned sharply. "Hush now. What's that?"

No one dared move or speak, ears attuned to the faint, incongruous sounds now drifting toward them across the tide, a chorus of male voices lifted in song, complete with pipe and fiddle accompaniment, the tune swelling steadily in volume to become instantly recognizable as that jaunty old favorite "Pop Goes the Weasel."

"Federal sailors," murmured Liberty. "Near, very near."

"One squeak out of anyone," warned Maury, "and he'll feel my fingers about his throat."

The ship's engines slowed; the music stopped. In the interval Liberty thought he could hear laughter, conversations even, though the words remained out of reach, indecipherable. Somewhere beyond what now appeared to be a painfully thin hull—"third of an inch of fine Birmingham steel," the captain had bragged—there obviously loomed a U.S. frigate and all the lethal potentiality that implied.

Affecting an imperturbable calm, he stoically awaited the first ball. After months of training himself to expect death in some pleasant sunlit meadow, Liberty was rather disconcerted by the prospect of such a visitation while trapped in a metal can afloat in a midnight sea.

Suddenly, from Tempie's corner came a tremulous keening, a solitary, animal cry such as is heard in the western forests in the dead of winter when the temperature drops and food is scarce, rising precipitously in volume until, amid a brief scuffling, it was, with a strangulated gasp, abruptly extinguished, the ensuing silence penetrated by Maury's distinctive accent, raw, menacing, "Quit your bawling, you miserable wench, or I'll cut out your tongue right here, right now, with this same blade I used to teach your mother a lesson or two. Now, nod your head if you'll hush, and I can let you go. Nod your head. All right, yes, that's good now, breathe easy, right, we're fine, we're all fine."

"Hardly the word I would use to describe our current condition," Liberty observed.

"And what word would you prefer, Dr. Johnson?"

"Oh, I don't know—'damned'?"

Then, all at once, the night fell in, a tearing noise went up and popped, and then commenced the deep crunching roars, one after another, of ejaculated iron. The Cavalier's engines shuddered to life. The water exploded.

"They've seen us," cried Maury, excited as a boy at the circus. "We're being fired upon."

"I'm familiar with the symptoms," muttered Liberty.

"Well, I don't reckon our present sequestration matters much at this point. What say we amble topside and take a gander?"

"Are the Yankees going to kill us all?" asked Monday.

"No, not all. You they'll lock in a cage and put on display in the White House. What do you think they're trying to do, you old fool, give us a peck on the cheek?"

An ominous whistling came rapidly upon their stern, alternating in pitch as it trailed, fading away.

"Hear that?" demanded Maury. "We're already outrunning 'em."

"I don't want to die," Monday pleaded.

"None of us do," confirmed Liberty.

"Monday, I leave this naughty child in your charge. Should any further problems arise, you have my personal permission to administer the proper correction."

"How do I do that?"

"With a ready hand, you dolt."

"What if she starts up with that blubbering again?"

"Remember Octavia?"

"Yes sir."

"Same way."

"But Master, Octavia was a mule."

"And a damned impertinent one at that. Just do as I command and God shall add another shiner to your hoard in heaven."

"Sure would like to feel a touch of those hard bits in my fist every now and again. I'm the poorest rich man I ever knew."

"I haven't time to dispute theological trivialities with a dunce. Just know that come Judgement Day we're all going to get paid."

"Oh really, reverend," declared Liberty. "Now there's a show I'd wait in line to see. Figure I'm due a considerable bounty for this particular skylark."

"Out the door with ye," ordered Maury, thumping his grandson on the shoulder. "It'll be hooks and hot cinders for you and your godless breed."

The imperturbable Captain Wallace was up on the bridge, casually pacing to and fro in a pair of carpet slippers, pausing at each turn to peer intently aft through a set of French field glasses. The sky was being lit at periodic intervals by a succession of rockets in whose stuttering glare could be glimpsed the dark, minatory shapes of two U.S. vessels steaming straight toward the *Cavalier*, in whose foaming wake shells were exploding harmlessly in great geysers of white water.

"Ah," Wallace pronounced with a grand gesture, as if welcoming latecomers to a Sunday social, "I fear our little bubble of excitement has burst. Look how they strain to catch us. There's not a cruiser in their navy can match our speed." Another shell dropped screeching into the waves some hundred yards astern. "See? We're already out of range and the interval can only increase. I was just about to send for you gentlemen, especially you, Mr. Maury, since as a former military man I thought you might enjoy a taste of the old powder again— from a suitably distant vantage, of course," the effervescence in his voice almost contagious.

"I never spoke of my service."

"You didn't? How odd. Well, sir, your bearing speaks for you, as well as your age. You are certainly of sufficient years to have participated in one or another of your country's numerous armed squabbles. You peace-loving Americans, when not busy killing each other, always seem to find yourselves engaged with foreigners of some stripe or another."

"Yes, mainly you people."

Wallace responded with a peal of laughter. "Well done, sir. I do appreciate a sharp tongue."

"Then attend to this, English. When I was a whey-faced youth back in '12, I did indeed carry a musket with the honorable George Croghan at Fort Stephenson, and, I'm proud to report, did dispatch several of you unsavory lobsterbacks to a godless infamy."

"Yes, but now we all wear gray, do we not? Oh look, there's a pretty thing." A shell, detonating prematurely, sent a shower of sparks glittering down into the sea. "I'm sure, Mr. Maury, you endured the hardship, the privation, the etc., etc. of the common foot soldier, but tell me honestly now, is there anything more thrilling in the annals of modern warfare than a spirited dash beneath the very iron snouts of a superior, all-but-encompassing enemy force? I shall miss the stimulation immensely. Peace, I'm afraid, is doomed to be a dreadful bore."

"And quite the unprofitable bore at that," interjected an out-of-breath newcomer, wheezing fitfully from the effort of maneuvering his ample bulk up the various staircases and ladders from below. A round, beef-colored man, he was, even in these desperately pinched times, conspicuously rigged out in a fine linen suit that was actually clean, with matching waistcoat and hat. Behind him stepped a tiny, dog-eyed woman as narrow in flesh as her companion was broad, her delicate frame all but swallowed up by a massive emerald gown to which had been affixed dozens of ribbons announcing various prizes in horse racing, marksmanship, spelling and pie baking.

"The Fripps!" declared Captain Wallace, as if reuniting with lost relatives. "Welcome. Our circle is complete. Allow me to introduce you to Mr. Asa Maury here and his grandson, Mr. Fish."

"The Maurys of Redemption Hall?" asked Mr. Fripp excitedly.

"The same," Maury answered with a curt nod.

"Well, if that don't beat all nature. You and I, I suspect, might be cousins. All my papers are packed, but, mind you, once we get to Nassau I promise to consult my genealogies. Look, Phoebe," he said, turning to his undemonstrative wife, "blood kin."

"Isn't everybody in the low country related to everybody else?" asked Maury.

"I know it can sometimes seem so, but, if I recall correctly, I believe one of your grandmother's sisters married a great uncle or something or other of mine and moved to Fib's Head back in colonial times."

"The tie seems rather slender, does it not?"

"That's what I shall determine once I lay out my charts, but I am rarely mistaken about such matters, am I, Phoebe? History is my pastime."

"I don't mess with that truck," replied Mrs. Fripp.

"As I was just saying," interjected Captain Wallace, moving adroitly to fill the awkward silence, "I had hoped you all might have an opportunity to at least get a glimpse of the fireworks, but at thirteen knots we're outrunning the show rather rapidly."

"Well, we would have been up here sooner, but—women," explained Mr. Fripp, with an indulgent smile toward his wife. "Even in the heat of battle all thought is ever upon appearance."

"Shut up," returned Mrs. Fripp.

"Oh, look!" Wallace pointed to the northwestern sky, where a sputtering ball of white light arced gracefully downward to its extinction beneath the waves. "How they'd like to give us a sound peppering."

"Magnificent!" pronounced Mr. Fripp, or Mr. G. D. Fripp, as he insisted on being addressed, wiping his large, shiny forehead with a perfectly pressed bandanna. "I've always enjoyed a good nightly bombardment. Reminds me of the Fourth, I suppose. Of course once those batteries commenced their devil's work upon Charleston itself, we had to vacate the city. Mrs. Fripp's nerves are as frail as glass. You know she can hear a sewing needle fall to the carpet from an adjoining room."

"Yes," confirmed the woman in question who had discreetly positioned herself as close to Captain Wallace as possible without giving offense, as if seeking shelter in the shade of his commanding presence, "and this pathological exaggeration of normal female delicacy has been, I dare to say, a thankless burden, an outright curse."

"Now, Phoebe," cautioned her husband, "don't go getting all lathered up again. We must ration the medicine we have until we reach the Bahamas."

"Tell me, madame," asked Captain Wallace, "when we were passing within earshot of that Federal ironclad, what could you perceive of the activity on board? With your keen senses you must have apprehended all."

"I heard some frightful out-of-key singing."

"As did we," added Maury.

"And the usual cursing, spitting and gambling that inevitably occurs whenever men gather together in large groups."

"Could you see," inquired Maury politely, "the very pips on their cards?"

Attempting to suppress his laughter, Wallace let out an equine snort, earning him an immediate glare from both Fripps.

"I would hope, Mr. Maury, that such an unseemly remark implies no discourtesy to my wife."

"No, no, not at all, G. D. I merely stand in awe before Mrs. Fripp's singular talents. I wished I possessed such sensory endowments."

"Easily said," commented Mrs. Fripp tartly, "when you have not endured at firsthand the suffering which accompanies such dubious 'gifts.'"

"Then I apologize, madame. I intend no ill will toward you or your husband. We are all in the same boat, so to speak."

"Excellent! Well turned!" exclaimed Captain Wallace, briskly rubbing together his large, callused hands. "May I suggest then that we repair to the wardroom where my personal chef, the noted Joe Cox, former head man at Delmonico's up in Gotham, or so he claims, has prepared a marvelous table d'hôte of such length and breadth as to astonish all. I have found that nothing quickens the appetite like a successful breaching of the line, particularly if one has drawn fire in the process. Tonight we feast on the joy of being alive."

A long table had been set with the precision and reverence of a communion altar, the damask of a purity few had seen since before the war, if then; the flatware of solid silver, the bone china from Boston and the food itself arrayed in quantities normally associated with a family Thanksgiving: oyster soup, baked sheepshead, roast turkey with egg sauce, roast beef, scalloped oysters, stewed kidneys, sweet potatoes, eggplant, turnips, parsnips, beets, stewed tomatoes, apple pie, raisins, chocolate and, placed at frequent intervals among the steaming platters, endless bottles of claret, burgundy, sherry, catawba and, of course, champagne.

"Captain Wallace," boomed Maury, "you have exceeded the bounds of extravagance. Reminds me of Christmas dinner at Redemption Hall back in yonder times when Father still presided over the clan."

"No short commons on this vessel," replied Wallace proudly. "Please, everyone, take your seats. I'm sure you're all familiar with the wearisome notion of our earth as a prison and we its inhabitants as condemned inmates who can never be certain when the man in the black hood is going to come knocking on the door. Well, if this be so, why fritter away our brief sojourn in funks and humours? Eat! Drink! Celebrate!" He raised the first of what would be numerous glasses of French wine.

"I see you are a gentleman of breeding," commented Maury. "Of what stock do you descend?"

"As British as black pudding, Mr. Maury. My family, apparently, was a tribe fatally prone to—how do you folks in Dixie so charmingly pose it?—'itchy feet.' Consequently, my heritage is a parti-colored coat of Irish, Welsh, Scottish, with a dash of Dutch thrown in for seasoning."

"Interesting. One might deduce from your carriage and demeanor that the strain would be somehow"—he took a delicate pause—"more wholesome."

"Do I strike you, Mr. Maury, as one diseased?" His eyes glittered in the gently shifting lantern light with an unquenchable, alert amusement.

"Surely, Captain, you must be cognizant that certain beneficial traits tend to become hopelessly diluted when submerged in foreign streams."

"Hadn't given the matter much thought, actually."

"A subject of fathomless depths upon which I can expatiate enthusiastically."

"Why don't we first occupy ourselves with the delights of this phenomenal meal," suggested Liberty rather hurriedly, reminding himself uncomfortably of his own ever-abustle aunt Aroline. "We have—what?—three days at least aboard this ship, time enough to investigate the perplexities of all the major sciences from alchemy to phrenology."

"Capital idea," seconded Wallace, again raising his glass and casting a roguish glance around the table. "A toast, then, to the Union. Now and forever."

Solemnly, Maury lowered his crystal. "Not even in jest, sir, not even in jest."

"But wouldn't you agree, Mr. Maury, that life would be an intolerably grim affair did we not indulge our fancy now and again?"

"An age of drollery this is not."

"Quite true. But I have discovered over the course of an uncommonly eventful existence that mental equilibrium is best maintained by learning to appreciate the chinks in things, the gimcrack juxtapositions, the slapdash air to even matter itself, learning, Mr. Maury, to spot the joke. A pertinent example: Back in '61, when I first shipped on this ill-starred Confederacy, skinnier, dumber, more arrogant than

I am now, I received a commission as a full-fledged privateer, letter of marque signed by ol' Jeff Davis himself. On our maiden voyage, about fifty miles east of Nantucket, we chanced to run across the USS *Giza*, a trim little bark who, at a single shot across her bow, judiciously showed her colors. Our first prize, and in a mad pitch of excitement we scrambled over her rails and actually attempted to pry open the cargo with our bare nails. And what do you think we found in all those precious barrels? Perfume, sir, a veritable lake of cheap eau de cologne the crew started guzzling down like rum until they realized what it was. I couldn't get the scent out of my nostrils for weeks. But let me tell you, I managed to extract a good chuckle out of that fiasco for days later and, frankly, also happened to turn quite a princely profit. Always a ready market for ladies' luxuries, even amid the smoke and screams, eh, gentlemen? And madame?" he added, with a fluid touch to the brim of his cap.

"I don't see why one should be denied whatever trifling comforts that chance to come to hand, whatever the circumstances," replied Mrs. Fripp, who along with her husband had pointedly ignored the table talk, preferring instead a direct assault upon the massive redoubts of food heaped before them. She had already begun reloading her plate for a fresh offensive.

"But such gratifications," observed Wallace, "become available only because people like me are willing to risk life and limb to go out and seize them."

"Bunkum," snorted Maury derisively. "You have the effrontery to present your shameless buccaneering as heroic and self-sacrificing when, in fact, you are merely acting for your own gain. I can't imagine a freckled opportunist such as yourself exhibiting even a passing interest in the Cause if putting coin in your purse weren't involved."

"At least I'm committed to going down with my ship."

"If you mean to imply, sir, that I am some sort of coward . . ."

"No, not at all. I'm simply suggesting that perhaps your own devotion to our beloved Stars and Bars might be constructed of thinner stuff than you imagine, thinner than greed, for example."

"At present, Captain Wallace, I am engaged in important research pertaining to southern ideals that must not be interrupted. Besides, I fear I am so constituted as to be wholly incapable of abiding any possible Yankee future."

"What?" questioned Wallace. "Are we all going to be required to wear shoes and eat with utensils?'

"Should Lincoln's clerks and shopkeepers prevail, Captain Wallace, we shall find ourselves beguiled into a time of tin soldiers, living in tin houses, rearing tin families. We shall be crucified upon the arms of the clock and then resurrected as machines. The world will be a passionless place devoid of honor, glory and, most of all, romance. And we will be bondsmen of the state, the church and the mill for all the numberless, anonymous days of our played-out lives."

"The whole country as a kind of exaggerated plantation?" remarked Wallace, who had been studying this vexatious passenger with enlarged interest. "But without the love, eh?"

"Bait me if you must, Captain Wallace, but heed this: the dollar is forged of a substance more indestructible than any iron. Shackles can come in many guises. And that is why we fight, sir—for freedom, only for freedom."

Wallace leaned back into his chair with a nautical squint, as if trying to read landmarks from a great distance. "You astonish me, Mr. Maury. That you have managed to live so long yet learned so little. Let's put the issue to our young friend here. The honest clarity of the eye uncorrupted. Tell me, Mr. Fish, what precisely do you understand to be the meaning of this nightmare your country is presently dreaming?"

"I'd prefer to keep my opinions on such matters private, if you don't mind."

"He's a Yankee," blurted Maury. "What do you expect him to think? They all champ on the ends of the same thoughts over and over again. Their views are manufactured on demand by a den of blind jews in a clandestine, windowless basement in the gnarled heart of New York City."

"Enchanting," pronounced Wallace. "I see your own thoughts incline to the partial and the apocryphal."

"But I heard the exact story myself," chimed in Mr. Fripp, laying aside the ham bone he happened to be gnawing on. "Only in my version the jews were also black."

"Same people who owned the companies which ran the slave ships," confirmed Mrs. Fripp. "They don't care what services they provide, or to whom, as long as their palms are properly crossed."

"And now," Maury continued, "they are scheming for the future I have already alluded to."

"Well," announced Liberty, in an unexpectedly commanding tone, wiping his lips with a napkin which, although apparently freshly laundered, tasted strangely of salt, "such enthusiastic speculation upon the affairs of the day tends to produce a benumbing effect on my brain, and, frankly, it has been a particularly long, arduous day. So, Captain Wallace, thank you for your generous hospitality. Mr. Fripp, Mrs. Fripp."

"If the boy is retiring, then so shall I," asserted Maury. "He's had difficulty sleeping alone since he was a baby."

"But we've had no coffee," protested Captain Wallace. "Or dessert."

"I shall look forward to indulging myself thoroughly at breakfast," replied Maury, rising from his chair.

"But apple pie," Wallace called to his departing guests. "Lemon pie, peach pie, cranberry tart, nuts, dates, figs, raisins, oranges, bananas . . ."

The morning arrived in a flood of intemperate heat and rude, all-encompassing light that rendered the prolonged visual study of any object, even one nearby and shaded, a task too tiresome to contemplate. The day seemed reduced to a succession of hours that nothing and no one on board could ever adequately fill. As if still crapulous from the sparkling conviviality and strong spirits of the evening previous, an uncharacteristic Captain Wallace spent his watch draped in a largely unapproachable melancholia from which he was occasionally aroused by the sighting on the far horizon of a topmast or a plume of black smoke, none of which, to the relief of the passengers, ever materialized into a closing cruiser or an angry frigate. Mr. G. D. Fripp announced sadly that Mrs. Fripp sent her regrets but would, due to the motion of the boat and her reanimated dyspepsia, remain confined to quarters until further notice. Monday, who had become convinced against all argument that the true destination of the *Cavalier* was the slave trading posts of Africa, denounced the ship as a wicked craft on a wicked errand and vowed never to speak again for the duration of the crossing, responding to orders or queries with mere grunts or impatient gestures. And Tempie would be neither touched nor addressed without breaking into dramatic fits of convulsive sobbing, unless, of course, she was sobbing already.

"Appears, my boy, only you and I among our little group retain the last vestiges of physical poise and civility," Maury observed to his brooding grandson as the two continued their morning promenade around the deck, winding their way between burlapped walls of baled cotton. "You know, Mr. Fripp informs me that most of this crop is his, the final harvest, as he and the missus plan to settle permanently on the island of New Providence in an astonishingly pink bungalow already bought and paid for. He paints quite a congenial scene, what with the sand, the palms, the Atlantic at your window, the immutable weather." He paused to lean against the rail, ponder the nervous swell and tumble of the sea.

"Then imagine how great his surprise," replied Liberty, "when, at the finish to our pleasant excursion, he claps his eyes upon the familiar harbor of Rio de Janeiro."

Seizing his grandson roughly by the arm, Maury pulled him close. "Now you hush up about that," he hissed wetly. "I swear, every time you open your mouth I find my hand moving instinctively for the revolver."

"I'm not afraid of you."

"So you've asserted. Monotonously. And if such is rightly the case, then you are not so wise as you sometimes appear. I know you regard yourself as unassailable because of your supposed indispensability to my work, but let me hasten to assure you that I shall permit nothing—nothing, do you hear me?—to hinder the final completion of this project. And if some unforeseeable event transpires which requires me to make some adjustments in the plan, why, so be it."

Their meanderings had led them unconsciously to a closet-sized space at the center of the cotton maze that Captain Wallace had ordered prepared as shelter for Mrs. Fripp should the *Cavalier* come under heavy fire and where they now faced each other no more than three feet apart. "Well," Liberty commented, "I believe the Confederacy might have made a grievous error when it did not immediately snatch you up for a general. I can see you even now, astride your mount, binoculars in hand, sending in wave after wave of brave boys up Seminary Ridge with about as much compunction as throwing another log on the fire."

"One feels an allegiance to one's duty, that is, if one has ever even deigned to rub elbows with such a quaint notion."

"Of course, I would expect that someone so entombed within their own mortal idiosyncrasies would be absolutely blind to any virtue whatsoever in another. And I refuse to be backed into the position of defending my character before an individual whose own sense of morality is practically nonexistent."

"I raised six children in the ways of the Lord from seedlings to flowering tops."

"And a fine job you made of it, too."

"All were taught their duty and all ventured forth to fulfill it."

"Even Mother?"

"A quick pupil. She mastered the lesson and then learned how to turn it inside out. If I said 'white,' she would invariably respond with 'black.'"

"Do you know the circumstances of her death?"

"A carriage accident."

So Liberty proceeded to serve up the details: the letter, the tears, the loss of composure, the reckless gallop, the bridge, the fall, the wheel spinning eternally through the affrighted air.

"So you hold me responsible for her release."

"You and Grandmother."

"But we weren't even present."

"Yes, you were. You've always been at her side, no matter where she journeyed, no matter how she was engaged."

"She was a headstrong girl, you know. There was no containing her."

"She was already in chains long before she left you."

"She did a fair job of breaking them."

"But not all of them, Grandfather, not all."

Maury permitted himself a long, audible sigh, as if a bellowsful of fresh air were flushing out the cavities in his head. Slowly his gaze traveled upward, inspecting with apparent interest the bulging walls of the chimneylike space in which they were enclosed, and on up to the framed rectangle of immaculate blue sky overhead, where his attention lingered as if awaiting the appearance of some object, any object, a cloud, a gull, a passing cannonball, to disturb the still perfection of all that incalculable emptiness. "I cannot confess to you," he said at last, "how often I so desperately missed her during the sad span of those lost years. What a precious, spirited lass she was."

"Why did you never come visit?"

"I was angry. She had betrayed me."

"But perhaps she was simply holding fast to the deeper meaning of virtues you had inculcated in her. Perhaps she was simply obeying her heart."

Maury responded with a skeptical grunt. "The heart can but lead you into calamity among the sharp pieces of this broken world. She was a child who possessed no proper conception of the prevailing winds of this life."

"Yet perhaps a fairer conception than any you could possibly entertain."

"Enough," asserted Maury, extending an upright palm. "I'll not dispute this issue with you again. You're but a child yourself."

"Ah," boomed out a genial Mr. G. D. Fripp, rounding the corner, and seemingly recovered from any slights and affronts he might have endured at dinner, "so this is where you two have managed to stow yourselves. When I didn't find you in your stateroom, I knew all I had to do was follow the sound of contentious voices. The Great Debate rattles on, I see."

"In a manner," replied Maury dryly.

"A soupçon of advice, then, from an antiquated cracker-barrel rhetorician such as myself: I enjoy, every now and again, a good metaphysical rip as much as the next blockhead, but why keep driving your plow over the same exhausted ground, risking figurative sunstroke and blisters for naught? Concerning the dialogue of the day, it would appear that, like it or not—and no one abhors the outcome more than I—Messrs. Grant and Sherman have delivered their premises to a rather convincing conclusion."

"They've concluded nothing," snapped Maury.

"Oh how I wish it were so, Mr. Maury, I honestly do. But what a fine situation to have arrived at, in the full richness of one's years, when merely to lay a head upon a pillow is to risk an infinite night of sweats and fidgets and horrid dreams that come thronging in like vultures to feed upon memories I would prefer remain unexhumed."

"Charming," pronounced Maury, looking for a courteous way around the man's extended girth. "But my grandson and I must get back to our stateroom. The servants have been alone much too long."

"No, please, don't go. I've been cooped up for hours with a sick woman who can no longer bear the sound of my voice. And last night I was visited again by"—he leaned forward to whisper confidentially—"one of those dreams."

"We'd be delighted to hear it," offered Liberty, avoiding his grandfather's caustic eye.

"Thank you, Mr. Fish. I have found that unless the excess is periodically drawn off the brain, certain distressing symptoms of a decidedly undomesticated variety tend to proliferate like weevils in the boll. Here, then, is my dream, a habitual bedside companion for many more years than I care to reckon. The scene is always the same. I am a child back at Arcadia some forty, even fifty summers ago, where it is always morning and the day has not yet begun to wilt and Father and Lomax are saddling up to go to a horse auction and Mother is in the sitting room reading *Robinson Crusoe* to little Lucy and I am upstairs in bed not daring to budge for fear of dislodging a moment of transport absolutely faultless in its construction and in all its particulars when I become progressively aware of an eerie halt in the order of things. Birds still chirp in the cypress, a fat fly buzzes against the ceiling, hounds bay from the hills, but the loudest sounds of all are those I am not hearing: no clink of chains past my window, no chant from the fields, no shouts from the quarters, no screeching in the kitchen, no whip cracking in the yard, and a chill lances through me like a shard of ice and I know for certain that I am going to die and then I awaken in the present in a disorganized state of great perplexity and fear, my mind for the moment not quite mine but a curious object on temporary loan from another. And the sensation, I assure you, gentlemen, is not one with which you would hanker to greet the coming day or hold any acquaintance whatsoever, no matter how brief. As you can probably judge, my bean's been feeling a bit slantindicular of late."

"Well, whose hasn't?" asked Maury. "I calculate, though, those sweet Bahamian breezes should sweep the marsh fog from all our heads."

"It is my fervent hope."

Liberty stared speechlessly at his grandfather, utterly unable to mask a rather complicated expression of sour incredulity.

"Hard to believe," mused Mr. Fripp, idly plucking a protruding tuft of cotton from a nearby bale, "that such an airy vegetative nothing could incite so much anguish and devastation. This is all that remains of Arcadia," he added, rolling the tuft between his fingers. "The Yankees, I suppose, will raze the place to the foundation, and once I sell this shipment to a factor in port, all material connections to the family estate will be severed forever." His suddenly brimming eyes threatened to overflow. "And, frankly, gentlemen, I honestly do not know if the dear missus can endure a single hour more confined to this rocking metal tub. I've questioned the captain persistently for even a fair estimate of our arrival, but on each occasion he has responded with a different date and time."

"Trouble yourself no further with the insufferable Wallace," advised Maury. "If he's not careful he might soon find himself piloting a barge on the River Styx. I can personally pledge to you that we shall reach our promised destination sooner than expected and that it shall be a happy astonishment for all."

"Thank you, sir," exclaimed Mr. Fripp, vigorously pumping Maury's hand. "Your words have lightened an oppressive and ever-shifting load. And, may I add, your mere presence on board lends strength to us all."

"Fate, Mr. Fripp, need not always be untoward. The Deity, in his veiled munificence, directed me to this ship, and I hold no doubt that He will guide each of our blessed souls safely into port."

"I'm certain you are correct, Mr. Maury. Please excuse my silly complaints and anxieties. It isn't often one stumbles upon a Christian brother whose conviction is quite so granite ribbed. Such an example makes infidels of us all."

"I am merely a pawn in the benevolent fingers of a greater Hand."

"I may as well confess to you, Mr. Maury, that upon first encounter Mrs. Fripp recognized at once the glare of piety radiating from your countenance, and Mrs. Fripp is an extremely devout woman whose ability to detect the divine in another is downright nonpareil."

"A talented lady in numerous departments," commented Maury.

"Quite so. And she will be gladdened to hear your reassuring assessment of our current position and probable future. In fact, it would surprise me not at all if she does not immediately abandon her bed and bucket to join us for supper in the salon."

"I wouldn't prod the poor woman into a state of health she has not yet authentically attained."

"No fear of that," replied Fripp, obviously eager to be off and relay the good news. "Phoebe does what Phoebe wants. No violating that commandment. And now, gentlemen, if you'll please excuse me, I must check in on our patient." He hastened away like a gambler intent on placing a last-minute bet.

"Queer sort of duck," mused Maury. "Seems quite capable and

solid at first glance, but then you deduce the stuffing is all feathers and balloon gas."

"Shouldn't wonder that you'd perceive every stranger as a probable charlatan," replied Liberty.

"Into the hold with ye," barked Maury, shoving Liberty clumsily on ahead of him. "It's time to review the next act on the bill."

Below deck, fumbling with the keys, muttering nonsensical oaths under his breath, Maury turned to his grandson and confessed, "Along with numerous other burgeoning ailments, my eyesight also seems to be failing. Used to be I could knock a squirrel out of a tree with a long rifle at a hundred yards. Now probably couldn't even see the critter."

"Hard luck," observed Liberty. "Imagine losing the ability to read skin tone correctly. Your whole flimflam goes up the flue."

But before Maury could compose a suitably cutting response, the proper key had been found, inserted into the lock, and the cabin door swung open upon the following informative study in mass and gravity: Monday, per usual, curled up asleep on the hard steel floor, his phlegmatic snores coincident with, and almost as deafening as, the *Cavalier*'s unfettered engines, and, suspended from an overhead pipe, Tempie's naked girlish body swaying pendulumlike in time with the roll of the ship, her stained and torn shift tightly tied in a determined complexity of knots around her now grotesquely elongated neck.

"What in damnation!" cried Maury, springing forward, a knife instantly in hand to cut down, with Liberty's assistance, his daughter, laying the limp body across the bale of cotton from which she had doubtlessly taken her last step into space. Maury bent anxiously over her, cocking an ear above Tempie's stupefied, gaping mouth, pausing as if to listen at the edge of an impossibly deep well. "Dead," he said, the pronouncement spat out like an unexpected pit in a pie. Liberty felt abruptly unbound, as though all his insides had been loosed and anatomized, and existence revealed as a rudderless spin through absolute darkness.

"You goddamn worthless coon!" yelled Maury, directing a sharp kick into the unprotected ribs of a dazed Monday, who still in the process of coming awake looked about in unblinking bewilderment at this contrary foreign place he couldn't, at the moment, remember having seen before and certainly never wanted to see again. "Damn you!" And out dashed another kick Monday tried unsuccessfully to dodge. "Get up off of your raggedy ass!" Maury leaned down, seized the shivering man by the collar and hauled him bodily onto the bunk. "Why I ever thought a superannuated trunk minder could conceivably mind a mere child for less than half an hour is a riddle His Omnipotence will have to explain to me in the hereafter. Now, what in tarnal hell happened in here?"

With aching slowness, Monday's gaze wandered from Maury to Tempie's stilled body, to Liberty, who refused to meet his eye, back to Maury, then down to the floor.

"You harken to me, you black son of a bitch. I don't care if you've taken thirteen vows of silence and had a conjur doctor's frog bone waved over your woolly skull. I want it explained to me in clearly understandable terms why there is a fresh corpse in my cabin."

Monday neither budged nor spoke.

"I await your lordship's response," said Maury scornfully, and then, quicker than sight, his open palm whipped out across Monday's gray-bristled cheek. "I'll have an answer, by God, before anyone leaves this room, dead or alive." And his arm, which was preparing to strike again, was abruptly halted in midair by Liberty's grip.

"That's enough," he declared, staring unflinchingly into the curdled heart of his grandfather's rage. "How much more violence need we endure? Isn't it obvious the poor man slept through this whole horrid tragedy?"

"Mr. Fish," warned Maury, reaching up to clutch Liberty's wrist, "kindly remove your hand from my person or I shall have to remove it myself."

"Listen, why don't we pretend the workings of civilization have actually had a meliorating influence on our barbarous culture and remove all our hands from one another, black and white alike, and keep them removed?"

Warily, without breaking the fervid sight lines that held them bound, grandfather and grandson physically disengaged themselves and stepped delicately backward.

"Need I remind you," said Maury, "that this man is my property and I will do with him as I please."

"No, you will not," replied Liberty, the muscle of his tongue fortifying each separate syllable.

"Don't speak to me as if I were some addlepated field hand. The last person to address me in such tones spent a month in bed nursing broken bones and spitting out teeth."

"I don't want to fight you, Grandfather."

"I ought to have known you'd betray me, too. Your mother and that cursed Yankee blood galloping through your veins." His attention remained steadfastly fixed upon the girl's carelessly arranged anatomy, roving methodically among the hills and dales of her cooling flesh, as if seeking some undiscoverable category of solace there in the extinction of this rare specimen, last of her breed, lost forever. "The whole world's polluted," he announced finally. Then, without so much as a glance, he ordered Liberty to report to Captain Wallace and inform him "what has transpired down in this iron cell."

At dawn Captain Wallace and off-duty members of the crew held a brief ceremony for Tempie, whose remains had been sewn inside a meal sack for formal deposit overboard. Liberty spoke of one he knew not well but comprehended enough to recognize that from birth she had been unfairly sentenced to a life so circumscribed she literally could not turn around without getting her limbs scraped, her soul chafed, so perhaps it was fitting that when finally sought, death was invited to make an appearance out here on the open sea, where amid the immeasurable flow of sky and flood there were no visible obstacles, only the clarity and space for one troubled spirit to find its way home.

Roused from her sickbed by the prospect of a funeral, Mrs. Fripp diagnosed herself as fit enough to totter up on deck and launch enthusiastically into a slightly discordant but still forceful rendition of her favorite childhood hymn, taught to her personally by her Mammy Silvey when she was but five years old, "Good-bye, I'll Meet You in the Kingdom, By and By."

Maury, of course, refused to attend the services, preferring to sit brooding in his stateroom with the bruised and mute Monday for company, and upon Liberty's return, without preamble or cause, he simply opened his mouth and began to speak, as if an underground torrent of words had been running through him for some time now and at this random moment just happened to erupt into daylight. "It's all gone to flinders, everything, you, me, Mother, Redemption Hall, all the pretty pictures, gone, and perhaps that's all our splendid life ever was, a procession of pretty pictures we poor deluded fools mistook for the actual scenes depicted.

"I've been anchored here all morning, lad, speculating and studying on this here bale for so many hours I have come to appreciate that this peculiar object is not, in fact, a 'bale' at all, but something else entirely. It's a . . . it's . . . I don't know what it is." He paused to release a stuttering sigh, his body seeming to visibly deflate. "It's a thing. That's the best I can do. It's a thing. This is a thing," pointing to his valise; "that's a thing," his tarnished wedding band; "you and I are things. And we should all be quite content with the stone certainty of that apprehension." He raised his head, found Liberty's sympathetic eyes. "Am I making any sense whatsoever?"

"Tempie's gone."

"I know, I know. But despite her forfeiture and this unfortunate lapse in my dialectics, the work can still go on. The work must go on. I will not be pulled down. The universe must offer me other terms. We simply begin again in what we can only hope"—the stirrings of a modest smile playing over his lips—"will be a more agreeable clime. So!" He clapped his hands against his knees and stood. "The time has come, I believe, for us to go make our visit to the captain." From a mahogany traveling chest he produced a pair of silver pistols and passed one over to Liberty. "I'll handle Wallace. You keep a weather eye on the crew. This could be a rather ramstuginous affair."

Liberty hefted the gun and examined the tooling. "You don't actually expect me to aid in the criminal commandeering of this ship?"

"Of course I do. Why else are we on board? Remember, despite the genetic confusion raging within, half of you is all Maury."

"The superior, undefiled half?"

"There are duties and obligations to the neglected side of this family you have not yet begun to remit."

"Yes, and there are mercies and moralities you owe a lifetime's worth of interest on."

"Such an all-fired pugnacious fellow you are—a quality, mind you, I admire mightily. Puts me in recollection of me. What an estimable soldier you must have made. Tell me, did you ever kill a single member of the—I reject, of course, the appellative 'enemy,' so let's try 'foe'—a single member of the 'foe'?"

"That's a private matter between me, my conscience and my God."

"If you had, you know, that dead reb might have been an uncle."

"And this hypothetical uncle might just as handily have killed a hypothetical nephew."

"Answer me this then. You absconded from your own army when the circumstances suited you, yet you have failed to make even a sole attempt to flee my own company, which I ruefully admit can often be found wanting a certain vital adhesive nature. Why?"

"Even the dullest clod could conclude straight off that a prodigy such as yourself required something more than a good deal of looking after."

"Well, then," answered Maury, chuckling like a parrot in the first honest expression of amusement Liberty had yet heard him produce, "we are come to common ground. Liberty, I like you. Now I know that such a sentiment issuing at this late hour from the two-sided mouth of an old horned reprobate like myself, even as he waves another piece in your face, may strike one as insincere, if not outright mendacious, but recollect, we were near total strangers from opposite sides of the hedge when we met. We needed room to sidle up to one another, appraise each other's scent."

"So I passed the inquest?"

"Like a Philadelphia lawyer. Which eminently qualifies you as an able practitioner of all manner of black arts and heroic derring-do. Here's your chance to act the true Confederate, indulge the rebel edge in ye. I know it's there. I've caught glimpses of our dear Stars and Bars flapping behind those furious blue eyes of yours. You're ready, I'm ready, the moment is ready. Wallace will be up on the bridge. If you can prevent any of the crew from entering—"

"No, Grandfather, I'm sorry, but I simply cannot," said Liberty, handing over the pistol. "In fact, I intend to inform Captain Wallace of your insane plot."

"You disappoint me, Liberty, you disappoint me mightily."

He did register a fleeting impression of Maury moving abruptly forward with the celerity of a maddened bear, but no impression whatsoever of the shiny barrel of Maury's revolver slashing downward to crease the left side of his head. At one instant he was in full attendance to the moment, in the next he was not. Later (whatever that odd word meant), consciousness seeping slowly back from wherever it had fled, he discovered himself gazing with a remedial scientific detachment down a perfectly aligned row of identically shaped, uniformly gray mushrooms, each, he now realized with deepening alarm, crucially lacking a stem. His befuddled brain was attempting to juggle these disturbing visual facts into some sort of rational sense when suddenly he understood that the geometrical phenomenon he had been examining with labyrinthine wonderment for what seemed days now was not some new form of plant life at all but an engineered row of steel rivets bolted to the floor against which his bleeding cheek now lay pressed. Staggering to his feet, he noted impassively, through the elusive prism of sight, that both Maury and Monday were gone. Head clanging, the world gone soft and pliant, every object sprouting a mysterious, fuzzy growth, Liberty made his tender way through the ever-shifting bowels of the ship and up the rubbery ladder to the bridge, where he happened upon a tense tableau that might have been entitled "The Tables Turned." With Monday glumly situated off to his left, Maury, a loaded revolver filling each hand, held Captain Wallace and two jittery members of the crew in an uneasy detainment which the collected captain appeared to be taking not all that seriously.

"I see you've not been too terribly damaged," remarked Maury after a quick glance at his grandson. He wiggled one of the barrels. "Take your place over there with your fellow apostates."

"Put down the guns," ordered Liberty in a tone normally employed to address rabid dogs. "You don't know what you're doing."

"Don't patronize me, boy. I have never acted with such clarity."

"Your grandfather," began Wallace in a sardonic drawl even more pronounced than usual, "is a man of many parts, not all of them, unfortunately, equally sound. He has been attempting to persuade us with, I must report, a limited degree of effectiveness, to alter our present course to one bearing on the exotic destination of," he peered politely in Maury's direction, "I believe it was Rio de Janeiro you mentioned, was it not? And frankly, I've been compelled to regretfully advise him that such a deviation is out of the question despite the Latin charms of said port, which I can assure you are quite considerable."

"If you prefer," warned Maury, "I can, with a twitch of my forefinger, expel you on the instant to a much warmer, livelier locale."

"By all means," responded the genial captain, "and once there I shall be sure to secure you a seat at the table. Now then," he went on, his mirth evaporating as swiftly as it had arrived, "hand over those preposterous weapons before someone, most likely yourself, suffers a grievous injury." He advanced a step.

"Hold!" warned Maury, waving the barrels recklessly about. "You wouldn't want an ugly hole in that fancy coat of yours, now would you?"

"Grandfather," pleaded Liberty, "turn yourself over. What possible chance have you? You're one against all."

"Tale of my life, boy. But one learns to carve a path through the ruck with the means at hand."

"Please. There's been enough distress inflicted upon this company."

"Yes," confirmed the captain. "Allow reason to prevail."

"Captain Wallace, I abandoned the constraints of reason back in my salad days, observing even then the utter impotence of logic before the actual workings of this fatuous world, and I will not be lectured at by a dewy-eared bantling nor dictated to by a fen-dwelling, gin-guzzling mutt such as yourself. Monday," he demanded harshly, "fetch that rope," indicating a tangle of line lying bunched in a corner, "and begin trussing up these fowl for the spit. I am now in command of this vessel, and I intend that all my orders be executed promptly and efficiently."

"As if a sole member of my crew," asserted Wallace, "would obey a single request of yours."

"That so, you black British bastard? Perhaps the spectacle of their beloved master bound and gagged with a pistol at his temple will provoke a salutary shift in their allegiances. Monday, you damn fool," he cried at the old man's ineffectual struggle to gather up all the cord from the deck, "don't dare tell me you don't know how to work a rope."

"But, sir, look here at all this devilment," complained Monday, displaying aloft a hopeless intricacy of knotted hemp.

"Liberty, go help that brainless jackass. Mary, Mother of God, the day I meet the man who knows his job and how to discharge it faultlessly is the day I fall to my knees and pray for immediate deliverance, because there'll be nothing wondrous left to behold on this benighted planet."

"If you weren't so preoccupied with abusing everyone around you," suggested Wallace, "perhaps the poor fellow might be able to satisfy your annoying demands. Perhaps that comely girl might still be with us rather than now being numbered among the majority."

"Liberty, tend at once to this limey son of a bitch. You may start by stuffing his hat into his mouth and tying it in tight."

Accompanying himself with a complete idler's repertoire of facial tics, vocal strains and hand pantomime designed to convey as wide a range as possible of truculence, resentment and undue imposition, Liberty finally managed to unravel the tarry cord and arrange it in a fistful of neat, dangling loops. "I'm going to need a knife."

"Can someone, anyone, please simply do as they are told," exclaimed a vexed Maury. "Just bind him up like the fallen despot he is, and I'll cut off the excess when you're through. I know I probably should have provided both you and Monday with written instructions, but he can't read and you can't think, which is why this mindlessly elementary affair is requiring twice as much time as it should. Light a fire under it, Liberty. We do happen to be conducting a mutiny here."

"Yassuh, Cap'n." Obediently, he shuffled a few steps, then turned and, without warning, swung out his arm, whipping the hank of rope straight across Maury's stunned face. One of the guns discharged, the ball whizzing perilously close to Liberty's ear as he, Wallace and the two crewmen lunged forward in concert, toppling Maury to the floor with a sickening crack, the captain sprawled atop the old plantation owner, pummeling his undefended head with startling savagery. "Don't hurt him!" begged Liberty, attempting to pry the flailing bodies off his grandfather. Retrieving the revolvers, Wallace clambered to his feet crying, "How dare he presume to seize my ship? My ship!" The crewmen hauled Maury roughly upright and held him in custody, so to speak, one on either side. Monday, who had wisely refrained from taking any role in this white folks' ruckus, now surveyed the aftermath from his secure vantage behind the helm, his jaundiced eyes, in a rare unmasking, sharply lit with exactly what he thought of these lurid, hollow creatures he had been forced to spend his existence among.

"Until a few moments ago," declared Maury, still wheezing from his exertions, "I continued to harbor great hopes for you, Liberty, but when Maurys begin striking out at Maurys, whatever the cause, nature herself is broached and our finer properties all but scuttled. It's that infernal willfulness in you, boy, puts the sand into every pie, and that is a dish I will not abide."

"Does that cussed pan of yours ever stop flapping?" demanded Captain Wallace. "I believe you could talk a preacher into a bawdy house," then addressing the stocky, bearded mate to Maury's port, brusquely ordered, "Get the shackles!" The instant the grip was loosened on him, Maury wrenched readily free, bolted for the hatchway with youthful alacrity and was gone. "Awfully damn spry for one of his years and infirmities," Wallace noted as all went scrambling in ragged pursuit.

They soon found the unregenerate secessionist precariously perched athwart the starboard rail, a mystic hiatus having descended over him, settling his haggard features—even the extensive patterning of wrinkles miraculously erased—into an earlier, milder version of his pitiless, eroded face. His hair and beard, flowing biblically in the high salt wind, appeared whiter than usual, spookily illuminated from within, as if the long-smoldering fervor by which every spite, every indignity, every canker of his obtuse life was tenderly fed had at last leapt the grate.

"Mr. Maury, sir, I implore you," urged Captain Wallace. "Please consult your senses. Is this the manner in which you choose to make a die of it? Is this the sorry end by which you wish to be remembered?"

"I'll not be placed in chains by any breathing soul on this miserable ball of mud."

"Grandfather," began Liberty, his voice remarkably steady, "even if you've no regard for yourself, consider the sentiments of your family."

"What family? I've lost three sons to this unpleasantness and haven't heard from the other in six months. Both daughters are gone, and Ida, poor woman, is gone in mind if not yet in body. All I have left, regrettably, is you. Why did I have to live so long only to witness a proud, noble line sputter feebly out into yankee-doodleism, negrophilia and cowardice?"

"But what about your country? The South's going to have to be rebuilt. Able-bodied hands will be scarce."

"My country is a fugitive exhibition of dwarves and changelings."

"Mr. Maury, sir," interjected Captain Wallace, "I must again request that you step away promptly from the rail."

"Free I was born and free I shall die," Maury announced defiantly.

Then, shooting one final, extended, quixotic glance deep into the place of perpetual soreness Liberty had come to think of, more or less, as his soul, Maury lifted his beseeching hands to the unsullied sky and abruptly cast himself backward into the clemency of the waves. Immediately boats were lowered and the ground searched until dusk, but without result.

"Formidable chap, your grandbub," mused Captain Wallace, studying the contents of a generous tumbler of aged bourbon poured from his rarely shared private stock, which he'd gladly broken out as "the most effective known treatment for loss, grief and general miasma." He and Liberty were closeted in his stateroom, attempting to achieve as elevated a state of inebriation as possible in the shortest amount of time. "Trifle deluded, perhaps, but then Dixie seems to breed these characters like rabbits. Always reminded me somewhat of home, you know, the cultivation of eccentricities being practically a national pastime back in Merry Olde." Then, noting Liberty's distracted gaze, he added hurriedly, "But listen to me rattling on like an old fishwife. Is your drink acceptable?"

"What? What's that?" asked Liberty, slightly startled, conscious only that at this moment the entire contents of his head totaled naught. "Oh yes, of course, best I've ever tasted." His own glass was largely untouched.

"This particular bottle was given to me in a sealed box by a rather high-toned member of the Wilmington gentry in exchange for a few delicate favors I granted his wife. Heard he died later in a jack epidemic, sweated for three full days at the end." Receiving no response to these enlightening comments, Wallace occupied himself by running his thumbnail along the grooves of a giant capital T floridly carved into the defaced surface of the table at which they uncomfortably sat. Neither could have gauged with any accuracy the duration of the silence. "Bum go to lose family," Wallace finally observed, "even if you've only been acquainted for a few days."

"He looked so strangely composed out there on the rail," said Liberty in quiet wonder, "so unearthly, as if he'd just awakened from a long nap."

"Am I wrong, or is this entire ill-advised catastrophe the result of one foolish old man's apprehension he was about to be transfigured into some sort of New England coffee grinder?"

"Well, Grandfather did ride a number of hobbyhorses simultaneously, but, yes, that was one pertinent fear."

"Wage slavery versus chattel slavery. I've heard the issue knocked about from bow to stern on every run. Guess which side of the argument prevails?"

"The question, it seems to me, involves the type and amount of coercion applied to guarantee a finished task."

"Then it's lucre or the lash, eh?" Wallace's eyebrows seemed risen halfway up his forehead.

"No, I happen to believe there is another, more compelling impulse of much greater potency."

"Yes," inquired the skeptical captain, "and exactly what carrot would that be?"

"Love."

"Love?" he asked blandly, the fixings of a smile failing to coalesce completely about his pale lips. He took another sip of bourbon. "In spite of your naïve sentimentality, you cannot possibly be serious."

"But I am."

"Do you mean to imply that common laborers could be persuaded to spend twelve hours a day stooped over in the fields under a boiling sun picking cotton out of love?"

"If they own the land, yes."

"Well." Wallace looked about the room as if searching for assistance. "I am dismasted, keeled, run aground. I need another drink. You Americans. What a perennial marvel. Scratch a mechanic and discover a dreamer within. What a tantalizing, impossible combination. Is it the climate, some quickening agent in the air, sends you all mooning helplessly through the woods, scavenging for God in every tree, paradise behind every rock? I am humbled by such inimitable enterprise. So then"—raising his tumbler—"here's to you, Mr. Fish; here's to your America. I suppose if there's even a fool's glimmer of a feasible utopia lying about unnoticed in the shadowy corners of this world, you are indeed the people to find it."

They clinked glasses and drank. And drank again.

An hour later, a flushed Liberty, now shirtless, was expostulating in a high, emphatic voice on the nagging dramatic question: was Othello brown or black? He strenuously championed the latter view, also insisting through lines cited from memory that it is Iago who is the true slave. Sometime later, when he heard himself accompanying Wallace in fractured refrain to the popular tune "Just Before the Battle, Mother," he figured it was time to discreetly retire and so, clutching an unopened bottle of rum—a gift to Monday from the good captain—and leaning periodically against the swaying bulkheads, stumbled cautiously back to his cabin. Monday remained where he'd been left, fretting over a porthole-sized portion of sea and sky, now ominously dark, in which he momentarily expected, despite numerous exasperated assurances to the contrary, the dreaded materialization of what he persisted in calling "Nasty Saw," surely the most treacherous slaving post in the entire history of treachery. The death of his master of forty years seemed to have affected him as little as the passing off of an afternoon shower because, as he patiently explained, indicating his scarred, misshapen head, "The man's still alive in here. He got to die inside, too."

Monday examined the bottle of rum closely, then returned to his vigil.

"You know, don't you," asked Liberty, in as sober a tone as he could summon, "that you are now free."

"So you say," replied Monday, face still pressed to the glass, his vow of silence never strictly enforced against Liberty.

"But I am not merely mouthing empty words. I am trying to inform you, if perhaps not too successfully, of a cataclysmic fact that should alter your existence forever and restore your life back to you."

After a significant pause during which this particular morsel was scrutinized from every possible angle, Monday turned gravely about and said, "I been hearing about this freedom business as long as rabbits got ears, and I have one question for you, Mister Liberty: which kind of freedom is this, anyhow?"

"What do you mean, which kind?"

"I mean, is this mockingbird freedom or mule freedom?"

"Which kind do you want it to be?"

Then, slowly breaking across Monday's face, the first genuine smile he had allowed himself since boarding the *Cavalier*. "I been dreaming I could fly since I was knee high to a splinter."

"Puts me in mind of Charleston," remarked Mrs. Fripp, absolutely entranced by the gradual thickening and spread of the southern horizon into a much-anticipated revelation of hills, of solid earth and an uncommon amount of green. Though improved sufficiently to allow her to take the air topside, Mrs. Fripp's condition remained tentative, G.D. hovering in solicitous proximity, trusty bucket in hand.

"New Providence," Captain Wallace announced, with a proprietorial sweep of his arm. "Though, Mrs. Fripp, as you may have marked, pictures up close do not always resemble their impression at a distance. While harbors are harbors the world round, the Bahamas, madame, are decidedly not the Carolinas. Nassau is a port with, shall we say, a colorful history, a reputation for revelry durable as the centuries, and while perhaps not quite so libertine as in the heyday of Edward Teach and company, whenever sailors cross courses with grand sums of specie, there's bound to be a debauch springing up somewhere in the vicinity. And, of course, the characters who feed upon the fringes of commerce are, inevitably, a genial and diverting lot: blacklegs, buggers, deserters, runaway slaves, cutthroats, knucks and mad sectarians. Hospitable fellows, one and all. Just beware of exhibiting your purse in public."

"Dare we step off the boat?" inquired Mr. Fripp, the captain's verbal sketch of the town already inducing certain fantasies he preferred not to indulge consciously.

"I neglected to mention the courtesans," added Wallace, running a cool appraiser's gaze over Mrs. Fripp from hair to toes. "Saucy women with big, bold eyes and slim, nimble fingers. A horn of plenty for any lady unfortunate enough to be caught in pecuniary embarrassment."

"What in the name of Satan and his gibbering hordes are you suggesting, Captain Wallace?" demanded Mr. Fripp, hastily searching his person for either his wallet or a weapon.

"Sheathe your sword, Mr. Fripp. Just another joke, that's all, a petty quip."

"Who is that remarkable man?" asked Liberty, his attention captured by the aerial acrobatics of a mate clambering about the rigging of the forward mast with an agility and grace astounding in one whose left arm ended at the elbow in a puckered stump.

"Quite the monkey, isn't he?" asserted Wallace. "Brother to a female acquaintance of mine in Savannah." His eyebrow lifted a notch. "Lost the wing at Antietam or some such hideous place. Couldn't bear sitting around home like a rusty hoe while the great boil continued on all around him. So, as a kindness to Fanny, I took the fellow on. Worked out rather well, as you can see."

"I must speak with him," said Liberty.

The renovated sailor, one Zachariah Dobbins, was immediately summoned and introduced to Liberty by the beaming captain, who obviously relished reuniting two old adversaries once met upon the selfsame field of battle and now, fortuitously, facing each other yet again upon the plates of his very ship.

"Was you in the corn?" Dobbins asked. He was a small, skittery type with no eyebrows and a tic in his right cheek.

"More like the threshing floor," answered Liberty. "Might be there still but for my own clumsiness. Tripped over my rifle just as one of your shells passed through. Took the head clean off the man next to me."

"Orn'ry doings."

"It was like you people rose right up out of the earth."

"Our colonel got the jimjams, you know. Stripped off his butternut, punched Lieutenant Berry in the nose, stole his horse and galloped off into the smoke. Often ponder whatever became of that damn fool."

"Sorry about your arm."

Dobbins shrugged. "Like you say, I might be there still. Left a mess of good boys on that ground. Seems like the whole country's a graveyard now."

"We can only hope the soil has now been sanctified."

"Sure woke snakes, though, didn't we? I thought we was going to walk off from this scrape with the ribbon, but you blue devils just kept coming and coming like all nature dogging us. How many of them are there of you, anyhow?"

"They turn them out daily by the batch up in those durn mills of theirs," joked the captain.

Dobbins shook his closely cropped head for a spasmodic beat or two, then paused with a vague, distracted air, as if listening for something rattling around inside. "We made a fist of it, by joe, but tell you true, I'm right content to be out of it. No hankering to see that particular elephant again, no sir."

"Nor I," agreed Liberty, and into the awkward interval that followed he impulsively thrust forward an arm, and after solemnly clasping hands the two veterans embraced.

"Sure glad I didn't kill you back there in Sharpsburg," said Dobbins, patting him affectionately on the back.

"Or I, you."

"My prayers are already so full, I'm afraid I wouldn't have room for even a quality Yankee."

"Don't sleep much?"

"About a hooter's worth."

"Same here."

"I figure that when the Good Lord tires of showing me them pictures every night He'll put them away in an iron box and bury it in a hole inside a hole at the deepest bottom of the ocean."

"It's been a slow freight, but peace is coming," Liberty said. "For all of us."

"I wonder what that will be like."

"Gentle, I suspect, very gentle. Mr. Lincoln will see to that."

"A half-breed in want of a goose's brains," declared Mr. Fripp, a moment after Dobbins had saluted his captain and returned to duty. "Come, come, Mr. Fish, don't you think the wisest policy to pursue regarding our insufferable public embarrassment is to run that boorish backwoods ape out of Washington on the same shit-greased rail he rode in on?"

"Gabriel!" cried Mrs. Fripp, in a rush of feigned indignation. "Your language."

"Though we may have lost the war, dear peach, the right to speak one's mind remains, I believe, blessedly at large."

"Not if you insist upon employing profanity."

"I'll employ whatever goddamn words I choose to express myself, woman."

"Now, now," cautioned the captain. "Don't force me to intervene. You've seen how skilled I am at negotiating settlements."

"Captain Wallace," exclaimed Mr. Fripp. "The wife and I have managed to handle our own affairs quite competently for some twenty-five years now, and I expect we're certainly more than capable of managing them for another quarter century without your nosy hindrance."

"Then please accept my apologies. I intended no offense. I cannot help noting, though, that you are about as touchy as a polecat in a washtub."

"I trust, then," interjected Mrs. Fripp rather acerbically, "that your beady-eyed attentiveness has also marked the state of my own nerves, which, I suggest, can be charitably described as 'tender.' And is it any wonder? The ghastly events of this voyage alone will follow me in nightmares to the grave, not to mention that vile war and its ruthless consumption of my land, my home, my family, my son. . . ." And she broke down in a fit of polite, muffled sobbing.

"Phoebe, please, gather yourself," urged Mr. Fripp. "Your condition." He held up the bucket.

"I'm a woman without a country," she wailed.

"But not without a husband," Mr. Fripp hastened to assure her, administering a succession of awkward caresses to her trembling back to no apparent consequence.

"'Weeping sad and lonely, Hopes and fears how vain,'" recited Captain Wallace in a soft, singsong voice, "'When this cruel war is over, Praying that we meet again.' Of all the memorable tunes, both spirited and melancholy, which you ingenious people have retrieved from conflict's wreckage, that's the one I require a couple healthy pulls of baldface afterward to help moderate the effect."

"But a sophisticated man of the world such as yourself," Liberty offered, "must realize that even when the guns are eventually stilled, the struggle will continue on."

"Indeed," proclaimed Mr. Fripp, momentarily diverted from his wife's subsiding crisis. "And what particular struggle is that?"

"The work to which my family has been devoted since long before my birth."

"Madness and piracy?"

"No, sir. Freedom and equality."

"What? Among the races? How preposterous!"

"He's one of them crackpot enthusiasts," explained an affable Captain Wallace.

"Well, it's certainly no enthusiasm of mine."

"That's why we've gone into exile," confirmed Mrs. Fripp, dabbing at her cheeks with a mess napkin.

"And well out of it, too, if the future is to resemble in any way Mr. Fish's vision. Imagine being forced to dine with a savage like Monday slurping from a bowl at your elbow. Want to spend an evening watching Sambo gnaw on a bone as you endure his ethiop views on the urgent affairs of the hour? The body shudders."

"How do you know you have not done so already," questioned Liberty.

"How's that?"

"Taken a meal with a member of the race, suffered his bad table manners, his outlandish tongue?"

"You're not suggesting—"

"Yes, and before me, how many others whose tainted company you might have enjoyed completely unaware?"

"Mr. Fish, I don't know whether you are gumming me or not, but it is precisely such loose palaver that in my day earned a man a pistol, a ball and a walk of twenty paces. I'll tolerate such chicanery not an instant longer. We are people of the first respectability. Come, Phoebe," he said, offering his wife a protective arm. "I believe we shall be more comfortable waiting out the debarkation in the privacy of our own cabin. Good day, gentlemen." And the couple departed without a backward glance, Mr. Fripp stiffly escorting his lady safely away from the hazard of civil contamination.

"Was that true" asked Captain Wallace, highly entertained by the energetic polemics.

"Was what true?"

"You seemed to imply that you were actually a mulatto of some degree."

Liberty shrugged. "I don't know."

The captain regarded his young, inscrutable passenger for a considerable moment, then broke out into his distinctive cackle.

"How can anyone know for certain?" argued Liberty. "Blood flows across time like water, going where it wants, when it wants, without respect to boundaries geographical, physical or social. Tributaries converge, branch, reconverge in a pattern that may not be so random as it appears. Life, I suppose, and ultimately it makes mongrels of us all."

"Well, mongrels . . ." mused the captain, before suddenly brightening. "The best kind."

"Yes," agreed Liberty, with a smile as wry and elliptical as his grandfather's. "The best kind."

Snow in big fat flakes was falling softly as spilled down when the crippled *Leopard*, laboring tentatively under only one boiler, crept almost soundlessly up through the Narrows, past the ever-shuttling channel traffic, and on toward Governors Island and the Battery beyond. An unfortunate encounter with a late winter squall some eighty miles off the Carolina banks had nearly swamped the over-laden vessel, rendering the incongruous cargo of sugar and wooden matches largely ruined and the cursing, half-naked stokers up to their knees in cold seawater.

Stationed in the bow, windburnt face lifted squarely into the thickening storm, stood a solitary, woefully underdressed figure in a resolute attitude that might even have appeared heroic to an observer too distant to mark the shivering limbs, the red, rheumy nose, the tearing sleepless eyes still teeming with collected imagery a reluctant mind refused, as yet, to process.

The snow fell, dissolving silently into the gray swell, and the ship chugged doggedly on. Up ahead, in the blank sky, appeared the first faint pencil strokes of a city, forming briefly, then vanishing to reform again like something vaguely recognizable glimpsed behind shifting folds of muslin—the idea of a metropolis, hovering tantalizingly apart on the very edge of embodiment. Liberty (for it was indeed he) turned away from the blizzard for a moment to wipe with the back of his bare hand the accumulating flakes from his brows and eyelashes. Too restless to remain snugly warm below decks, he had wanted to experience this impending return to a favorite city with the unguarded fullness of his inner apparatus, to expose himself thoroughly to whatever snares and traps New York might have set for him in his unknowing heart. But now, as the Leopard drew near and the city began solidifying before him in all its thrusting magnitude, he realized, to his disconcerting surprise, that he felt nothing whatsoever, nothing but the bitter air.

This voyage back from the Bahamas had been a particularly trying business, confined aboard a faltering ship with a ludicrously tyrannical captain and a desperate crew few of whom ever spoke to Liberty but to bark out colorful insults regarding his nationality, his patriotism, his ancestry. His berth on this unhappy vessel had been secured by Captain Wallace who, within an hour of the Cavalier's arrival in Nassau harbor, had recognized the familiar lines of a British steamer coaling nearby, and, alluding mysteriously to an unpalatable favor once performed for the Leopard's flinty master, persuaded his old shipmate to allow Liberty to ride deadhead back to America. Monday had already announced with a sorrowful but obstinate solemnity that he believed he had quite had his fill of all the American states, north and south alike, their deceits, their impieties, their incessant quarrels, and that he wished to give these fragrant English isles a go. The Fripps, of course, acknowledging none of their fellow creatures but the local cotton factor and the porters struggling with their abundant baggage, hopped into a waiting carriage and rushed off to Government House for a call on a former business partner, now conveniently serving as royal governor—a patently childish social snub upon their maritime companions which produced no effect at all on Liberty for whom big bugs or bed bugs, it was all the same to him.

Now, as Liberty disembarked into the wintry alien wonder of his native country, he found himself rudely accosted by a mettlesome indigent dressed in pieces of clothing from at least three different suits and hobbling furiously at him across the icy cobblestones on a single primitive crutch. He seemed to have been posted in that specific spot in ordained anticipation of Liberty's arrival.

"Yes, yes, don't play me false now," bellowed the stranger, offering up a hand so begrimed he seemed to be wearing a glove. "We shared a canteen in the shade of Piney Branch Church back there at Spotsylvania. Remember those ruddy cheeks of yours as clear as my own dear mother's picture."

"But I've never been anywhere near Spotsylvania," protested Liberty with the mild caution typically employed in the presence of bedlamites, rogues and other freethinkers.

"Sure you was," insisted the stranger. "Why, 'twas you, me and Indian Bobby Stones the very ones carried Uncle John himself over to the ambulance. Never forget that queer little smile pasted to his lips, the neat black hole under his left eye."

"I never saw General Sedgwick in my life, alive or dead. Or, as I've already indicated, any parcel of Spotsylvania Court House and environs, for that matter."

"Sell my own sweet sister to strut about the world on a pair of pins sound as yours," the stranger went obliviously on, frankly admiring the length and sturdiness of Liberty's young limbs. "This one of mine ain't fit to kick a dog. Here, grab my crutch for a wink." He then formed the hard nugget of a fist and began pounding with dramatic severity upon the thin shank of his uselessly dangling right leg. "Damn loin's dead as a tree stump from the hip down." He looked Liberty hard in the eye and muttered flatly, "That was Spooner's Mill." He paused. "Ever hear tell of it?"

Liberty allowed he had not.

"No, no one has. Don't suspect anyone ever will, either. Memorable enough for me, though, I can guarantee you that. How about you there? Appears you somehow managed to scamper through this shindy with nary a scratch."

The snow fell between them like a cheap, disintegrating curtain.

"I was fortunate," admitted Liberty, attempting to conceal his discomfort behind a wan smile.

"No, you wasn't, that's for true. It's how it was writ down in the book before you, me or anybody was ever born. It's how you was writ from the beginning, the character you was dictated to impersonate through all the daylong turnings of the pages."

"Seems you've got more than a touch of the metaphysician in you."

"What else have I to do with my needless hours than abuse this battered old head?" he asked in a sudden pucker.

"Perhaps in the next story you'll be assigned a better part," suggested Liberty delicately.

"Flapdoodle. I'm done with stories. I hope to end in a place where stories are no more because human contention is no more."

"I believe I've dreamt of such a place myself."

"It's a place outside the book."

"The best places always are."

"Yes," replied the stranger, then abruptly distracted, began looking anxiously about as if he had momentarily forgotten just where he was. "Listen, lad," he went on quickly, "I apologize for putting the bite on you, but if you should happen to have any excess specie secreted about your person and might be willing to offer a small donation to one Chester Cribbs for the purchase of a spanking new limb I would thank you most kindly—as would the Lord."

"Now, answer me plain, Mr. Cribbs, do I strike you as an individual who is likely to possess even a single unwanted copper?"

"No," Cribbs promptly replied, "frankly you do not, but it has been my experience observing the nefarious traffic along these docks that you can't always be certain who's juggling a pocketful of rocks and who is not. Besides, no hurt in the asking now, is there? Don't know how else an ancient bereft veteran like myself could ever lay in all the Vs and Xs necessary to get my leg revivified."

"What do you propose to have done?" asked Liberty, mentally calculating the largest possible sum he could spare from the modest amount Captain Wallace had generously provided him for the long trip home.

"Well, I hear about this fellow down Philadelphia way, crafty professor of some stripe or other, used to be a doll maker, busies himself now mending broken bodies. They say he's invented this wiry style of contraption straps around your knee, got a damn hooter-sized engine fixed to it, makes your leg go up and down slicker than a well pump. Give me one of them, I'd go dashing up and down Broadway like a schoolboy on a freak."

"Now there's a vision the city needs to behold," agreed Liberty, handing over a quarter eagle he reckoned he could afford.

"Bless you, sir!" exclaimed Cribbs, examining the coin in his creased palm as if it were a fragment of the True Cross. "May the angels guide you sure and steady to the last encampment."

"I'm already there," answered Liberty, honoring Cribbs with a smart salute.

The journey north (packet to Albany, rail to Rome, Concord coach to Delphi) passed in an oddly pleasant restorative mist. His head was empty. He spoke only when spoken to. People, villages, whole alabaster landscapes traversed his stare unregistered, and when finally he stepped down from the last carriage, he barely recognized the contours of his own hometown. In his absence the once intimate shops and offices and houses, absurdly untouched by shot and shell, seemed to have been subtly altered, the buildings perceptibly reduced in size, the streets narrowed.

Cold, alone, feet so numb he might as well have been limping about on wooden pegs, the first feathery stages of a bad catarrh or ague or worse tickling lamentably at the back of his throat, Liberty turned up the near impassable road that led homeward. Keeping true to the wheel ruts, he presently entered the enchanted wood where, as a boy, he had played with an almost disturbed intensity, now the black trees and branches stood shorn and spidery upon a pale sky like an unintelligible message scribbled in a palsied hand. The storm had blown off, and already poking aggressively through the soft uniform mantling were the stained layers of granite outcroppings, fallen timbers, misshapen boulders, the essential hardness of the world beginning to reassert itself. Liberty trudged stolidly onward.

As he hiked up the buried lane toward the magnetic gingerbread house in which he had been born and bred, he spied beside the barn a stooped, angular figure hewing wood with an organized fury, the sound of the ax bit like a measured succession of rifle reports echoing sharply through the thin air. Even at a distance his father appeared decidedly older, enveloped in a more grayish aura. He, too, seemed alarmingly diminished in size.

At the sight of this tattered stranger plodding toward him unbidden and unannounced, Thatcher paused in his work. Then, flinging aside the ax, he rushed eagerly forward to embrace the son he had not seen in three interminable years.

"You look thin," he observed, holding Liberty back at a critical arm's length.

"As do you."

"Well." Thatcher was peering steadily into his son's face with a concentration so fierce Liberty had to avert his gaze. "Well," he said again.

"I guess I'm a deserter," Liberty confessed.

Thatcher smiled. "I'm certain the grand blue leviathan requires no further assistance from you."

"They might believe otherwise."

"I honestly doubt that. Seems incredible that the long-anticipated jubilee has come at last but so, apparently, it has. Yet enough," he added, wrapping a firm arm about his son's newly muscled shoulders. "We can discuss these momentous matters later. Let's go inside. You must be fatigued beyond endurance."

Upon hearing her nephew's distinctly elastic voice in the hallway, Aunt Aroline darted from the kitchen, shrieking out his name repeatedly, and then, seizing him by the ears, proceeded to fill every inch of Liberty's startled face with wet kisses.

"Aroline, please," begged her younger brother, "let the boy catch his breath."

"A glorious day, Thatcher, an eruption of divinity into our lives. Our heavenly petitions have been answered."

And though she apparently could not help but continue to grin at him like an institutionalized fool, Liberty noticed that she had become, or perhaps always had been, a curiously birdlike creature of fine bones and plentifully wrinkled skin whose increasing transparency over time permitted to shine progressively forth a spiritual radiance of astonishing authority.

"You look so dreadfully peaked," she remarked. "What farm slop did they feed you in that wretched army? Tell you what, Liberty honey, the mess of pottage I've been preparing all day shall remain a mess of pottage because I'm going to fix you your favorite dinner—roast joint and a Marlborough pie. How does that sound?"

"About as peart as rain on a rooftop in July," he replied, quoting fondly from his aunt's seemingly inexhaustible stock of quaint expressions that had served to season his childhood and the world beyond childhood with meaning and mystery.

"Now you two get on into the parlor," ordered Aroline, ushering her amused brother and nephew brusquely forward, tears beginning to collect in her nervous, faded eyes. "The fire's fresh, and, Liberty, that old hairy chairy of yours," referring to a juvenile favorite hair-bottomed rocker, "has practically gone to pasture waiting for a rider of your exuberance." Her voice having grown discernibly breathless, she suddenly wheeled about and vanished, apparently requiring a quick infusion of air from an unoccupied room.

"Same as ever," Liberty noted affectionately.

"After you've been here a while," commented Thatcher, "I'm afraid you shall find the, uh, slippages becoming ever more common."

The legendary rocker proved to be much too noisy and vertiginous for Liberty's adult nerves, so father and son settled comfortably into a pair of matching Windsor chairs before the crackling hearth. Above the mantel the ancient family clock continued, as it had always done, to sever off the minutes with dependably audible precision.

"I've been to Redemption Hall," Liberty announced quietly.

"I expected as much," replied his father. "The night you ran off with the Fowler boy I suffered a dream which was to trouble me for many nights to come. I saw you practically sauntering at a brisk constitutional pace not just oblivious to the surrounding hordes of vigilant snakes and reptiles but actually frolicking fearlessly among the venomous creatures. I saw you astride a grinning gator, piloting an entire fleet of the fanged amphibians toward some distant dubious conclusion. And when I belatedly recognized that you were grinning, too, I became quite agitated. You were the autocrat of the alligators."

"Well, you always claimed I possessed an unwholesome and decidedly un-Fishlike mesmerization with things sovereign and ecclesiastical."

"I knew this damn war would devise a way, no matter how labyrinthine, of depositing you in that accursed place."

"I had to go."

"I know."

Liberty then related, in as temperate and objective a tone as he could maintain, the whole sordid account of what he had found in Carolina, of the melodramatic events aboard the *Cavalier*, of the fate of Grandfather Maury. As he spoke, Thatcher seemed to slump visibly in his seat. "Worse even than I could imagine," he muttered.

"His head bobbed to the surface once before the final descent, his infatuate will, I suppose, keeping him afloat to direct one last shot of malice straight to my heart."

"Such hatred is a near unquenchable force."

"In his case it required an entire ocean."

Thatcher sighed. The clock ticked tartly on. "Let's go visit your mother."

She had been buried in the midst of her scrupulously tended flower garden beneath, so Thatcher explained, a summertime quilt of unendurable color; now the sole evidence of once-thriving life lingered only in the brown brittle weeds piercing winter's dreary monochrome like a fusillade of fallen arrows. A well-trodden path had been worn in the snow between house and plot. The simple stone, topped by a thick white crust, read:

ROXANA MAURY FISH

1822–1862
Beloved Wife and Mother
Freedom's Warrior

"I'm so sorry I wasn't here," confessed Liberty.

"There was nothing you could have done."

"Except, perhaps, the one thing . . ."

"Yes, you and those damn envelopes. It was as if you were trying to protect her from enemy fire."

They stood together in joined solitude and pretended to study the barren ground as the sere branches around them rattled in the chill wind.

"She would have been so proud of you," declared Thatcher.

"I didn't do anything different from any man on either side."

"But you were her son."

Liberty said nothing.

"Stay as long as you wish," advised Thatcher gently. "I shall be inside."

Sometime later Liberty looked up with a start, wondering where his father had gone. He hardly noted the dripping woods, the churning sky, the solitary doe in the clearing on a distant hill picking its way daintily through the high drifts, but he could hear his mother's voice, her firm podium voice, as clearly as the squirrels chattering at him from the nearby trees: "Like flowers listing toward the sun we ever incline, each separate one of us, black and white alike, despite the obstacles abounding, toward the virtues, the necessities, yes, the absolute pleasures of our own personal Fourth of July, physically, mentally and spiritually. This is the handprint of the Creator upon our natures." Then Liberty knelt down in the snow, kissed the palm of his own hand and pressed it against the cold marble.

As he rose and turned to go, he saw, standing respectfully back in the shadows of the open doorway at the rear of the house, a wizened little man leaning heavily upon a cane.

"Euclid!" cried Liberty, dashing recklessly across the frozen yard to lift his old friend dramatically aloft in a fervent bear hug.

"Enough, boy, enough," protested Euclid, tapping Liberty sternly on the back with his stick.

"But look at you now, you've changed not at all."

"Liberty, you couldn't get away with fibbing me at the age of six, too late to take it up now."

"All right, you've shaved your head."

Euclid ran his fingers over the phrenological wonder of his bare skull. "Spirit told me to. I should be setting out any day now and traveling light is traveling easy."

"Traveling where?"

"Canaan Land, of course."

"Isn't it a trifle soon to be making that trip?"

"I'm not the chap who works up the schedules." He reached over and gripped Liberty's unshaven chin. "I see the boy's just about gone from your face."

"I'm an old man, Euclid, full of an old man's thoughts."

"I always suspicioned you'd come through."

"More than I ever knew."

"Now come," he beckoned rather curtly, leading Liberty with painstaking deliberation down the precarious, uneven steps to his private quarters in the cellar where, in the earthen floor at the far end of the room, beneath a highly detailed map of the Erie Canal, had been constructed a miniature model of the entire waterway from Albany to Buffalo, complete with working locks and wait houses and relay barns, bridges and towpaths, including even snubbing posts, and all the major villages along the route represented by clusterings of little enameled cottages.

"I am," marveled Liberty, "utterly flummoxed. The time, the diligence, the sheer act of such an undertaking lies thoroughly beyond comprehension."

"Don't matter none," explained Euclid. "I was conjuring up a spell. I was fired by the extravagant notion that if I put an honest hand to this job and never flagged, every hour I worked on my ditch would be an hour no bullet could find you."

"A few came mighty close, Euclid, but then, I am a master dodger."

"And this," declared Euclid proudly, "is for you," producing from his pocket a stunningly executed, hand-carved replica of a genuine canal boat, accurate in all particulars, trimmed in bright blue and gold, and across the stern in florid cameo and layered in gilt the word "ROXANA."

"Euclid, please, you're piling on the agony," protested Liberty, turning the perfectly crafted object over and over again in his trembling hands.

"Then, what say, baby doll, we baptize this ark." From a sawbuck table Euclid fetched a pitcher of water and, bending down with a grunt, carefully filled his modest creation to the berm. "Your mother, you know, spoke often of her tremendous desire to see Niagara Falls. Near to Buffalo, eh?"

"Near enough."

Then both got down on their knees in the dirt on either side of the "Grand Western" and began taking polite turns nudging the little packet along, halting dutifully before each lock while Euclid manipulated the gates, then onward again, passing under the numerous low bridges, Liberty occasionally crying out the warning "Everybody down!" Euclid with one of the many tiny figures he had fashioned to populate his imaginary country reenacting a drunken captain's comical spill into the drink, and drifting dreamily on past all the fabled towns, Schenectady to Herkimer, across the Long Level, Rome to Syracuse, through the Montezuma marshes, Rochester to Lockport, until finally, giddy and wet, they arrived at the bustling terminus.

"Done!" proclaimed Euclid with an almost postprandial satisfaction. "We made it safe to Buffalo."

"And the Falls a mere coach away."

And, so saying, the two men reached across the canal and clasped hands, muddy fingers and all.

"Kindness of such magnitude, I fear to admit, embarrasses me greatly," said Liberty, unable for the moment to meet Euclid's dark, penetrating eyes.

"The quality your aunt knows as adhesiveness need never be tethered or hobbled," Euclid explained. "She's a gentle beast who will neither run off nor do harm."

"A quality conspicuously absent lately from my own congealed portion of the world."

"Then, Liberty, baby doll, you got to feel free to help yourself to another platter."

That night, nestled snugly into his own high feather bed beneath the only roof he had ever called his own, he was, without any awareness of a transition, plunged precipitously into dreams of terrific violence that shuddered him awake hours later to a quaking darkness and bedclothes damp with sweat, unable to locate precisely where or even who he was. Then he remembered. It's America, he thought, and you, whoever you are, will be all right. It's America, and everything was going to be fine.

A NOTE ON THE TYPE

The text of this book was set in Monotype Joanna, a typeface designed by Eric Gill, the noted English stonecutter, typographer, and illustrator. It was released by the Monotype Corporation in 1937. Reflecting Eric Gill's idiosyncratic approach to type design, Joanna has a number of playful features, chief among them the design of the italic companion as a narrow sloped roman.

Composed by Creative Graphics, Allentown, Pennsylvania
Printed and bound by Berryville Graphics, Berryville, Virginia
Designed by Wesley Gott